2017

CHRISTMAS
in a
COWBOY'S ARMS

sourcebooks
casablanca

The publisher acknowledges the copyright holders of the individual works as follows:
Father Christmas © 1995, 2011, 2017 by Leigh Greenwood
A Chick-a-Dee Christmas © 2017 by Rosanne Bittner
The Christmas Stranger © 2017 by Linda Broday
A Texas Ranger for Christmas © 2017 by Margaret Brownley
A Christmas Baby © 2017 by Anna Schmidt
A Christmas Reunion © 2017 by Amy Sandas

Leigh Greenwood's *Father Christmas* was originally published in 1995 in the United States by Leisure Books, an imprint of Dorchester Books.

Published by Sourcebooks Casablanca, an imprint of Sourcebooks, Inc.
P.O. Box 4410, Naperville, Illinois 60567-4410
(630) 961-3900
Fax: (630) 961-2168
sourcebooks.com

Printed and bound in the United States of America.
OPM 10 9 8 7 6 5 4 3 2 1

Contents

Father Christmas 1
    Leigh Greenwood

A Chick-a-Dee Christmas 101
    Rosanne Bittner

The Christmas Stranger 207
    Linda Broday

A Texas Ranger for Christmas 289
    Margaret Brownley

A Christmas Baby 357
    Anna Schmidt

A Christmas Reunion 423
    Amy Sandas

FATHER CHRISTMAS

Leigh Greenwood

*For Brandon, who never
got to celebrate Christmas*

One

"I've got to be a fool to come here. I should be headed for California, where nobody would ever find me."

Joe Ryan glanced over at his dog, Samson. The big, yellow, short-haired mongrel was sniffing among some rocks, a growl in his throat, the hair on his back standing up.

"Stop looking for coyotes and listen to me."

The dog looked up but almost immediately turned back to the tangle of boulders and desert broom.

"You keep poking your nose into every pile of rocks you pass, and you're going to find a wolf one of these days.

"Maybe you can talk to him," Joe said to his horse, General Burnside. "He never listens to me."

Joe rode through the Arizona desert with care. He kept away from the flat valley floor, where a man could be seen for miles. Rather than stop for water at the cottonwood-lined San Pedro River, he looked for springs and seeps. He had shaken the posse before he left Colorado, but the law would soon figure out where he was. He planned to be gone by then.

"I can't imagine why Pete wanted a ranch in this country," Joe said aloud. "Even a coyote would have a hard time making a living."

He had fallen into the habit of talking to his dog and horse just to hear the sound of a human voice. He'd seen few people since he broke out of a Colorado jail a month earlier.

Sometime after midday, Joe pulled up just short of the crest of a small ridge. He paused to light a cigarette and let his gaze wander over every part of the landscape. When he was satisfied that there was no movement, he started forward. Using the cover of juniper thickets, scattered mesquite, and greasewood, he crossed the ridge and rode into a basin.

Pete Wilson's ranch lay below.

Joe studied the land closely as he rode in. It was good land. It would be hot in summer, but there was plenty of food for cattle. A small creek passed close to the house. He was surprised Pete had had enough sense to choose such a good spot. His former partner hadn't struck him as a far-sighted man. Impatient and bad-tempered was a better description. But then, a shrewish wife could ruin any man. And from what Pete had said, Mary Wilson was a thoroughgoing harridan.

Well, it didn't matter to Joe. He meant to find the gold, clear his name, and be on his way. It wasn't cold for December, but he was looking forward to the warm breezes of California.

"Come on, Samson. Let's get it over with."

Pressing his heels into the flanks of his lanky, mouse-gray gelding, Joe started toward the ranch.

∿

Mary Wilson struggled to sit up. The room spun violently before her eyes. She closed them and concentrated hard. She had to get up. She was too weak to stay here any longer.

"Get the horse," she said to the blond child who watched her with anxious eyes. "Don't try to saddle him. Just put a halter on him and bring him to the porch."

"He won't come to me," Sarah Wilson said.

"Offer him some oats. I'll be outside in a moment."

The child left reluctantly. Mary didn't like forcing Sarah to fetch the animal, but she had no choice. She wasn't even sure she was strong enough to make the twenty-two-mile trip into town. She didn't know how she could be so weak without being ill. She had felt fine until two days ago. Then her strength had just vanished. Taking a firm grip on the bedpost, she pulled herself to her feet. The room spun more rapidly than ever. Gasping from the effort, Mary refused to let go of the bedpost. She *would* stand up. She *would* make it to town. She had thought she had more time. The baby wasn't due for another month.

She attempted to take a step, but her swollen stomach unbalanced her. She used a chair to steady herself. No sooner had she regained her equilibrium than she heard Sarah scream. Fear gave Mary the strength she lacked. She stumbled across the room to the rifle she kept on the wall next to the door. She took it down and managed to open the door about a foot. Leaning against the doorjamb, she pushed herself forward until she could see into the ranch yard.

Sarah came flying up the steps. She almost knocked Mary down as she buried herself in Mary's skirts. Mary's gaze found and locked on the rider who had reached the corral. What she saw frightened her.

A stranger dressed in buckskin and denim, astride a huge gray horse and accompanied by a large dog, was riding into the yard. A big man with very broad shoulders, he wore a gun belt and carried a rifle. His hat was tilted too low to allow her to see much of his face, but his chin and cheeks were covered by several weeks' growth of dark-blond beard. He rode right up to the porch.

Sarah tightened her grip on Mary's skirts. Mary's hold on the doorway began to give way. She leaned her shoulder against the wood to keep from falling.

The man came to a stop at the steps. He didn't dismount, just pushed his hat back from his forehead and stared hard at Mary. Mary found herself looking into the coldest blue eyes she'd ever seen.

"This Pete Wilson's place?" the man asked.

His voice was deep and rough. It didn't sound threatening, but it sounded far away. The ringing in Mary's ears distracted her. She felt her muscles begin to relax, and she tightened her grip on the rifle. "Yes," Mary said.

"You his wife?"

"I'm his widow. What can I do for you?"

The man's face seemed to go out of focus for a moment. Then it started to spin very slowly. One moment he was right side up, the next upside-down. Mary fought to still the revolving image, but it only moved faster.

Then she saw nothing at all.

∽

Joe wasn't surprised when Mary Wilson met him at the door with a rifle. He *was* surprised to see she was pregnant. He was even more surprised when she fainted. Damn! Now he'd have to take care of her. He knew absolutely nothing about the care and handling of extremely pregnant women.

Still, he was out of the saddle and up the front steps almost before her body had settled on the floor. He scooped up the unconscious woman. Despite her condition, she weighed very little. She looked white, totally drained of color. That wasn't good.

He kicked open the door and entered the small stone cabin. Looking around, he saw a rope bed in the corner. He carried her to the bed and eased her down. She rolled onto her side. He put his hand on her forehead. She didn't feel hot. If anything, she seemed too cool. She looked more exhausted than anything else. Thin in the face. Almost gaunt. Maybe the baby was taking everything she ate. She looked big enough to be carrying a colt.

He pulled the blanket over her. Pete had lied. She was

a pretty woman. There was nothing harsh or shrewish about her face. He'd never seen any female who could look that pretty without painting herself and putting on a fancy dress. She reminded him of some kind of fragile bird—but one with the heart of an eagle—standing guard over her chick.

She lay there, helpless. He wanted to touch her again—her skin had felt so soft under his hand—but the sight of the child cowering in the corner behind the bed caused him to back away.

"Is she sick?" he asked.

The child just stared at him, her eyes wide with fear. She pressed close to Mary but well out of his reach.

"Speak up, girl. I'm not going to hurt you. I want to know if she's sick or if she faints all the time."

The child cringed and practically buried herself in the crack between the bed and the wall. He noticed that her eyes kept going toward the doorway. He turned. Samson had followed him inside and flopped down a few feet from the door.

"Outside," Joe ordered, with a wave of his hand. "You're scaring the kid."

The dog whined in protest.

"Maybe later, but right now you're not welcome. Out."

With a protesting woof, the dog got up and ambled outside. He lay down directly in front of the open door, where Joe would have to step over him to get out.

Joe closed the door on Samson. "Nosy brute. I guess I spoiled him. I don't suppose you have a name," he said to the girl, "something I can call you?"

The child continued to stare.

"I didn't think so. You got anything to eat around here? I'm hungry. I haven't had a decent meal since I went to jail."

Still no answer. Joe was confused about the child.

Pete had talked about his wife a lot—that was how he'd conned Joe into teaming up with him—but he hadn't said a word about a daughter. Was this kid Pete's or Mary's?

"What does your ma like to eat?"

No answer.

"How about you?"

It was clear that the child wasn't going to say anything, so Joe decided to look around for himself. He found a little coffee, sugar, salt, some tea, beans, bacon, and flour. Some canned goods lined a shelf against the wall. He glanced back at Mary. She looked as if she needed something sustaining. "Do you have any milk?" Joe asked the child.

She continued to stare.

"Look, I'm not going to hurt you. I'm going to fix something to eat, but I need a little help here. Your ma's looking right run down. You want her to get better, don't you?"

The child nodded, and Joe felt a little of the tension inside him relax. It wasn't much progress, but it was a beginning.

"Do you have any milk?"

The child shook her head.

Hell, he thought, every ranch or farm kept a milk cow. What was she going to feed the baby if her milk ran dry? "How about eggs?" Come to think of it, he hadn't seen any chickens when he rode up. What kind of place was this, anyhow?

The child didn't say anything, but she cautiously left her corner, approached the door, and opened it a crack. With a sharp intake of breath, she jumped back.

Joe crossed the room in a few strides. "Dammit, Samson, I told you to get out of here." The dog got up and moved off the porch. "Go on. Find me a rabbit or something for supper."

Samson disappeared behind the house. After peeping around the corner to make sure the dog wasn't waiting to attack her, the kid headed toward a shed that seemed to serve as a barn and chicken coop. Joe figured he'd better stay outside just in case Samson came back. He stuck his head inside, but Mary hadn't moved. When he turned back, the child was out of sight.

Hell! He was on the run from the law, and he had a pregnant woman and a child who wouldn't talk on his hands. He hadn't been around a respectable woman in years and didn't know what to do with one.

The kid emerged from the shed, cast a worried look around for Samson, and ran across the yard toward the house. She slowed and came reluctantly up the steps. Looking up, she held out her hands. She had an egg in each.

If it hadn't been for the long hair, Joe wouldn't have been able to tell if she was a boy or a girl. She wore a red-checked flannel shirt and black pants. Her shoes looked more like boots several sizes too large. There was nothing feminine or appealing about the child.

"Put them on the table," Joe said. "I've got to get a few things from my saddlebags." He should unsaddle General Burnside and give him a good rubdown, but that would have to wait. He unstrapped his saddlebags. He had started back up the steps before he turned back for his rifle. He didn't think there was anybody within twenty miles of this place, but he'd feel better if he had his rifle with him.

The kid had retreated to her position behind the bed. Joe placed his rifle against the wall and tossed his saddlebags on the table. For now he'd have to use his own supplies. He had plenty of beef jerky. He didn't know anything like it for building up a person who was weak.

"Water," he called out to the child. "I need water." When he heard nothing, he turned around. She was pointing to a bucket. He looked inside. It was half-full. It was also tepid.

"Fresh water." Joe held out the bucket.

Reluctantly the child came forward, took the bucket, and headed outside again.

Joe hadn't had time to pay attention to his surroundings. Only now did he notice the dozens of drawings covering the walls, all of them black ink on white paper. There were drawings of a town somewhere in the East, of the ranch and surrounding countryside, of the child, of Pete. Even of the stone cabin.

The winter scenes were the most incredible. Even in black and white, they had the power to evoke memories of winters back home in the foothills of North Carolina. The snow weighing heavily on pine boughs, icicles hanging from the roof of a wood-frame house, a woman leaning over the porch rail, barnyards made pristine by a blanket of snow.

Joe pushed the recollections aside. Not even a mantle of snow could turn his past into a happy memory.

He moved along the wall, studying each picture in detail, until he stumbled over a bunch of twigs. "What the hell!" he muttered. He had knocked over a bundle of hackberry branches tied together. A few red berries showed among the dense green foliage. Each branch ended in a sharp, strong thorn.

A muffled cry from the doorway caused him to turn. The kid dropped the bucket and threw herself at the bundle of twigs. The water spilled out and quickly disappeared down the cracks between the floorboards. Joe watched, unbelieving, as the kid set the bundle of twigs back in the corner.

"That's Sarah's Christmas tree," Mary informed him in a weak, hesitant voice.

Joe hadn't realized Mary was conscious. He drew close to the bed, scrutinizing her. She seemed okay, but he intended to make sure she stayed in bed.

"That's a bunch of hackberry branches, for God's

sake," he said, unable to understand why the kid continued to fuss over them, pulling and twisting the branches until she had arranged them to her satisfaction. "They ought to be tossed on the fire. She could kill herself on those thorns."

"Sarah is determined to have a Christmas tree, and that's the best she could do."

"Why didn't she look for a jojoba? At least it doesn't have thorns."

"She wanted the red berries. Her mother used to tell her about decorating for Christmas with holly."

"You should have stopped her."

"Who are you?" Mary Wilson asked, changing the subject. "What are you doing here?"

"I'm Pete's old partner."

She started to throw back the covers.

"Lie still."

Joe's peremptory order stilled Mary's hand in midair. He pushed her arm down to her side and jerked the blanket back in place.

For a moment she seemed on the verge of defying him. Probably learning he was Pete's partner wasn't enough to make her trust him. But if she was afraid, she didn't show it. More likely she'd show her talons.

"I'm about to fix me something to eat. I need that water," Joe reminded the kid. She reluctantly left her tree to pick up the bucket and go back outside.

"Does the kid talk?" he asked.

"Yes."

"She got a name?"

"Sarah."

"Who is she?"

"Pete's daughter. Her mother died. I was his second wife."

Sarah entered the cabin with the fresh water. Joe took the bucket over to the worktable. "Make sure your ma doesn't get up," he said over his shoulder. "Maybe if you sing to her, she'll go back to sleep."

"I can't... You shouldn't..." Mary began.

"Probably, but I'm doing it anyway," Joe said. "Sing!" he commanded the child.

Turning away from the two females watching him in open-mouthed bewilderment, Joe opened his saddlebags and began to lay out their contents. He was surprised when he heard a very soft voice begin to sing. He knew just enough to know the kid was singing in French.

He wondered what had made Pete Wilson leave such a family—a daughter who was petrified of dogs, wouldn't talk, and sang lullabies in French; a beautiful young wife who was so weak she couldn't stand up and was going to have a baby any minute, if he could judge from the size of her.

Memories he thought he'd forgotten came rushing back. Damn! He hadn't thought of Flora in five years.

He didn't know why he should now. The two women had nothing in common.

Flora had been vibrantly, noisily alive. She laughed, sang, cried, shouted, always at the top of her voice. He had been wildly in love with her, but she hadn't been willing to settle down. She had liked flash, excitement, money, action—all the things Joe had learned to avoid.

Mary was nothing like that. She was fair, thin, faded, and extremely pregnant. Despite that, she had a feminine allure. Soft skin, thick eyebrows and lashes, generous lips, the curve of her cheek, the expanse of her brow— all combined to give her an appearance of lushness completely at variance with her condition.

This woman would never want flash or excitement. She would work hard to build a home that nurtured a man, that he would shed his blood to defend.

She'd be the kind of woman his grandmother almost was.

After Joe's father disappeared and his grandfather died, his grandmother had raised him. Sometimes, when she spoke of her husband, there was a light in her eye, a softening in her voice and touch, that spoke of a time when she had been happy and content. But most often she was harsh and demanding, the woman she had become to survive on her own, to hide her grief over the kind of woman her daughter had become.

Joe was sure Mary would never be like that. She had the strength and staying power it took to endure ill fortune.

Pete Wilson was a fool.

∽∞∽

The sound of soft singing gently drew Mary out of the darkness that clutched at her. She opened her eyes. She must have fainted again. Sarah knelt by the bed, her hand gripping Mary's, as she softly sang one of the French lullabies her mother had taught her.

A noise caught Mary's attention, and she remembered the man. Pete's partner. He was at the stove. Then she realized that the cabin was warm. She hadn't been able to cut wood for a week. She had done her last cooking with twigs Sarah had gathered.

It was tempting to lie back and let him take care of everything. She was so tired. She couldn't tell what he was doing at the stove, but he moved with quiet confidence. Then she caught the delicious aroma of coffee.

He was cooking!

Her stomach immediately cramped, and saliva flooded her mouth. It had been almost two days since she had eaten a full meal.

"You never did tell me your name," she said.

The man turned. "Joe Ryan. Stay put," he ordered when she attempted to sit up. "The corn bread's not ready yet."

"I can't lie here while you fix supper."

"Why not? You couldn't do anything if you did get up."

Mary had never seen a man cook. She'd never even seen one in the kitchen except to eat. A good woman didn't get sick. There was no time. She remembered that. She'd heard it all her life, especially after her mother died and she'd had to take over managing the household.

"You don't have to take care of me."

Joe looked at her as if she were talking nonsense. "I considered leaving you lying in the doorway, but I figured I'd get tired of stepping over you."

"What did you fix?" Mary asked.

"Beef and corn bread. It's not fancy, but it's good."

"I appreciate your feeding Sarah. It's been a while since I've been able to fix her a decent meal."

"Or eaten one yourself," Joe said as he began to ladle the stew into two plates. "I don't suppose you have any butter?"

"No. I haven't been able to catch the cow."

"I guess the kid will have to drink water. Do you like molasses?"

"We both do," Mary answered. "I always did have a sweet tooth."

Joe opened the oven and took out a pan of corn bread. "I made it soft. That's the way my grandma used to make it."

He hadn't had corn bread this way in years.

He scooped corn bread out of the pan and put some on each plate. He covered each portion with a generous helping of molasses. "Get your water if you want it," he said to Sarah. He moved a chair next to the bed.

"I can get up," Mary said.

"I told you to stay put."

"I'm not an invalid."

"Then why did you faint twice today?"

"I'm sorry."

"I don't mind that," Joe said. "I just mind you acting like you're well. It's not sensible. I don't like it when people don't act sensible."

"Then what is the *sensible* thing to do?" Mary asked, slightly put out.

"Lie back and let me feed you. Then go to sleep until supper. You're worn down. I'm surprised you didn't faint before you reached the door."

She would have if it hadn't been for Sarah's scream. Only fear for the child had gotten her that far. She had passed out the minute she realized Joe didn't mean them any harm. She watched as he picked up the table and moved it next to the chair.

Then he placed both plates on the table. He placed a spoon beside one. He pulled up a second chair, and Sarah slid into it.

"Eat," he said to Sarah.

"Go on," Mary said when the child hesitated. "I'm sure it's as good as anything I could make."

"I'm a good cook," Joe said. "You sure you can sit up?"

"Of course." Mary managed to pull herself into a sitting position. She hoped he didn't know how close she was to fainting again.

"Lean forward."

She couldn't. He lifted her up and placed the pillows behind her.

"You're weak as a damned kitten."

"I was on my way to town when you got here."

"You wouldn't have made it out of the damned yard."

She would have loved to disagree with him, but she doubted she would have made it out of the house. "I would appreciate it if you would watch your language in front of Sarah."

"She's heard worse if Pete's her pa."

"Not since I've been here."

"You stopped Pete's cussing?"

"No, but he did make an effort to curb his tongue."

He looked as if he was considering her in a new light. Mary wasn't at all certain it was a flattering one.

"Open up. Your dinner's getting cold."

Mary half hoped she'd be able to tell him how truly awful it was, but the first taste confirmed his opinion of himself. He was a fine cook. It was all she could do to wait until he brought a second spoonful to her mouth.

"Eat a little corn bread. I put two eggs in it. As soon as I can find that cow, we'll have some butter. Beef's good for building a body up, but nothing works like eggs and butter."

Sarah looked up at Joe, glanced at Mary, then back at Joe. Mary was delighted to see her plate already empty.

"Get yourself some more if you want, kid," Joe said.

Sarah filled half her plate with stew, the rest with corn bread.

"For a little thing, she sure can eat." Joe put a spoonful of stew into Mary's mouth. "For a woman who was about to meet her maker, you sure talk frisky."

"I'm afraid any frisk I had disappeared long ago," Mary said, feeling a little as if she'd been chastised, "but I do have a sharp tongue. That's been a problem all my life." She swallowed another spoonful of stew. Her stomach didn't hurt anymore. Much to her surprise, she was beginning to feel full. She leaned back on the pillows.

"You haven't told me a thing about yourself," she said. "I don't even know why you're here."

"That can wait. All you have to do now is eat and sleep. It would help, though, if you could convince the kid to talk to me."

"The *kid* is named Sarah."

"Maybe, but she doesn't answer to that either."

"Talk to the gentleman, Sarah. It would be rude to remain silent, especially after he's been kind enough to cook our dinner."

"I'm not kind, and I'm not a gentleman," Joe said. "At least, no one ever thought so before."

"Maybe you never gave them reason, but you have me. Thank you."

"The only thanks I want is to see you eat up every bit of this food."

"I'm feeling rather full."

"That's because your stomach has shrunk to nothing. Eat a little more. Then we'll let you rest until supper."

By the time Mary managed to eat everything on the plate, she was exhausted. She was also hardly able to keep her eyes open. The hot food, the warmth in the cabin, and the knowledge that she was safe combined to overcome her desire to stay awake and question this unusual man.

"You must tell me what you're doing here," she said as she slipped back down in the bed. Joe adjusted the pillows under her head and pulled the covers up to her chin.

"Later. I'm going outside now so you can get some rest." He picked up his saddlebags and headed toward the door. He turned back. "Tell the kid she doesn't have to be afraid of Samson. He never did more than growl at a kid in his life."

"I'll explain it to *Sarah*," Mary replied.

Joe disappeared through the door. A moment later she heard him start to whistle.

Mary nestled down in the bed, but she couldn't sleep. She had never met a man in the least like Joe Ryan. She couldn't imagine him being Pete's partner.

Mary had disliked her husband. She was ashamed to admit it, but now that he was dead, it seemed pointless to continue pretending. He'd been mean, thoughtless, frequently brutal. She had never been able to imagine why her uncle had thought his stepson would make her a good husband. Not even her uncle's affection for his wife could blind him to the fact that her son was a cruel, selfish man. Her father should have protected her, but he was eager to get her out of the house. One less mouth to feed. Mary had been relieved when Pete left to prospect for gold in Colorado. Not even learning she was pregnant had made her wish for his return.

"Look out the window and see what he's doing," Mary said to Sarah.

"He's just looking," Sarah told her.

"At what?"

"Everything."

"The horse?"

"Yes."

"What's he doing now?"

"Looking in the shed."

"Anything else?"

"He's digging a hole next to the shed."

That made Mary uneasy. Any partner of Pete's was likely to be of poor character. Stealing horses from a helpless woman would probably be a small thing to him.

"Bring me the pistol," she said to Sarah. The child got the pistol from its place in the dresser drawer and brought it to Mary.

Mary checked to see that it was loaded. "Tell Mr. Ryan I would like to see him."

Two

JOE RUBBED THE LAST OF THE DRIED SWEAT OFF GENERAL Burnside with a handful of straw. "I shouldn't have left you standing this long," he apologized to his mount, "but I had to dig a few holes first. No gold buried next to the shed."

He tossed the straw aside. They both contemplated the corral. "I suppose you might stay in that if you'd been ridden so hard you were wobbly in the knees." He pushed on a rotten rail. It broke into two pieces and fell to the ground. "I guess I'll have to hobble you."

Samson trotted up from his round of inspection. "Did you find any likely places to bury gold?" he asked the dog as he put hobbles on General Burnside. "I hope you didn't eat any of those chickens. Apparently the coyotes consider them their own personal property." He shook his head at the gaping holes in the chicken fence.

He walked to the shed, a large structure open in the front and the back. In between was a room entered through a door from the house side. Much to his surprise, Joe found wire for the chicken yard and a large number of rails for the corral. From the dust on them, they had been there a long time. Apparently Pete hadn't lacked the money or the materials to keep up the ranch, only the will to use them. Joe looked around, but saw no likely place to hide a strongbox. He'd look under the floorboards, but he doubted he'd find anything. Too obvious.

"I don't know why Pete thought panning for gold was

easier than fixing a few fences now and then," Joe said. All the tools anybody would ever need were scattered around the shed. "It's a hell of a lot harder to build a sluice box and defend it from some rascal who'd rather shoot you than build his own."

He walked back out into the December sun, pulling his hat lower over his eyes. He glanced toward the house. The gold had to be there, but was it inside or out? He'd have to make a thorough search.

He could see the kid watching him through the window. Funny little kid. Odd she should be afraid of dogs. It was almost as if she was afraid of him, too. Her mother wasn't. In fact, she'd sent the kid to tell him she wanted to see him. He'd obey the summons once he'd finished in the yard.

"Don't know why Pete left a woman like that," Joe said to Samson, who followed at his heels. "She's got a bit of an edge to her, but she's got standards. A woman ought to have standards. Gives a man something to live up to." He tested the poles in the chicken yard. They needed bracing. "I can't believe Pete was such a lazy skunk."

The broken fence irritated him. It was such a little job, so easy. But it wasn't his responsibility. He looked up into the hills beyond the ranch house. If the gold was up there, he'd probably never find it.

He didn't think Pete had told his wife about it. The place didn't look like five dollars had been spent on it, certainly not twenty thousand. No, Pete had buried it here, because he didn't have time to bury it anyplace else before he was killed in a card game over a pot worth less than two hundred dollars. Only a fool like Pete would do something like that when he had twenty thousand buried.

His irritation made it even harder to ignore the broken fence. "Oh hell, I might as well fix it. Why should the coyotes have all those chickens?"

He was silent while he braced the corner poles and replaced others that looked ready to break. Then he cut out the broken sections of wire, leaving clean sections to be replaced. "Can't say I look forward to catching all these chickens," he said to Samson as he wired a new piece of fence into place. "But she'll need eggs to get back on her feet. After the baby comes, she won't have time to be chasing them down."

He finished one section of wire and began cutting a piece to fit the next gap.

"Can't figure why a woman like that would marry Pete, the lazy son of a bitch. She wasn't brought up out here. You can tell that from her voice. It's soft, sort of gives the words a little squeeze before she says them. You know, leaves off a few letters here and there. Virginia or Carolina. After bringing her all this way, why did Pete run off and leave her, especially with a baby coming? It's a terrible thing for a woman to be alone."

He finished the last piece of wire, tested his work, and found it strong enough to withstand coyotes and wolves.

"A lot of good work was done on this place some time ago, Samson. The man who built that cabin knew what he was doing. This shed, too. But everything is in bad need of work now."

Joe hadn't been on a farm since he was sixteen. He'd thought he hated it. But as he had grown older, he'd come to treasure his memories of the years he'd spent with his grandmother. But that kind of life needed a family, and he'd had none since she died. He'd never found a woman who made him want to stop drifting. He'd never found the right kind of place. Despite the sagging corral, the shingles missing from the roof, loose hinges, broken windows, this place seemed the right kind, Mary the right kind of woman.

No use letting those thoughts take root in his mind. He'd be gone in a few days. This place needed a man here day after day, a man who loved it as much as the man who built it had. Maybe Mary Wilson could find her a better husband this time. She sure was pretty enough. Dainty and feminine. She was the kind of woman to mess up a man's thinking, start him to doing things he didn't want to do.

Like fixing a chicken yard.

Joe went into the shed and started tossing out fence posts and corral rails until he got down to the floor-boards. They came up easily. The ground looked as if it had never been disturbed, but he took a shovel to it anyway. Half an hour later, he knew Pete hadn't buried the gold under the shed. He replaced the floorboards, but balked at dragging all those posts and rails back inside.

"Hell! As long as I've got everything out, I may as well fix the corral. I'm going to need someplace to put that damned cow once I find her."

Joe picked up the poles and started for the first gap in the rails. He wasn't able to get thoughts of Mary out of his mind. Nor of the farm he hadn't seen in seventeen years. In his mind they just naturally seemed to go together.

◦◦◦

Mary woke up feeling better than she had in days. She was strongly tempted to get up and have some more of the stew. But she resisted. She was going to tell him to leave. She couldn't have a stranger of unknown character hanging about the place.

"He's coming!" Fear sounded in Sarah's voice and showed in her eyes. She bolted from the window into the corner between the bed and the wall.

Mary felt tension mount within her. It was a lot easier to plan to tell Joe to leave than actually do it. The sound of his footsteps on the porch made her flinch. The grating sound of the door frayed her nerves.

He entered with a plucked chicken in his hand.

"I figured the coyotes could do without this cockerel," he said as he walked over to the table and laid the chicken down. He poured part of the water into a pot, the rest into a basin.

"More water," he said to Sarah, holding out the bucket.

Sarah glanced at Mary. Mary nodded her head, and Sarah inched forward to take the bucket. However, she froze when she opened the door.

"Your dog," Mary said.

"We've got to do something about that."

Joe sent his dog to keep his horse company. At least that was what he told him to do. Mary doubted the animal would actually obey.

"Do you want this chicken cooked any special way?" Joe asked, going back to the table and beginning to prepare the chicken for cooking.

"No." She had meant to tell him to go at once, but he had taken the wind out of her sails. She was acutely aware of his overpowering male presence. Just watching him move about the cabin in those tight pants caused something inside her to warm and soften. The feeling unnerved her. She found Mr. Ryan very attractive. Stranger or not.

"You never did tell me how you and Pete came to be partners, or why you decided to come here now."

She shouldn't be asking questions. It would just postpone the inevitable. She decided to sit up. It was impossible to talk to this man lying down. She felt at such a disadvantage. Unlike her attempt earlier, Mary was able to sit up and position the pillows behind her.

"It was more an accident than anything else." Joe spoke without facing her as he worked over the chicken. "We had claims next to each other. A mining camp is a dangerous place. Men who find color sometimes disappear or turn up dead. I watched Pete's back, and he watched mine. When our claims played out, it made sense to take what gold we'd found and hire on to guard a shipment of gold to Denver."

He started cutting up the chicken and dropping the pieces into the pot.

"I don't remember anything after the first mile."

Joe had paused before the last sentence. He went back to work, cutting through the joints with short, powerful thrusts of the knife.

"I woke up in my bedroll with the sheriff standing over me and empty gold sacks on the ground next to me. I was convicted and sent to jail."

He finished cutting up the chicken, wiped his hands, and set the pot on stove. He looked straight at Mary. "Pete set me up. He stole that gold. When I found out he was dead and the gold never found, I broke out and came here. This must be where he hid it."

Mary was too stunned to speak. He couldn't possibly expect her to believe that. She had never thought much of her husband's honesty, but she couldn't believe Pete had been a common thief.

She started but discarded several responses. "That's absurd," she finally said. "Pete didn't steal any gold. He didn't hide anything here."

"He did both. I mean to find it and clear my name. Besides, part of that gold is mine. Some is yours."

Mary wondered how much gold was hers. She needed to hire someone to help with the ranch. There was so much she couldn't do, especially with a baby. Of course, he might not be telling the truth. She wasn't going to get excited about the money until she saw it.

Joe started a fire under the chicken. When he was satisfied that it was well caught, he opened the window and tossed out the dirty water.

Sarah entered with the fresh water. Joe placed the bucket on the table, and Sarah retreated to her place in the corner.

"You don't have to hide from me," he said.

Mary thought he sounded as if his feelings were hurt.

"Why don't you rummage around on those shelves and see if you can find some canned fruit or vegetables," he told Sarah. He took out some coffee beans and put them in a pan to roast on the stove. Next he measured out rice and set it on the edge of the stove. Then he cleaned the table and set out plates.

Mary didn't know what to do. Her hands closed over the gun under the covers. She had to tell him to leave. It was out of the question to let him stay. He had to go now. It would soon be night.

"I find it hard to believe Pete did what you said. But if he did, I'm truly sorry." She didn't know how to say there were times she had come close to hating her husband. "It was very kind of you to fix us something to eat, but you needn't stay any longer.

"I'm much stronger now. I'm sure you'll want to make it to town in time to get a room in the hotel."

Joe looked at her. She felt a flush burn her cheeks. She would swear he was laughing at her. Inside, of course. His expression didn't change.

"If you're trying to get rid of me, you're wasting your time. As soon as I find the gold, I'll head out for California, but not one day before. As for a hotel, I don't dare go near town. Somebody might recognize me."

"There's no gold here. Pete was home only one night after he came back from Colorado. He went off again the next day and got himself shot."

"Don't worry, I don't mean to stay any longer than I have to. And if you're worried about your reputation, your condition is protection enough." He directed a frankly amused look at her. "I wish you'd put that pistol back where it belongs. It's not a good idea to sleep with a loaded gun."

Mary didn't know why she brought the pistol out

from under the covers. Maybe it was the fact that he seemed to be able to read her mind. Maybe she felt she ought to do something and nothing else had worked. Whatever the reason, she found herself pointing the pistol at Joe.

"If you're going to shoot me, get on your feet first. I'd hate to have it known I was killed by a woman so weak she couldn't stand up."

"I can stand up," Mary insisted. To prove her point, she threw back the covers and started to get to her feet. Immediately she felt faint.

Joe caught her before she fell.

"I never met such a foolish woman in my life. Stay in that bed, or I'll tie you down. You can shoot me when you feel better. Meantime, you'd better give me this." He took the pistol from her slackened grasp. "Next thing you know, you'll drop it and put a hole through the chicken pot. I'm not chasing down another rooster."

Mary started to laugh. The whole situation was too absurd. Nothing like this happened to ordinary people. She was ordinary, so it shouldn't be happening to her.

She certainly shouldn't be experiencing this odd feeling. It almost felt as if she wanted to cry. But she didn't feel at all sad. She felt bemused and bewildered. Her brain was numb. Here she was, completely helpless, and she had tried to shoot the only human who had come along to help her.

She must be losing her mind. This man, this stranger, had taken the gun from her hands, put her to bed, then gone back to fixing her supper. And he planned to stay until he found the gold he insisted Pete had hidden here.

He was always ahead of her. That was a new experience for Mary. She had never known a man to act intelligently. She wasn't even sure she thought men could be intelligent, but Joe was. He was kind, too, despite his gruff manner.

"The kid has found some peaches," Joe announced. "I hope that's all right with you."

"I like peaches," Mary said. The aroma of roasting coffee beans permeated the cabin. The smell made her mouth water.

"Supper will be ready in less than an hour. Time for a nap. You can dream of ways to spend your share of the gold when I find it."

Again he had read her mind. The first thing she intended to buy was a dress for Sarah.

❧

"Dinner was delicious. You could make a living as a cook."

"Don't much like cooking."

"But you're so good at it."

"If I have to eat it, I want it to taste good. Just put those dishes in the sink, kid. If you cover them with water, most of the stuff will soak off by itself."

"Why won't you call Sarah by her name?"

"Why won't she speak to me?"

"I don't know."

"Neither do I."

"I thought a man like you would have an answer for everything."

"Hell, there's more I don't know than I'll ever be able to figure out."

"That doesn't bother you?"

"I know what I need. The rest would just clutter up my head."

The clatter of plates caught his attention. "Well, I think I'll see about fixing up a bed for myself."

Mary figured she must have looked startled.

"Don't worry about me crowding in here. Samson and I will bed down outside. I don't like being closed in, in case somebody comes looking for me."

He stood and stretched. "I've had me a full day. I imagine I'll sleep tight. Leave the chicken and coffee right where they are, kid. All they need is a little heat, and they'll be just as good tomorrow. Don't worry about locking the door. With Samson around, nothing's going to come near the house."

Mary wondered how he knew she was planning to lock herself in.

Joe backed into Sarah's tree and knocked it over. Uttering a sharp oath, he bent to set it up. Sarah was there before him. She cast him a glance that was at once fearful and accusatory.

"I asked you to watch your language," Mary reminded him.

"I did," Joe said, looking aggrieved. "I could have said much worse." He rubbed a spot on his leg. "That damned tree stuck me."

"I appreciate your restraint."

"No, you don't. You're like every other woman God ever made. You smile and mumble about restraint, but you keep after a man until you get exactly what you want. I had a grandmother just like you. Sorry about your tree, kid."

"She has a name."

"And I'll use it when she talks to me. 'Night, ma'am."

When the door closed behind him, Mary felt the strength go out of her body just like water from a sink when the plug was pulled. The man energized everything around him. Now that he had gone, she felt exhausted. Being full of hot food didn't help.

"Leave the dishes in the water, Sarah. I ought to be able to get up tomorrow. We can do them then."

"I'll do them now," the child replied. "He wouldn't leave them."

No, he wasn't the kind of man to leave things undone. He seemed methodical, capable, dependable, yet he was drifting through life, able to do any job required of him, but never stopping to put down roots.

Mary had decided not to marry again. Her father and Pete had taught her that a bad husband could destroy all the love and comfort around him. But if she ever changed her mind, she meant to find a man she could depend on to stay in one place year after year. That wasn't Joe. Yet somehow she kept thinking about him.

"Is he really going to sleep on the ground?" Sarah asked.

"That's what he said."

"Is he going to be here tomorrow?"

"Why do you ask?"

"I like him. He's nice."

"Then why don't you speak to him?"

"Pa never liked it when I talked. He said girls ought to keep quiet because they have nothing to say."

"Your father didn't think much of women. It seems to be quite the opposite with Mr. Ryan. I've never in my life seen a man pay so much attention to a woman's comfort."

"Do you think he'll stay?"

"He said he would stay until I was stronger."

"I mean all the time."

A warm feeling flooded through Mary. "He means to go to California. He's only staying out of politeness."

"I wish his dog would go to California."

"I'm sure he won't hurt you."

"He's so big."

"So is Mr. Ryan, but you're not afraid of him, are you?"

"I don't think so."

Mary felt a silent chuckle inside. "I don't think I am either. Now it's time to go to sleep. I have a feeling Mr. Ryan will be up early in the morning."

❧

"That's one beautiful woman," Joe said to Samson. He took a last puff on his cigarette and rubbed it out. "A man like me ought not stay around here too long. I should head for California as soon as she can get out of bed without falling over."

The night had turned cold. Millions of stars glimmered in a cloudless sky. The saguaro cactus cast black shadows against the horizon. The spidery arms of an ocotillo contrasted with the broomlike arms of the paloverde and the more dense ironwood and mesquite. An owl hooted. Some field mouse wouldn't be around to see the dawn.

This place made him uneasy. It was like a home, the kind that folded itself around a man and made him want to stay put. It made him think of his mother and the time he saw her last. He was just sixteen when she threw him out for the man she was living with. Five months later she was dead.

"There are two kinds of women," Joe said to Samson as they walked across the ranch yard. "There's the kind that's hot to get married but doesn't like men the way they are. They pretend they do, but as soon as the preacher says a few words over them, they set about changing their husbands into something they like better than what they got. Stay away from them. They'll either drive you to drink or drive you out of the house."

Having changed his mind, Joe climbed into the loft and spread it over the straw. Samson looked up as if he were waiting for Joe to invite him in, but Joe didn't.

"Then there's the other kind, the kind that use men and let men use them. They destroy themselves. Like Flora. Nothing was ever enough. She always had to have more. Until one day she just burned herself out."

Samson sat down on his haunches. Joe leaned back on the straw and smiled. It sure beat his rock-and-sand bed from last night.

"Of course Mary is different from either one of them. She's pretty enough to make a man forget his responsibilities. She's so delicate and fragile, you want to protect her. You saw me. I couldn't wait to cook her dinner and fix up her chicken yard.

"But she's strong. She's got staying power. Once she picks out a man, she won't throw him out no matter how much work he needs. She'd even have made something of Pete if the fool had stayed."

Joe told himself he should have been looking for gold instead of mending fences and chasing chickens. This woman was going to get him into trouble yet. He turned over, didn't like his position, turned back again.

"Of course she tried to be brave, to pretend she wasn't scared to death. She could hardly hold the gun. I doubt she'd have had the strength to pull the trigger if a wolf had been coming through the door. Makes you want to hold her close and tell her nothing's ever going to hurt her again."

Joe sat up and glared at Samson.

"And that's how they get you," he said. "You got to keep alert. Because if that's not enough, they throw in babies and little girls. That Mary Wilson has got a quiver full of arrows. The first man who sets foot on this place won't have a chance. He'll be Mr. Wilson before the dust settles."

Joe flopped back down. *He* was the first man to set foot on this place.

"That's why I'm heading out to California the minute I find the gold."

Some time in the night Joe awoke to the sound of a crescendo of growls. Then he heard a yip cut off in midcry.

"Samson, I sure wish you could smell gold as quick as you can coyotes," he commented before he turned over and went back to sleep.

Three

JOE WONDERED IF MARY AND THE KID ALWAYS SLEPT THIS soundly. Mary had locked the door, but it had been a simple matter to enter through the window. He'd searched almost every corner of the cabin, and neither of them had awakened. He would have liked to think this trusting slumber was due to his presence, but if it was, it would vanish the minute they found out what he had done.

Joe didn't like going through Mary's things. It made him feel like a sneak, but he had to search every part of the cabin. It was stupid to let scruples stop him now. Still, he was uncomfortable when he opened a drawer to find it filled with undergarments. He almost closed it again. It hardly looked big enough to hide one bag of gold. He closed his eyes and ran his hands under the neat piles of garments to the bottom and back of the drawer.

Nothing.

He felt his body relax. He hadn't realized he was so edgy. Nor did he know why. Mary was a virtual stranger. Searching her home shouldn't bother him at all. But seeing and touching her clothes produced a feeling of intimacy he didn't welcome. It made him acutely aware of her physical presence. His body's response embarrassed him. He was a decent man. He shouldn't feel this way about a pregnant woman.

He quickly finished the wardrobe and turned his attention to the trunk. It wasn't locked. The top shelf needed no search to see there was nothing there. He had his hands deep among the dresses and blankets underneath when he heard a pistol click. He turned to see Mary sitting up in the bed, the cocked pistol aimed at him.

"What do you think you're doing?" she asked.

"Searching for the gold." He didn't think she would shoot him, but he couldn't be sure. He boldly finished running his hand along the bottom of the trunk.

"I told you I knew nothing of the gold," Mary said.

"I had to make sure for myself."

"I ought to shoot you."

"You'd have trouble getting rid of the body. And if you didn't kill me, you'd have to take care of me."

The kid woke up. She was frightened to find Joe in the house, Mary holding a pistol on him.

"I ought to turn you in to the sheriff."

"I'd be gone before he could get here. And I'd come back."

Mary kept the pistol pointed at Joe a moment longer, then slowly lowered it. He felt the tension in his muscles ease.

"You really think Pete stole that gold and buried it here, don't you?"

Joe began to put Mary's things back in order. "There's no other explanation for what happened. He came here right after the trial. It hasn't turned up anywhere else, and it wasn't on him when he was killed."

"He certainly didn't give it to me."

Joe closed the trunk and got to his feet. "I can see that, unless you're the kind who can sit on a fortune for six months and not spend a penny."

Mary looked him in the eye. "I could sit on it for a lifetime. I won't touch stolen money."

He believed her. There was a quality about her that said she would have nothing to do with a dishonest man.

Joe went to the woodbox and started picking up

pieces of wood to start a fire in the stove. "Well, it's not inside the cabin, so you don't have to worry about me going through your things again."

"Despite your actions, I think you're honest."

Joe laid the fire carefully. Her response was unexpected. At best, he'd supposed she would only tolerate him. What else could she do? She was alone, down in bed, twenty-two miles from town, with no one to help her but a six-year-old kid. But to decide he was honorable! She must be up to something.

"No need to go flattering me. I know what I am. I never pretended to be anything else."

"And just what are you, Mr. Ryan?"

Joe lighted the coal-oil-soaked stick he had placed at the center of the wood. A pale yellow flame illuminated the inside of the stove, casting flickering shadows onto its sooty walls.

He had avoided that question for years. He wanted to think he was like everybody else—worthy of dreams, worthy of success. But Flora said he was nothing but a two-bit drifter, a poor and overly serious one at that.

"Nothing much, ma'am. I guess you could say I'm drifting along, looking for a reason to stay put. Kid, I need some eggs for breakfast. See what you can find." He poured water into the coffeepot and put it on to heat.

"Where is your dog?" Mary asked. "You know she's afraid of it."

He went to the door and looked outside. "He's gone," he said to Sarah. "Scram."

The child stuck her head out the door, looked around, then darted outside.

"Don't you want to be something else?" Mary asked after Sarah had gone.

He poured out a handful of coffee beans and dumped them into a grinder.

"I want my name cleared," he said over the noise of

the grinder. "Once a man is branded a thief, it doesn't matter what else he is. People can't see anything else."

"Isn't there anybody who can speak for you?"

"It won't do any good. I broke jail. As long as the gold is missing, nothing else matters." He poured the freshly ground coffee into a pot.

"Then I hope you find it."

"Enough to help?" He unwrapped the bacon and began to cut thick slices from it.

"I don't know anything."

"You can try to remember everything he did while he was here, every movement, every word he spoke. Even his expression, his mood." He pulled the curtain across the alcove where Mary slept. "You'd better get dressed. Breakfast will be ready in half an hour."

⟨∞⟩

"What was that noise last night?" Mary asked.

She was seated at the table, a cup of coffee in front of her, waiting for Joe to finish filling her plate. He had tried to keep her in bed, but she had been determined to get up. He had insisted on helping her walk. She didn't need his help, but it was nice of him to offer. The least she could do was lean on him.

"It was Samson," Joe said, setting down a plate with bacon, one egg, and a thick slice of bread in front of Sarah and another in front of Mary. "You won't be troubled by coyotes any more. Give him a month, and there won't be one within ten miles."

"It's a shame you can't leave him here when you go to California. We could sure use him."

"Can't do that. If Samson stays, so do I."

The statement had been made in jest—at least Mary thought so—but the effect on each of them was electric. Mary realized that she had practically issued Joe an invitation to remain at the ranch indefinitely. Judging from his expression, he had considered accepting it. What shocked Mary even more was the realization that she wanted him to stay. She didn't know what kind of arrangement they might be able to work out, but the idea of having Joe Ryan around all the time was a pleasant one.

"Eat your breakfast," Joe said. "There's nothing much worse than cold eggs." He glanced over at Sarah. "We're going to have to do something about that cow. A kid like you should be drinking milk. You're nothing but skin and bones."

"Sarah has always been thin," Mary said.

"Thin is okay. Skinny as a stick isn't," Joe said. "You know where that cow got to?"

Sarah nodded.

"As soon as we clean up, you show me. I refuse to let an old cow turn her nose up at me."

Mary watched him clear away the breakfast things, talking to a mute Sarah as if they were old friends. He didn't act like any man she'd ever known. In some ways he was just as dictatorial, just as unconcerned with her feelings as Pete had been. In other ways, he was the kindest, most thoughtful man she'd ever met. He was certainly the most helpful.

He must be up to something.

After Pete was killed, Mary had realized that she had never been able to trust men or depend on them. She had looked toward this Christmas as the beginning of her new life—just her, Sarah, and the baby.

Then Joe had showed up and she had started to question her decision. She found herself thinking *if all men were like Joe*, or *if I could find a husband like Joe*… The fact that he was an escaped criminal, a man on the run, didn't seem to weigh with her emotions. It didn't even weigh much with her mind.

She tried to tell herself to be sensible, but she couldn't. Maybe it was the baby. Her mother used to say pregnant women were prone to being emotional and sentimental. Her mother also said love nourished life. Nobody had ever nourished Mary like Joe. Whatever the reason, she liked him. She didn't want him to go away.

∽∾

Joe had reached the conclusion that six months in jail had made him crazy. There was no other way to explain why he was leading a milk cow and talking to a six-year-old girl who wouldn't say a word to him. He ought to be turning the place inside out. Failing that, he ought to be on his way to California. Some U.S. Marshal was sure to be on his trail by now.

But here he was, walking through the desert with a cow and a kid as if he didn't have a care in the world. Yep, he was crazy.

"You got to be firm with a cow," he said as they reached the yard. "They're real stubborn, especially if you're little. My grandma had an old black-and-yellow cow who used to chase me until I beat her with a stick. Never had any trouble after that. Get me that bucket I left on the porch.

"You got to tie the cow's head close to the post," he said when Sarah returned with the bucket he had washed and set out on the porch earlier. "That way they can't turn around. Won't fight so much if they can't see. Now fetch me the stool."

Joe felt silly sitting on the tiny stool, but he had to show the kid what to do. After that, she could do all the sitting.

"You got to watch her at first," Joe said. "She's been on her own and won't like being milked." The cow kicked at Joe when he started to wash her teats. Joe slapped her on the hip. "Let her know you won't put up with any nonsense." He pushed on the cow's hip, but she wouldn't move her leg back. "Keep pushing on her until she moves that leg," he told Sarah. "It's easier to milk her that way."

Joe pulled on a teat. A stream of warm milk hit the bucket. He jerked the pail out of the way just as the cow kicked at him. He smacked her on the hip again.

"She'll do that a few more times before she figures out you mean business. Cows are stubborn, but they're not dumb. Has she got a name?"

The kid shook her head.

"She's got to have a name. How will she know when you're talking to her?" Joe thought a moment. "How about Queen Charlotte? She acts like a queen, and she's just as ugly as the real one."

Sarah nodded her agreement.

"Good. Now it's your turn."

Sarah looked reluctant.

"You can't let her know you're afraid, kid, or she'll keep on kicking until you give up. Come on, sit down."

Sarah sat. She reached out a tentative hand.

"Don't be timid. You're the boss."

Sarah squeezed the teat three times before the cow kicked the bucket over.

Joe smacked Queen Charlotte on the hip and moved her back into milking position. "Now try again." Seconds later the cow kicked again. Sarah stood up.

"Here, let me show you," Joe said, taking his place on the stool. "I haven't done this in nearly fifteen years, but it's something you don't forget. Move over, Queen Charlotte," he said to the cow. "You're about to get the milking of your life. You kick this bucket one more time, and I'll feed you to Samson piece by piece."

Sarah giggled.

Through the window, Mary watched, bemused, as Joe milked the cow, talking to Sarah and the cow equally. When Samson wandered up, Joe included him in his conversation, introducing him to Sarah just as if he were an equal.

The man fascinated Mary. The more she saw of him,

the more she wanted to know about him. She was drawn to him in a way that defied her notions about the feelings that could exist between a man and a woman. He touched a part of her that had lain silent all these years, the loving and longing part that Pete had nearly killed. She wanted to reach out and touch him, as though physical contact would recapture the youthful dreams she'd nearly forgotten.

She found herself looking at his body, admiring the shape of his thighs, the curve of his backside, the power of his shoulders. She had never felt this way about Pete. She had never looked forward to their nights in bed, nor had she missed them after he left. But Joe touched something deeper in her, far beyond anything Pete had touched. She found herself blushing, wondering what it would be like to sleep with Joe.

Samson tried to lick Sarah's face. The child was still frightened of the huge dog, but Joe made her hold out her hand for Samson to smell. Then she had to pat him on the head. Sarah was still wary, but Joe had broken the back of her fear.

Joe laughed, and the sound sent a frisson of pleasure racing through Mary. It was a deep, rolling sound, a sound that promised something very special to the person who could find the source and tap into it.

She picked up her pad and began to draw. In a few moments, she had preserved forever some of the magic of this morning.

∞

Joe looked over Mary's shoulder as she drew a picture of Queen Charlotte and General Burnside staked out in the meadow beyond the barn, mountains in the distance.

"It's incredible," Joe marveled. "I don't see how you do it. You put a few squiggly lines here, a few more there, and you have a picture. All I'd have would be a bunch of squiggly lines."

Mary laughed, pleased with the compliment. Pete had never liked her drawings. He had considered them a waste of time. "It's not very hard. You just have to practice."

"Hell, I could—Sorry, I can't seem to control my tongue. It doesn't hardly know how to talk without cussing."

"That will come with practice, too."

"Maybe. What do you do with all those pictures?"

"What should I do with them?"

Joe looked at the drawing again. "Sell them. I know hundreds of miners who'd pay plenty to have something like that to brighten up their walls. You could make more money than you can running cows on this place."

"I'm perfectly content to stay here running cows. Besides, I like to do drawings for people I know. I ought to be doing some for Sarah. She wants to decorate the house for Christmas."

"If that pathetic tree is any example," he said, indicating Sarah's bundle of thorns, "she ought to give up the idea."

"If you understood about her mother, you'd understand why it's so important to her."

"Then tell me. I won't figure it out otherwise."

"Sarah's mother died when Sarah was four. I don't know why Pete married her. He seems to have hated everything about her. He got rid of everything that belonged to her or reminded him of her. According to Sarah, her mother loved Christmas and would spend weeks getting ready for it. She used to spend hours singing to Sarah, telling her stories about *Père Noël*. Last Christmas was Sarah's first since her mother's death. Pete wouldn't let her decorate, have a tree, or do anything for Christmas. To Sarah, that was like taking away the last link with her mother. She likes me, but she adored her mother. Christmas is all she has left of her. It's terribly important to her."

"Pete was a real bastard," Joe said. "Why in hell did you marry him?"

Mary ignored the curses. "Pete's stepfather was my uncle. He thought Pete would make a good husband for me. My father was anxious to get me out of the house. One less mouth to feed, one less female to contend with. I guess I was tired of waiting for a man who didn't exist."

Joe gave her the strangest look. Mary badly wanted to know what he was thinking. She wondered if he'd ever been in love, if he'd found his perfect woman. He seemed lighthearted, but beneath that she detected a cynical streak. He didn't believe in goodness. That was odd, considering he had so much of it in him.

"If she's hoping that ratty old tree will attract her *Père Noël*, she's looking down an empty chute."

"Please don't tell her that." Mary looked to where Sarah sat churning cream for butter. "She thinks if she believes hard enough, *Père Noël* will find her."

Joe shrugged and headed toward the door. "I don't know anything about *Père Noël*, but I do know about horses and cows. I'd better do some work on that corral."

"You don't have to do that."

"If I don't, you won't have any milk after I leave. It'll never hold Queen Charlotte the way it is now."

Still amused by his habit of bestowing fanciful names on his animals, Mary asked, "When are you leaving?" She was stunned to realize that she had known this man less than twenty-four hours, but she no longer thought in terms of his leaving.

She liked him. He might be a criminal, but she liked him.

No. He was an escaped convict, but she couldn't believe he was a criminal. He'd fixed three meals for them, perfect strangers he owed nothing, especially if Pete had set him up. He had spent hours helping Sarah, even though the child wouldn't speak to him. He had even praised Mary's drawings.

He was rugged, curt, and given to cursing, but

underneath all that roughness he had a generous nature. He showed a wonderful understanding of her and Sarah. On top of that, he took better care of her than any man she'd ever known, including her father. Why shouldn't she fall in love with him? He was exactly the kind of man she'd always hoped to find.

No, she had to be mistaken.

She couldn't love him. She was letting his kindness go to her head. Maybe it was being pregnant. Her mother had warned her that pregnancy could do strange things to a woman.

Mary redirected her attention to her drawing pad. She needed more Christmas pictures for Sarah. Drawing would give her something to do and keep her mind off Joe and the foolish notion that she might be falling in love with him.

That evening after dinner, Mary tacked up the drawings she had done during the day. She wondered if they would mean anything to Sarah. The child had never known anything but the desert. To Mary, nothing about the desert spoke of Christmas. She had done a few drawings of the surrounding hills and mountains, but she had been in Arizona only eleven months. Christmas to her was the snow-covered pines and oaks of her native Virginia, magnolia, and bright holly berries.

It sounded strange to hear rain on the roof—it had been raining since late afternoon. Even more strange to Mary, everything would look the same tomorrow. In this land, rain didn't bring the green she longed for.

"It's a shame you don't have any paints," Joe said, inspecting a drawing before he handed it to her to put on the wall. "It just doesn't look like Christmas without color."

"Pete would never buy me any. No paper either. This is my last pad."

Pete used to get angry when she drew. But when she

was drawing, she could pretend he didn't exist. Joe was a part of her drawings. He was already in several.

He liked to watch her. He said it pleased him to see the lines come to life, capturing a living scene. Her pleasure increased because of his. He would laugh and point to a cactus or a ridge that had just come into being. For a few minutes, it would seem he almost forgot the gold and the sentence hanging over his head.

At times like that, it was terribly hard to remember he'd soon be gone.

"Would you mind heating some water so Sarah can have a bath?" she asked.

Joe gave Sarah an appraising glance. "The kid *is* rather dirty."

Taking a bath was not a simple operation. A fire had to be lit in the stove and water brought in from outside and heated in every available pot and pail. The tub had to be cleaned out and brought in from the shed. Last of all, the water had to be poured into the tub. Mary hadn't been able to do this for months. Cloth baths just weren't the same as soaking in a tub of hot water.

"What about you?" Joe asked.

"I'll take cloth baths until after the baby comes," Mary said. "I hate to ask you, but you'll have to go outside until Sarah is finished."

"I do all the work, then I'm the one who gets to sit shivering on the front porch?"

"I'm sorry, but it wouldn't seem right to—"

"Never mind. I need to dig a few more holes anyway."

The door opened with a protesting squeak. Joe reminded himself to put some bacon grease on it in the morning.

∞

"You can take the bathtub out now," Mary said.

She was framed in the doorway, golden light behind her. Joe thought he'd never seen anyone so beautiful.

Her thick, dark hair—very sensibly done up at the back of her head, with a few curls loose to soften the look— seemed jet-black in the dark, her skin nearly white by comparison. Her eyes glistened luminous and wide in a face that seemed too delicate for a land known to be hard on women.

Joe got up off the porch steps. His joints felt stiff. It had stopped raining, and the stars had come out, but the night was too cold for sitting on stone steps. He was surprised to see the kid still in pants. "Why isn't she wearing a dress? Girls ought to be clean and sweet-smelling, all curls and ruffles and bows. She still looks like a boy."

"She doesn't have any dresses," Mary said.

"Why not?" Joe asked. He'd never heard of a girl having no dresses. It didn't seem right.

"Pete wouldn't buy her any. He said she'd only tear them up and have to wear pants anyway."

"I wish I'd known. I'd have beaten the hell out of Pete when I had the chance." He caught Mary's stern look. "I'm sorry, but it's enough to make a man cuss to see a little girl as pretty as the kid have to look like a boy because her bobcat-mean pa wouldn't buy her a dress."

Mary brushed Sarah's long auburn hair to help it dry faster. "I mean to do something about it as soon as I'm able."

Joe decided they ought to do something about it now. "You got some ribbon?"

"Yes."

"How about some good-smelling powder?"

Mary smiled. "Yes. What do you want it for?"

"I want you to put the powder on the kid, the ribbon in her hair."

"Open the trunk and hand me the round box on the top. And a piece of red ribbon if I have any."

Joe found the box easily. The ribbon was another

matter. He found a tangle of red, but it was too narrow for Sarah's hair. He chose a yellow ribbon instead. "You can use the red to make bows for the tree," he said. His grandmother had done that when he was a little boy. He handed the yellow ribbon to Mary, then turned to the tree. It was a pathetic mess. He couldn't put bows on that. His grandmother would rise out of the grave and come after him.

"We've got to have a better tree than that," he said aloud. "That's a disgrace. Are there any pines or junipers nearby?" he asked Mary.

"There're some up in the hills."

"After breakfast tomorrow, I'll see what I can find." He turned to see Sarah staring at him, eyes wide. The yellow ribbon was just the right shade to set off her hair. "See, I knew you were a pretty little thing. Pretty enough to have little boys giving each other black eyes over you." He squatted in front of her. "Would you like a real tree?"

Sarah nodded her head vigorously.

Mary had dusted Sarah's shoulders with white powder. Joe bent over and took a sniff.

"Pretty as a picture, and you smell good, too. I know your mama would be proud as a peacock to see you. Now all you need is—"

Sarah threw her arms around Joe and hugged him until he thought she was going to cut off his air. Slowly he let his arms slide around her. Her body seemed much too slight for such intense feeling. He didn't know how to react. In his whole life, he'd never had a child hug him.

For a while he thought she wasn't ever going to let go. Then, quite as suddenly, she unclasped him and hid herself behind Mary.

"I was going to say all you need is a dress," he said, "but you're pretty enough without it." He stood up. His muscles felt as strange as his voice. "I guess it's time

I get myself over to the shed. Samson doesn't like to go hunting unless he knows I'm tucked up tight."

❧

Joe needed some time alone. He was feeling at sixes and sevens. He was strongly attracted to Mary. That he understood, that he knew how to combat. But this business with the kid hugging him until she nearly choked him had caught him off guard. Mary had weakened him, and the kid had closed in for the kill.

Not kill exactly, but he was down and sinking fast.

He no longer thought Mary had anything to do with Pete's thievery. If she found the gold, he was certain she would hand it over to him. She hadn't even been interested enough to ask how much of it was hers.

Despite the way he'd forced himself into her life, she had been gracious. She hadn't been pleased when she found him going through her things, but she seemed to understand why he'd had to do it. That was a hell of a lot more than he'd expected. Flora would have screamed like a wildcat. His mother would have hit him up beside the head. Mary had accepted his explanation and put her gun away.

No woman had ever taken his word for anything. Except his grandmother.

Mary had every reason to throw him out, but she greeted him with a smile sweeter than a spring sunrise. She talked to him about little things, things you talked about with people you felt comfortable around.

But now the kid had hugged him and his comfort had fled. There was something about a kid hugging you that was unlike anything else in the world. There must be a special soft spot in every man reserved for little girls. He had seen men who wouldn't hesitate to commit almost any evil reduced to tears by the plight of a child, but he'd never suspected that he was similarly susceptible. But he was, and the kid had scored a bull's-eye on her first throw. He wanted to march right back in there, give her a hug, and promise her that Christmas was going to be just as wonderful as she hoped.

But he couldn't. He had to find the gold and be gone before then. The longer he stayed, the greater the danger that the law would find him. He was foolishly letting Mary and the kid distract him from his goal. He'd spent no more than an hour looking for the gold today.

He dropped to his bed in the straw and pulled his bedroll around him. He'd start checking beneath all the stones in the yard tomorrow. After he and the kid found a decent Christmas tree. He couldn't stand the thought of her pinning all her hopes on that bundle of twigs.

And Mary and her baby?

That was a tough one.

Four

THE KID WAS HELPING JOE FIX THE CHIMNEY WHEN HE heard Mary mutter something under her breath. He looked around the corner of the cabin to where she sat on the porch.

"The preacher and his sister are coming," she said, "Brother Samuel and Sister Rachel Hawkins."

Joe hadn't intended to fix the chimney this morning, or any other morning. He had been inspecting the cabin to see if any stones showed signs of having been removed recently. A few stones in the chimney were loose.

Once he realized that there was nothing behind them but more stones, his excitement had died down, to be replaced by a dull fear that he would never find the gold. Then he decided to reset the stones properly rather than just shove them back into place.

He had almost finished the job when Brother Samuel and Sister Rachel drove into the yard. Joe could tell at a glance that he wasn't going to like them.

From the look of things, they weren't going to like him any better. Brother Samuel frowned as though he'd just come upon a condemned sinner and didn't like the smell. Sister Rachel looked as if she'd never had any fun in her life and was determined that nobody else would have any either. They were both dressed in black.

Joe didn't like black. It depressed him. Seemed it had depressed Brother and Sister Hawkins, too.

Samson had been lying next to Mary's chair. But

when the Hawkinses got down from their buggy, he rose to his feet, a growl deep in his throat.

"Good morning," Mary said, greeting the pair without getting up. She patted Samson until the growls stopped. "It's awfully kind of you to drive so far to see me."

"It didn't seem so far," Brother Samuel said. "The morning is brisk, the sun heartening."

"I've been expecting to see you in town," Sister Rachel said. "You know my brother can't think of you out here alone without becoming distressed." Brother Samuel helped his sister mount the porch steps. She walked around Samson to take the chair Mary offered her. Brother Samuel chose to stand.

"I know I look as big as a cow, but I've got another month," Mary told her. "Besides, if all goes well, I mean to have the baby here."

"Surely you don't mean to have it by yourself."

"Oh, no. I'll hire someone to stay with me."

"I'd feel so much better if you would move to town now," Brother Samuel said. "I'm most concerned about you."

"I can't afford the cost of putting Sarah and myself up in a hotel for a month."

"I'm sure the ladies of Pine Flat would be glad to offer you and Sarah places to stay."

Joe wondered why neither brother nor sister offered to take Sarah and Mary into their own home.

"I couldn't be separated from Sarah," Mary replied, "not after her losing both her mother and her father. Neither could I settle myself on anyone. I won't have a friend in the world if I start doing that."

"You'll have a friend in us no matter what you do."

"We'd offer to keep you with us," Sister Rachel said, "but we're away from home nearly all the time."

"Nonetheless, you can stay with us if it will convince you to come to town."

Joe noticed that Sister Rachel didn't look quite so enthusiastic as her brother. He guessed Brother Samuel was in the habit of offering haven to people and leaving Sister Rachel to do all the work.

"I didn't know you had hired a man to work for you," Brother Samuel said, eying Joe.

"Oh, he's not a hired hand. He's Pete's old partner…"

Mary's lips formed Joe's name, but she didn't say it.

Brother Samuel didn't come down the steps to shake hands with Joe. The inclination of his head was the only acknowledgment he made of their introduction.

"Pete's been dead six months. What's he doing here now?" Sister Rachel asked.

"He's here to…" Mary's voice trailed off.

"…to settle a partnership," Joe said, leaving his work and coming around the corner.

"Then why are you fixing the chimney?" Sister Rachel demanded.

"It needed fixing."

"It's not suitable!"

"I'm not a stonemason, but I think it'll hold up for a while."

"My sister means it's not suitable for you to be staying with a single woman without proper chaperonage."

"I should think her belly and the kid are chaperones enough."

Joe's answer was mild enough, but he felt anger boiling up inside him. Who the hell was this man to come in here and stick his nose in their business? Joe had read the Bible, and he didn't remember anything giving preachers permission to interfere in other people's affairs. Sister Rachel's shocked response to his answer amused him. The old biddy would probably fall down dead if a man so much as kissed her.

"In that case, I don't imagine you'll be staying long," Brother Samuel said. He didn't appear to be quite as shocked as his sister. He seemed angry. Joe suddenly wondered if the reverend brother had designs on Mary for himself. She was certainly pretty enough to tempt a man, even a cold fish like the reverend.

"I probably won't be here longer than a couple more days," Joe said. "Mary was a little run-down when I arrived. I'd like to be sure she's back on her feet before I leave."

"Why didn't you tell us you were unwell?" Sister Rachel asked. "I'd have come right away. In fact, I'll stay with you now. Samuel will just have to do without me for a few days."

"That's not necessary," Mary hastened to assure them. "I'm feeling much like my old self. I know your brother depends quite heavily on you, especially during the Christmas season. No, I'm fine now."

"If you're sure."

Joe would have sworn Sister Rachel was disappointed. Maybe she would have appreciated some relief from the heavy duties of the season.

"Will you be stopping by town when you leave?" Brother Samuel inquired of Joe.

"Probably," Joe replied. "I imagine I'll need to pick up a few things."

"We have other calls to make, so we'd better be on our way," Brother Samuel said to Mary as he helped his sister down the steps. "I'll be looking for you in town in a day or two," he said to Joe. "I know you wouldn't do anything that might damage Mrs. Wilson's reputation, but you can't be too careful. People will talk."

"They'd better not within my hearing," Joe answered.

Brother Samuel looked as though he hadn't expected that answer. His smile was uncertain.

"We'll be expecting you and Sarah in town to stay right after the New Year," Sister Rachel said to Mary. "If not, I'm coming to stay until after the baby arrives."

"I'll let you know," Mary said. She got to her feet but didn't go down the steps.

Joe went back to his work, but he kept watch until Brother Samuel and Sister Rachel had disappeared over the ridge. "I wonder where Sister Rachel left her broomstick?" he said to no one in particular. "Bound to be faster than that old buggy."

Mary laughed, then tried to pretend she hadn't.

∽∞∾

Mary eased down on the bed and leaned against the mound of pillows. She had to do some serious thinking. She couldn't have Brother Samuel thinking she would become his wife. He had never asked her, but she couldn't fail to notice the look in his eye.

She had been given no opportunity to dispel his illusions, but she would never marry him. She felt lucky to have survived her marriage to Pete, and she had no intention of putting herself in that trap again.

She wanted a quiet, stable life, not one manipulated by a man.

Yet she didn't want Joe to leave. She had felt her heart lurch when he said he'd see Brother Samuel in town in a couple of days. Already she had come to depend on him, to look forward to his company.

It was impossible not to compare the two men. Brother Samuel was an ardent man, even a passionate one, but his passion had nothing to do with the flesh. Being around Joe had made Mary very aware of her physical nature. It was impossible to look at him and not feel the magnetism of his presence. He was simply the kind of man who made a woman achingly aware of her femininity. Even pregnant, he made her feel desirable.

Mary decided that was a dangerous situation. It would undoubtedly be safer if Joe did meet Brother Samuel in town and then continued on to California. But she knew her life would be very empty if he left.

Her mother had warned her she wouldn't always be able to find love where she wanted it. Was she looking for it with Joe?

∞

Joe was jealous. There was no point in denying it. From the moment that man drove into the yard, he had felt it gnawing at his insides. He hadn't recognized it at first, but he did now.

He was jealous of the Reverend Brother Samuel Hawkins.

He looked around. There was nothing that could remotely be considered a Christmas tree. Sarah rode behind him, her little pinto struggling to keep up with his big gelding. Samson loped ahead, on the lookout for coyotes. The low hills were covered with a scattering of vegetation—mesquite, catclaw, and ironwood all looking much alike; ocotillo and prickly pear cactus; spiky agave with their tall blooming stalks; assorted grasses and bushes.

But no pines or junipers.

They would have to go higher if they were to find a Christmas tree.

Could he be falling in love? He couldn't allow that to happen. But wasn't that what being jealous meant? He'd only loved two women, and both of them had sent him away. Mary had tried—even held a gun on him. He didn't know if she had changed her mind, but he knew he wasn't the kind of man she wanted or the kind who would be good for her. She'd send him away in the end.

"What do you think of that tree?" he asked Sarah. It was a pitiful excuse for a tree, but it was a pine.

She shook her head.

"Look, if I'm going to traipse all over this mountain looking for a tree, you're going to have to talk to me."

The kid watched him out of silent eyes.

"You ought to know by now I won't hurt you. Even Samson likes you."

She still didn't speak.

"Okay, let's go back."

Before he could turn General Burnside around, she said, "It's not pretty," just as if she'd been talking all along. "Let's go higher."

As they wound their way up the mountainside, Joe decided that women got the hang of being female at an early age. Boys didn't figure out what it meant to be a man until much later. By the time they started courting, the girls had a ten-year head start. It was like shooting fish in a pond.

He headed General Burnside up a slope toward a patch of green about a mile away. Samson disappeared down a canyon.

Joe was letting himself get distracted. A dangerous thing. It was time he went back to looking for the gold and got out of here. He was getting too settled.

He was starting to like where he was.

He'd forgotten what being on a farm was like. For years he'd thought only of his mother and the man she threw him out for. But being here reminded him of the things he had liked about the farm. It seemed strange to him now, but he liked the way he was living. He didn't even mind the chores. He was beginning to get ideas about how to improve things, ideas about what Mary ought to do come spring. He'd enjoyed teaching Sarah how to milk Queen Charlotte. Hell, he'd sworn he'd never milk another cow after he left the farm. But there was something solid and comfortable about their big brown bodies. And it sure as hell was nice to have butter to put on his biscuits.

"Do you like that man?" Sarah asked.

"What man?"

"The one who came to the house this morning."

"No reason to dislike him."

"I don't like him. He makes Mary sad."

"How's that?"

"She gets all jumpy whenever he comes. She mumbles a lot after he's gone. I think she's afraid of that woman."

"I think your ma is just afraid they'll try to take too much care of her."

"Mary doesn't need anybody to take care of her. She has me."

Joe thought it was a nice thing for a little girl to say, but Sarah had no idea just how much a woman needed someone to take care of her. He didn't see how Mary was going to make out by herself.

"Do you always call your ma Mary?"

"Mary says she loves me like a mama, but she knows I have a real mama who's gone to heaven and is waiting for me there."

That would teach him to stick his nose in where it didn't belong.

"I bet she'd like it, though. She won't think you're forgetting your real ma, but women like to be called Ma. It's just not the same when you call her Mary."

"If you were married to her, would you want me to call you Pa?"

That nearly knocked him out of his saddle. No messing around. The kid had cut to the heart of the matter.

Joe wanted to marry Mary. He had fallen in love with her when she fainted while pointing a rifle at him. He'd just been dancing around the issue since then, trying to fool himself and everybody else.

"Yes. If I were married to Mary, I'd want you to call me Pa. I'd like having a little girl like you. I know Pete's your real pa, but I'd want you to call me Pa because that's how I'd feel about you."

Joe realized that he'd stayed away from women

because he didn't believe in love. He'd never felt it. His mother and Flora had talked about it all the time, but he didn't want any part of the destructive emotion they felt.

Mary and Sarah loved each other in an entirely different way. Wasn't it possible they could love him as well?

Don't be a fool. You're on the run. You can't stay here or anywhere else.

"Let's look up there," Sarah said, pointing to a clump of green even more distant than the one he had picked out.

Samson climbed out of the canyon and came to join them.

"Why is Christmas so important to you?" Joe asked.

"Mama told me she was going to die," Sarah began. She looked up at Joe. "But she said she wouldn't really be gone. She said she was going to stay with *Père Noël*, far away where I couldn't see her. She said *Père Noël* brought things from mommies to their little girls so they would know they hadn't forgotten them. She said she would send me something every Christmas."

Sarah looked away.

"Last year Papa said we couldn't have Christmas. He said it was foolish. He said *Père Noël* was a lie and Mama was just telling me a story so I wouldn't cry. He said she was gone away and I'd never hear from her again. He wouldn't even let me put a ribbon on the door so *Père Noël* could find our house."

She looked up at Joe once more.

"He didn't come. I put out my shoes, but there was nothing in them. Do you think Papa was right?"

Joe decided that if anybody'd ever deserved to die by slow torture, it was Pete Wilson. "No. *Père Noël* probably couldn't find you among all these cactus. I'm sure he's got all your presents saved up. He's going to look extra-special hard this year to make sure he doesn't miss you again. We'll put an extra-big bow on the door. We can leave a light in the window, too. We're a long way from town, you know."

"You really think he'll come?"

"I'm sure of it. Now we'd better find that tree and get back home, or we'll never get it decorated."

They had climbed several thousand feet. There were pines and junipers all around to choose from.

Sarah stopped and pointed to a ledge fifty feet above their heads. "There, that's the tree I want."

⟡

Mary saw them when they topped the ridge a mile away—Joe on his big gelding, a big man silhouetted against the landscape; Sarah on the pinto, a little girl who looked even smaller next to Joe; Samson, sniffing rocks in his never-ending quest for coyotes. And the tree. It was tied to Sarah's pony. It almost enveloped the child.

The baby turned over. Mary put her hand on her stomach. She was feeling funny today. The baby seemed to have moved lower in her body. It caused her to waddle like a duck. Just the thing to make a man like Joe look on her with approval.

She had given up pretending she didn't like him. Watching him riding patiently with Sarah conjured up even warmer emotions.

She loved Joe Ryan.

She still found it hard to believe a man like him existed. All the other men in her life had ended up being pretty much alike—rotten. She had given up hoping to find anybody different. Then, just when she felt she could carry on alone, Joe Ryan had come into her life and upset everything. He was exactly the kind of man she wanted.

But she couldn't have him.

If she were a sensible woman, she would marry Brother Samuel. He wasn't a warm man, but he was a kind one. He would prove to be stubborn in many ways, but a clever woman could probably handle him quite easily. And she was a clever woman.

But she didn't want Brother Samuel, even if he weren't a preacher, even if Sister Rachel weren't his sister. She wanted an escaped convict who was on the run. That made her real clever.

They stopped. Apparently Joe had to readjust the tree. She wondered where they'd found it. They had been gone for most of the day. It was nearly eight o'clock. The sun had dipped beyond the western hills, leaving streaks of orange, mauve, and a deep purply-black across the sky. She had become worried about them. She had been sitting on the porch for nearly two hours.

The fire in the stove would have gone out. Dinner would be cold. But that didn't matter now. Joe would be home in a little while. She could warm everything up.

Yes, Joe was coming home. This was where he belonged, where she felt he wanted to be, where she wanted him to be. But the world outside wouldn't let him stay.

She picked up her pen and began, with swift, sure strokes, to create a picture of Sarah and Joe silhouetted against the evening sky.

While she waited, she had tried to think of what she might do to help him. She had racked her brain for any possible clue to where Pete had hidden the gold. She had even thought of hiding Joe. There were miles of hills in which a man could lose himself. But she knew Joe wouldn't agree to that. He had come here to clear his name. He would never consider marrying her until he had.

And she wanted to marry Joe. She wanted him to be her husband, her lover, the father of the child she carried, the other children she hoped to have. She didn't know what she could do, but she made up her mind not to give up hope. She'd never thought a man like Joe existed, but he did. There had to be a way to keep him.

She flipped the page and began a second picture as Joe and Sarah rode into the yard.

Sarah seemed hardly able to contain her excitement. She flitted around the cabin, talking enough to make up for several months of silence.

"I bet it's the biggest Christmas tree in Arizona," she said.

Joe leaned the tree against the wall, then made a stand for it. It almost reached the ceiling. The branches spread out three feet on either side of the trunk.

"I'm sure it is," Mary agreed.

"We found dozens of other trees," Joe told her, "but she wouldn't be satisfied with any of them. She had to have the one growing on the highest ledge."

"It was the prettiest."

"You should have seen me clambering up the rocks like a mountain goat," Joe said. "Nearly broke my neck."

"It's beautiful," Mary said, "but a smaller one would have been nice. There's hardly enough room left for us."

"You can put lots of pictures on it," Sarah said, "lots more than that other old tree."

That other old tree had been shoved into the stove, its existence forgotten and unlamented.

"Joe said we could put ribbons all over it," Sarah told Mary. "I can't reach the top. Will you lift me, Joe?"

"If you don't stop dancing about, he's liable to hang you from the ceiling," Mary said.

"No, he won't. He said he'd like having a little girl like me. He said if he was married to you, he'd want me to call him Papa."

The escalation of tension was tangible. Joe kept his eyes on his work. He laid the tree on its side and measured the stand to make sure it fit. "Any marrying man would like a kid like Sarah," he said as he drove a nail through the stand into the bottom of the tree. "She rides like she was born to it." He drove in a second nail. "She'll probably learn to rope cows before she's ten."

"Will you teach me?"

The tension increased another notch.

Joe nailed one of the braces, turned the tree over, and nailed the second. "It's like Brother Samuel said, it's not proper to have a man like me hanging around." He nailed another brace. "I should have left by now." He nailed the last brace. He stood the tree up before he dared glance at Mary. "Some men just aren't born to settle down."

Joe set the tree in the corner.

Sarah's face broke into an ear-to-ear grin, and she jumped up and down, clapping her hands in her excitement. "It will be the most beautiful tree in Arizona. I know it will."

"We'll certainly do our best," Mary said, coming out of her trance. "I'll make the bows. You and Joe can tie them on."

"Give me one. Give me one," Sarah begged, too excited to be silent.

Mary quickly made a bow and handed it to the child.

"Lift me up," Sarah said to Joe. "Lift me high."

Mary's fingers flew, cutting ribbon and making bows as fast as she could, but nearly every other fiber of her being was focused on Joe. Time and time again he lifted Sarah as if she weighed nothing, good-naturedly joining in her excitement, talking to her as though she was the most important person in his life.

The child blossomed under his attention. It was hard to remember the scared, silent, hollow-eyed child she'd found when she became Pete's wife. Joe might think he wasn't meant to settle down, but he had the key to Sarah's heart.

And her own. She watched those powerful arms

lift the child and longed to feel them wrapped around her. She saw his smile, felt the warmth of his caring. His presence transformed everything around him—her, Sarah, the cramped and cold cabin. Mary felt warm and protected. She felt happy and content. She felt a longing so intense that it blocked out the pain in her back.

"That's all the ribbon," she said. "It's time for the pictures. Make sure you tie them on the tips of the branches so they'll hang right."

"You can do that," Joe said.

"I think I'll watch."

Sarah took her hand and pulled. "Please, you help too."

Mary started to get up, but the pain in her back grew worse.

"I'd better sit down. I think I did too much today."

"I told you I'd fix dinner when I got home," Joe said, worry clouding his eyes.

"You've done that often enough. Besides, I thought you'd like something warm after a long, cold ride. Only then I let it get cold."

"We came home too late."

Home! He'd said it. He couldn't be as untouched as he acted. He might not think he was a family man, but that was probably because things hadn't worked out for him in the past. That didn't mean he couldn't be a family man now.

The ugly fact of his uncompleted prison term reared its head, but Mary pushed it aside. Given time, they could find an answer to that. The real problem was how Joe felt.

She shifted position to ease the pain in her back. She wished the baby hadn't settled so low. It made it easier for her to breathe, but it put extra pressure on her spine.

Almost instinctively she reached for her drawing pad. Of all the scenes she had rendered with her pen, this was the most important. She regretted having no colors.

Without them, there was no way to capture the golden quality of the light that illuminated the cabin. It was impossible to show the drab, ordinary nature of Joe's clothes in contrast to the vibrant love of life that glowed in his eyes. It was impossible to show the transformation that had taken place in Sarah.

Most important of all, it was impossible to show the difference he had made in her life. Black and white had been all she needed before. That was how she'd viewed the world. But Joe had changed all that. He had brought spirit and passion into her life. He had brought love.

It was impossible to show that without color.

She looked down at her drawing. She hadn't missed anything—the cabin, the tree, Sarah, even herself in the corner. But Joe was at the heart of the picture. Without him, this would have been just one more in a long string of dismal evenings.

"Your mother is drawing again," Joe said to Sarah. "Let's see what she's doing this time."

Mary turned the page over quickly. "I'm trying to get you two and the Christmas tree in the same picture. That one didn't turn out the way I expected. Stop trying to look over my shoulder. I can't concentrate when you do that."

"I can't help it," Joe said. "I can't get over the way you make a picture appear—like magic."

Nothing like the magic you've wrought, Mary thought.

But as Mary turned her attention to her drawing, she realized that there was something missing.

There were no presents under the tree.

Joe thought about the presents, too. He imagined Mary had something hidden away for Sarah, but it couldn't be much. She hadn't been able to get to town, and Christmas was only three days off.

He paused on his walk to the barn. The night was radiant. The full moon flooded the landscape with light.

It wasn't the warm light of the day, and it was too weak to vanquish the shadows, but it was beautiful nonetheless. There was a ghostly stillness that was comforting, as though all the troubles of the world were held at a safe distance by some almighty hand. Countless stars winked in the dark canopy of the sky, their tiny lights friendly and cheerful.

Samson trotted up. "Are you taking the night off?" Samson licked Joe's hand. "Don't come oiling up to me. I know you like Mary better than me. I can't say I blame you, but I'm not going to forgive you, either. I know she's prettier than I am, but we've been together for six years. I even rescued you from that drunken old squatter. I was planning on taking you to California, and look at the thanks I get."

The dog gamboled around him, wagging his tail and barking playfully. "Don't think you're going to talk me into letting you share my bed. You'll just get me up in an hour to let you out."

Fifteen minutes later, settled into his bedroll with Samson nestled beside him, Joe thought about the presents that weren't under that tree. He knew Sarah didn't expect much, but that wasn't the point. Presents would mean that *Père Noël* had come. Presents would mean her mother still remembered her, still loved her.

Either he was going to have to be Father Christmas, or Sarah would be disappointed again.

Then there was Mary. She probably didn't want anything. She certainly didn't expect anything, but for her, Christmas would be a new beginning. Especially with the baby. He wanted to give her something to celebrate that new beginning, but he couldn't think what. He certainly didn't have anything in his saddlebags. Even if he could find her share of the gold, that wouldn't be it either. What he wanted to give her couldn't be found under any tree, but he didn't allow himself to dwell on that.

He would go into town tomorrow and hope no one recognized him.

∽∾∾

"Are you sure you have to go?" Mary asked next morning when he told her he was going into town.

"I've got a few things I need to buy before I leave. And I told Brother Samuel I'd see him in a couple of days. He's liable to come out here again if I don't show up."

She didn't care about Brother Samuel. She could put up with a hundred of his visits as long as Joe was here. She was afraid he meant to ride out and never come back. She was afraid that going to town was only a ruse to cover his leaving forever.

"You've got to hurry back," Sarah said. "You don't want to miss Christmas."

"That's not for two days," Joe said. "That's enough time to go to Tucson and back."

"I don't want you to go to Tucson," Sarah said.

"I won't. Now be sure to milk Queen Charlotte, gather the eggs, and take care of your ma. She's not feeling too well."

Joe had noticed that the moment he walked in the door. He always noticed.

"I'll leave Samson here to take care of you. Now I've got to be on my way. If I don't leave soon, I won't get back before midnight."

Mary felt some of the anxiety leave her. He wouldn't go off and leave his dog. He had to be coming back. But she didn't feel entirely reassured. She wouldn't be until she saw him riding back over the ridge.

Five

PINE FLAT WASN'T MUCH OF A TOWN. THERE WEREN'T ANY pines in it, either. The town had been thrown up on a flat piece of desert between mountains. A dry wash ran along the base of the near ridge. The unpainted, weathered wood of the buildings stood out in stark contrast to the backdrop of orange-gray rock, pale-green cactus, and sapphire-blue sky.

Joe pulled the brim of his hat low over his face. He rode down the single street quietly and slowly. He didn't want to attract attention. It was after twelve o'clock. He'd timed it that way, hoping most people would be eating their midday meal. The fewer who saw him, the less chance there was of anyone recognizing him.

He stopped in front of Jones Emporium because it was the largest store in town. He wasn't sure what he wanted to buy. He didn't have much money. He had plenty in a bank in Denver, but he couldn't touch that. He wouldn't have any now if he hadn't been in the habit of keeping a little gold dust back every time he made a shipment. After breaking out of jail, he'd made a quick trip to his claim to dig up the gold before heading south.

He hoped the law still thought he was hiding somewhere in the Colorado mountains.

"Wish me luck," he said to General Burnside as he dismounted, "and keep your eyes open. If you see the law, go to bucking and whinnying for all you're worth. If they catch me now, they'll be auctioning you off before the month's out. No telling what kind of sidewinder might buy you."

Inside the store, four oil lamps suspended from the ceiling couldn't dispel a gloom made worse by dark wood and no windows. "Do you have any dresses for a six-year-old girl?" Joe asked a young female clerk.

"How big is she?"

Joe held his hand barely above his waist. "About this high."

"Over here," the young woman said, leading him to a table covered with dresses. She showed him three of the correct size, a blue serge, a yellow party frock, and a dark blue dress with a white pinafore.

Joe bought all three.

"You got anything to make a house look like Christmas?" he asked. "Red ribbon and stuff like that?"

"Not much," the girl said.

Joe bought ribbon, colored paper, and streamers of colored crepe paper to wrap around the tree.

That was when he found the set of paints.

"This all you got?" he asked. He opened the box. Inside were sixteen little compartments containing a rainbow of colors.

"It's the last one," the salesgirl said.

"I need some drawing paper."

He was in luck. They had several pads. He bought them all. He also bought a baby's rattle, a white dress the girl said could be used for a christening, and a thick blanket. His grandmother used to say all babies caught cold in the winter. He didn't want Mary's baby catching anything.

He also bought some canned fruit, a jar of jelly, a ham, a side of bacon, and a sack of flour. He bought Sarah a box of bath powder and a mirror; he bought Mary a box of scented soap and a small cameo pin.

He also bought himself a coat. It would be a long, cold trip to California.

"You got quite a haul there," the man behind the

counter said when Joe had added stick candy and a small box of chocolates to his pile.

"I don't get home much," Joe said. "Almost missed Christmas."

"They'll sure be glad to see you this time," the man said as he sorted Joe's purchases and added up the prices. "You'll want this wrapped up?"

"Good and tight," Joe said. "I'm on horseback."

"Better be a strong horse," the clerk said as he gave Joe the total.

Joe took out a small bag of gold dust. "Got some scales?"

"I'll have to get Mr. Jones," the clerk said.

Joe fidgeted while the clerk found the proprietor. He forced himself to remain outwardly calm while Hiram Jones peppered him with questions as he weighed out the proper amount of gold.

Joe was anxious to get out of town. He had drawn too much attention to himself by the amount of his purchases and paying in gold. He wanted to be gone before Mr. Jones and his clerks had a chance to spread the story.

He cussed aloud when, just as he had loaded his purchases and mounted up, Brother Samuel Hawkins came striding down the boardwalk. The man eyed Joe's bundles with suspicion.

"That seems like a lot to be carrying all the way to California," Brother Samuel observed.

"It's mostly Christmas presents for Mary and the kid," Joe said, damning Brother Samuel for his nosiness. "I decided I couldn't leave just now. Nobody likes to be alone at Christmas. Besides, with the baby coming, Mary hasn't been able to get to town to buy anything for the kid."

"*Mrs. Wilson* needed only to ask my sister or myself. We would have been more than happy to make any purchases for her."

Joe gathered up the reins and started General Burnside walking down the street. If the Reverend Brother Samuel wanted to talk to him, he was going to have to keep up.

"She probably didn't want to bother anybody. She'll most likely be mad enough to chew splinters when she sees what I've done. But I couldn't do anything else. Sort of in Pete's memory, you know."

The Reverend Brother looked as though he didn't like the answer but didn't know quite how to punch a hole in it. "My sister and I were planning to visit on Christmas."

"You come right ahead. I'm sure she'll be glad to see you. Now I gotta be going. General Burnside here is getting impatient to be home before dark."

"I believe my sister and I will come out this afternoon."

Joe pulled General Burnside to a halt and leveled a stony glance at Brother Samuel. "Now why would you be wanting to do a thing like that? You were just out there."

Brother Samuel didn't look quite so self-assured now. "I tried to explain how important it is to be scrupulous with Mrs. Wilson's reputation."

Joe could feel cold anger start to build in him.

"There's nobody I know of doubting Mary except you."

"I don't doubt Mrs. Wilson!" Brother Samuel exclaimed.

"Sounds like it to me. I thought preachers were supposed to have faith in good people."

"Not everybody is so high-minded."

"Then I wouldn't care a whit about what they thought."

"I have to care," Brother Samuel announced. "I intend to ask Mrs. Wilson to marry me. My wife's reputation must be above reproach."

Joe glared at the preacher. He was a little beetle of a man, an insect dressed in black. How dared he think of touching Mary, much less marrying her. She was too good for him. He would be too stupid to know what he had found. He'd try to hedge her in with restrictions and rules and protocol and everything else he could think of to squeeze the life and soul out of her.

Joe didn't want Brother Samuel to marry Mary because he wanted to marry her himself.

"Mary's reputation is good enough for you or anybody else," Joe said, his anger rising. "I'll break the neck of any man who says otherwise."

"I said nothing like that! I merely said—"

"You've said too much. You'd better go home to your midday meal. Hunger is making you sound out of temper."

Joe turned his horse and nearly rode into the sheriff.

"Howdy," the sheriff said. "You're new in town, aren't you?"

It took Joe a moment to calm his anger enough to answer in an even voice. "Just passing through."

"You've got quite a load for a traveling man."

"Christmas," Joe said. "For friends."

Brother Samuel started to introduce the two men. The sheriff's name was Howells. "I just realized I don't know your name," Brother Samuel said to Joe.

"Hank Frazier," Joe said. "I used to be Pete Wilson's partner. Just stopped off to give my respects to his widow on my way to California."

"It's a sad thing to happen to a new bride," Sheriff Howells commented. "She hardly got here before her husband was killed. Then to find herself expecting a baby."

"The Reverend here seems to think he's the one to lend her a helping hand," Joe said.

"She could do worse," Sheriff Howells said. "Much worse."

"Well, that's none of my concern," Joe said. "Nice to meet you, Sheriff, but I got to be on my way."

Joe pulled his hat a little lower on his head and walked

General Burnside out of town. He couldn't decide which worried him more: the possibility that Mary might marry Brother Samuel or the chance that the sheriff had recognized him.

"This is what comes from getting hooked up with a woman," he told General Burnside. "Normally I wouldn't care who a pregnant woman married. Never cared two hoots about kids, especially little girls. Now look at me. I've spent nearly half my money, I still haven't found the gold, and I'm running around town talking to a sheriff who probably has my picture on his wall. Worst of all, I'm jealous of some beak-nosed fool who calls himself Brother Samuel Hawkins."

Joe rode for a few miles in silence.

"I can't marry her. Everything was against it from the start. It's done nothing but get worse since. Besides, who's to say she would have me? Any sensible woman would choose the Reverend Brother Samuel over me. Now that's a lowering thought. Samson would be laughing out of both sides of his mouth." Of course women preferred almost any kind of man to an ex-convict. You couldn't get much lower than that without killing a man. And if Joe could have gotten his hands on Pete right after the conviction, he might have done that.

∽∾

Joe was late getting back. Mary had expected him by midafternoon. It was dusk now, and there was still no sign of him. She knew she shouldn't try to milk the cow, but she needed to keep busy. It helped keep her mind off Joe's absence. And she needed to be outside, away from all the Christmas decorations.

"You sure he's coming back?" Sarah asked for the dozenth time. She was more worried about Joe than Mary was.

"Absolutely," Mary said. "Now help me down these

steps. Queen Charlotte is probably in a fret to be milked by now."

Mary paused on her way across the yard to let a pain in her back pass. The pains had been getting worse all day. She had started to worry that something was wrong with the baby. It wasn't supposed to come for another month. Between worry about Joe and the baby and trying to reassure Sarah that Joe would be back, she was nearly frantic.

"He wouldn't leave Samson," she said to Sarah. "Now stop fretting and fetch the cow."

When Mary reached the shed, she turned to the shadowy corner where Joe slept. She could see his bedroll spread out over the deep straw. She felt even closer to him here.

Without warning, a pain wrapped itself around her and squeezed until she was sure she would faint. Clutching her belly, she fell to her knees. The pain let up long enough for her to call for Sarah before it struck again. It was blinding in its intensity. She couldn't move. She couldn't think. She could only sink to the straw.

The baby was coming!

"Joe will be home soon," she told Sarah as the frightened child hovered over her. "Everything will be all right then."

❧

By the time the cabin came into view, Joe had made up his mind to leave the next day. He had given up any hope of finding the gold. Maybe he could come back, but for now, his time had run out. Sooner or later people would forget him.

Even Mary.

He was surprised not to see a light in the cabin. It was only dusk, but it would be dark inside. It seemed unlikely that both Mary and Sarah would be taking a nap at this time of day.

He urged General Burnside into a trot. The packages bounced noisily, but he didn't slow down. He urged his horse into a canter when he saw the cow standing in front of the shed, lowing in distress.

Something was wrong. He was headed toward the house when he saw Sarah emerge from the shed.

"Where's Mary?" he called as he slid from the saddle.

"In the shed," Sarah said. The child looked badly frightened.

"What's wrong?" Joe said, heading toward the barn at a run.

"She fell down and can't get up again," Sarah said. "She said the baby's coming."

Inside the shed, Joe dropped to his knees next to Mary. He could hardly see her in the dim interior. "What are you doing here?"

"I can't move."

"I've got to get you inside. You can't have this child in a cowshed." Joe slid his arms under her. "Brother Samuel would have apoplexy."

Mary groaned when he picked her up. She groaned even louder when a pain struck.

"You had no business leaving the house," Joe said as he carried her across the yard. "Open the door, Sarah. And turn back the bedcovers."

Mary moaned, but she seemed relieved to be inside.

"How long have you been in pain?"

"The really bad ones started this afternoon, but my back has been hurting ever since last night."

"You mean you were getting ready to have this baby this morning and you didn't tell me?"

"I didn't know. It's not due for another month. I thought I had a backache."

"How long is having a baby supposed to take?"

"It depends. Maybe five or six hours."

"You mean I don't have time to go back to town for Sister Rachel?"

"No," Mary said. The word was changed into a howl by the pain. "You're going to have to help."

"Me!"

"You and Sarah."

"But I don't know anything about having babies."

Mary tried to smile. "It pretty much happens by itself. All you have to do is keep telling me it will soon be over and that it'll all be worth it because I'll have a beautiful baby to show for it."

"Shouldn't I get hot water and things like that?"

"You won't need water until time to clean up."

Joe decided the baby had *better* come pretty much by itself. He was too dumbfounded to do anything but stand around wringing his hands. Mary was equally helpless as one pain after another gripped her in its coils.

"You're going to have to catch the baby," Mary managed to tell him between gasping breaths.

"In what?"

"Your hands."

Joe looked down at his hands as if he'd never seen them before and didn't know what they were for.

"Sarah will help you."

But Sarah was even more upset than he was. The poor child didn't know what was happening. He couldn't help her. He didn't know what was happening either.

Instinctively he reached out to take Mary's hand. She took hold of him as if he were a lifeline and she a drowning sailor. He had no idea a woman could be so strong. When the pain hit her and she squeezed his fingers, he expected to come away with a collection of broken bones.

He directed Sarah to gather towels, put water on to heat, and find the extra blankets. But each time the pain hit Mary, Sarah would stop, her gaze shifting between Joe and Mary. Only when the pain had passed and Mary's face was once again reasonably calm would she move.

Joe had never felt more helpless in his life. It was even worse than watching himself be convicted for a crime he hadn't committed. Then he had had his anger to sustain him, his plans for what he would do to Pete Wilson when he got out. Now he easily understood why men got drunk and left birthing babies to the women. Joe wasn't a drinking man, but he wished he had a drink right now. As Mary's pains got worse, he found himself wanting a whole bottle.

"Help me sit up a little," Mary said. "I need a pillow under my back."

Just as Joe slid his arms around Mary, she screamed in pain.

"What!" he said, jumping back. Sarah was hitting and kicking and scratching him for all she was worth.

Joe decided they had both gone mad.

"No!" Mary managed to say as the pain started to recede. "He's not hurting me."

Sarah didn't stop until Joe took her by the shoulder and pushed her away from him. Even then she would have bitten him, if he hadn't jerked his hand back when he saw her go for him with bared teeth.

"It's all right," Mary said, reaching out to pull the child to her. "He's not hurting me. It's the baby."

"You mean, she thinks I did that?" Joe asked.

"Her father used to hit her mother. I saw him hit Sarah once. I told him if he ever hit her again, or me, I'd kill him."

Joe looked at Sarah and felt anger surge through him. He wasn't proud of a lot of things he'd done, but he'd never hurt a child. "Why the hell did you think I'd hurt Mary?" he demanded.

"She doesn't," Mary assured him. "She's just frightened. She doesn't know what to think."

"Do I look like I'm beating her?" Joe demanded, his own worry finding release in anger.

Sarah stared up at him, frightened.

"I'm trying to help her have this baby," Joe said, "and I don't know what the hell I'm doing. I can't figure it out if I've got you biting and scratching like a bobcat."

"She won't," Mary said, hugging the child to her. "You won't, Sarah. I'm going to scream a lot more. Joe's helping. You've got to help too."

As though to prove her words, Mary went rigid and cried out. Joe jumped to her side, holding her hand, supporting her until the pain released its grip.

"The baby is almost here," Mary said. "See if its head is showing."

"Huh?" Joe said, stunned.

"See if it's showing. If it is, you've got to get ready for it."

"Can't Sarah do it?"

"No."

Joe had never been shy around women, but this was different. He felt that in some way he was violating Mary, and that went against his grain.

"What am I supposed to look for?"

"The muscles have to relax to allow the baby to pass. If you can see the top of its head, you know it will be born soon."

It was easy for Joe to clear his head of coherent thoughts. He didn't have any. To pretend he wasn't doing what he *was* doing was more difficult.

"I see it," he said, so excited he forgot his embarrassment. "I can see almost the whole top."

"Good," Mary said. "Then I might not die before it's born."

Another excruciating pain caused her to cry out.

"Hold her hand," Joe told Sarah. "I think it's getting ready to come."

It seemed to Joe that the pains came one right after another, giving Mary no time to rest or recover in between. Then it was all over, and he held a baby girl in his hands. He stared down at the child, unable to believe he had just witnessed the birth of another human being, the beginning of a brand-new life. He had looked like this once. So had Mary, Pete, and Sarah. Someday this baby would be a grown woman and have her own children.

It was amazing, incredible, unbelievable.

The baby's cry brought Joe out of his daze. "It's a girl," he said, handing the infant to her mother. "And she looks like you."

Mary was exhausted, but she managed a smile. "She doesn't look like anybody yet. But she's beautiful just the same."

"She's all messed up," Sarah said.

Mary laughed. "Yes, she is. Why don't you help Joe clean her up?"

"Me!" Joe was counting himself lucky to have done nothing wrong so far. "I'll bring the water to you," he said. "I don't know a thing about washing babies."

"It's simple."

"Maybe, when I'm not shaking so much." He held his hand up in front of him. It was quivering.

Mary managed a weak smile. "Maybe you'd better let Sarah bring me the water."

Joe turned away from the bed and came up short. Samson sat by the door, his gaze following every movement. Outside, General Burnside and the cow stood with their noses to the window, their breath fogging the panes. They looked as if they had been watching the entire proceedings. "I forgot all about them," he said, turning to Mary. "The presents are still tied to the saddle, and Queen Charlotte hasn't been milked."

"Then you'd better take care of them," Mary said. "Sarah and I will try to have everything cleaned up by the time you get back."

Joe stumbled out the door, too dazed by the events of the last few hours to be aware of the cold or that Samson had followed him. Like a man in a trance, he caught up General Burnside's reins. Queen Charlotte followed on her own.

"Did you see what just happened?" he asked the animals. "Mary had a baby. It's a tiny little thing, so tiny you can hardly imagine it growing up into a real person."

He began to untie the ropes that held the packages to General Burnside's back.

"One minute there were just three of us. Next minute there were four. A brand-new person, just like that." He snapped his fingers.

Samson was sniffing the packages, with particular attention to the ones containing the ham and bacon.

"She's got little tufts of black hair all over her head. She's all wrinkled up from being squeezed inside Mary. Can't be too much room inside a little woman like that, even for a tiny baby. Leave that alone," Joe spoke sharply to Samson. "That's Christmas dinner."

He put all the packages inside the shed and closed the door on Samson. He unsaddled General Burnside and turned him into the corral.

"Okay, it's your turn, Queen Charlotte." He patted her side as he settled himself on the milking stool. He looked again, then ran his hand carefully along her side. "Looks like you'll be having a little one come spring," he said, the streams of milk beginning to hit the pail with rhythmic smoothness. As the milk filled the pail, the high ping thickened until it more closely resembled a rip in a piece of fabric.

"You get busy on those coyotes," he said to Samson. "We can't leave any hanging around. We don't want Queen Charlotte here to lose another calf. And no telling what they might do to a baby girl. No, sir, you get up off your haunches and get going."

Almost on cue, a coyote yip-yipped somewhere in the hills close by. A second answered.

"See, I told you there was work to be done." But Samson had already disappeared into the night on silent feet, a growl deep in his throat.

Joe finished milking the cow and let her into the corral. He looked toward the house, at the light shining brightly through the window in the dark night, and felt a wonderful sense of peace. The horse and cow were in the corral, the chickens were safe in their pen, and it was warm and secure inside the house where Mary, Sarah, and the baby awaited his return. Everything he'd ever wanted was right here.

Only he had to leave.

But he couldn't, not until he was sure Mary and the baby were all right. He was worried about her. She looked so worn out. Sister Rachel was coming on Christmas. He couldn't leave until then.

Tomorrow was Christmas Eve. He had to help Sarah make a bow for the front door. And he wanted to see her open her presents on Christmas morning. He wanted her to have some pretty dresses, but the biggest reason for staying was to see the expression on her face when she unwrapped them.

He wanted her to know her mother still remembered her.

He'd stay until Christmas. Then he'd go.

Six

MARY HAD NEVER FELT SO HAPPY OR CONTENT. SHE HELD her daughter in her arms, the infant nursing contentedly. Sarah bustled about helping Joe fix breakfast for all three of them. Nothing more was needed to make Mary's life complete. It was all here in this small cabin.

She loved Joe. She was comfortable with that now. It would never change. But she knew he couldn't stay. It would mean capture and return to prison with very little chance that he would get out for a long time.

"Have you been thinking of a name for her?" Joe asked.

"I had several in mind."

"Like what?"

"Elizabeth. Anne. Ruth."

"They're such sober names. Don't you think a greedy little puss like her ought to have a different kind of name?"

The baby nursed with noisy, slurping sounds. "What did you have in mind?"

"I haven't known many good women, but I think Holly's okay."

"Holly," Mary said half to herself. "It is a nice name. It makes her sound strong, bright-eyed, and ready to fight if she needs to."

"Like right now."

Mary was changing Holly to the other side, and the infant screamed her anger at having her meal interrupted.

"I think Holly is a fine name," Mary said. "I'll always think of you when I call her name."

The silence that fell made them both painfully aware that their time together was drawing to a close.

"You haven't found the gold."

"No."

"What are you going to do?"

"Go to California. Somewhere else, if I have to. Maybe after a while I can come back and look for it again."

She knew he wouldn't. If he didn't find it now, he would never come back.

"When do you have to go?" She didn't want to know the answer, but she had to ask.

"Christmas. I got a few presents in town."

Her eyes filled with tears. Her husband had caused him to be sent to jail. She had caused him to risk being caught. Still he had taken the time to buy presents for them. How could anybody believe he'd stolen that gold? "You didn't have to do that."

"It's not much, just some little things."

The baby finished eating. She rewarded Mary with an enormous burp. "That's what you get for eating too fast," Mary said, but her smile and tone turned her censure into words of love. "Here, why don't you hold her while I eat?"

"Me?" Joe said.

Mary smiled. He always seemed to be saying that, like there were things he'd never considered he could do. "She's a lot nicer to hold now than she was last night."

"I don't—"

"All you have to do is put her in the crook of your arm. Come here, and I'll show you."

Joe approached reluctantly.

"Put your arm across your chest," Mary said.

He did, and she placed the baby in his arm. He immediately clamped her against his chest with his other arm. He was certain he would drop her before he made it to the chair so he could sit down. Holly looked up at him with the biggest black eyes he'd ever seen.

Joe walked to the chair with small, stiff-legged steps. He felt as if he'd never walked before, as if his legs had forgotten how. He practically fell into the chair. Holly continued to look at him with her big eyes.

"She ought to go to sleep in a few minutes," Mary said as she prepared to get up.

"Stay in that bed." Joe's order was so sharp that Holly started to cry. He held her a little closer and, miraculously, she stopped. "You're too weak to get up," he said in a hushed voice. "Sarah can bring your breakfast to you."

"I feel fine. I—"

"You can get up this afternoon. For now, you stay where you are."

Satisfied that Mary would remain in bed, Joe turned his attention back to Holly. Mary had dressed her in a soft flannel gown that was twice her size. She looked too small to be real. He rubbed her cheek with his callused finger. It was incredibly soft. She opened her mouth wide and yawned. She took hold of his finger with her hand. It looked absurdly small, too small to encircle his finger.

She closed her eyes but continued to hold on to his finger. He thought her pug nose was cute. He supposed it would grow to look like her mother's, but it was just the right kind of nose for a baby. He compared her fingers to his own. She had the same number of joints, the same wrinkles at the knuckles, fingernails—everything he had, only so much smaller.

She was asleep in his arms. It almost made him want to cry, and she wasn't even his kid.

Something turned over inside Joe. This was what he wanted—Mary, Sarah, and Holly. He wouldn't ask anything more of life if he could have that much. He understood love now. He could trust his feeling for Mary and hers for him. Holly had made him understand that he could love and be loved.

"You better give her to me," Mary said. "You need to find that gold."

Joe's gaze locked with hers. "If I do?"

"Then you won't have to leave."

Joe couldn't speak for a few minutes. "Are you sure? I've never had a family. I might not be good at it. I'll always be an ex-con."

"I don't care. I never met a man like you, Joe. I didn't think there was one. I don't know why you should be so different from Pete, my father, and all the other men I've known, but you are. Sarah knows it. Even Holly. Look at her sleeping. She knows she's safe as long as you're holding her."

Joe hadn't thought about it that way, but he knew there wasn't much he wouldn't do to protect this child. He managed to lever himself out of the chair without waking Holly. He handed her over to Mary.

"I'm going to make her a cradle. She ought to have a bed of her own. Then I'm going to turn this place inside out. I've still got twenty-four hours to look for the gold."

❧

"Is Joe going to leave?" Sarah asked.

"I hope not," Mary said.

"Why can't he stay?"

Mary was reluctant to tell Sarah the truth, but she knew she would have to learn it some day. "Pete stole some gold and blamed Joe for it. They put him in jail. He broke out so he could find the gold and prove he didn't steal it. Pete buried the gold here, but Joe can't find it. He has to leave, or they will put him back in jail."

"Can't we go with him?"

Mary felt excitement leap within her. Why hadn't she thought of that? It was so simple, so obvious. "Would you want to go with him?"

"Joe's nice. I want him to be my papa. He said he would like having a little girl like me."

"I'm not sure he would let us go. Joe's a very proud man. He'd probably feel he couldn't share his name with us if he couldn't do it without fear of being put back in jail. If he could just find the gold, everything would be all right. Can you remember anything unusual Pete did when he came home?"

Sarah shook her head.

"I know you were afraid of him, but please try to remember. Anything might help Joe. Now you'd better finish cleaning up. I'm going to take a nap. I promised I'll be strong enough to help with dinner."

But Mary's thoughts weren't on dinner or getting stronger. She was trying to think of some way to convince Joe to take her and the children with him.

Joe had never built a cradle, but it wasn't a difficult task. There were tools for everything in the shed. He bet Pete had never used half of them. "We can't have Holly sleeping on Mary's bed," he said to Samson. The big dog sat watching everything he did. "She's pretty quiet now, but she won't be for long. She could roll right out of that bed."

He tested the cradle. "The runner isn't smooth enough," he told Samson. "You can't expect a baby to go to sleep when you're bouncing it all to bits." He turned the cradle over and started to file down some of the ridges. "Of course, she can't stay in this cradle forever. As soon as she's able to pull up, she'll have to have a crib. We don't want her falling out on her head."

Samson yawned.

"I know this isn't as exciting as hunting coyotes, but you don't have to be rude. Go talk to General Burnside if you're so bored."

But Samson just yawned again, rested his head on his paws, and continued to watch Joe.

"I think that'll do it," Joe said when the cradle finally rocked smoothly. "It doesn't look very fancy, but it'll give her a place to sleep." Joe picked up the cradle and started toward the cabin. "Well, come on," he said to Samson when the dog didn't move. "I don't think Sarah's scared of you anymore. At least, she won't be if you behave yourself. Just go inside, lie down, and keep quiet."

Samson followed Joe into the house. Sarah did look a little apprehensive, but when the big dog lay down, she looked relieved.

"It didn't seem a good thing, the three of you sleeping in that bed together," Joe said as he set the cradle on the floor next to the bed. "Somebody could roll over on that baby and never know it."

Tears pooled in Mary's eyes. "That was very thoughtful of you, Joe."

"You want me to fix it for her now?"

"No, I'd rather hold her."

"Well, I'll be outside taking the place apart if you need me," Joe said as he backed out of the room. "Just give a yell if you need anything."

❧

"Now, Samson," Joe said once they were outside, "I want you to put coyotes completely out of your mind and concentrate on gold. Unless you want to wear out your feet trotting all the way to California, we got to find it before nightfall."

The hours of the afternoon stretched longer and longer. Mary could hear Joe as he moved about the ranch, digging, sounding for hollow spaces, cursing when another idea proved to be as useless as the previous ones. She prayed he would find the gold. She knew she would never find another man like Joe. She could never love anyone else the way she loved him.

She marveled to herself. She had known him less than a week, yet it seemed they had always known each other. It was as if they were the missing halves of each other. Now that they were together, it was as though they had never been apart.

She looked down at Holly. She wanted more babies—Joe's babies.

"Did you find anything?" Mary asked Joe when he came in, a full milk pail in hand, to begin supper. She knew the answer, but she kept hoping he would say something to give her hope. She couldn't give up yet.

"No, but I got a few more places to look."

"It'll soon be dark."

"I can use a lantern."

"You're never going to find it, Joe. You know that."

"There's always a chance that…"

"If you haven't found it by now, you won't. You might as well accept it."

"I can't."

"Why?"

"Because it means I'll have to leave you."

"You could take us with you."

Joe turned sharply. "No."

"I wouldn't mind."

"I would. I couldn't have you following me all over the country, wondering if the law was going to catch up with me one day or the next."

"It would be better than never seeing you again. I love you, Joe Ryan. I never thought it would be possible to love anybody like I love you."

Joe fell down beside the bed, took Mary in his arms, and kissed her. "I love you. Too much to turn you into a vagabond."

"I won't mind."

"I know you'd try. You might even succeed, but you'd never like it. You long for stability, permanence, a feeling things will be the same tomorrow and the day after. It wouldn't be fair to Sarah and Holly, or any children we might have. I've been wandering since I was sixteen. It was hard for me even then."

"Then you've got to keep coming back until you do find the gold. Sarah and I will help look. You can't give up."

"Where is Sarah?" Joe asked.

"I don't know. I thought she was with you."

"I haven't seen her all afternoon. When did she leave?"

"While I was taking a nap."

"That was more than six hours ago."

"Did she take the pinto?"

Joe looked out the window. "He's not in the corral. I can't believe I didn't hear her leave."

"You were concentrating on finding the gold."

"I was wasting my time," Joe said. He turned to the stove. "If she isn't back by the time supper's ready, I'll go look for her. It's getting cold. Wouldn't be surprised if it freezes tonight."

Sarah returned before supper, but all she would say in response to where she'd been was, "I was looking for some branches to make a Christmas wreath."

"You have no business being gone by yourself so long," Joe said. "You nearly scared your mother out of a year's growth."

"Did I scare you out of a year's growth, too?"

Joe decided that things turning over inside him was going to be a regular occurrence as long as he was around Mary and Sarah. "You scared me out of two years. Look here," he said, pointing to the hair at his temples. "I'll bet you can see gray hairs."

Sarah looked. "No."

"Well, you will if you do anything like that again."

"I won't."

"Promise?"

"Promise."

They spent the rest of the evening decorating. Joe cut the crepe paper into thin strips and ringed the tree with them. Sarah made big bows out of the ribbon. Joe helped her tack those up on the windows. Then they made a wreath, wired several pinecones in it, tied a huge bow to the bottom, and attached it to the front door. Mary cut out scenes in colored paper, and they pasted them on the windows. By the time they finished, there was hardly a part of the cabin that didn't have some sign of Christmas.

"There's nothing left to do but put a lantern in the window, go to bed, and wait for Christmas morning," Joe said, rubbing his hands together.

"Are you sure *Père Noël* will find us?" Sarah asked anxiously.

"Sure," Joe said. "With that wreath on the door and the lantern in the window, he can't miss." Joe looked at Mary. She was putting an extra blanket over Holly. The baby slept soundly in the cradle.

"I guess it's about time I said good night," he said.

Mary straightened up. "I don't want you to go."

"Mary, I already told you I can't—"

"I mean tonight. I don't want you to go tonight."

"But I can't sleep here. Brother Samuel would be horrified."

"The Devil take Brother Samuel."

"We can only hope," Joe murmured.

"If this is to be your last night, I want you to spend it with us."

Joe stood still. He'd been thrown out of many places in his life. People had turned their backs on him, but he'd never been invited in. He ought to go. If they came for him in the night, he'd be trapped here. Worse still, Mary's reputation would be ruined.

But he wanted to stay. More than anything in his whole life, he wanted to stay in this room with these people. If tonight was all he was to be granted, then he would take it.

"I'll put my bedroll by the door. That way—"

"I want you to sleep here," Mary said, patting the bed, "with Sarah and me."

"But you've just had... Sarah won't... Sister Rachel would fall down in a dead faint if she knew."

"I'm not asking for anything more than to be near you."

"Are you sure?"

"Absolutely."

"Okay, but I'll sleep on top of the covers."

Joe was prey to so many conflicting emotions, he hardly knew what he felt. He had never slept with a woman without touching her. He vowed he'd cut off his right hand before he touched Mary. She'd just had a baby, for God's sake. Besides, he was leaving tomorrow. He couldn't make love to her, then walk out of her life. Maybe other men could, but he couldn't.

And he knew he wouldn't be back. He would never find the gold. He accepted that now. Without the gold, he could never ask Mary to be his wife. He couldn't accept that. Something inside wouldn't let him give up. Maybe he could look again in the morning. Maybe he could come back in a few months.

Maybe.

But all he had—all he might ever have—was this night. He moved closer to Mary, reached out, and took her hand in his. He felt as if he was fighting for his share of her attention. Holly wouldn't settle down. Finally he released Mary's hand, put his arm around her, and pulled her to him. Holly settled between her breasts and went to sleep. Sarah reached up to take hold of the hand Joe had around Mary's shoulder. In moments she was asleep as well.

"This wasn't what I had in mind," Mary whispered as she clasped Joe's free hand.

"Me either," Joe whispered back. He kissed her hair. "But I wouldn't trade it for anything in the world."

It was far more than he had expected. So much less than he wanted. He told himself to concentrate on the moment. It was warm and wonderful. It just might be enough to last him for a lifetime.

Mary woke when Holly began to stir. She fed the baby before her cries woke Joe or Sarah. Even in sleep, Sarah held tightly to Joe's hand. Mary wanted to do the same thing for the rest of her life. Joe had gone to sleep with his head on her shoulder. She felt almost crushed by the love that surrounded her. And it all came from Joe.

Joe woke at dawn. The cabin was cold. Taking care not to wake Mary, Sarah, or the baby, he eased out of bed. Still in his stockinged feet, he opened the stove and began to lay a fire. "Shut up, Samson," he said when the dog started to whine. "I'll let you out shortly."

In a few minutes he had water on for coffee. He looked outside. The ground was covered with a light dusting of snow. It was closer to a white Christmas than he had ever had growing up. He shoved his feet into his boots, grabbed the milk bucket, and eased the door open on silent hinges he'd oiled two days ago.

The frozen ground crunched under his feet. "Queen Charlotte's just going to love getting milked this morning," he said to Samson, who frisked about, his breath making clouds in the frigid air.

The cow did mind being milked, but Joe milked her under the shed out of the wind. She showed her appreciation by kicking only once. Joe set the milk on the porch. "Let the cream rise to the top and freeze. Used to do that back in Carolina," he told Samson. "Sweetest cream you ever did taste." He fed and watered General Burnside, then got his presents from the shed.

Mary was at the stove slicing bacon when he entered the cabin, loaded with presents. She stopped, her knife suspended in midair. "What have you got there?" she asked.

"Just a few things I thought you and Sarah might like."

Mary put her knife down, went to the trunk, and opened it. She took out a handmade doll and a pair of white shoes. "I couldn't afford to buy anything but the shoes. I was going to make her a dress."

"It doesn't matter. I got her some."

Mary watched as Joe stuffed each of Sarah's shoes as full as he could get with powder, a mirror, candy, ribbons, and all the things the girl in Jones Emporium assured him a little girl would want. "So that's why you risked going to town."

"No, it isn't. I—"

Mary put her hands on his shoulders, stood on tiptoe, and kissed him hard on the lips, her knife dangerously close to his jugular.

"Don't tell lies, not even little ones. It's Christmas."

The word worked its magic, and Sarah and Holly woke up at the same time.

Sarah's gaze went straight to the tree. She rubbed her eyes, looked, and rubbed them again. "*Père Noël* really did come," Sarah said, staring at her shoes.

"I told you he wouldn't miss the light in the window," Joe said. "Now, you can't open anything until after breakfast. I'll take that while you feed the baby," Joe said, removing the knife from Mary's hand. "Sarah, you can set the table."

Joe tried not to think that this was the last time he would sit down to eat with Mary and her family. He tried to tell himself this was the high point of his stay. He would concentrate on enjoying it. He would have more than enough time to think about what he would be missing.

Joe gave Mary the rattle, dress, and blanket for Holly. Sarah emptied her shoes, exclaiming over everything she found. But when she opened the package Joe handed her with the three dresses inside, she shrieked so loudly that he thought she didn't like them. She bounded up, threw herself across the room, and hugged him until he thought he couldn't breathe.

"Every pretty little girl ought to have a dress," Joe said. "I just bought you a couple of spares. Here, put this one on," he said, handing her the party dress. "And don't forget to powder yourself real good," Joe said as Sarah retreated behind the curtain. "I like my little girls to smell good."

"You shouldn't have spent all your money on us," Mary said, her eyes filling with tears.

"I bought myself a coat. I've got plenty left."

"You're telling lies again."

"Enough, then." He reached back into the welter of brown paper and handed Mary the box of scented soaps. While she was thanking him for that, he handed her the books of drawing paper, the pens, and ink. Before she had recovered completely, he handed her the set of colored paints.

She just sat there, her hand over her mouth, tears pouring down her cheeks.

"Next Christmas, I want every one of those drawings to be in color," he said, a huskiness in his voice. He cleared his throat. "Christmas should never lack color, even in Arizona."

"Oh, Joe," Mary said, and threw her arms around him.

Joe found himself hugging Mary and Holly at the same time. Holly objected. Loudly.

"Be quiet, child."

"No, she's right," Joe said, pulling back. "No point

pretending. We've got to face up to it. This is the last we'll see of each other for a time."

"Joe," Sarah said.

But Joe didn't answer her. Mary was clinging to him, and he couldn't summon the willpower to let her go. He buried his face in her hair, willing himself to remember this moment forever.

"Why won't you let us go with you? It won't be a hardship, not like it will be living here without you."

"Mary, I already explained why I can't do that."

"Joe," Sarah called.

"Just a minute," Joe said to her. He wanted to memorize the feel of Mary in his arms, the smell of her. "I'll come back, I promise. Maybe by then you can remember something that will help, but I can't take you with me while this stolen gold is hanging over my head."

"Joe!"

"What is it?" Joe said, finally turning to Sarah. "Can't you see—" Joe froze. Sarah was dressed in her party dress, a ribbon in her hair, the white shoes on her feet. She was beautiful. She looked like a little angel.

But that wasn't what mesmerized him. She was holding her hands up toward him. In them was a bag of the missing gold.

"Can you stay now? Can you be my papa?"

Seven

MARY SAW THEM LONG BEFORE THEY TURNED INTO THE yard—Brother Samuel and Sister Rachel, accompanied by Sheriff Howells. She wrapped the baby in Joe's blanket, put her in her cradle, and put on water for coffee. She threw a heavy woolen shawl, the last of Joe's presents, over her shoulders and met them at the door.

"You poor woman," Sister Rachel exclaimed as soon as she stepped inside. "We came the moment the sheriff told us." She threw her arms around Mary and embraced her.

"To think you've been alone with him all this time," Brother Samuel said.

"Saints preserve us!" Sister Rachel exclaimed, patting Mary's flat stomach. "What happened to the baby?"

"She's asleep in her crib," Mary said. "Apparently I miscalculated when she was due."

"But how…who…when?"

"Two days ago. Joe and Sarah helped me."

"You let that strange man, that *criminal*, help you!" Brother Samuel exclaimed.

"I didn't have much choice. He found me in the shed unable to get up."

"Poor woman. And all the time you didn't know what he was."

"I know exactly what he is," Mary said, proud, calm, and happy. "He's the man I'm going to marry."

Sister Rachel and Brother Samuel practically threw

Mary down in a chair. "Having the child so unexpectedly must have brought on brain fever," Sister Rachel said.

"He's an escaped convict, Mrs. Wilson," Sheriff Howells added.

"Suppose he didn't steal that gold?" Mary asked. "Would you have to take him back?"

"Well, I don't know. He did break jail."

"But he broke out so he could find the gold and prove he didn't steal it. Wouldn't that be reason enough not to send him back?"

"If he can come up with the gold, the transport company would drop the charges. They'd probably give him a reward, too."

"That's a perfectly absurd question," Brother Samuel said. "Of course he has to go back to jail."

"I never trusted him, not from the first," Sister Rachel said.

But Mary wasn't to be sidetracked by Brother Samuel or Sister Rachel.

"So if he can return the gold and prove he didn't steal it, do you promise not to send him back to Colorado?"

"Yes, ma'am, but I can't promise Colorado won't still charge him with breaking jail."

"But why should he be punished for that when he shouldn't have been in jail in the first place?"

"You got a point there, ma'am. I think we could work things out. Of course, he might have to go up there a while later to talk to some people, but I don't imagine they'd hold anything against him. If he can prove he didn't steal that gold, that is."

Mary got to her feet. "How about coffee? I've made a new pot."

∞

Joe had expected to see Brother Samuel's buggy in front of the cabin, and he wasn't surprised to see the sheriff's horse as well. He balanced the strongbox across the saddle in front of him. His and Mary's gold was safely stowed in the bottom of his saddlebags.

"How did you know where to find the gold?" he asked Sarah, who rode beside him.

"Papa showed me the cave once. He threatened to put me in it if I was bad."

"Why didn't you tell me last night?"

"I wanted to surprise you."

"You sure did that."

"Are you going to be my papa now?"

"It depends on what the man riding that horse says." Joe pulled up in front of the house. The sheriff and Brother Samuel came out to meet him.

"You want to give me a hand with this box?" Joe asked.

"That the stolen shipment?" the sheriff asked as he came down the steps.

"Yes."

"Where did you find it?"

"I didn't. Sarah did."

"Papa hid it in a cave," Sarah said.

"How did you know?" The sheriff took the box from Joe. Joe dismounted and helped Sarah down.

"Last night Mama said Joe would have to go away if he couldn't find the gold. She told me to try to think of everything Papa did when he was home that time.

"That's when I remembered him sneaking out of the house."

Mary came down the steps. "You called me Mama."

Sarah threw her arms around Mary's neck. "Joe said you'd like it."

"I do," Mary said, hugging the little girl tight to her chest. "I like it very much."

"Pete set me up," Joe explained to Sheriff Howells. "But he was killed before he could come back and get the gold. It's all there. See for yourself."

Mary came to stand by Joe, one arm around him, the other resting on Sarah's shoulders. "The sheriff says you won't have to go back to Colorado. He said you can stay here."

"You sure about that?" Joe asked him.

"I don't see why not. They've got their money back. The way I see it, they owe you something for being locked up all that time."

"You think I can get that conviction taken off my record? I don't want my kids' pa to have a record."

"Ought to be able to do that, too."

Joe turned to Brother Samuel. "I want you to marry us."

"Right now?" Sister Rachel asked. It was almost a shriek.

"Yes, right now," Mary confirmed.

Brother Samuel looked horrified. "I can't do that."

"Why not?" Joe asked. "You're a preacher, and you have two witnesses."

"You don't have a license."

"Please?" Mary asked.

"I can't without a license," Brother Samuel repeated, looking belligerent.

"Mary can't travel into town for a while yet," Joe said. "And I don't intend to set one foot off this ranch until she does. Unless you want me to ruin that reputation you were so worried about, you'll marry us right now."

"It wouldn't be right. I can't—"

"Oh, shut up, Samuel, and marry them," the sheriff said. "We can make out the license when we go into town. I'll bring it out tomorrow. I think we've caused this man enough trouble as it is."

❧

"I still can't believe it," Mary said that evening as she snuggled down next to Joe. "I swore I'd never get married again. Wait until I tell my family."

Holly was asleep in her cradle. Over in the corner, Sarah had burrowed deep into Joe's bedroll. Samson lay next to her. Joe and Mary occupied the bed alone.

"I'm not sure Brother Samuel believes it, and he married us."

"Poor man. I thought he would choke on the words. He looked miserable."

"Not half as miserable as you'd have been if you'd married him."

"I never would."

"Let's forget about Brother Samuel and Sister Rachel. From now on, it's just you and me."

"And Sarah and Holly."

"And General Burnside and Samson."

"And Queen Charlotte and her calf-to-be."

There seemed to be no end to the love that surrounded Joe. But that was the way it ought to be. Love was what Christmas was really about.

About the Author

Leigh Greenwood is the award-winning author of over fifty books, many of which have appeared on the *USA Today* bestseller list. Leigh lives in Charlotte, North Carolina. Please visit his website at leigh-greenwood.com.

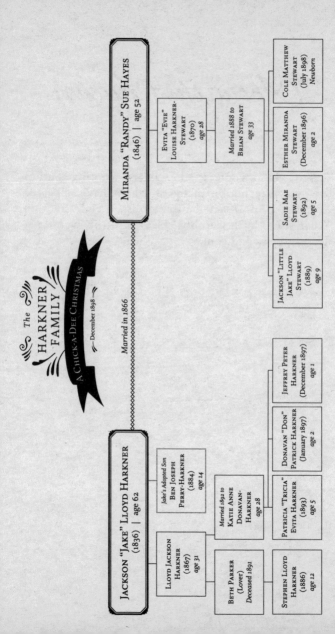

The
HARKNER
FAMILY
A CHICK-A-DEE CHRISTMAS
~ December 1898 ~

JACKSON "JAKE" LLOYD HARKNER (1836) | age 62

Married in 1866

MIRANDA "RANDY" SUE HAYES (1846) | age 52

LLOYD JACKSON HARKNER (1867) age 31

Jake's Adopted Son
BEN JOSEPH PERRY-HARKNER (1884) age 14

BETH PARKER (Lover) Deceased 1891

Married 1892 to KATIE ANNE DONAVAN-HARKNER age 28

STEPHEN LLOYD HARKNER (1886) age 12

PATRICIA "TRICIA" EVITA HARKNER (1893) age 5

DONAVAN "DON" PATRICK HARKNER (January 1897) age 2

JEFFREY PETER HARKNER (December 1897) age 1

EVITTA "EVIE" LOUISE HARKNER-STEWART (1870) age 28

Married 1888 to BRIAN STEWART age 33

JACKSON "LITTLE JAKE" LLOYD STEWART (1889) age 9

SADIE MAE STEWART (1892) age 5

ESTHER MIRANDA STEWART (December 1896) age 2

COLE MATTHEW STEWART (July 1898) Newborn

A Chick-a-Dee Christmas

An Outlaw Hearts Novella

———— •◦• ————

Rosanne Bittner

Foreword

Because the fourth book to my Outlaw series, *The Last Outlaw*, was published just one month before this Christmas story, I decided to bring back the wonderful characters from my Outlaw books, picking up their lives at their first Christmas following a terrible family ordeal that took place in *The Last Outlaw*. Because the event in *The Last Outlaw* left the Harkners with much to celebrate and to be thankful for, a Christmas story is perfect for them.

A Chick-a-Dee Christmas is about a family that has known tragedy and triumph, a family spawned by outlaw/lawman Jake Harkner, who once knew nothing about love, whether giving it or receiving it. His saving grace was the love of a good woman, his beloved Miranda, who taught Jake everything he'd never known about love, guiding him on a journey of hope and support and God and light...dragging him from the depths of hell into a world he once never imagined he could enjoy, and a beautiful, loving family of whom he never felt worthy.

I think you will love this delightful story, although it has its dark moments. This is a story about how a once-ruthless man, who can kill in the blink of an eye—especially when defending his family—can take on an entirely different personality when it comes to his loved ones. For those who know how ruthless Jake Harkner can be, watching him with his grandchildren, especially his two little granddaughters, is almost comical. They bring out a side of Jake that most don't realize exists.

I hope *A Chick-a-Dee Christmas* will make you want to read the full series of books about Jake and his "Randy"—how they meet in *Outlaw Hearts*, and on through thirty-two years together in *Do Not Forsake Me*, *Love's Sweet Revenge*, and *The Last Outlaw*. It's a family saga filled with love and devotion and forgiveness and the adventure created when facing incredible challenges that come with settling America's Great West.

One

Late November, 1898…

COLE DECKER KNOCKED ON THE FRONT DOOR OF JAKE'S log home. "Riders comin' in," he yelled.

Jake got up from his favorite big red leather chair near the stone fireplace and ordered his adopted son Ben to stoke the fire and add some wood to it. His wife, Miranda, peeked through a front window.

"Jake, they're all strangers," she told him. "Only one of them looks familiar, but I can't place him."

"Probably looking for work." Jake walked to the front door, where his famous .44s hung over the doorway, too high for Jake's several grandchildren to reach, but at six feet four inches, Jake had no problem reaching them. He strapped them on.

Ben, fourteen, threw a couple more logs on the fire. "Be careful, Pa."

"Don't worry."

"Grampa, will you get hurt again?"

The question came from Jake's six-year-old granddaughter, Sadie Mae. Hardly a night went by that one or more of the grandchildren wasn't staying overnight with their grandparents. Last night it was Sadie Mae, who belonged to Jake's daughter, Evie, and five-year-old Tricia, one of his son's several children. The little girls played with dolls near the hearth in the kitchen while their grandmother cleaned up from breakfast.

Jake winked at them. "No, sunshine, I won't get

hurt again. We have lots of good men guarding us. I'm betting that rooster out in the henhouse is more dangerous than those men out there."

Sadie Mae smiled, her dark eyes twinkling and her dimples deepening. She was the official egg gatherer, and she considered all the hens in the chicken coop hers and called the baby chicks "chick-a-dees." She took pride in the fact that the ornery rooster, who was this very moment crowing, never came after her or pecked her when she gathered eggs. But the proud, cocky master of the henhouse—whom the children called Outlaw—seemed to have it in for Jake Harkner. They'd had their differences, and the rooster usually won, although if it weren't for Sadie Mae, Jake would gladly shoot the strutting monster and boil it for dinner.

Jake leaned down and pulled on worn leather boots he kept by the front door, wincing with pain as he did so. Inwardly he cursed the leg he'd broken a little over a year ago in Mexico. It had never been properly set, thanks to the men who'd captured and tortured him and left him for dead. The leg would likely plague him with pain the rest of his life, sometimes keeping him up at night, other times reasonably bearable. He took his fleece-lined corduroy jacket from its hook and put it on, then stuck his Stetson on his head.

His wife touched his arm, and he saw the same look in her eyes he always saw when she feared someone was out to kill him just because he was Jake Harkner. He leaned down to give her a quick kiss. "Cole is out there, and probably a couple of other men who brought the others in. It's okay, Randy. Just keep the girls inside." He paused to light a cigarette, then opened the door and went out onto the wide veranda that wrapped around the front and both sides of their huge log home.

Both girls ran to a front window to watch. "There's Jake," Sadie Mae told her cousin, pointing out her big brother. Once called Little Jake, the proud young man who worshipped his infamous grandfather almost beyond measure was nearly eleven now, and he preferred to be called just Jake. To clear up any confusion, his grandfather was now called Big Jake, although to all the children he was simply Grandpa.

Outside, five men sat on their horses in front of the house, all of them wearing six-guns and sporting rifles tied to their saddles. They all wore winter jackets, varying from wool to leather to corduroy, two with wide-brimmed hats stained from summer sweat, the other three wearing wool hats, one with earflaps that hung loose. Behind them sat two cowhands who worked for the J&L, guards who always watched for strangers on the Harkners' vast spread. Few made it onto the J&L without being noticed, and almost none made it all the way to the homestead without a J&L cowhand escorting them, rifle in hand. Jake and Lloyd wanted it that way to make sure their wives and children were always protected.

Their best ranch hand, Cole Decker—known as Uncle Cole to the Harkner grandchildren—remained standing on the veranda when Jake stepped out. He watched the riders carefully. Young Jake moved to stand next to his grandfather, but Big Jake knew how dangerous that could be if any one of these men was really here to make a name for himself.

"Move a bit away, Jake," he told the boy, watching the riders as he spoke.

Young Jake obeyed, eyeing the men closely, always ready to defend his grandfather and his sister and cousins and grandma and anybody else in the family who might need protecting. There was not an ounce of fear in the young man, and he never failed to make sure others knew it, even if they were bigger than he was.

"Something I can do for you boys?" Big Jake asked

the visitors. He kept his cigarette between his lips as he spoke.

"Just lookin' for work," the apparent leader answered. He was a medium-built man who looked hard and experienced.

"We don't have any work," Jake told him. "I know the government is moving in and changing things. A few ranches have folded, but not the J&L—and it damn well won't. Part of the reason is we keep the help down to the fewest we can that still allows us to keep things going, so I'm sorry, but we can't hire anyone." Out of the corner of his eye, Jake saw his son riding toward them from where he'd been stacking wood behind a shed.

"How about horses?" the leader asked. "We could use a couple of fresh ones."

"You have a name?" Jake asked him.

The man nodded. "Porter Evans. Maybe you've heard of me."

"You worked for Cal Bennett. He sold out to us."

Porter's horse shifted and whinnied, its hooves mixing a light snow with unfrozen dirt underneath it and creating mud. November had brought heavy snows in the higher elevations of the Rockies, but here in the foothills there wasn't much on the ground, and the sun was actually peeking out from behind a few clouds. "Might you be Jake Harkner?" the man asked.

"I might."

Porter nodded. "Everybody knows who runs the J&L. Two ex–U.S. Marshals, one of them an old outlaw who ought to be sittin' in prison, seems to me." He grinned. "That man must be you."

Jake drew deeply on his cigarette and took it from his lips. He kept all five men in his sights. He pushed the side of his jacket back behind his six-gun. "Everybody has a right to his opinion, and you're probably right that I should be in prison. But right now I'm standing here a free man and telling you there's no work. As far as horses, that's up to my son, who just rode up."

A very handsome younger man with straight black hair that hung nearly to his waist approached them, riding a big roan mare. Porter eyed him, figuring him to be about thirty. He looked back at Jake. "Looks more like an Indian to me."

"His choice," Jake answered. "He never did like to sit still for a haircut."

"What's going on, Pa?" Lloyd asked. He remained on the horse as he turned the animal to face the visitors.

Jake nodded to Porter. "That man there is Porter Evans. He and the men with him used to work for Cal Bennett. They're looking for work. I told him we don't need the help right now, but they're asking about horses."

Lloyd eyed the men just as warily as his father did. The family had been to hell and back more than once, which brought out a natural defensive attitude. "I can spare a couple of horses. But I'll only take one man with me to look at them. The rest of you can stay here."

Porter nodded. "I'll go."

Lloyd glanced at one of the J&L men sitting behind the others, rifle in hand. "Come with me, Terrel. Cole and Vance can stay here with the others." He turned his horse and rode off with Porter and Terrel. One of the other visitors pulled his wool jacket closer around his neck and shivered. He was a big, heavy man who sat on a horse that looked like it should be pulling a plow rather than carrying a man.

"It's cold out here," the man grumbled. "You got any coffee inside that house?" he asked Jake.

"I do." Jake scanned all of them again. "But I'm afraid I don't normally ask strangers inside my home. The wife's a bit skittish. You can understand why."

"Yeah, she's probably been through hell, being

married to a man like you," one of the others, a much younger man, sneered.

Jake eyed him darkly. "Mister, this being the day after Thanksgiving and still sort of a holiday, I'll ignore that remark." He turned to the bigger man. "You and your men can go on over to the bunkhouse. The men will have coffee over there, and you can go inside and warm up."

The young man who'd made the remark about Jake's wife moved his horse closer, rudely shoving a couple of the other horses aside. He was a small-built man, which reminded Jake of something he'd told his grandsons and adopted son once. *Some men are like little dogs—meaner than the big ones. They're quicker on defense and they'll bite for no good reason.*

"My name is Tommy Tyler. You ever heard of it, Jake Harkner?"

Jake almost laughed at the young man's cocky confidence. He was little more than a kid, but a smart-ass young man with a gun could be more dangerous than a grown, seasoned man, who generally had a lot more sense. "A hot temper and foolish words can get you in a lot of trouble, kid," he told the young man, eyeing him carefully.

"Well, now, everybody knows *you* have a hot temper too, Jake Harkner. Only you're gettin' a little too old to be able to back it up."

"Is that so?"

Tommy moved a hand to his six-gun. "Yeah. That's so."

"Don't even think about it, Tommy," the heavier man warned. "That there is Jake Harkner, and you ain't near good enough to take him on. Get on over to the bunkhouse."

Tommy eyed Jake a moment longer. "I think there ain't never gonna be a better chance to take this man on. When a man gets older, he gets slower."

"He ain't the kind that age affects him," the heavy

man told him. "I'm thinkin' Jake Harkner ain't one second slower than he ever was. Now get your ass to the bunkhouse!"

"Yeah, ain't nobody faster than my grandpa," young Jake boldly told Tommy. "You'd better get on out of here, or my grandpa will shoot you down so fast you won't even get your gun out of its holster."

"Jake, that's enough!" Big Jake ordered. "Go on in the house."

The boy raised his chin and eyed Tommy a moment longer before reluctantly going inside.

Tommy continued to stare at Jake, who held his gaze steadily.

"Tommy, I really don't want to kill a man today," Jake told him. "We're still in a holiday mood, and you're awfully young."

"I think you're just scared I'll pull this gun on you," Tommy sneered.

"Suit yourself, son," Jake told him.

Tommy hesitated a moment. Jake could tell he was trying to drum up the courage to back his threats. Then the kid went for his gun. In a split second Jake's gun boomed and Tommy's hat flew off his head. Staring in shock, the others could hardly believe how fast Jake drew. They never even saw it. Tommy stared wide-eyed at Jake, his hand still on the butt of his gun, which had not even cleared its holster.

Jake held his .44 steadily on the boy then, pointing it directly at Tommy's head. "Mister, there was a time when I would have blown your stupid brains out—*gladly!* But two of my little granddaughters are watching, and I don't think they should see that kind of a mess!"

Lloyd was already charging back to the house from the distant corral, where he'd been showing horses to Porter Evans.

"Get the hell off the J&L," Jake growled at Tommy,

"before I change my mind about not putting a hole in your forehead! One of you other men take his gun. He can have it back when all of you leave. He's goddamn lucky I'm letting him leave in one piece!"

The heavier man turned his horse and faced Tommy. "Hand over that gun belt, you stupid sonofabitch!" he ordered.

Tommy backed his horse, contemplating not obeying the order. Finally, he angrily removed his gun belt and threw it on the ground, glaring at Jake. "Merry damn *Christmas!*" he sneered. He glanced at a front window then, noticing two little girls watching him. He made a little jerking move and shouted "Boo!" He chuckled when one of the girls screamed, then grinned at Jake. "Maybe one of them little cuties can come out here and pick up my hat for me," he goaded. "Then again, maybe you could send out that wife of yours. I hear she's somethin' to look at—your daughter and daughter-in-law, too. Have the wife leave her coat off so's we can all see those curves."

He laughed and turned his horse, heading for the bunkhouse. Bum leg and all, Jake charged off the veranda and ran up to Tommy, grabbing the young man off his horse from behind and throwing him to the ground with surprising force for a man a good forty years older.

"Pa, wait!" Lloyd reached the house and dismounted, but not before Jake picked Tommy back up and landed a big fist between his eyes, sending him sprawling again.

"Do you really think I'll let you go warm up at our bunkhouse after a remark like that?" Jake roared.

Lloyd held back. When Jake Harkner was this angry, there was no stopping him, especially if he was defending someone in the family.

Jake picked Tommy up once again and pistol-whipped him across his cheek. Tommy cried out with pain as his body whirled sideways and again landed in the snow.

"You bastard!" he screamed at Jake. "I think my cheekbone and my nose are both broke!"

"And you think I care?" Jake reached down and picked up the younger man by his coat collar and the back of his pants and threw him over his horse. "If I ever see your face again, it will be in a lot *worse* shape when I'm through with you!" he warned. He slapped Tommy's horse on the rump and yelled "Ha! Git up!" Blood from Tommy's nose and cheek dripped onto the ground as the horse took off at a gallop. "*Follow* him!" Jake ordered one of the waiting ranch hands. "Make sure he fully leaves J&L property!"

"Sure, boss." Vance turned and rode after Tommy, keeping his rifle within reach.

Lloyd stepped closer to his father. "Pa, are you okay?"

Jake turned, dark clouds hovering in his eyes. He winced with pain from his leg as he shoved his six-gun back into its holster. "I've been *better*!" He leaned down and picked up his hat, then ran a hand through his hair before putting it back on. "And don't make any remarks about me being too old to get into a fight. I can handle myself just fine when somebody threatens my *wife* or *grandkids*!"

Lloyd just shook his head. "I'm not saying a damn word. But you should have let me take care of this one, Pa. You could make your leg worse."

Jake sighed and flexed his right hand, rubbing at his knuckles. "You were off at the corral, and this couldn't wait." He took another cigarette from inside his jacket. "And to hell with my leg! That smart-mouthed little sonofabitch needed to be taught a lesson!" He heard a little girl from inside the house crying. It sounded like Sadie Mae. "*Damn* it!" he grumbled under his breath. He lit the cigarette. "Now I've gone and made Sadie Mae cry." He took a deep drag on the cigarette and cursed himself for losing his temper in front of the granddaughters, as well as spouting profanity, which too easily poured from his lips when angry.

The man who'd ridden in on a plow horse dismounted with a grunt and picked up Tommy's gun belt. He carefully approached Jake and Lloyd. "I'm sorry about this," he told them. "*Real* sorry. Tommy thinks he's Billy the Kid or somethin'. The rest of us didn't come here to make trouble, and that's the truth. We're just lookin' for work and horses." He put out his hand. "My name is Lenny Tucker."

Jake read men well. This one he could trust. Lloyd shook the man's hand but Jake held back. "You'll understand that right now my right hand isn't feeling too good," he told Lenny.

Lenny nodded.

"Pa has a temper when it comes to strangers threatening the family," Lloyd added.

"I seen that," Lenny said with a faint smile.

"I don't mean to seem inhospitable for not letting you into the house," Jake told Lenny. "As you can see by what just happened, men with my reputation have to be careful. Inside that house is a very beautiful woman who has been through too much and is pretty wary of strangers. Plus I have two little granddaughters in there. I'd just as soon not bring in a bunch of strange men with muddy boots and all."

"I don't blame you, Jake." Lenny could easily see the truth to the stories. Jake Harkner blew a man's head off in Denver a couple of years ago because the man had shot his son. And over a year ago he'd foiled a bank robbery in Boulder, killing something like five men and wounding two more, all on his own. What a fool Tommy Tyler was. "Is the invite to go warm up at the bunkhouse still open?"

Jake looked at Lloyd. "I told them they could get coffee at the bunkhouse and take an hour or so to warm up."

Lloyd sighed and faced Lenny. "It's all right. When I rode over here after that gunshot, I told your man Porter to stay put. He's picking out a couple of horses. Go warm up, but you'd best be on your way in an hour or so. And I don't want to see that little bastard my father just chased off come back around the J&L again."

"We'll make sure of it. But ain't any of us who'll want him hangin' with us anymore, so after we head south for a couple of days, we're leavin' Tommy behind. We can't be responsible for a troublemaker. We figured if we couldn't get work here, we'd head on down to Colorado Springs, where it's warmer in winter."

"Can't blame you there," Lloyd told him.

Lenny turned to Jake. "Thanks for letting us go over to the bunkhouse and warm up. I have to say it's an honor to meet you, Jake. I'm just sorry for the trouble." He turned and hoisted his heavy frame back onto his horse. "Come on, boys." They started away, and Lenny called back to Jake, "Merry Christmas!"

Jake ordered Cole to go with them and keep an eye on things.

"Sure, Jake." He walked behind the riders, his hand on his six-gun.

Jake glanced toward the distant corral where Porter Evans was leading a horse around with a rope. "Watch yourself," he told Lloyd.

"Did that stupid kid *draw* on you?"

"He did, except his gun never cleared its holster."

"What an idiot." Lloyd grinned and shook his head. "They never learn, do they?"

"Seems not." Jake turned and tossed his cigarette into the snow, noticing Evie and Katie, Lloyd's wife, were both standing outside their nearby homes, watching. "You'd better go reassure your wife and sister that everything is fine," he told Lloyd.

"Should I send Brian over? You need any doctoring?"

"Hell no! He'll just insist again that I take something for the pain in this damn leg, and I'm not doing it!"

Lloyd put his hands on his hips. "Well, maybe it's the pain that makes you so ornery."

Jake held his gaze and smiled a little. "Maybe. But most pain medicine has whiskey in it, and you know how I feel about that. I'd rather suffer than turn into a drunken bastard like my father was. I have a lot of vices, but whiskey has never been one of them. And my temper is bad enough *without* drinking. I'll go inside and tend to those girls. I hate for them to see something like this, but I didn't have much choice. It's pretty bad when a man's reputation filters all the way down to his grandchildren."

"Pa, you've been a changed man. Don't let this take you back to blaming yourself for everything. You want me to come in to get Tricia and take her home?"

"No. I'll talk to her and Sadie Mae both." He studied his son, which was like looking at himself, other than the younger man's long hair. As far as Jake was concerned, Lloyd represented the best of whatever part of himself was good and worthy. A man couldn't ask for a more loyal and loving son, nor one more able to run an eighty-thousand-acre cattle ranch and still help tend to a big family. "Go talk to the women and then sell those horses. Make sure all those men leave sooner than later."

Lloyd nodded. "You know I will. You go nurse that hand, and I know your leg is giving you fits after what just happened." Lloyd turned and remounted, riding over to where his wife and sister stood waiting. Jake noticed Evie's husband, Brian, coming out of the house then…a good man and a physician. God knew this family and the ranch hands kept the man busy enough, but sometimes Dr. Brian Stewart traveled to other ranches to care for wounds from fights and accidents or to help deliver a baby. Jake shook his head at the thought of his amazing family…all the beauty and talent and love that surrounded him. He'd never understand why he had been so blessed.

He sighed and went back up the steps of the veranda, deciding he'd better try to get rid of his anger before he went through the door. Sadie Mae was still crying.

Two

J

AKE WENT INSIDE THE HOUSE TO SEE RANDY CONSOLING Sadie Mae, while young Jake stood near the fireplace, his hands still in fists. "You okay, Grandpa?"

Jake sighed, removing his hat and coat and unbuckling his gun belt. "Jake, you have to stop goading men like that cocky little cowboy," he warned his grandson. "Let me or Lloyd or your father take care of them."

"I didn't like how that Tommy looked at you," young Jake said, pouting. "I could tell he wanted to draw on you, Grandpa. I just wish I was big enough to handle a gun myself."

"Don't be so anxious to have a gun in your hand. You know how I feel about that, Jake. As for Tommy Tyler, I've been around men like that all my life, and I damn well knew he was going to be stupid enough to draw on me. You don't need to be defending me when it comes to something like that. It just distracts me, because I don't want you to get hurt. That's why I sent you into the house."

The boy blinked back tears. "I just get scared, Grandpa. I don't want anything to happen to you. Last winter we all thought you were dead, and that's the worst thing I ever felt. I don't ever want to see you dead."

Jake reached out and touched the boy's cheek. "No smart-mouthed little runt like Tommy Tyler will ever get the best of your grandfather, Jake. As far as me dying, that's up to God, not to me *or* you. But when it happens, and it will, you have to accept that everybody gets older and everybody dies, Jake. I'm just glad I was given the chance to have a family first and the best grandsons a man could ask for in you and Stephen. I appreciate how brave you are in defending me, and I know you'll do the same for your mother and sister someday."

Young Jake suddenly hugged him. "Are you mad at me?"

Jake grinned. "It never lasts long, Jake. I love you too much."

Sadie Mae and Tricia stood watching their grand-father, still sniffling over the scare of Jake's booming gunshot and the fight that followed. Jake patted his grandson's shoulder, then let go of him and glanced at Randy, who just stood there with arms folded, smiling softly through tears.

"Are *you* all right?" she asked.

Jake sighed deeply, rubbing at his neck. "I will be." He looked down at his namesake. "Jake, you didn't do anything wrong. Go on home and comfort your mother. Evie is probably upset."

"Okay." Young Jake gave his grandfather a quick smile before darting away. "Wait till Stephen finds out about this," he said excitedly, referring to Lloyd's son. Young Jake and Stephen were close, though Stephen was three years older. "He's way out north of here helping some of the men spread winter feed. He'll be sorry he missed the shoot-out!" He ran out the door and Big Jake removed his coat and hat, then his guns. He hung them back over the door and glanced at his worried wife.

Randy walked up and embraced him. Jake hugged her close and kissed her hair. "This sure isn't how I figured the morning after Thanksgiving would turn out," he told her.

Randy looked up at him. "Thank God you're okay," she told him, moving her hands over his arms while she studied her husband's handsome face. "But, Jake, you really shouldn't go throwing men off their horses and landing into them like that. You might have hurt your back or your leg."

He rocked her in his arms. "Don't be underestimating me, woman," he teased.

Randy smiled. "After what we shared last night, I'm not underestimating a thing. I just want you to use some common sense because of that leg, Mr. Harkner."

"I'll be fine. I just hope I don't end up regretting the fact that I let that young sonofabitch ride off alive and well."

Sadie Mae spoke up then, new tears forming on her cheeks. "That man looked at me with mean eyes, Grampa. He scared me."

Jake gently pushed Randy away and walked over to where the girls stood near the circular stairs that led to the loft bedroom he shared with Randy.

"And now he's gone and won't be back," he assured the frightened girl. He leaned down and managed to pick up both girls, one in each arm. "No more crying," he told them. "Grandpa is just fine."

"Why did that man want to shoot you?" Sadie Mae lamented.

"He was just a stupid kid who wanted to brag he was faster than Jake Harkner."

"Are you hurt?" Tricia asked him.

Jake carried them to his big leather chair, thinking how he would have preferred to kill Tommy Tyler. But times were changing, and he was trying to change with them, although it was very frustrating for a man accustomed to dealing out his own form of justice.

"I'm just fine," he told the girls. He winced with pain as he lowered himself into the chair and let the girls each sit on a knee. He loved how different they looked. Tricia's hair was bright red and curly, like her mother's— Lloyd's wife, Katie. She had bright blue eyes, and her nose and cheeks were scattered with freckles. Sadie Mae had long, dark hair like Jake's lovely daughter Evie, who was tall and slender and ravishing, an example of the best of Mexican and white blood. Sadie Mae had dark eyes and a smile that would melt the heart of the worst man who ever walked. She smiled almost constantly, and when she did, her whole face lit up and the sweet dimples in her cheeks grew deeper. Both girls still had that little-girl chubbiness about them, and Jake loved them beyond measure.

Sadie Mae hugged him around the neck and laid her head on his shoulder, her lips near his ear. "Grampa, why do some men want to hurt you?" She started crying again. "I don't wanna be without you."

"I'm right here," Jake assured her, "and I'm okay." He gave her a quick kiss on the cheek, glancing at Randy then. The words he'd just spoken rang the same as when he'd had to reassure his wife the same way two winters ago, after she'd suffered an attack by men seeking revenge on Jake Harkner.

Don't let go, Jake.

I'm right here. I won't let go.

He still saw that look in her eyes sometimes. He'd never forgive himself for all the things Randy Harkner had suffered because of him.

"I'm okay and I'm right here," he repeated, this time to his wife.

She quickly wiped at her eyes and turned away to finish cleaning up the kitchen. Jake turned to his granddaughters. "Let's read a story together," he told them. "I'll let you two read it to me, because your mothers have taught you well. I'll bet you read better than Grandpa does. So I'll let you try first." He reached to a table beside his chair and handed a children's storybook to Tricia. "Do you know that when I met your grandmother, I was a grown man and still hardly knew how to read?"

"Didn't you go to school, Grampa?" Sadie Mae asked.

"Well, I had a pretty mean father and he wouldn't let me go. So I learned to read later in life, when I watched and listened to your grandma teach your mother, Sadie Mae." He squeezed Tricia close. "And your father, Tricia."

"Grampa, will you take me and Tricia to town to buy Christmas presents?" Sadie Mae asked. "I wanna buy Mommy a hairbrush 'cuz she has long, pretty hair."

"Yes, she does." Jake was glad for a conversation that kept the girls' minds off of this morning's violence.

"I get two cents every day for getting all the eggs," Sadie Mae said proudly. "I saved my pennies for Christmas."

"Me, too!" Tricia piped up, both girls sometimes vying for their grandfather's attention. "Mommy pays me for beating the rugs and helping with dishes."

"Well, then, you two must be pretty rich. You can both get your mothers something nice."

"What do *you* want, Grampa?" Tricia asked him.

"All I want is smiles on your faces, so I already have my present." Both girls gave him their best smiles and giggled.

"Don't tell Mommy I'm getting her a hairbrush," Sadie Mae told him. She put a finger to her lips. "It's a secret," she said in a near whisper.

Jake grinned. "I'll remember that. I know how much you like secrets, Sadie Mae."

Sadie Mae clapped her small hands over her mouth and giggled. Randy wiped her hands on a towel then and walked over to stand behind Jake while Tricia read to him. She leaned down and kissed her husband's cheek, thinking what a contrast he was now compared to only minutes earlier, when he went after Tommy Tyler. There was a time when Jake Harkner would have shot the young gunslinger down even though Tommy never even got his gun out of its holster.

She suspected the only thing that stopped him

this time was knowing his little granddaughters were watching. She was still trying to get used to the Jake Harkner who was struggling to change with the times… but she knew that deep inside, the ruthless outlaw was constantly trying to break the chains of civility. Facing his brutal past last year, when he found his mother's grave in south Texas, had helped soothe some of the old anger deep inside. Finding love through family, and especially his grandchildren, had helped even more, but sometimes a man's past could be so ugly that rising above it completely was impossible. He was, after all, Jake Harkner, the man who'd been so brutalized the first fifteen years of his life that he'd killed his own father to escape.

No man completely conquered such a past.

Three

"IT'S THAT INCIDENT EARLIER TODAY, ISN'T IT, JAKE?" Randy rubbed liniment on her husband's aching left leg, always wanting to cry at the odd bump in his shinbone. Imagining the hell he'd gone through alone in Mexico sometimes kept her awake at night. Sometimes he still thrashed around in bed because of nightmares from it, let alone the pain that often kept him awake.

"What do you mean?" Jake asked.

Randy began wrapping a stretchy gauze around his leg. Sometimes it felt better when supported with a tight wrap. "I can always feel it when we make love, my darling husband. The anger comes through in *how* you make love."

Jake lit a cigarette. "I'm sorry. Did I hurt you?"

Randy smiled softly. "Of course not. Heaven forbid Jake Harkner should hurt a woman." She started a second layer of gauze. "You were just more forceful, like you wanted to prove to yourself someone like Tommy Tyler wasn't going to interfere with your pleasure or your wife or in any other way disrupt your life." She tied off the gauze then and met his gaze. "You forget that after almost thirty-three years, I know your every single mood, the meaning of your every movement, every look in those handsome dark eyes…how you're feeling when you touch me and make love to me."

Jake looked her over lovingly, but then Randy caught a hint of the old Jake as he took a deep drag on his cigarette. "I should have killed him. You know I don't like leaving an enemy alive. We've been through enough to know the kind of damage that can do." He set the cigarette in an ashtray beside the bed. "I hate this New West. A man can't be a man anymore."

Randy laughed lightly, this time a genuine laugh. She ran her hand gently over his leg, leaning down and kissing it. "There isn't a person living who would ever accuse Jake Harkner of not being a man! You are so incredibly masculine that I still worry about women going after you when you go into town for supplies. Wasn't it Gretta Decker who said you reeked of sex?"

There it was! The smile she loved. She'd managed to get his mind off of Tommy Tyler.

"Yeah, well, that notorious prostitute from Denver is now married to our own cowboy Cole Decker and living in a cozy little cabin only a half mile away right here on the J&L."

Randy straightened and pulled her robe a little closer around her nakedness. "Yes, and they seem so happy, but I can't help being a bit wary when you have to go over there to see Cole, especially if he's not home," she teased.

Jake laughed. "They're great together, aren't they? I actually don't think Gretta would ever cheat on that man, in spite of her past. Besides, Cole is my best friend, let alone the fact that I would never want to have to answer to you for something like that."

She leaned closer. "So big, bad Jake Harkner is scared of his wife?"

"You bet I am." He held out his arms. "Come here, Mrs. Harkner."

Randy smiled as she stretched across his bare chest, always admiring her husband's fine build, still solid for a man his age—a man most others still didn't care to cross. He'd proven earlier today that was smart thinking.

Jake stroked her hair. "I'm glad Cole is happy, after what he and I went through last winter…and I'm glad for Gretta. She's been an amazingly good wife to him. I think this is the life she always wanted."

"I think so too." Randy kissed his neck, and Jake rolled her onto her back and moved on top of her.

"And there are still times when I can hardly believe I'm actually still alive and lying in this bed with the most beautiful woman in Colorado."

"Even though I'm in my fifties?"

"No one would ever guess that. And in my eyes, you're the frightened twenty-year-old I met back in Kansas... and later bedded in the back of a wagon somewhere on the plains, losing my soul and heart forever."

Randy ran a finger along the thin, now-faint scar down the left side of his face, from a wound suffered years ago when he was a marshal in Oklahoma. *So many years. So many scars.* The worst were the scars on his back, some from the beatings he took from his drunken father when he was a little boy, and more from being beaten with a bull whip over a year ago in Mexico, when he was left for dead in the desert.

"Much as you hate the word, Jake, you *are* a hero to a lot of people. I don't know how you've survived so much, and I hate it when something happens like today that forces you to revisit that lingering anger and hatred down deep inside. You've come so far. Letting that man go proves how you've grown and changed."

He kissed her once more and moved to her side, pulling her close. "I'm just sorry for all you've been through putting up with me." He pressed his hand against her belly and gently rubbed it. "You gave me this great big family. If not for Lloyd and Evie and all the grandkids, I'd be the same lost, lonely man I was when we met—or most likely dead a long time ago. And you're right. I can't help feeling angry over what happened earlier. I just hated for those sweet little girls to see and hear that, especially so near the holiday. I hate being the one who keeps bringing up the ugly side of life around here without even trying."

"You can only live your own life being the wonderful father and grandfather that you are, Jake." Randy scooted up and kissed his neck. "Those little girls think you're the greatest thing that ever walked. *All* the grandchildren think that, and rightly so." She sat up straight then. "Let's take all the children into Brighton next week, if weather permits. They're anxious to buy Christmas presents for their parents and each other. We'll separate them, keep brothers and sisters apart so they can buy for each other. They love the trip into town, and it will help get all of us into the Christmas spirit and forget what happened today."

Jake picked up his cigarette and took a last drag before pressing it out. "Whatever you want." He grinned, pushing her robe aside where it had fallen open again, revealing lovely breasts. "Right now I'm thinking I could make love to you again." He moved a hand inside her robe. "It helps me forget about the pain in my leg."

Randy smiled. "Jake, we just did this."

"So?" He rolled her onto her back again. "No kids are here tonight, and I'm not getting any younger. We'd better take advantage before this old man can't do this anymore."

Randy laughed lightly. "That will be the day!" She ran her hands over his arms and shoulders. "I don't see any old man. I see a very virile, handsome, strong man who *does* reek of sex."

Jake kissed her deeply. "You're my best medicine, Randy. *Tu eres mi vida, mi querida esposa.*"

He met her mouth in another deep kiss, a man who knew exactly how to make her want him all over again. That hadn't changed in all the years they'd been together. Jake Harkner wasn't just good with guns.

Randy's robe came off, and she tried to remember if,

in all the years they'd been together, she'd ever said no
to this man.

Four

IT WAS QUITE A PROCESSION WHENEVER THE HARKNERS chose to bring the whole family into Brighton for shopping. People in the street always stopped to watch, each with his and her own opinion of Jake. *Still an outlaw at heart…a hero for saving Boulder citizens when that bank was robbed…a lawman who still thinks he can take the law into his own hands…dangerous…must not be easy being married to a man like that… The whole family is so loving and loyal to him. They saved him from a hanging in Denver, you know… But he blew a man's head off in front of a hundred people! They say he adores his wife—that he would easily kill for her… He adores ALL women, I heard, especially prostitutes… I sure wouldn't cross him… The newspapers said he was tortured and left for dead last year in Mexico—went there to rescue some young girl who'd been kidnapped.*

Whispers. Quiet laughter. Curious stares. Distrust. Admiration. Most men liked to brag that they knew Jake Harkner, had met him. He was, after all, famous—"the last outlaw" some called him. Most women fluttered and twittered and smiled with nervousness around him. His smile usually melted their hearts and left them speechless…and wondering what it was like to be married to "a man like that."

Bells jingled merrily on the harnesses of the two horses pulling the large four-seater sleigh driven by Brian. Randy, Evie, Sadie Mae, and the girl's two-year-old sister, Esther Miranda, were also along. Evie held her six-month-old son, Cole. Joining the packed family in the sleigh was Katie and her little girl, Tricia, two-year-old son, Donavan, and one-year-old son, Jeffrey Peter. Katie's parents from Oklahoma also lived on the J&L now, and her mother, Clara, had come along to help with the babies.

The packed four-seater sleigh slid through town to the sound of the jingling harnesses and the girls' and women's laughter. Tricia and Sadie Mae had begged to make the trip in the sleigh because there was enough snow and it rode better than a wheeled wagon—and because "sleighs are more fun!" the girls insisted.

"Lord, when that bunch comes to town, it's an all-out parade," Win Becker said to his wife. The Beckers owned the local hardware store. They stood at their front window to watch.

"Should be a good day for us, Win," Tessie Becker answered. "They'll be needing plenty of supplies to get through the rest of winter. Heavier snows will set in soon, and they'll be holed up on the J&L till spring."

"Ole Amos at the feed store will have a good day too," Win replied. "Those Harkners have money, that's sure."

"Some say it's money Jake's son inherited from his first wife when she died," his wife commented. "I think her pa was a wealthy rancher who lived way south of here. It's quite a past those Harkners have, all from way back when Jake Harkner was a wanted man and went to prison. His wife waited for him all those years. Most women would have given up on him."

"She's quite a woman. God only knows what she's been through."

"And she's so beautiful and tiny and sophisticated. She sure is a contrast to that husband of hers."

Behind the sleigh came two buckboard wagons for supplies, driven by Cole and Terrel. Alongside the wagons rode Stephen and young Jake. Ben rode just behind them, all three boys on their own horses, sitting as tall as possible to feel more like men.

"You can tell those boys are proud to be related to Jake Harkner," Tessie mentioned. Bringing up the rear was Jake himself, riding beside Lloyd. They separated and rode at a faster lope to catch up alongside the big sleigh. It took nearly a day and a half to reach Brighton from the J&L, and the whole family had spent the night at a rooming house established on a neighboring ranch belonging to Henry Hill, with whom the Harkners had become good friends. Brian had saved Hill's son's life earlier in the winter, when the boy took a bad turn after a case of the measles.

The sleigh approached the Sherman Inn, one of only two hotels in Brighton. The supply wagons clattered on down the street.

"We'd better prepare some rooms," Margaret Sherman told her husband. They stood on their front stoop, and Margaret waved to Jake as he dismounted. The Harkners usually stayed at their place when the whole family came into town, usually only once or twice a year.

"They must be here for supplies and probably to shop for some Christmas presents," her husband, Clint, added. "I'm glad you already put up a tree. Those little girls will love it."

"I'll get the rooms," Jake told Lloyd. "The women can go ahead and shop for whatever they need." He tied his horse and glanced at Brian. "Brian, can you see to the women? Lloyd can go with you to keep an eye out."

"Jake, just a little shopping for now," Randy called to him. "We'll come back in about an hour, when the rooms are ready, and put the babies down. We all need to rest a while after that long trip."

"I figured as much."

Brian turned the sleigh to head for a dry-goods store on the other side of the street.

"We're gonna buy Christmas presents!" Tricia called to the Shermans.

"That's real nice, honey," Margaret Sherman called back.

"My present for Mommy will be a secret!" Sadie Mae added, giggling.

Bells jingled and more giggles filled the air as the sleigh sailed back down the street.

"I'll meet you at the stables, Pa," Lloyd told Jake before following the sleigh. Stephen, young Jake, and Ben rode after them.

Jake stepped up onto the front stoop and nodded to the Shermans, then put out his hand to Clint. "We'll need at least five rooms, Mr. Sherman. The family just keeps getting bigger."

"Well, that must make you right proud, Jake," Margaret told him, looking up at Jake and smiling. She was short to begin with, but Jake towered over most average men and women. "You have a beautiful family!"

"And I don't deserve any of them. If anybody had told me thirty years ago that I'd end up like this, I'd have shot them for being crazy."

Margaret sobered a little at the remark, wondering if Jake Harkner used to shoot men for no good reason. She smiled nervously and invited him inside to sign for the rooms.

Jake turned to watch Lloyd and Brian help the women out of the sleigh. Tricia and Sadie Mae screamed and laughed and tossed snow at each other before running inside the dry-goods store. He smiled, loving their excitement. He took a good look around then before going inside, always wary, always watchful, always alert.

Five

SADIE MAE STUDIED THE WIDE SILVER-HANDLED hairbrush. She tugged at Randy's skirt. "Grandma!"

Randy knelt down beside her granddaughter. "Look!" Sadie Mae said. "Can I get that for Mommy for Christmas?"

"How many pennies do you have, Sadie Mae?"

"A hundred!"

"And how much is that in dollars? Remember what your mother and I have been teaching you?"

Sadie Mae nodded, grinning. "It's a whole dollar!"

Randy smiled. "Very good, Sadie Mae! Let me see how much it is." She walked over to the clerk, speaking quietly. "Mr. Cunningham, no matter what the price, please tell Sadie Mae that hairbrush she wants is just one dollar."

The man grinned and nodded. He quickly wrote the real price on a piece of paper. One dollar and eighty cents. Randy dug into her handbag for the eighty cents. "Thank you!" She walked back to Sadie Mae, who was still ogling the hairbrush. Tricia stood beside her and she pointed it out to her cousin. "I'm getting that for Mommy! Don't tell!"

"I won't." Both girls giggled. "I found some real pretty ribbon for my mommy," Tricia said. "She likes to tie her hair with ribbons. Daddy likes it that way."

"Your daddy has long hair, too," Sadie Mae told Tricia. "Maybe we should get *him* some ribbons!"

Both girls giggled even harder, picturing Tricia's big, tall, dark father wearing fancy ribbons in his hair.

Randy reached them and told a very happy Sadie

Mae that the brush was only one dollar. Sadie Mae clapped her hands and handed Mr. Cunningham a little drawstring bag with her hundred pennies in it. "Can you wrap it in brown paper so Mommy doesn't see it?" she asked. "Grandma brought us here without our mommies so we could buy them presents."

"Sure, I can wrap it."

"Tricia, let me help you while Mr. Cunningham wraps Aunt Evie's brush," Randy told her redheaded granddaughter. She walked to a counter where bright ribbons were displayed.

Sadie Mae felt happy. Everyone was buying presents! Her cousin Jake needed new boots. Her uncle Ben needed dress pants for when the traveling preacher visited. Cousin Stephen might get a new rifle. Her grandmother wanted new curtain material, and her aunt Katie wanted a jewelry box. The list was long, and everyone knew what others needed or wanted, but no one knew if that particular item would become a Christmas present or just a needed supply. Most of the real presents would be a secret until they were unwrapped Christmas morning.

And Sadie Mae loved secrets! She looked out the window and saw a red bird, which totally fascinated her. With joy in her heart, she headed out the door to get a closer look, deciding to follow the bird if possible while her grandmother helped Tricia shop for Katie. The bird fluttered around the corner and into an alley.

Sadie Mae looked around, noticing her father coming up the steps to go into a hat store next to where her grandmother shopped. He was carrying Sadie Mae's baby brother, Cole.

"Stay close, Sadie Mae," Brian warned. "I have to go inside." He walked into the hat store, where Evie shopped with Katie and Katie's mother. Sadie Mae loved babies and was proud that she often watched her baby sister and baby brother and year-old cousin, Jeffrey Peter.

After her father disappeared into the store, Sadie Mae glanced at the alley where the bird had flown. Following it just around the corner seemed safe enough. She looked to see her grandpa Jake standing outside the Sherman Inn talking to the owners just three or four buildings away and across the street. She couldn't wait to tell him about the hairbrush she'd bought for her mother, but first she wanted one more look at the red bird.

She darted around the corner, and the red bird flitted from a barrel farther down the alley. Sadie Mae ran after it to the back of the building, then stopped cold. A man wearing a gun and a black hat was bent over another man. The other man's face was bloody.

"That'll teach you to cheat me at cards!" the man with the gun said, jerking the bloody man up.

"I didn't cheat you!"

"The hell you didn't!" The man with the gun pulled back a fist to hit the bloody man again, then paused when he noticed Sadie Mae. He just stared at her a moment, and Sadie Mae stared back, frozen in place. He looked familiar.

The man with the gun shoved the other man onto his butt and turned toward Sadie Mae, stepping closer.

Sadie Mae's eyes widened. It was *him*—the gunman who'd tried to shoot her grandfather back when those men visited the J&L.

The man with the gun grinned. "Well, well, well," he said, squinting a little to study her as he knelt nearby.

Sadie Mae couldn't make her legs move. She just blinked, her throat feeling tight. The man with the gun scared her, not just because she knew he'd just beat up another man, but because he had an ugly, still-unhealed cut on his right cheek where her grandfather had hit him with his gun. One eye was still black, and his nose looked crooked. Did Grampa break it when he hit this man with his fist?

"You look familiar," the man with the gun told her.

Sadie Mae swallowed. "You're that bad man who tried to shoot my grampa!" Sadie Mae told him, her little hands moving into fists. "My grampa beat you up! You're mean!"

The man grinned wickedly. "*That's* why you look familiar. You're one of the little girls who was watching through the front window." He laughed from somewhere deep in his throat. "You're Jake Harkner's granddaughter, aren't you?"

Sadie Mae pressed her lips together, refusing to answer.

"Well, now, you listen here, you little brat," the man told her. He leaned in closer, leering with the Devil in his dark eyes. "You'd better not tell your grampa or anybody else that you saw me beat up that man over there. If you do, I'll *kill* you, got that? I'll wrap my hands around that little throat and squeeze till you can't breathe any more. And after I kill you, I'll go after your grandpa and I'll kill *him*! And then I'll find a way to hurt your *mommy*, so you'd better not say a word, understand?"

Tears streaming down her chubby cheeks, Sadie Mae nodded. "I remember your name. You're Tommy Tyler, and you're a *bad* man," she told him, jerking with sobs at the words.

Tyler poked at her chest. "So is your grandfather! He killed his own *daddy*! Did you know that? He killed a *lot* of men and did a lot of bad things. And if you tell on me and he comes after me, the law will *hang* him! He'll—"

Tommy didn't finish. He heard the click of a gun hammer behind him.

"Touch my granddaughter again and you're a *dead* man!"

Jake Harkner's deep, hard words interrupted Tommy, who froze, still kneeling.

Sadie Mae burst into tears. "Grampa, he said he was

gonna kill you and me and Mommy! And he said if you hurt him, somebody will hang you!"

Jake kept his gun pressed against the back of Tommy's head. "Nobody is going to hang me, Sadie Mae. You go find Grandma and tell her to get the sheriff. Right now, Sadie Mae. Do as I tell you!"

The girl's whole body jerked in a sob as she wiped at her tears, then ran off.

Jake pressed the barrel of his gun to the back of Tommy's head. "Pull that gun out and throw it aside," he told the young man.

"*Shoot* him, Harkner!" Tommy's bloodied victim demanded as he got to his feet. "The sonofabitch deserves it!"

"Stay out of this!" Jake ordered. "If you're able, go help my wife find the sheriff so he can throw this bastard in jail!"

The wounded man ran off and Jake kicked Tommy's gun aside.

"How...how did you find us?" Tommy asked.

"I'm not easily fooled, Tommy Tyler!" Jake growled. "A man like me is always aware of his surroundings, and I keep a close eye on my family! I saw Sadie Mae run into this alley and I came over here the back way because it was quicker. It's a damn good thing I did! Do you have any idea how badly I want to pull this trigger?"

Tommy closed his eyes and swallowed. "Please don't."

"It wasn't that many years ago that I *would* have!" Jake growled. "You ever touch my granddaughter again—or scare her or make one wrong move against *any* member of my family—and before I kill you, I'll make you *wish* you were dead! If we were alone right now, I'd blow your goddamn head off and bury you out in the foothills, and no one would ever know what happened to you! Right now you're the luckiest man who ever walked, but this is the *last* time I'll let you live! One more incident like this and I'll kill you in the slowest, most painful way possible, even if it means prison or a hanging! Understand?"

Tommy slowly nodded.

Jake suddenly jerked him up by the back of his collar and literally threw him against the wall of the dry-goods store. With a strength that surprised Tommy, he stiff-armed him, pinning him to the wall and half choking him while he held his six-gun against Tommy's eye. "If you have a grudge against me, then you face *me* with it, understand? Not a little girl! Come against me in an honest gunfight again, Tommy Tyler, and I'll put a hole in you so big, people will be able to see *through* you! *Nobody* makes my little granddaughter cry!" he growled. He shoved the gun barrel harder, making Tommy grimace with pain and terror. "Maybe if all I do is push this eye out, they won't hang me! What do *you* think?"

Tommy fought tears. "Go ahead! I can take it! My pa beat me plenty, so I'm tough, like *you*!" His words came out in a raspy whisper because he couldn't take a full breath.

Jake just stared at him a moment, then pulled the gun away. "Where *is* your father?"

"He's *dead*! Killed by another drunk two years ago, and I never shed one tear!"

Jake towered over him. "How the hell old are you?" he asked.

"Eighteen!" Tommy sneered. "Old enough to take care of myself and to carry a gun!"

"Well, let me tell you something, Tommy Tyler! When I was your age I was a lot like you, and it would take me *days* to explain the hell I've been through my whole life because of it! If I can save even one kid from that hell, it's worth it." He kept Tommy pressed against the wall, glaring at him to get his point across. "I'm trying to teach my sons and grandsons the right way, so they never have to go through what I've gone through!

And I'm telling you right now to change your ways or you'll be damn miserable and alone your whole *life*! Even if you're surrounded by people who care about you, you'll be alone. Alone because you'll live with black memories that never let go. So I'm giving you a chance to *think* about that! I've let you live twice. Don't count on that happening three times, understand?"

Tommy slowly nodded.

"Keep your sorry little ass away from my family! I'm giving you the best damn Christmas present you'll ever get! I'm giving you your *life*!"

"Pa!" Lloyd came running down the alley. "Mom said—"

"He made Sadie Mae cry!" Jake told his son, keeping his dark eyes on Tommy.

"Leave this to the law, Pa. Sheriff Bosley is coming. Some man with a face all bloodied told him Tommy Tyler beat on him and held a gun on him. Bosley will arrest him for assault, and he'll be out of our hair."

Jake just remained standing there with a tight grip on Tommy, finally lowering his gun into its holster.

"Pa, we're in town and there is *law* here!" Lloyd reminded him. "Don't do something crazy."

In moments, Sheriff Bosley and Tommy's victim came running down the alley, followed by a small crowd of onlookers. The news that Jake Harkner had a man pinned down in an alley had traveled as fast as a bullet.

"Jake, let the sheriff take care of this!" Randy pleaded then. She appeared at the end of the alley and slowly walked closer. "Sadie Mae is fine."

Always calmed by his wife's voice, Jake finally let go of Tommy, who stood there sweating and now crying.

Jake glanced at the sheriff. "Lock him up, and don't let him out until my family and I leave town, understand? I can't guarantee I won't *shoot* the little bastard next time!"

"Sure, Jake."

People whispered and stared as Jake walked past them and up to Randy, who saw an odd devastation in his eyes. "I just saw *me*," he told her. He grasped her arm and pulled her away from the crowd. "He's a cocky, angry little shit like I was at his age—full of hate and a desire to feel important because his father beat the pride right out of him! He told me I could beat on him all I wanted and he didn't care, because his father had toughened him up." Jake turned away.

"Jake." Randy put a hand on his arm. She knew what the ugly memories of his own father did to him...the beatings...the mental abuse.

"I'm all right," Jake told her. "I tried to tell him... to explain the hell he'll always live with if he doesn't straighten himself out. I don't know if it helped. I just know it's almost Christmas and maybe...I don't know...maybe I was supposed to say something to him. I hope I won't regret letting him go." He lit a cigarette, obvious anger and frustration in his dark eyes. "Go rest at the hotel," he told Randy. "You and the other women can finish your shopping later today and tomorrow morning."

"Jake, you did the right thing."

"*Did* I?" He turned away and sighed. "I'd better not see that little sonofabitch anywhere near one member of my family again! But part of me says I should help him."

"Good! That's a good sign of how much you have healed from your past." Randy moved around to face him. "With Christmas near and the children around, you did the right thing, handing him over to Sheriff Bosley."

Sadie Mae stood at the corner between her parents at the end of the alley. She clung to Evie's skirt and burst into tears. Evie knelt down to try to soothe her. "It's all right, Sadie Mae."

Jake tossed his cigarette into the snow and hurried over to where they stood.

"Daddy and Grampa will be mad at me," Sadie Mae whimpered. "Daddy told me to stay close, but I saw a pretty bird and I chased it. I thought maybe it had little babies like the chick-a-dees at home."

Still holding baby Cole in his arms, Brian knelt down to his daughter. "Sweet pea, I'm not mad. But you do have to mind better, when it comes to running off. I only give you those orders for your own good." He took her hand. "Give Daddy a kiss."

Still sobbing, Sadie Mae kissed Brian's cheek, then looked up at her grandfather, who sometimes seemed like a giant to her. "I'm sorry, Grampa. Did that man hurt you?"

Jake rubbed at his eyes and sighed before leaning over to pick the girl up. "No, Sadie Mae, he didn't hurt me. And the sheriff took him away, so everything is fine."

"I'm sorry, Grampa," she whimpered. "I got you in trouble."

Jake wrapped his arms around her, looking at Randy as he patted her back and let her cry on his shoulder. "Sadie Mae, Grandpa gets *himself* in trouble. I don't need someone else to do it for me. You didn't do anything wrong, and nobody can hurt Grandpa, so you stop crying, okay? If you keep crying, you'll make *me* cry."

"Big men like you don't cry, Grampa." Sadie Mae's words came out slowly as she kept her head on his shoulder.

"Oh, you'd be surprised, Sadie Mae."

"Did you cry when your daddy used to hit you?"

Pain stabbed at Jake's heart. Did she remember Tommy Tyler's words? That he'd killed his own father? "Sometimes," he answered. He could tell the girl was getting sleepy, exhausted from the emotional ordeal. "Did you get that present for your mother?" he asked her.

"Yes," she answered drowsily. "Don't…tell her, Grampa. It's a secret."

"I won't tell." Jake kept Sadie Mae in his left arm and

reached out with his right to put an arm around Randy. "Come on. I'll go to the hotel too, and we'll all rest."

"I'm for that," Brian answered. "This son of mine needs to be fed."

"It's not that far," Jake told Brian. "Let's just walk there. You can leave the sleigh hitched right here for now."

"Let me carry Cole for you," Lloyd told his brother-in-law. He took the sleepy boy into his arms.

Randy stood on her tiptoes and kissed Jake's cheek before ducking from under his arm. "You go ahead. I'll get Katie and Clara."

Evie grasped her mother's arm as Jake walked off with Brian. "I'm proud of how Daddy handled this," she told Randy. "He can't make his own laws anymore."

They walked together then with Lloyd toward the rooming house. "He knows things have to change," Randy answered Evie, "but I think something happened here that hit him deeply, Evie. He saw his younger self in Tommy Tyler. That helped him hold back. He could have shot it out with Tommy again and would have had the right, but he let him go. He still fights that deep anger, but I think he understands himself better, if that makes any sense."

"It does. We just have to keep praying for him so we don't lose him again. It's just a shame, all of us here to have fun buying Christmas presents, that this happened at all."

Lloyd glanced back to see the sheriff marching Tommy Tyler off to jail. He turned to his mother, towering over her with the same big frame his father had. "If Tommy Tyler ever shows his face again around Pa, I'm not sure what Pa will do. He only held back for the sake of Sadie Mae."

"I know. Keep an eye on him, Lloyd. He talks to you."

Lloyd leaned down and kissed his mother's cheek. "I'll go find the boys and herd them over to the hotel after I hand Cole off to Brian again. We all need some rest."

"We'll meet you there with Katie and Clara," Evie told her brother. "Young Jake won't like having to nap. He has far too much energy, but he'll just have to do as he's told. And he'll probably wish he'd been here to see his grandfather in action. I swear, I have already lost complete control of my son, and he's not even quite eleven years old."

Lloyd smiled. "Like grandfather, like grandson."

"Lloyd Harkner, you belong in that same picture. And the older you get, the more you look like our father in every way," Evie teased.

Lloyd turned to watch Jake and Brian nearing the hotel. "Not every way. I don't have his memories, and thank God I don't." He turned to his sister. "Little Sadie Mae sure does love him, though. He's crazy about her and Tricia. It's almost comical, when you think about the life he's led and how ruthless he can be. He has so many personalities, I sometimes don't know which Jake I'm talking to."

"I'm just glad he's here with us for the holidays," Randy told her son and daughter. "This will be the merriest Christmas we've ever had." She saw Tommy Tyler resist a little when the sheriff shoved him into the jailhouse. "At least I *hope* it will be."

Six

"JAKE?" RANDY CALLED HIS NAME IN A NEAR WHISPER. She pulled her robe tighter around herself and retied it. It was 1:00 a.m. and everyone in the hotel was in bed. Somehow she knew Jake wouldn't be. He stood at the end of the hall looking out a window that faced the side street. He turned to face her, wearing only his denim pants and an undershirt and no shoes.

"You should be sleeping," Jake told her.

"And not you?"

Jake shrugged. "Too many nights sleeping under the stars over the years and keeping one eye open for varmints, sometimes the human kind."

Randy walked silently on her own bare feet to stand next to him so they could talk quietly. "I know you too well to think you'd be sleeping," she told her husband. "I had a feeling today's events would eat at you."

"Yeah," he answered. He pulled her close. "But I'm also awake because I miss you too. I'd rather be lying next to you right now instead of having about six arms and six legs tossing and turning in the same bed. I'm too old and have too many aches and pains to sleep with Stephen and young Jake and two-year-old Donavan."

Randy smiled and moved her arms around him, resting her head against his chest. "Yes, well, I'm fighting Tricia and Sadie Mae. That's the only bad part about these trips. The kids are all getting so big, we'll have to rent more rooms next time." She leaned up and kissed his chin. "It's the leg, isn't it?"

Jake sighed deeply. "It's always the leg. Young Jake tosses and turns and ends up sideways, poking me with a foot. It's impossible to sleep with him." He moved his arms around her. "It's also Tommy Tyler. That first time at the ranch, I just reacted to him wanting to get into a gunfight and then the way he talked about you. And today, I saw him making Sadie Mae cry and I wanted to kill him for it. But when he told me to go ahead and beat him…"

"You saw yourself at his age," Randy finished for him, still resting her head against his chest.

"One big difference. I got into gunfights and fistfights and had a smart mouth…but I never would have teased little girls or threatened women."

"Even so, there is a lot of anger and rebellion in that young man. Maybe in his case he didn't have such a loving mother. Maybe he was beaten by both parents."

Jake sighed deeply, rocking her in his arms. "Maybe. All I know is, I was just about his age when I killed my father." He kissed her hair. "Part of me wants to try to talk some sense into that little bastard, and I don't know why."

Randy leaned back and looked up at him. "Jake Harkner, you *have* changed. Do I dare believe you are actually able to control that anger and funnel it into helping someone?"

He frowned. "Don't get your hopes up."

Randy smiled. "Believe me, after thirty-three years I know better." She stepped back but kept hold of his arms. "You see a chance to stop a young man from going down the path you took at his age. There is nothing wrong with that. You're always preaching to our grandsons about the same thing, and you and Lloyd went a few rounds back in the day when you tried to stop him too." She reached up and touched his face. "Jake, do you remember Evie's words before you left for Mexico?

When she was praying for you, she asked God to make you understand that the way you handle guns is actually a talent that can sometimes be used to help someone. You came very close to losing your life to save a girl you didn't even know. For all the bad in you, there is so much good, and you can help young people. It shows through beautifully when you talk to your grandsons. They are growing up respectful and brave and will be good men who can handle themselves well. Maybe the Good Lord doesn't want you to stop there. Maybe He sent Tommy Tyler to you. That young man has invaded our lives twice now in just a couple of weeks. Maybe you can help him."

"Yeah, well, he needs the shit kicked out of him, and now that I know he's only eighteen, that's hard for me to do. He's just a kid."

"Then let the men at the bunkhouse straighten his tail out. Give him a job at the J&L. A couple of weeks living with those tough J&L men will make him see the light, I'll bet."

Jake finally grinned. "You have a point."

"Talk to Lloyd about it."

"We'll see." He pulled her close again. "How about if I go into your room and we make up some kind of bed on the floor so we can both get some decent sleep?"

Randy laughed. "When those little girls wake up, they'll be climbing all over us, so if you want to sleep in there, get ready for a rude awakening in the morning."

"I'll manage. At least I can hold you for a while. You always say you can't sleep without my arms around you." He leaned down and kissed her deeply. "I've gotten so I can't sleep without holding you. After all those months of pain and missing you, I can't get enough of you anymore."

Randy put her arms around his neck. "Good. I like hearing that."

They kissed again.

"Too bad we can't be alone," Jake lamented.

"You'll just have to wait until we get back home, Mr. Harkner."

"And you're still too beautiful to resist, Mrs. Harkner."

"Well, that isn't going to last much longer," Randy answered with a smile. "I'm working hard at preserving what's left."

"And you're doing a good job. You are very well preserved."

They both laughed and headed into Randy's room, where Tricia and Sadie Mae slept sideways in the bed. Randy shook her head.

"I couldn't get back into that bed now if I wanted to." She grabbed extra blankets and pillows she'd ordered earlier, certain this could happen. She threw them on the floor. "Not the most comfortable bed in the world, but let's try to get some sleep." She and Jake managed to make a bed out of blankets and rugs and finally settled in together.

"I'm not sure I can do this two nights in a row," Jake complained. "I am going to try to get an extra room for tomorrow night. This family is getting too damn big."

Randy snuggled her back against him, and Jake pulled her close.

"This is just as comfortable as that wagon we were in the first night you made love to me," Randy told him, smiling at the memory.

"Yeah? Well, there are two little girls nearby, so don't remind me of that first night, woman. It's too hard on me."

Randy kissed his arm. "Then go to sleep."

"Easier said than done." Jake sighed deeply. "Do you hear that?"

"Hear what?"

"The silence." He kissed her hair, thinking how thick and golden it still was, and brushed out long, the way he liked it. "Back in the old days, we would have heard the tinkling of barroom piano music, the screeching laughter of whores, and the yelling and fighting of drunks—maybe even shooting in the streets." He hugged her closer. "Things sure have changed out here, haven't they?"

"It's called law and order, Jake."

"Yeah. I used to set my own laws and had my own ways of keeping order."

"You certainly did, and it usually got you into trouble. I'm enjoying the peace and quiet of the normal life we have now. After the last couple of years, I don't think I could take much more, so leave the law to men who wear badges."

"I used to wear one. And Boulder still wants me to be their sheriff."

"Jake! You promised—"

He leaned over and cut off her words with a kiss. "Don't worry. I'm too damn happy with you and the family on the J&L. Last winter I thought I might never see Colorado or my family again." He kissed her neck, her hair. "Go to sleep."

Randy settled against him, wondering if she would ever get over the glory of being in his arms again…where she was always, always safe. The whole family was safe, as long as "Grandpa Jake" was around.

Seven

"ARE YOU *CRAZY*?"

"Poor choice of words, son. You already know I've been a little bit crazy my whole life. Must be from getting my brain knocked around so much as a kid." Jake spoke with a cigarette between his lips as he headed for the jailhouse.

"Pa!" Lloyd reached out and grabbed his father's arm. "Slow down!"

Jake turned to face him, taking the cigarette from his lips.

"You know what I meant," Lloyd told him. "That kid in there is huge trouble! He'll be getting into fights with my son and with young Jake and very likely Ben every five minutes. They won't put up with his shit and neither will the men."

"Good! That's what he needs. Besides that, when young Jake is mad, he can beat up a grizzly. Stephen is already growing practically as tall as you, and he wrestles down steers. He can hold his own. And I don't need to tell you about Ben. He could probably beat up both of *us*! The kid is a moose. There isn't a person alive who'd believe he's only fourteen. All three of those boys have been toughened up by ranch life, and they have the Harkner spirit of defense—even Ben, in spite of not having a drop of my blood in him." Jake turned and started walking again. "Besides, I don't intend to let that little bastard Tommy get close to a gun *or* the houses. He'll live out at the bunkhouse, and you know damn well how fast the men out there will shake his tail out. They'll have him wetting his pants."

"Damn it, Pa, *why*? Why are you doing this?"

They stepped up onto a boardwalk and Jake faced his son again, taking another drag on his cigarette before explaining. "Because it's a way for me to atone for my past. For once I'm going to *help* a shit-bag outlaw instead of *shooting* him, which he's very lucky I haven't already done."

Lloyd closed his eyes and sighed. "Pa, sit down on this bench over here before you go into that jail. Will you do that? The J&L is mostly mine, so I think I have a say in this, don't you?"

Jake buttoned his wool jacket closer around his neck, studying his very brave and loyal son's dark eyes. He couldn't imagine any father being more proud of his son. He sighed deeply and put the cigarette between his lips again. "All right. I'll grant you have a point." Jake walked over and sat down, stretching his left leg out to relieve some of the pain. "I already know what you're going to say."

"*Do* you?" Lloyd sat down beside him, resting his elbows on his knees. He removed his gloves and set them aside, then rubbed his hands together to get the circulation going. "Pa, why in hell do you think you need to atone for anything? You're almost sixty-three years old and you quit your outlaw ways over thirty years ago. You paid for it with four years in prison and just about that many more years as a U.S. Marshal in the most hellish and dangerous country a man could ask for. You saved Mom's life when you two first met. You shot it out with seven men to keep them from killing me and Mom when I was a baby. You still have pain in your hip from taking a bullet then. And later, after I abandoned the family and went kind of crazy, you literally risked your neck to save *me*. You risked your life again to save Evie at Dune Hollow."

"So did you. You were shot."

"That doesn't matter. We're talking about *you* now. I know you hate that, but I'm not done yet." Lloyd stopped to light his own cigarette while his father sat quietly smoking. He took a long drag before continuing. "You saved young Ben from being beaten near to death by his father, and then you adopted him and have treated him like your blood son ever since. Evie and I couldn't ask for a better father or a better grandfather to our kids. And in Denver you nearly got yourself hanged for killing the man who shot me. You didn't even know if I was dead or alive. You just reacted out of your love for me. Then you stuck by Mom with a patience I never knew you had after what she suffered two years ago. No man could have been kinder or more loving to his wife."

"What's your point, Lloyd?"

"My point is that you have nothing to atone for. You've already done it, over and over. You risked your ass again foiling that bank robbery in Boulder—probably saved some innocent lives."

"That's just because they had hold of your mother and my granddaughter."

"No, it isn't. You would have done it anyway, even if they weren't involved. Don't say you wouldn't have. And then you truly did nearly lose your life going to Mexico to rescue a young girl you didn't even know, and you did it for the highest-paid prostitute in Denver—a woman few men would bother helping. But her daughter was in a horrible state and you couldn't stand it, so you went down there and ended up with a broken leg and beaten with a bull whip and you're still in pain from that. So don't be talking about how you have to atone for anything. What's the *real* reason you want to hire on Tommy Tyler?"

Jake took one last drag on his cigarette and threw the stub onto the boardwalk, then stepped it out. "Because in all the things I've done, I've always killed or hurt the bad guy, if that's what you want to call them. They all deserved it, but I was hardly any different from them the first thirty years of my life. I never gave any of them one chance to change his ways…the way your mother gave me the chance to do the same. And in this case, the bad guy is only eighteen. By the time I was eighteen, I'd killed my father and was running with the worst of them."

"You didn't have any choice when you killed your father."

"Maybe not, but that damn legacy has been with me all my life. I finally shed myself of the ugly memories when I went down to Texas and saw that my mother and little brother got a proper burial and a proper headstone. But I don't think that was the end of it. I think God wants me to do one more thing. And yes, those words came out of Jake Harkner's lips. I have a chance to save a young man from going down the road I took, and I'm going to try. For one thing, if I don't face this head on, that little bastard might decide to backtrack on me and still come back and try to bring harm, to me or someone I love. I'm going to cut him off at the pass and surprise him by offering him a job…with some damn hard-set rules."

"He'll laugh in your face."

"Maybe. But unless he wants to sit in jail and then have no money and no place to go when he gets out, he'll take my offer. I saw something in his eyes, Lloyd. I saw myself…the little boy who really wanted nothing more than for someone to care about him and offer him a little help. And in that moment I saw my father beating up on me, like I was beating up on him. It stopped me, and I felt something…someone…telling me to do something about it. I don't know how else to explain it."

Lloyd finished his own cigarette, stepping it out as he rubbed at his eyes. "All right. But I'd better never see that little sonofabitch anywhere close to Sadie Mae or

Tricia—or trying to pick a fight with one of the boys. And I'll tell the men not to go easy on him, so don't expect any forgiveness or kind treatment from Cole or Terrel or any of the rest of them."

"I don't *want* them to treat him kindly. I just want them to treat him like they treat each other, unless he steps out of bounds. If he smarts off or tries to start something, he deserves whatever they do to him. If anybody can make a man out of a smart-mouthed little troublemaker like Tommy Tyler, it's the men on the J&L. He'll soon learn to stay straight or wish he had."

Lloyd leaned back and stretched out his legs. "Fine. Go get the little bastard. Tell him when we leave in the morning, he's going with us…tied up in the back of one of the wagons. I won't let him sit a horse and try riding off scot-free."

"Agreed." Jake leaned forward, watching a snowflake drift down to his boot. "Lloyd, maybe the kid has never had a decent family Christmas. I want him to see what our family Christmases are like. If he straightens up enough by Christmas, we'll let him join us for presents and dinner."

Lloyd removed his hat and ran a hand through his hair. "I can hardly believe Jake Harkner is talking." He rose, pulling his long hair out from under his jacket before putting his hat back on. "Please let me be the judge of that. We want this to be the happiest Christmas possible. Do you agree he can't be there if I say so? He hasn't even seen Evie or Katie yet. You know how beautiful they will look to a wild little eighteen-year-old like that. If he says one word to make them uncomfortable or looks at them wrong, I'll beat the shit out of him myself. You won't have to feel guilty for being the one to do it. Hell, you're the one who jumped all over him back at the ranch for making that remark about Mom. You're expecting an awful lot to happen in just a little under three weeks."

Jake rose and faced him. "I know. It might not work at all, but at least I'll know I tried."

"Yeah, well, I'd better get back to Katie. Today I get the joy of watching Donavan and Jeffrey while she shops with her mother and Evie. Jeffrey is already trying to walk and Donavan is into running off on me, so I'll have my hands full. I'll let you talk to the sheriff."

Jake nodded, smiling a little. "Thanks for agreeing to this."

"I just hope I don't regret it."

"You think I don't feel the same way?"

Lloyd studied his father and the lines in his face that spoke of too many hard years. "I love you, Pa. If not for being so damn glad to know you're alive, I'd object to this, but I can tell it's important to you."

They shared a look that said, *I'd die for you in an instant—no hesitation—if it came to that.* The bond was set hard and fast.

"Thanks," Jake told his son.

They gave each other a quick hug and pat on the back before Lloyd left. Jake took a deep breath and stepped into the jailhouse.

Eight

IT WAS QUITE A PARADE HEADING HOME. THE NIGHT before they left, a choir from the local Methodist church went caroling about town, stopping in front of the hotel to sing carols to the entire Harkner brood. Jake's very Christian, faithful daughter Evie joined in the singing, as did Tricia, Sadie Mae, Katie and Randy, who all joined the choir when they left to sing elsewhere.

Today the two supply wagons were stuffed with Christmas presents and winter supplies...and one Tommy Tyler, who sat with one wrist chained to the wagon bed, his lips tight with indignation. He glanced at Jake whenever he rode into sight, trying to figure out why in hell the man had decided his punishment should be to come and work at the J&L. The rules were stiff, and he wasn't so sure he'd abide by them. Then again, the look in Jake Harkner's eyes when he talked about taking him to the ranch was enough to make a man queasy. He had no doubt that if he disobeyed, either Harkner or his men would set him straight.

I'm doing this to give you a chance at a good life, Jake had told him. *I was just like you at one time, and if I can stop one young man from going through the hell I've been through in my life, it's worth the chance.*

Tommy had never known a decent family life. His mother had run out on him and his father when he was only two, and his alcoholic father had beat him often, telling him he was the reason his mother left. *You worthless little bastard,* the man often called him. *You probably ain't even mine!*

What did he need with family? What did he know about living straight and holding a job for longer than a couple of weeks? And why in God's name should someone who hardly knew him and who didn't even like him take him to his own home and take a chance on him? He hated to admit it, but deep down inside he was impressed by the Harkners, the way they all seemed so close, the fact that their patriarch was the infamous Jake Harkner himself, the very man he'd been stupid enough to draw on when he first rode onto the J&L.

Jake's grandsons rode up alongside the wagon then, the younger one who was also called Jake handing out a canteen.

"My grandfather said you should take a drink," the young man told Tommy.

A disgruntled Tommy reached for the uncorked canteen with his free hand.

"Grandpa says you better not say or do anything against my little sister and my cousins—or my mom or aunt Katie or my grandma. You better remember that."

Tommy handed back the canteen after taking a swallow of water. "Those are big words for a little kid," he sneered.

"I'm not a little kid," young Jake declared. "You make a wrong move and it won't be just me. My cousin Stephen will be on you, and my uncle Ben. He's big and strong. And then my uncle Lloyd will probably join up and so will Grandpa and some of the men. You don't know how mean they all can be."

"I hear Ben isn't your legal uncle at all."

"He sure is. My grandpa legally adopted him."

"Why?"

"'Cuz he was being beat on with a belt by his father. Grandpa beat up his father and he took Ben away from him and adopted him. Grandpa knows about bein' beat on by your pa. It makes him real mad. That's why he's helpin' you."

"Why should he care?"

"He just does, that's all. But he won't put up with you bein' disrespectful to the men or any of the women."

Tommy grinned. "I hear one of the men married a high-class prostitute, and she lives on the ranch with him. You sure your grandpa doesn't sneak over there and pay her visits? I hear he has a soft spot for wild women."

"Gretta is a nice lady and our friend. My grandpa helped her daughter down in Mexico and he was almost killed. Gretta is Cole Decker's wife now. Even if she wasn't, my grandpa loves my grandma an awful lot. Him and Gretta are just friends 'cuz women like that were good to him when he was little. He just likes to help people is all."

Tommy shook his head. "Boy, oh boy, that sure doesn't sound like the Jake Harkner I've always heard about. I've always heard he likes wild women and is mean as a snake and sneaky as one. He's killed a lot of men and never regretted any of it. Why would a man like that want to help people?"

"'Cuz a lot of people helped him over the years. He told us he just wants to do somethin' to make up for it, but don't take that for granted. He'll turn on you in a minute, if you talk bad or do somethin' to anybody in the family."

"Jake!" Young Jake heard his grandfather yell out to him. "Get away from Tommy and mind your business."

"I'm just makin' sure he knows not to make trouble," Jake told his grandfather, sitting a little taller in his saddle and adjusting his hat.

Big Jake grinned. "He knows it. Ride on ahead and watch for holes and such so we don't lose a wheel and get stuck out here in the cold."

"Sure, Grandpa." Young Jake rode off, and Big Jake kicked his horse into a gentle lope and rode closer to Tommy.

"I'll unchain you as soon as we get onto J&L land. If

you choose to run off, you'll be in a bad way. A storm is coming and we're trying to hightail it home before it hits. You might as well make up your mind to stay at the bunkhouse and be glad you're inside and warm."

Stephen and Ben rode up to Jake then.

"Grandpa, when can we cut a Christmas tree?" Stephen asked, his voice croaking a little between a young boy's voice and a much older boy's voice.

"Let's wait about a week," Jake told him. "We're taking Tricia and Sadie Mae with us this time. I promised them."

Both boys rode off, and Tommy watched Big Jake, thinking what a man of contrasts he was. Today he was all grandpa, yet from all he'd heard, he could be as ruthless as the worst of them. He could tell just from his own run-in with the man. This was a strange situation he'd fallen into. He wanted to hate Jake Harkner...but part of him also liked the man, and that made him angry.

Nine

JAKE WALKED INTO PEPPER'S BARN, AS THE NEWEST BARN on the J&L was called. It was named after one of the top hands, who'd died trying to rescue some of the horses when the old barn burned down. It was something the family seldom talked about…and something that haunted Jake. His wife was dragged off by outlaws that night while he and the men fought the fire. He'd damn well found her, and those men had suffered the worst of Jake Harkner's rage. He'd made sure no one would ever know what happened to them.

It had taken these nearly two years since for Randy to be strong and vibrant again…and for them to get back on solid ground in their own relationship.

Jake walked up to Tommy Tyler, who was cleaning out stalls. He told himself to keep his temper in check because he'd vowed to help Tommy, not kill him, which he sorely wanted to do at the moment.

Tommy paused and turned to see Jake standing there. He backed away a little.

"You don't look too good," Jake told him, studying the young man's battered face. One eye was black and swollen. He had a deep cut on his left cheek and a split lip.

"I don't *feel* too good," Tommy answered. He swept some manure and hay aside. Jake noticed he did so gingerly.

"Bruised ribs?" he asked.

Tommy remained turned away and sighed. "Yeah."

"Good."

Tommy paused, then turned to face Jake. "Look, I spoke out of turn, all right? You here to finish me off?"

"I'd love to do just that, but I promised myself I'd give you a chance, so I'm trying real hard not to light into you with a shovel. Cole tells me you were mouthing off about the women—that you said what you'd like to do with my son's wife. He didn't tell Lloyd, because I can guarantee we'd be burying you out there in the foothills right now if he knew. He didn't want me to bring you to the J&L in the first place, so don't make me regret it. Katie Harkner is one of the finest women and best mothers I know— and yes, she's beautiful. Don't think Lloyd doesn't know some of those men's thoughts about her, and about my daughter and even my wife. But there's one big difference between those men's thoughts and yours."

Tommy raised his chin defiantly. "How can there be any difference?"

"Because every man on this ranch has a deep respect for all three women, and even for Cole's wife. Gretta went through things when she was young that she doesn't like to talk about. When you understand what some people have been through, you start seeing them in a different light. That's why I brought you out here, Tommy. When I wrestled you down in that alley, you said something that made me want to help you—but not when you insult married women who are nothing short of angels."

Tommy looked away. "A man can't help taking a second look and enjoying his thoughts. And don't tell me you don't think the same thing when you see a pretty woman."

Jake leaned against a support post. "Thinking something and saying it out loud or acting on it are two different things. And for reasons it would take me all day to explain, I have a deep respect for pretty much *all* women, including Gretta. So if I ever hear you've been around her and tried to force yourself on her because of what she used to be, I'll make you wish you were never born, and you'll go right back to jail after that. You likely know what happened to my daughter back in Oklahoma, because it's in that book about me. And my wife has been through hellish things you'll never know about. Lloyd's wife, Katie, is the sweetest person who ever walked, and it hasn't been easy for her being married to a Harkner man, especially when Lloyd rode with me as a marshal. And you'd best remember that my daughter, Evie, is the closest thing to an angel you'll ever meet. It's her Christian faith that got her through something worse than death, and it's that faith and her prayers that have got this family through some really rough times. So don't ever let me hear about you insulting any woman on this ranch. Understand?"

Tommy stared at the dirt floor.

"Look at me, Tommy Tyler."

Tommy sighed again and raised his gaze to meet Jake's eyes, eyes that told him he'd better take note...or else.

"I asked if you understand what I'm telling you."

Tommy nodded. "I understand."

"Those men over at the bunkhouse gave you just a hint of what I'll do to you if you step out of line again. And that goes for teasing or scaring my granddaughters too, or trying to pick a fight with any of my grandsons or Ben. I told you all of this when I brought you here. I won't repeat any of it a second time, and you don't want to know what will happen if you force me to. Overall you have it pretty good out here."

Tommy rubbed at his sore jaw. "Except for shoveling shit."

Jake grinned a little. "Just part of the chores, Tommy. You make trouble and you'll be *eating* that shit instead of shoveling it. And don't think I won't shove some into your mouth if you insult a woman. Got that?"

Tommy just stared at him a quiet moment. "Yeah. I got it."

Jake took a cigarette from an inside pocket on his fleece-lined jacket. He struck a match and lit it, taking a deep drag. "You're a smart, good-looking young man who can have a damn good life if you want it. You can't begin to know how much I'd like to do things different if I could go back in time, but we only get one chance at this life. I'm giving you *your* chance to make the best of it." He kept the cigarette between his lips as he turned to go.

"Jake," Tommy spoke up.

Jake turned.

Tommy looked at the floor again and shuffled his feet a little. "I don't know why in hell you care, but nobody has ever cared about me before. It makes me mad, because I'm afraid to believe it's true. So I do things and say things…" He shrugged.

"You do and say things to hurt those around you because you want to make sure *you* don't get hurt. Do you think I don't understand that? My wife could tell you a hundred stories. It took me years to truly realize she really did care and wasn't going to leave me the minute I did something stupid." Jake took a drag on his cigarette. "And I care about you, Tommy, but I don't tolerate bad behavior from my sons and grandsons, and I sure as hell won't tolerate it from you."

Tommy nodded. "I'll watch it after this."

"Is that your form of an apology?"

Tommy shrugged, smiling a little. "I guess so." He finally met Jake's gaze again. "Will you tell the men I apologized? I kind of like most of them. It's no fun having all of them give me the cold shoulder. I was starting to enjoy their company."

Jake nodded. "I'll tell them." He started to leave again.

"One more thing," Tommy asked.

Again Jake paused and turned. "What is it?"

"I, uh, my ma ran out on me when I was little, and you know what my father was like. There was never any Christmas for me growing up. We never had a tree or anything like that. I was just wondering if…" He sighed and looked away again. "I'd kind of like to go along when you cut down a Christmas tree. I know it's probably a family thing, but I'd just like to see what it's like… hunting for just the right tree and dragging it back home."

Jake studied him a moment. There he was…the little boy, Jake Harkner, who wanted nothing more than a real family. "Fine with me, but I'll have to walk it by my grandsons and Ben and Lloyd."

"Sure. If they don't want me to go, I'll understand."

Jake nodded. "Finish what you're doing here. The men will be eating out at the bunkhouse soon. You'll want to be there while the food is good and hot."

"Sure." Tommy picked up a shovel and walked back into one of the stalls. "You'll tell those men before that, won't you? About me being sorry?"

Jake grinned. "I'll tell them." He left, trudging out into a recent heavy snowfall. He'd never admit it to anyone else, but it felt kind of good to put out a helping hand to someone like Tommy, instead of a mean fist.

Ten

"GRAMPA, DON'T LET GO OF ME. BUCK IS SO BIG!" TRICIA snuggled her back against Jake, who held her close with his left arm while guiding the big gelding with his right. The horse had a black mane and tail and black feet and was otherwise a solid doeskin color.

"You know I won't let go, baby girl," Jake told her.

Strands of Tricia's bright red curly hair stuck out from under her stocking hat, and her cheeks were a ruddy red from the cold.

Interestingly enough, Sadie Mae had chosen to ride with Tommy Tyler. When she heard he'd never known a real Christmas or had a Christmas tree, she actually felt sorry for the very same young man who'd scared her to death in the alley back in Brighton. She was so, so much like her mother in spirit, with an angel-like ability to love the unlovable.

Which is probably why that damn old rooster in the henhouse leaves her alone, Jake thought. It was as though that demon bird recognized the special goodness about Sadie Mae, which made sense, because the wicked beast hated Jake and attacked him every chance it got. As much as the ornery, strutting cock saw the goodness in Sadie Mae, he saw the outlaw in Jake. In fact, the kids had named the rooster Outlaw. Jake dearly wanted to shoot it or twist its head off, but he didn't dare because it would break Sadie Mae's heart. The situation was a matter of wonderful jokes among the family. Even Tommy had laughed about it when Sadie Mae told him the story of the conflict between Jake and the rooster on their ride out here to find a Christmas tree.

Forgiveness. Sadie Mae had the ability to forgive, just like Evie. His beautiful, Christian daughter had forgiven the men who'd so sickeningly abused her back at Dune Hollow in Oklahoma. That was one of the darkest times in Jake's life, and when he got through rescuing her, there weren't many of those men left alive for Evie to forgive. But forgive them she did. How he'd produced a daughter of such faith and beauty he would never under-stand, other than it all must have come from Randy's blood, not his.

Bells jingled as they rode, Tricia having insisted that jingly bells be tied around several of the horses' necks. Their "hunting party" consisted of Jake and Tricia, Tommy and Sadie Mae, Stephen, young Jake, and Ben. They brought plenty of rope to drag a tree back with them, and the boys all carried rifles "just in case." Young as they were, they all knew how to use them. A man never knew what he might come across out here in the Colorado foothills.

The girls giggled and sang Christmas carols, but the boys refused to join them, sitting tall in their saddles as though grown men didn't sing songs. Jake quietly studied young Jake, who rode a bit ahead of him and to his left. The boy had Jake's own spirit, which worried him a little. He was extremely defensive of his mother and father and siblings, and easily angered to the point of putting up his fists. Since he was old enough to talk, he'd made it very clear that he was proud to be a Harkner and hoped to be "just like Grandpa" when he grew up.

No, you don't, Jake thought. *Nobody wants to be just like me.* Young Jake had always all but worshipped him, which had turned out to be dangerous more than once. Back in Guthrie, when he was only three and still called Little Jake, he'd run right down the street thinking to defend his grandfather when Jake was in the middle of a shootout with wanted men. Jake had taken a bullet in the thigh while shielding the boy.

Of all three boys, young Jake yearned the most to be a man, even though he was the youngest of the three. Stephen and Ben were a little more accepting of the gradual process that took, although Stephen was already tall and strong for his age, and Ben already had a man's build. He'd exploded in growth at around eleven, and Jake was beginning to wonder if the boy would ever *stop* growing.

"Grampa, look at that one!" Tricia yelled then, pointing to a huge pine that was far too big for a Christmas tree. "Can we have that one?"

"Tricia, that tree would never fit in Grandpa's house. We'd have to cut a hole in the roof."

"But you have a big, high ceiling!"

"Not *that* high!"

They did have a big house—a huge log home Jake had had men build for Randy, with enough bedrooms for grandchildren to stay over any time they wanted…and a loft bedroom where he'd made love to his beautiful, faithful wife too many times to count. Randy deserved that house. It was the first home they'd owned and settled into in all their years of marriage…years of being on the run, working different jobs, time in prison. At last his wife had a "forever" place to settle.

"That one!" Sadie Mae shouted then, pointing to a scraggly tree barely four feet high. "It looks sad, Grampa."

"Trees don't have feelings," young Jake scoffed.

"Yes, they do," Sadie Mae argued.

"Sadie Mae," Jake called to her, "that tree isn't lonely. It's growing right beside its mother tree. See? We'll let that tree get bigger and stronger before we cut it down, okay?"

"Okay."

They moved into thicker pines, dismounting and separating to look for just the right tree.

"Nobody go too far!" Jake told them as he lifted Tricia down. Tommy led Sadie Mae around a small hill of mostly boulders, and the boys began their own search in another direction, each one keeping a rifle in hand, as did Jake. Tommy had no rifle because Jake wouldn't allow him to carry a gun yet.

"Grampa, we found one! We found one that's just right!"

The shout came from Sadie Mae, who was with Tommy on the other side of a huge, rocky mound that hid them.

"Come, see, Grampa!"

"I'm coming." Jake took Tricia's hand and kept his rifle in his other hand as he led the girl toward the boulders. It was then he heard it—the growl of a cougar. And Sadie Mae's screams.

Eleven

"Run, Tricia!" Jake ordered, letting go of her hand. "Run back to Stephen! Everybody stay back!" He headed around the boulders, ignoring the pain in his bad leg as he plowed through the snow, horror filling him at the sound of the deep-throated growling of a cougar and the hideous cries of Tommy Tyler. His gut tightened at the realization that Sadie Mae's own screams had stopped.

"Sadie Mae!" Jake screamed her name as he made it around the other side of the small hill. He couldn't see or hear her. All he saw was Tommy, curled up on his knees against one of the boulders, a cougar clawing at his shoulder. *Jesus, where is Sadie Mae!* He had to kill the cougar, but the bullet could go right through, into Tommy. Was Sadie Mae under him?

Sonofabitch! The memory of the young girl he'd loved at fifteen flashed through his brain in a millionth of a second…his filthy alcoholic father raping her. He'd shot John Harkner to stop him from hurting Santana, but the bullet had gone right through his father's neck and killed the girl too. That could happen again. He could kill both Tommy and Sadie Mae.

"Grampa! Grampa!" he heard someone screaming behind him. The boys must be watching.

"Don't shoot!" Jake ordered them.

Screams everywhere—the boys, whinnying and frightened horses, Tricia, Tommy.

Jake knew he had no choice. He cocked and raised his

.30–30 Winchester. A six-gun might not do the job… but the risk! The risk! The big cat was moving violently over Tommy. Sadie Mae must be under him! One of the other kids could be next! He aimed…and prayed…and fired…cocked it again…fired again.

Finally, the cougar quieted and stopped moving. It collapsed on top of Tommy. Jake tossed his rifle and ran to the bloody scene. "Sadie Mae!" he screamed. "Boys, help me!" He tugged at the heavy cougar, one of the biggest cats he'd ever seen. Ben and Stephen helped drag the big cat off of Tommy while young Jake dug at the snow and dirt under Tommy, looking for his little sister.

"Sadie Mae!" The boy screamed her name. "She's underneath Tommy! He was trying to protect her! Sadie Mae!"

"Be careful, Jake," Big Jake warned. At the moment he felt removed from reality. That couldn't be his Sadie Mae lying there looking dead when he rolled Tommy's body off of her. Not Sadie Mae! Not any one of his grandchildren! He couldn't bear losing them. What if he'd shot her!

Tommy groaned, blood pouring from a huge tear in his right shoulder, so big that the sleeve of his coat was completely ripped away.

"Ben!" Jake shouted as he pulled the sleeve all the way off Tommy's arm and then used it to press against the gushing wound.

"What should I do, Pa?" Ben asked.

Young Jake knelt beside his little sister. "She's dead! She's dead!"

"Don't be so sure, Jake!" Big Jake told him. *She can't be dead! She can't!*

The boy lifted Sadie Mae a little, and Jake immediately guessed what had happened. The rock under her head was stained with blood. "Tommy must have tackled Sadie Mae to cover her and protect her. It looks like her head hit that rock," Big Jake told the boy, struggling to stay calm himself. "She's probably just unconscious." *God, let me be right.* The girl's eyes were closed and she looked so tiny and limp. "Stephen, get a blanket off any horse that didn't run off, and wrap it around Sadie Mae. And bring me one for Tommy!"

"Yes, sir!" Stephen ran to get the blankets.

"All of you need to do what I tell you, understand?" Big Jake told Ben and young Jake and Tricia, who was sobbing.

"We will," Ben answered.

Stephen ran back with the blankets and hurried over to where young Jake sat in the snow with Sadie Mae in his lap. He helped young Jake gently wrap his sister into the blanket. Stephen winced at the sight of blood on the sleeve of his cousin's corduroy jacket where he'd been supporting Sadie Mae's head. Stephen bunched up the blanket a little under the girl's head to help support it more comfortably. He brought the other blanket over to Jake then and wrapped it around and under Tommy as best he could.

Jake kept pressing hard on Tommy's gaping wound while Tommy lay shivering and staring in shock. "How many horses are left?" Jake asked his grandson.

"Just two," Stephen answered, his dark eyes tearing. "I tied them up good so they can't run off like the others."

"Good. I want you to take one of them and try to find the other three. Gather them up and get them back here and tie them, but try to build a good fire here before you leave. We need to keep Tommy and Sadie Mae warm as best we can. I'm going to have Ben ride for Brian and bring him and Lloyd back here along with a wagon. Brian will need the fire in case we have to cauterize Tommy's wound."

Stephen immediately began gathering kindling as fast as he could.

Jake looked over at his adopted son. "Ben, I want you

to take Tricia and ride back to the homestead as fast as you can! I can't let go of this compress on Tommy or he'll bleed to death. And I don't know how bad Sadie Mae is hurt. It might be bad for her, if we move her around too much or try to carry her home on a horse. I don't know that much about head wounds. And there is no way to get Tommy back without a wagon. He's bleeding too much. Ride fast, understand? Bring Lloyd and Brian back here along with a wagon. Tell them Tommy's wound is bleeding so badly it might need to be cauterized. Brian will know what to do."

"Okay, Pa," Ben answered.

"And hang on good and tight to Tricia!" Jake shouted. "We don't want any more accidents!"

"Sure, Pa."

Tricia kept bawling Sadie Mae's name as Ben picked her up and carried her off to one of the two remaining horses. He plopped her on it, mounting up behind her. He turned the girl to face him so she could wrap her arms and legs around him and hang on better. He moved his left arm around her then for even more support and kicked the horse into motion. "Hang on, Tricia!"

Ben rode off, and Stephen fought tears as he hurriedly gathered more kindling. "The wood is wet, Grandpa," he told Jake.

"Just put plenty of kindling under those bigger logs, and some branches with dried pine needles on them. Dead pine is best. It burns hot."

Stephen did the best he could, then took matches from Jake's coat pocket and lit the kindling. Once he got the fire going, he hurried off to see if he could find the other three horses.

Suddenly all was quiet, other than young Jake's quiet sniffling. He rocked his sister in his arms, and Jake kept up the pressure on Tommy's ugly wound. There was so much blood on the rocks and in the snow and soaking

Tommy's jacket that Jake couldn't tell how many other places the cougar had managed to sink claws and teeth into the young man, let alone the fact that Tommy could have a bullet in him...from Jake's rifle. The thought that he might have shot Tommy or Sadie Mae...

He glanced at Sadie Mae, wanting to hold her. "Jake, take the blanket away a minute. Look your sister over and make sure my bullet didn't go through that cat and Tommy and into her. She has a good chance of being all right if she isn't shot."

Young Jake wiped at his eyes and pulled the blanket away a little, noticing Sadie Mae's coat was intact. He felt down her legs and over her tummy and chest. "I don't think she's shot, Grandpa, but she's all bundled up in wool leggings and coat. It's hard to tell for sure, but I don't think so."

"Just keep her warm then, and don't let her move around if she wakes up." *Please do wake up, Sadie Mae!*

Tommy groaned and opened his eyes, staring blankly at Jake. "What...happened?" he asked in a near whisper.

"Cougar," Jake told him. "I can't let go of this wound, Tommy, or you'll bleed to death. Just lie still. Ben went to get Brian. He'll know what to do."

Tommy closed his eyes again. "Hurts...everywhere."

"I damn well know all about pain, Tommy."

Tommy opened his eyes again, this time wide with fear. "Sadie Mae! I...remember...big cat...didn't have a...rifle. I tried to protect...Sadie Mae."

"I know. She hit her head, Tommy. She's unconscious but has no other wounds. You probably saved her life. I owe you for it."

Tommy looked over to where young Jake sat, holding his sister. He looked up at Big Jake then. "You should... be with your...granddaughter. Just let go of me and... go to her."

"I can't let go of this wound. You'll bleed to death."

Tommy grimaced as he rubbed at his eyes with his left hand. "Why...do you care?"

Jake shook his head. "Damned if I know. I guess it's my turn to care about somebody besides those in my own family and maybe a couple of the men I'm closest to on the J&L."

"Like Cole Decker..."

"Like Cole Decker," Jake repeated. "We're damn good friends. He knows things about me most men don't." *Keep talking! Don't think about the fact that Sadie Mae could die!*

Young Jake pulled Sadie Mae a little closer. "Wake up, Sadie Mae," he said, weeping.

Tommy looked over at them. "I'm sorry," he told the boy, turning to look up at Jake again. "I didn't mean for her...to hit her head. It all happened...so fast."

"I know," Jake told him. "It's okay."

"I...should have seen...that cougar."

"Tommy, we've had plenty of run-ins with cougars here on the J&L. A cougar is a cougar. They're good hunters for the very reason they can sneak up on you without a sound, so don't be blaming yourself. If anyone's to blame, it's me, for not keeping everyone together. The list of things I blame myself for is pretty damn long. This whole thing was supposed to be a fun adventure for the kids, especially the girls."

Jake suddenly choked up, wanting to scream. *Sadie Mae, don't die! Don't die! I couldn't live with that!*

"You said...I wasn't to blame," Tommy said, his voice growing weaker. "So you aren't...either."

Jake couldn't stop the tear that slid down his face. "You have no idea how many things I'm to blame for, Tommy." Jake sniffed and quickly wiped at the tear by arching his shoulder to rub his cheek on the corner of his wool jacket.

Tommy closed his eyes and grew quiet again. His

face looked hideously white, but his lips looked blue. Jake pressed harder on the wound. He was not a praying man, but he prayed now, closing his eyes and hanging his head.

Jesus, please don't take my Sadie Mae. No sweeter innocence ever lived. Of all the times you've let my useless hide live, don't choose now to take someone so sweet and with her whole life ahead of her. Take me instead, Lord. Take me.

He was still afraid Sadie Mae was shot. If they found out his baby girl was dying from his own bullet, he'd have to turn his gun on himself and pull the trigger. He couldn't survive that. *Not another Santana, Lord. Not another Santana.*

Twelve

"PA!" LLOYD CHARGED UP ALONGSIDE BEN, WHO'D shown him the way. He jumped off his horse before it even came to a halt, running up to Jake, then glancing over at young Jake holding Sadie Mae. "Oh my God." He hurried over to the dead cougar, grabbing its tail and dragging it farther away to make room. He quickly covered it with snow to help keep the smell from frightening the horses.

Brian charged up on another horse and ran over to his son and daughter, kneeling beside them.

"Sadie Mae," the man groaned, setting his doctor's bag beside him.

"Dad, I think she's dead," young Jake cried.

Brian fought his own tears as he felt her throat in hopes of feeling a pulse. "She's not dead, Jake," he told his son. "Lift her to a sitting position if you can so I can examine her head. Ben said she hit it on a rock."

"She never woke up," young Jake said, weeping.

Lloyd knelt beside his father while Brian examined Sadie Mae. He saw the devastation in Jake's eyes. "Pa, let me take over."

"I can't let go."

"Yes, you can. You look ready to pass out, and I know you want to go to Sadie Mae."

"Brian will have to cauterize this wound, or he'll bleed to death. He saved Sadie Mae from that damn cougar's teeth and claws. It's just too damn bad—" Jake's voice caught in his throat. "God can't let that little girl die, Lloyd. It's not fair, me sitting here alive and her maybe dying."

"Pa, don't go there. He's not going to take someone as sweet as Sadie Mae."

"Won't he? Losing Sadie Mae would be worse punishment for my sins than flat-out dying myself."

"You listen to me, Pa!" Lloyd grasped his arm. "You're alive because the whole family loves and needs you. Don't be questioning the why. God decided that already. Now let go of Tommy and go to Sadie Mae. I'll help Tommy."

Jake kept hold of Tommy's wound for another few seconds. "I didn't see that goddamn cougar, Lloyd. Didn't see it. Didn't hear it. And I'm scared to death my bullet went through that sonofabitch and into Tommy and Sadie Mae. Tell Brian..." His voice choked then, his eyes filling with tears. "It might be like with Santana. Tell Brian to first make sure she's not shot. Sometimes a bullet can be hardly noticed. Check her back. That's where the bigger hole would be if..."

"Pa, stop it." Lloyd turned to Brian. "Brian, check her all over. Pa's scared maybe his bullet went through the cat and into Sadie Mae. I'll check Tommy." He took the blanket away from Tommy and ran his hands over his entire body, then opened his coat for another inspection. "There's nothing here, Pa. You know what a good shot you are. You got the cougar and nothing else." He squeezed his father's shoulder for reassurance. "Where's my son?"

"Stephen went after the horses that ran off. He's okay."

"She's not shot," Brian told them then, devastation in his voice. "She's just unconscious, and I don't know for sure what to do for that, other than to scoop up some snow and put it against the back of her head to slow the bleeding and swelling."

Jake seemed to wilt then at the news.

Cole came rattling up then with a wagon. Everyone moved fast after that. Cole took care of packing the back of Sadie Mae's head with snow, staying beside her to keep adding snow as it melted, while Brian checked out Tommy, who came awake again.

"Don't...bother with me, Dr. Stewart," he told Brian. "Stay with...your daughter."

"There isn't a lot more I can do for her at the moment, and you probably saved her life, Tommy. The head wound isn't your fault. She could have been torn to pieces by that cat, and it looks like it did a good job of trying to do that to you."

Jake finally let go of the wound. The pain in his leg from crouching for so long hit him hard. He grimaced as he crawled over to Sadie Mae. "Let me have her, Jake," he told his grandson.

Everything happened in a kind of daze after that. Jake pulled his granddaughter into his arms, a sniffling young Jake standing next to him with his hand on his grandfather's shoulder. He raised his chin, trying to pretend to be a man about all of it.

"I wish I could kill that damn cougar all over again," the boy said angrily. "If he was still alive, I'd go shoot him!"

Cole kept adding snow to the back of the girl's head. He looked into Jake's eyes, knowing what this meant to the man. "She'll be okay, Jake. It's like Lloyd said. If God let your worthless hide live after what happened in Mexico, he ain't gonna take this little girl, understand?"

Jake managed a weak smile. "At least you put it more bluntly."

"That's the only way to talk to a man like you, you old sonofabitch. This girl's got the Harkner blood, and Harkners have the ability to survive just about anything. She'll be okay. Them chickens back home and even that damn ornery rooster need her to take care of them."

Jake just kept holding Sadie Mae while Brian took

the fireplace poker from the wagon and heated it up. Minutes later the air was filled with Tommy's screams. Jake well knew the pain of having a wound cauterized. He cringed at the memory of Brian doing the same thing to him years ago when he took that bullet in the thigh.

Stephen rode back to their camp, pulling all three extra horses with him. Jake was proud of how Ben and both Stephen and young Jake were turning into dependable young men who could probably take over the J&L right now if they had to.

He carried Sadie Mae to the wagon then, managing to climb into the wagon bed in spite of the pain in his bad leg. He sat down with her in his arms while Brian finished bandaging Tommy as best he could.

Cole and Lloyd and Ben managed to lift Tommy into the wagon, and Ben climbed in to help prop blankets under Tommy's head. Brian also climbed into the wagon, examining Sadie Mae again.

"The bleeding has finally stopped," he told Jake. "We just have to pray she wakes up. Let me have her, Jake."

Jake didn't want to let go, but Brian was her father. He was also a rock for the whole family—the calmest, most steady, most reliable man Jake had ever known. And patient. The poor man had been through hell marrying into the Harkner clan, and no better man walked when it came to being a husband to Evie, his beautiful daughter who'd suffered so badly. Most men couldn't have handled what happened to her, but Brian Stewart wasn't most men, and there was no doubt how much he loved Evie.

He handed Sadie Mae over to her father and watched them both as Cole whipped the reins to turn the wagon and head for the homestead. Stephen and young Jake followed, bringing along the rest of the horses.

Jake could hardly wait to see and hold his wife. He needed her right now, that steady strength that was

Miranda Harkner. He still found it amazing how many beautiful people God had brought into his worthless life.

And Evie…if ever anyone's prayers could work miracles, it was Evie's. There would be a lot of praying going on. And right now Jake couldn't think of a better Christmas present than for Sadie Mae to open her eyes and give him one of her dimpled smiles.

Thirteen

THE NEXT TWO WEEKS SEEMED ENDLESS AND HOPELESS. Jake, Randy, Brian, and Evie took turns holding Sadie Mae for hours at a time, each one sitting in Jake's favorite red leather chair in front of the fireplace in the great room. It was warm there. Besides that, Jake wanted Sadie Mae to see the big decorated Christmas tree that stood in the corner on the same wall as the fireplace. Cole and some of the other men had gone out and cut it down for the family, doing all the work of trimming off bad branches and building a bracket to attach to the trunk. It sat in a big washtub filled with water and was tied to hooks in the log walls to keep it from falling over.

Katie and Ben and the grandsons had all helped decorate it while Brian and Evie spent their time tending to Sadie Mae, Evie taking breaks to feed baby Cole. Katie's mother took care of two-year-old Esther and helped care for Katie's little ones so Katie could spend more time at the main house.

Everyone took turns holding Sadie Mae, talking to her…soothing her…waiting for any sign of consciousness. They'd had to put diapers on her, and Brian managed to force-feed her and get milk and water down her throat, which gave all of them hope. All bodily functions were working, and she actually swallowed when they fed her and made her drink.

Jake held her now, staring at a crackling fire in the hearth. Randy approached him. Randy. His strength. His reason for being. The woman who'd created all of this for a man who didn't deserve anything. She knelt in front of him, resting one arm on his knee and stroking Sadie Mae's hair. "She looks so peaceful and sweet," she commented. "Even when she isn't smiling, you can see her dimples." She looked into her husband's dark eyes. "It's not your fault, Jake. It isn't Tommy's either. You know that."

Jake sighed. "I know." He craved a cigarette, but he wouldn't let go of Sadie Mae. He figured he needed to start smoking less anyway, but it was damn hard when he was this upset. It was in times like this that he smoked even more. "I just keep remembering that day I found her crying because she broke all those eggs. She has such a soft heart, like Evie. And I remember how she giggled when I went into that henhouse to gather more eggs and was attacked by that damn rooster and half the hens. She thought that was so funny—big bad Grandpa, cussing and swearing and fighting off a bunch of chickens. She's so damn attached to those cackling little monsters and what she calls their little chick-a-dees. That's what I've begun calling her in return—my little chick-a-dee." His eyes teared. "My God, was that last year, or the year before? So much has happened since then."

"It will be two years this coming spring," Evie spoke up. She sat in a nearby chair nursing six-month-old Cole Matthew under a blanket. "And you keep the faith, Daddy. There isn't a moment that goes by that I'm not praying for my daughter. God brought you back from the dead and home to us last winter. This year his gift to us will be Sadie Mae."

Brian sat in a wooden rocker next to Evie. He reached over and squeezed her shoulder. "You doing okay?"

Evie looked at her husband lovingly. "As long as I have you."

"I'm worried the stress will affect your ability to feed the baby."

"He's a big eater, but I'm doing okay."

Jake was always amazed at the strength and love between his daughter and her husband. They hadn't panicked over Sadie Mae, but he knew they were both suffering inside and trying to stay strong for each other and for the rest of their children. Young Jake remained quiet and somber. Today he was at the bunkhouse, where the men were inventing things to keep him occupied and cheered up.

He thanked God for Katie's parents, who'd moved to the ranch from Oklahoma last summer. Clara Donavan helped keep the rest of the little ones busy baking cookies and making decorations. She and Randy and Katie had wrapped most of the gifts, which sat stacked under the big tree. All that was left now was for Sadie Mae to wake up.

Jake leaned down and kissed the girl's eyes. "Wake up, chick-a-dee. Please wake up."

Randy leaned in to kiss Sadie Mae's cheek, then rose to walk behind Jake. She bent down and kissed his cheek, too. "You hang on, Jake. I know your every thought, and you're thinking it should be you lying here near death. Tommy feels the same way—that it should be him. That young man has changed so much. God had a purpose, bringing him into your life and you into his. Don't think for one minute there isn't a purpose for everything he gives to you and does for you."

Katie came inside then with Lloyd and Tricia. They'd left Donavan and baby Jeffrey Peter, who had just started walking, with Clara.

"Any change?" Lloyd asked, walking over to his father. "No."

Lloyd knelt down next to the chair and kissed Sadie Mae's hair. "Tommy is a lot better. Won't be able to use that arm much for quite a while, but there's no infection, and he's up walking around—sore as hell in all the places where he took some pretty bad cuts and gouges, but he'll make it."

"Good. He's turning out to be a good man."

"Thanks to you. You raised me to be a pretty good man, too, Pa. See how important you are to this family?"

Jake shook his head. "If you say so."

Tricia petted her cousin's dark hair.

"Wake up, Sadie Mae," she said to the girl sadly. "I got nobody to play with, and I love you." Her lips puckered in a sad pout as she looked at Jake. "You still love me too, don't you, Grampa?"

Jake frowned. "Tricia, why would you ask that?"

"'Cuz you hold Sadie Mae all the time."

"That's because she's so sick, Tricia. I would love to hold you right now, but it's my turn to sit with Sadie Mae." Jake smiled inwardly at how both girls were constantly vying for his attention.

Brian kissed Evie's cheek and rose to walk over to Jake. He took Sadie Mae into his arms. "Go ahead outside with Tricia, Jake. Take her for a walk or something. See how popular you are? The kids are all practically fighting over who gets to spend the most time with Grandpa."

Jake managed a grin and rose. "There was a time when *nobody* wanted to be around me." He waited while Brian sat down, then leaned over to kiss Sadie Mae's forehead again. "I love you, chick-a-dee," he said softly into her ear. He straightened and turned, pulling Randy into his arms for a moment. They left the words unspoken, but they missed each other, being together alone at night, holding each other. If Sadie Mae died, nothing in life would be the same. It was too much. Too much. The family had suffered more than any family should have to suffer, and that was what saddened Jake the most.

"It's okay, Jake." Randy stood on her tiptoes and kissed his lips.

So many years. So many great times. So many terrible

times. Even his Randy had suffered, but here she stood, loving him, supporting him. He put a hand to the side of her face and kissed her once more. "Get some rest of your own," he told her.

"I'm baking your favorite bread. Surely you want me to finish that first."

He smiled. "I wouldn't mind." He kissed her once more, then walked to the door and took down his jacket, pulling it on and putting on his wide-brimmed hat. "Leave your boots and leggings on, Tricia," he told her. "We'll go for a walk." He left his six-guns hanging on a hook over the door. Tricia hurried over to him, and Jake picked her up.

As always, bright red curls stuck out from under Tricia's knitted hat like tiny springs. The girl threw her arms around Jake's neck. "I love you, Grampa. Sadie Mae will be okay. Aunt Evie is like an angel. That's what Daddy says, so she'll be okay 'cuz Aunt Evie is praying for her."

Everyone in the room shared a smile.

Jake kissed Tricia's cheek. "You're probably right, Tricia," Jake told her before walking out the door.

Everyone looked at each other as Evie pulled little Cole from under the blanket and kept the blanket over herself as she held the baby against her shoulder to burp him. "I know what you're all thinking, and I agree," Evie told them. "If Sadie Mae dies...well...I don't even want to think about it. But besides me and Brian and young Jake, Daddy will be devastated. He can't bear the thought of any one of us dying before him. He's come so far. But if we lose our Sadie Mae, none of that will matter."

"But he's so much stronger now, Evie," Randy told her. "I've seen it and felt it. We'll all get through this." She knelt beside Sadie Mae again, touching her soft, pudgy cheek. "God won't let her die. He can't." She brushed at tears. "He just can't." *Jake, I can't lose you now. Not after all these years and all we've been through together.*

Fourteen

"I'm sad, Grampa."

Jake carried Tricia off the front porch. "So am I, baby girl." He walked past Randy's many roses planted all around their log home. The bushes were barren now and mostly buried in snow. Come spring they would open their glorious blooms of red and pink and yellow and white. No one was better at growing roses than Randy Harkner. He just hoped Sadie Mae would be awake and alive to help her grandmother tend them.

"It's cold, Grampa."

"I know." Jake opened his jacket and wrapped her into it. "Now I can keep you warm and you can keep me warm. Let's go to the barn and look at the new colt that was born last night. Do you want to see a baby horse?"

Tricia brightened. "Yes! Oh, yes!"

Jake winced with the pain in his leg as he carried the girl to a huge new barn a little distance from the house. The fresh air felt good, and showing Tricia a new colt would help take both their minds off of Sadie Mae.

He carried Tricia to the stall where the new horse stood beside its mother on spindly, unsteady legs. It let out a funny little whinny that made Tricia giggle. "He has a white face, Grampa, just like his mommy."

"He sure does. And look how well muscled he already is…perfect form. He'll make a good cutting horse someday. That's what his mother is. Her name is Marble, because the colors in her coat swirl around like a marble."

"That's a good name. Can I name her baby?"

"We'll have to ask your daddy. These horses belong to him."

"He'll let me name it if Mommy tells him he has to. Daddy does everything Mommy wants."

"Is that so?" The thought brought a smile to Jake's lips. "I'll have to ask Lloyd if that's true." He set Tricia on the wide board atop the wall of the stall, where she could observe the colt without going inside. "I can't wait to hear his answer." He thought how much fun it would be when he brought up what Tricia said in front of the whole family. He loved teasing different members of the family, especially Katie. Her fair skin would turn beet red. And it was also great fun to tease Lloyd, always so serious and stoic. Father and son were constantly jabbing at each other in a "one-up" contest.

"Sit still there, Tricia. I don't want you to go inside the stall. Mothers of any breed get a little ornery when they think they have to protect their young. Marble is gentle, but you can't be too sure when a female animal has just had a baby. It's usually when they have their young along that female grizzlies attack."

Jake lit a much-needed cigarette, taking a deep drag and throwing the match into a small bucket of water that hung nearby for matches and cigarettes. He thought about Lloyd again, how their jabs at each other were nothing more than a form of loving each other. It gave him a good feeling to know Lloyd would be there for the family once he himself was gone from this earth. *Lord God, don't you dare take that little girl before me. Don't you dare.*

He stood near Tricia and let her watch the baby horse, which wobbled toward her and let out another small whinny.

"Can I pet him, Grampa?"

Jake moved an arm around her from behind to make

sure she wouldn't fall inside. "Sure you can. Marble looks pretty calm." He let Tricia pet the horse while he finished his cigarette and thought how Sadie Mae would also love to be out here watching a new baby horse. Little girls loved animals and babies. Sadie Mae's special love was for the baby chick-a-dees.

Baby chick-a-dees.

It hit him then. He took one last drag on his cigarette and let go of Tricia just long enough to drop it into the bucket of water. He came back and lifted Tricia into his arms again. He kissed her cheek. "Tricia, I have an idea how maybe we can help Sadie Mae."

"How, Grampa?"

"Baby chickens! She loves baby chickens!"

Tricia smiled and nodded her head, the springy red curls jutting from under her cap bouncing when she did so. "What are you going to do, Grampa?"

"We'll go get a few baby chicks from the chicken coop and take them into the house. Maybe their peeping will wake her up."

Tricia's big blue eyes turned to saucers, and Jake thought how she and Sadie Mae were as different in looks as night and day.

"That's a good idea, Grampa!" Tricia told him, her blue eyes sparkling. "Let's go get some baby chicks."

"Well, now, there's the problem, Tricia," Jake told her as he headed out of the barn. "Do you remember what happened to me the last time I went in that henhouse?"

Tricia giggled. "Everybody teased you, Grampa. That old rooster came after you, and you had scratches all over your face. Sadie Mae told us you said a bunch of bad words!" she answered.

"That's right. I haven't gone near the chickens or that henhouse since then. That mean old rooster hates me, Tricia. He behaves for Sadie Mae, Evie, and your grandmother, but not for anyone else."

"Let's get Mommy then, or Grandma."

"Well, your mommy is busy feeding your new baby brother, and Grandma has a little cold. I don't want her to come out here and breathe the cold air. You and I will have to do it."

"We could try to explain to the rooster that we need the baby chicks for Sadie Mae. Maybe he would understand. He minds me too, so I can go in with you."

"I don't think you should go in. If Outlaw decides to attack, the chickens will all go wild and you could get hurt. I'd like to shoot that beast, but Sadie Mae would be awful mad at me if I did that, and we need the rooster to make baby chickens."

"How does he do that, Grampa?"

Jake realized he'd talked himself into a corner. *The way Grandpa loves on Grandma,* he thought with a grin. "Well, mama chickens get scared when the rooster isn't around," he lied, using an authoritative ring as he spoke. "So scared that they won't lay eggs that will hatch. When mama chickens are scared, their little brains produce something inside them that stops the eggs from ever hatching. Those chickens like the rooster's protection. He's kind of like me and your daddy—watching for bad things in order to protect you and all the people we love."

Tricia pouted her lips. "Mommy says Daddy is brave and strong, like you, Grampa. And he's handsome like you, she says."

Jake grinned. "She thinks I'm handsome?"

"Yes, she does. But she says Daddy is the most handsome of all."

Jake laughed. "Of course he is. He's a lot younger. And your daddy is a better man that I'll ever be because he grew up surrounded by lots of love."

Tricia put a small hand to Jake's cheek. "I'm sorry your daddy was mean to you, Grampa. How come your daddy didn't love you?"

The old pain tried to return. "I guess he was just not a very happy man, sweetheart. No one will ever really know, and it was a long, long time ago. Right now we need to worry about Sadie Mae and how we can help her. Let's see if that mean old rooster will let me put a couple of chicks in my coat pocket. And if there is a bucket sitting around, we'll gather a few eggs for Grandma. We all miss Sadie Mae being the official egg gatherer."

Tricia puckered her lips. "Will Sadie Mae wake up, Grampa? I miss her."

"Sure she will." Jake fought the sickening dread inside that he might be wrong. He held Tricia close and headed for the chicken coop.

Fifteen

ALL WHO WERE IN THE HOUSE LOOKED TOWARD THE front door, a bit startled when it suddenly burst open and Jake walked inside followed by Tricia, who held a basket of eggs. Jake slammed the door against a rising cold wind and turned to hang up his hat.

Everyone stared at the deep scratches on his face and hands.

"Jake!" Randy walked up to him in alarm, glancing at the eggs. She couldn't help laughing then. "Don't tell me you went inside the henhouse!"

"I damn well did," he answered, stomping snow off his feet.

Lloyd burst into more laughter. "What the hell for, Pa?"

"Daddy, you look like you've been in a bar fight," Evie told him. She sat rocking a sleeping Cole.

Even Brian grinned, in spite of still sitting in Jake's chair holding his unconscious daughter. "Jake, we all needed to find something to smile about. You've done a good job of that."

"Look, Grandma!" Tricia said to Randy. "Look at all the eggs we got!"

"Well, my goodness, that's wonderful, Tricia! Go set them in the kitchen, sweetheart."

Tricia headed to the kitchen with the eggs. "Grampa said a bunch of bad words again," she tattled. "He wouldn't let me go in there 'cuz of old Outlaw, but he got all these eggs and then he got the baby chicks!"

Randy looked at Jake. "Baby chicks?"

Jake nodded. "Baby chicks."

"You brought baby chicks into the house?"

"I thought maybe if Sadie Mae heard their peeping…"

"Daddy, that's a wonderful idea!" Evie exclaimed.

Lloyd rose. "Yeah, well, it looks like our father literally risked his life again for someone he loves."

Jake grinned. "Just about."

They all laughed. It felt good to laugh.

Jake leaned down and kissed Randy, then whispered in her ear, "I want to make love to you."

"Jake Harkner!" Randy exclaimed aloud. "What has gotten into you?"

Jake laughed lightly. "The fresh air, I guess. And I feel good about this."

"About what?" Katie asked, opening her arms to Tricia as her daughter came bounding up to where she stood in the kitchen. She took the basket of eggs from her daughter and then hugged her.

"We got the baby chicks for Sadie Mae to wake her up!" the girl told Katie.

It was then they all heard the chicks peeping. Jake reached into his coat pockets and pulled a baby chick from each one. "Fix up a basket or a box near the hearth," he told Randy. "We have to keep these things warm."

Randy thought what an incredible contrast it was to see her husband so gently holding the baby chicks in his big, rough hands…hands that had fought hundreds of men, hands that had held those infamous guns as an outlaw and then a lawman, hands that could crush those chicks in a second. She hurried into the kitchen to find a basket, then put a towel inside. She brought it back to Jake and he gently set the chicks into it.

"Take them over to the hearth and warm them up a little," Jake told her. "We'll hold them close to Sadie Mae and let her hear their peeping." He removed his coat and sat down to pull off his boots.

"Pa, that's a great idea," Lloyd told him again. "And you'd better clean up those scratches on your face. God knows how much chicken sh—" He hesitated. "Chicken droppings that old rooster stepped in on his way to do battle with you."

They all laughed again.

Jake glowered at Lloyd. "Maybe I should put a few scratches on *your* face—which Katie thinks is quite handsome, according to Tricia."

Katie blushed and Lloyd grinned. "I could add something to those scratches, Pa," he joked.

"Try it. I'm still not so old that you could take me in a fistfight."

"Oh, you're old enough. You're just too damn mean. But something tells me old Outlaw is meaner."

The entire incident helped bring a little joy and laughter to all of them. Jake just shook his head and grinned. "Pull these boots off, will you?" he asked Lloyd. "It hurts my leg when I bend it up to try to do it myself."

Lloyd knelt to pull them off and Jake held on to a chair, wincing with pain as his son slid off the left boot. The young man remained kneeling where he was for a moment. "I wish I could take away your pain, Pa."

Jake raised his other foot. "I know you do, but it's over and done and I'm alive. Get this other boot off so we can see if those chicks help Sadie Mae."

Lloyd pulled off the other boot, and father and son hugged each other briefly before walking over to the fireplace where Randy had set the basket of chicks. The tiny yellow birds were peeping nonstop now as they tumbled around inside the basket.

"Stephen and young Jake will probably be over here soon," Lloyd said. "I'll have one of them go get some feed for the chicks."

Jake turned to Tricia. "Come on, baby girl. You take one and I'll take one, and we'll hold them by Sadie Mae's ears."

Tricia obeyed. "Be careful, Grampa," she whispered, as though this was a time now to be very quiet and very serious. Jake and his granddaughter took the chicks to the big leather chair where Brian sat holding his daughter. The rest of the family gathered in a big circle around the chair. Tricia stood at the side closest to Sadie Mae's head and held the baby chick close to one of her cousin's ears. Jake leaned in and held the other chick to Sadie Mae's other ear.

All of Brian Stewart's doctoring and constant love and care couldn't do for his little daughter what the baby chicks did. Sadie Mae lay there as still as always, at first. Then she moved, just a little. Her eyes didn't open. She didn't talk.

But suddenly...she smiled.

Jake knelt down, holding the chick in one hand and taking hold of Sadie Mae's hand with the other. She wrapped her small hand around one of his fingers and squeezed.

Jake pulled her hand to his lips and kissed it, and quietly wept. Part of him wanted to go out to the henhouse and hug that damned rooster.

Sixteen

It was the best Christmas the family could remember. Last Christmas they all thought Jake was dead and would never come home. Now here he was, alive and well, and Sadie Mae was awake and talking. She still had trouble pronouncing certain words, and she'd forgotten some of her reading, but Evie was reteaching her, and she was learning fast, a sign that the damage was minimal. The child was back to gathering the eggs, and never once did she have a problem with the infamous Outlaw.

This Christmas day, every man at the bunkhouse was invited to stop by Jake and Randy's home to pick up a plate of turkey and apple pie. Sadie Mae herself handed each one a full loaf of her grandmother's fresh-baked bread, her fetching, dimpled smile warming the hearts of the worst of them. Tommy Tyler was invited to the main house to celebrate Christmas for the first time in his life. Cole Decker was there too, with Gretta.

Over his years as an outlaw and then a lawman and infamous gunman, Jake Harkner had indeed picked up some very unusual friends—characters the average God-fearing person would have nothing to do with. The rough bunch who worked the J&L would all stand in front of a bullet for anyone in the family, even though some of them, including Cole, had committed crimes back East and were probably wanted there.

Presents were exchanged, and Evie carried on about the beautiful hairbrush Sadie Mae had given her. Katie unwrapped colorful hair ribbons from Tricia, and others opened gifts of mirrors, lovely dress material, thread, kitchen utensils, shaving kits and mugs, socks, scarves, boots, handmade shirts, doll babies, knitted baby blankets, fancy hair combs, skin creams, and necklaces. There was a new rifle each for Stephen, young Jake, and Ben.

A big family meant a lot of gifts and a lot of bedlam and a lot of laughter. Tommy noticed how they all gravitated around the family patriarch, the dark and dangerous Jake Harkner, who today showed no sign of the ruthless man he could be if necessary. His grandsons Stephen and young Jake stayed close to him, and Tommy had observed in his time here at the J&L that it was young Jake who most resembled his grandfather in looks and in spirit and in a determination to make sure everyone knew they'd better never mess with one member of the family. Someday the boy was going to be someone no man dared cross.

Through most of the festivities, Jake sat quietly watching. Randy sat beside him, occasionally reaching over and taking hold of his hand as she laughed and carried on about all the gifts the others were receiving. She knew her husband's thoughts, how he was wishing he could have had Christmases like this as a child. She felt at her throat for the ruby necklace Jake had put on her minutes ago, his Christmas gift, her birthstone.

Lloyd presented Katie with a diamond ring to go with her plain, gold wedding band. In return Katie announced to the family that she was carrying what would be child number five for the couple. That brought cheers and considerable teasing, since over the last four years it seemed Katie was constantly pregnant.

"Tricia told me why Katie puts up with you, son," Jake spoke up after lighting a cigarette.

"Oh? Why's that?" Lloyd asked. "Or have I just stuck my foot in my mouth?"

"You just stuck your foot in your mouth."

Lloyd closed his eyes and shook his head. "Let's have it."

"It's not so bad," Jake answered with a big grin. "She just said that whatever Katie wants, she gets. You do whatever Katie asks."

Katie blushed deeply, and Cole and Brian both whistled amid laughter from everyone else.

"Oh, and you're very handsome," Jake added.

That brought more pink to Katie's face.

"Daddy, don't forget what our friend Peter Brown's wife called him," Evie declared. "A Greek god."

Shrieks of laughter.

"You're leaving out the fact that she called Pa magnificent," Lloyd threw in, trying to turn the attention from himself.

Jake took hold of Randy's hand then. "Well, come spring, this magnificent man is taking his beautiful wife on a trip," he told the family.

Randy looked at him in surprise. "A trip?"

Jake studied her lovingly. "You've never been back East since you and I left Kansas for one hell of a life together," he told her. He turned to the others then. "It's time your mother knew some true leisure and pampering. I'm taking her on a train trip East. That's her other Christmas present from me. We'll visit Jeff Trubridge in Chicago and probably lawyer Peter Brown." He paused for just a moment. "And his wife," he added.

Lloyd understood why his father had added Treena Brown to the remark. There was a long story behind the tenable friendship between Jake and Peter, whom they'd come to know back in Guthrie. Attorney Brown had saved Jake from prison and hanging more than once, but he'd also been in love with Randy for years, and Jake damn well knew it. Peter had never dared to act on his feelings, but it was because of Randy that he'd so often offered his services to help Jake out of deep trouble. The two men held a deep respect for each other, but there would always be that unspoken rift between them. Jake liked to subtly remind others that Peter had a wife of his own now.

"We might as well visit Peter's castle of a home north of Chicago," Jake added. "Because of what's going on with ranching and the cattle business, I'd like to visit the Union Stockyards and see what the future holds. We have to stay on top of things if we want to hang on to this ranch. And we might even head south from Chicago and go back to Kansas, where we first met." He looked at Randy. "Maybe we can find that supply store where all this started...and where you shot me because you were so afraid of the wanted outlaw who barged in, waving a gun."

Randy's eyes teared. "Oh, Jake, I don't know what to say."

"You deserve a trip and some pampering. You've worked so hard your whole life and have known too much tragedy. And after coming out here, you've hardly ever been off this ranch. It's time we both saw a bit of the civilization going on back East and had some time together—just the two of us."

Randy broke into tears. "That's the best gift I could have asked for." She rose from the chair beside him and leaned down to kiss him.

"Daddy, it will be so good for both of you to get away," Evie told them.

Jake squeezed Randy's hand as she straightened. "Don't be crying," he told her. "It will be fun for both of us. Maybe your good friend Peter Brown can set us up with some fancy doctor who can do something with this leg of mine."

Randy put a hand to her chest. "That would be wonderful!"

Tommy Tyler watched and listened and was touched by the closeness he'd seen in the Harkner family since arriving on the J&L, and especially since he was wounded.

Jake's son-in-law had given him excellent care, even during the time the man's own daughter could be dying. He'd never experienced a more enjoyable day or a better example of love and family closeness than this Christmas. Evie had even given him a Christmas present—a hand-knitted wool scarf with a matching cap. He'd enjoyed a delicious meal and watched family members hold hands while Evie led them all in Christmas carols.

Randy wiped at tears and took a few deep breaths to gain her composure, then walked to the grand stone fireplace and took a letter from where she'd left it on the mantel. She unfolded it, explaining to Tommy it was from a dear friend, a reporter in Chicago who'd written the book about Jake, *Jake Harkner, the Legend and the Myth*.

The myth is that Jake Harkner is mean and ruthless, Tommy thought. *And he can be, but no one would ever guess that deep inside, there is a goodness that would surprise people.* He figured he would never get over the contrast between the legend and the man who sat in this room today taking part in a family Christmas. And watching him interact with his wife…any man could tell he practically worshipped the woman, but Randy Harkner worshipped her husband in return.

"Jeff is one of those we will be visiting on our trip East," Randy told Tommy. She smiled at Jake. "Jake, he'll be so surprised and happy! And we can finally meet Jeff's wife and family." She studied the letter a moment. "This letter is just to tell us everything is fine with him and his family and he hopes the same for us. He's sent us a copy of an article he wrote in the *Chicago Journal*," she told the family. "He cut it out and included it with the letter." She unfolded the article and began reading it.

"I am writing this column to praise a man who has proven that the power of love can pull a man from the pits of hell into love's light…" Randy read.

Tommy watched the family as they all nodded. Evie

shed quiet tears. Katie reached over and grasped her husband's hand, and Lloyd in turn hugged Tricia close. The girl sat on his lap with her head resting against his chest and seemed to be almost asleep.

Tommy glanced at the pistols that hung on a hook over the front door, feeling sick now at realizing he'd pulled a gun on Jake Harkner. How sad that most people had no idea the kind of man he really was.

"I have grown to love all of them," Randy read as she neared the end of the beautifully written article about how far Jake Harkner had come since he and Jeff first met. Tommy found himself wishing he could meet the reporter, Jeff Trubridge. The man had actually ridden with Jake and Lloyd when they were U.S. Marshals back in Oklahoma. Tommy wished now he could have experienced riding beside Jake Harkner in going after the worst of the worst in No Man's Land.

"Many blessings and happy holidays to a family that well deserves it," Randy finished reading.

"Daddy, that was a beautiful article," Evie spoke up. "I'm glad Jeff sent us a copy."

Tommy found it touching that Jake's grown daughter still called him Daddy. The word just didn't seem to fit Jake Harkner's reputation.

"Tommy, we have one more gift for you," Randy said then. "We are so grateful for how you risked your life to keep that cougar's vicious claws from digging into our beautiful Sadie Mae."

Tommy frowned. "But she got hurt anyway."

"You still saved her from death," Evie reminded him, "or if she'd lived, what would have very likely been awful pain and horrible disfigurement. The claws that gave you those awful wounds could have dug into Sadie Mae's face."

Tommy shook his head. "Ma'am, the only present I want is being able to sit right here and be part of a family

Christmas and eat the best bread and pie I've ever tasted. I don't need anything else."

"Well, you're getting something anyway," Lloyd told him. "That new colt out in the barn is yours. He's going to be a really fine horse. And you have a job here on the J&L for life, if you want it. I was against Pa bringing you back with us in the first place, but one thing Jake Harkner is good at is judging a man, and he saw something about you he figured was worth taking a chance on. As usual, he was right."

Tommy felt like crying. He took a deep breath and swallowed as he ran a hand through his thick, dark hair. "I don't know what to say. That's a beautiful colt. I've never even known a real Christmas, let alone getting such wonderful present."

"Well, there is one stipulation," Lloyd added, smiling.

"What's that?"

"You have to let Tricia name the horse. She asked if she could, and I said yes. So you're stuck with the name."

Tommy frowned, glancing at Tricia. "Let's have it, Tricia," he said.

Tricia grinned and climbed down from her father's lap. "Me and Sadie Mae named the baby horse together," she told Tommy. "But first Sadie Mae has to give you *her* Christmas present."

Sadie Mae came running from the kitchen with a small box in her hand. Both girls approached Tommy, giggling.

"I kept it a secret all day!" Sadie Mae told Tommy before glancing over at her grandpa Jake. "Didn't I, Grampa?"

Jake grinned as Randy stood behind him now, rubbing his shoulders lovingly. "You sure did, Sadie Mae. That's the longest I've seen you keep a secret inside."

"Sadie Mae loves secrets," Evie told Tommy. "Sometimes she's almost naughty about it."

Sadie Mae and Tricia both giggled. Sadie Mae handed Tommy the box then. "Merry Christmas," she told Tommy.

Tommy already suspected what was inside the box when he heard a little peep. He opened it carefully to find a fuzzy little yellow baby chick. He had no idea what he'd do with such a present, but he was touched, knowing what baby chicks meant to Sadie Mae. He didn't want to hurt her childish joy, and he felt sick inside at how cruelly he'd teased her in the alley back in Brighton.

"Sadie Mae, this is the best present I ever got," he told her, reaching into the box and petting the baby chick with one finger. "I mean, that horse, he's a wonderful gift, but this here little chick is something I'll have to take care of real gentle-like." He looked at Sadie Mae. "I'm sorry I was mean to you that day back in Brighton."

"It's okay," the child told him. "That's why I gave you the chick-a-dee, so you have to love it and learn not to be mean."

Tommy grinned. "Thank you, Sadie Mae. I'll keep it at the bunkhouse and make sure the men help me keep it warm and fed. Those rough no-goods will tease me to death, but I don't care. I'll manage."

Sadie Mae clapped her hands and smiled, turning to Tricia. "Tell him the horse's name, Tricia," she said excitedly.

Tommy waited for the dreaded news. There was no way a little girl was going to give the colt a suitable masculine name that would reflect the pride and power the horse would one day display.

"Chick-a-dee!" Tricia answered, both girls giggling uncontrollably then.

The rest of the family laughed.

"That's a great name, Tricia," Big Jake told the girl.

"Yeah," Lloyd added. "I can't wait till you tell the men that colt's name, Tommy. It will be really fitting when he grows into a magnificent stallion."

They all laughed more, and Tricia and Sadie Mae jumped up and down, clapping their hands.

Tommy just shook his head. "Chick-a-dee it is," he told the girls.

Ben got up to add wood to the fire, and outside a gentle snow began falling. The thick, wet flakes began coating the dark pine trees throughout the homestead and into the foothills of the Rockies with a lovely white blanket, bringing a velvety look to the glorious scenery. It also brought a deep quiet to the grand mountains, which jutted up from the snow in purple and gray magnificence. The only sound that came from the Harkner homestead was laughter, where inside there sat a ruthless wanted man with two little girls on his lap hugging him around the neck and kissing his cheeks.

From the Author

I hope you have enjoyed my story, and that upon reading it you will want to read all four of my Outlaw books and learn how it all started...the love story of Jake and Miranda Harkner...the story of one man's journey from darkness into light, and those who helped him along the way. The books are *Outlaw Hearts*, *Do Not Forsake Me*, *Love's Sweet Revenge*, and *The Last Outlaw*.

About the Author

Award-winning novelist Rosanne Bittner is highly acclaimed for her thrilling love stories and historical authenticity. Her epic romances span the West—from Canada to Mexico, Missouri to California—and are often based on personal visits to each setting. She lives in Michigan with her husband, Larry, and near her two sons, Brock and Brian, and three grandsons, Brennan, Connor, and Blake. You can learn much more about Rosanne and her books through her website at rosannebittner.com and her blog at rosannebittner.blogspot.com. Be sure to visit Rosanne on Facebook and Twitter!

THE
CHRISTMAS
STRANGER

A MEN OF LEGEND NOVELLA

—◆◆◆—

Linda Broday

One

North Texas, 1878

THE HOWLING DECEMBER WIND WHIPPED AROUND HANK Destry, doing its best to knock him from the saddle. His numb hands could no longer feel the reins. Seconds later, his blue roan stepped into a snow-covered hole and went down to one knee before rising to struggle on. One more obstacle to overcome would probably do them both in.

Mother Nature was throwing everything she had at him to test his mettle.

Hank shivered in the freezing cold, trying to ignore the stinging sleet hitting his face. He tugged the collar of his threadbare coat up around his ears and studied the barren land, looking for some kind of shelter. The blizzard limited his vision to ten yards, and no dry place appeared in sight. Darkness would soon fall and he didn't know how much farther he could ride. He was worried about the condition of his horse, Boots, more than himself. Boots and his dog, Beau, were all he had.

An old man had once told him that when all hope seemed lost, cinch up your britches, set your sights on the horizon, and keep moving. That's what Hank had been doing his whole life—just putting one foot in front of the other, trying to stay ahead of trouble. He'd all but given up hope for better. There didn't appear to be a place for him.

The border collie walking alongside glanced up and whimpered.

"I'm doing the best I can, Beau. I'll find shelter soon." Hank squinted and scanned the inhospitable landscape again. "Just a little farther. I promise." He prayed he could deliver on that. The animals didn't deserve to suffer because he couldn't take care of them.

His eyes stung from the twisting wind, and he'd long lost the feeling in his feet and hands. Hank cursed the fact he had to be out in this storm at all. But he had nowhere to turn back to. The roads behind him were barricaded by mistakes and misfortune. There was nothing but pain and hurt back there. Forward was the only direction left—if he survived these freezing temperatures.

Surely he could find one place that welcomed a down-and-out man like him.

A few miles farther, he slid from the saddle and crumpled to the frozen ground. Snow drifted around him.

Directions didn't matter much anymore. The only way was down.

His eyes drifted shut and he no longer felt the bitter cold.

✿

Sidalee King tucked a third warm blanket around Mamie Tabor. The old woman's rheumy eyes found hers. "Miss Mamie, please let me take you home with me. This place isn't fit for a woman, especially a sick one. I'm worried about you. And it's almost Christmas."

"Child, this place's as good as any. I won't be a burden." Mamie patted Sidalee's hand. "I feel terrible that you had to traipse through this weather to tend to me. You'll catch your death."

"I don't think I've ever known a more cantanker-ous woman." Sidalee tenderly smoothed back the gray strands. Miss Mamie reminded her so much of her grandmother who had long passed. Mamie had seen eighty-four years come and go. Sidalee had discovered her by accident living in an abandoned line shack on the Lone Star Ranch almost two months ago.

"When my son, George, gets here, he'll take me home with him," Mamie murmured.

Sidalee prayed he came soon. His mother needed him. "Did he live near you? Maybe we can send someone for him."

Confusion filled the old woman's eyes. "I can't recall. But I know he'll find me."

She coughed and the sound came from deep in her chest. She needed to be looked after, but her son seemed the only person left of her family. Miss Mamie had said that after she and her husband, Albert, lost everything they had in a house fire, they hitched up a wagon and came looking for someplace to start over. Except Albert died along the way. Lord only knew how Mamie had managed to roll him into a shallow grave and place rocks over him to keep the animals from scavenging. Then the horse had run off, leaving her afoot. She walked to the line shack that Stoker Legend had abandoned when he bought more land and built another crude shelter farther out.

And now she waited, though whether death or her son would come first was anyone's guess.

"Don't worry," Sidalee reassured herself as much as Mamie. "George'll come. Take some more of my cough cure." Sidalee reached for the mixture of honey and lemon she'd brought and spooned some into Mamie's mouth.

Misery filled her gaze. "You got better things to do than tend to a sick ol' pitiful woman, child. Now git along before this weather gets worse."

"Why are you trying to rush me out? Are you tired of my company?"

"Nope. I jus' don't want you to get caught out in this mess halfway between here and home." Mamie forced a smile. "I never met a girl with as much kindness as you. You're an angel." Another coughing spell took Mamie's breath.

Sidalee held a cup of water to her mouth and watched her sip. She glanced around the small one-room dwelling. It was clean enough inside, but with the dirt floor, drafty window, and a roof that leaked, it wasn't fit for habitation. Yet Miss Mamie had dug in her heels and wasn't budging. Not only that, she'd made Sidalee promise not to tell anyone about her. But she was sure Stoker Legend should know. The big rancher would come and take Mamie to a warm place where Doc Jenkins could look after her. And that's exactly what she needed.

Stoker Legend was different from most ranchers. She'd never seen a more compassionate man, and he treated the people who worked for him like family. He would care for Miss Mamie.

Yet Sidalee wouldn't go back on her word. She rose and added more wood to the fire. The supply was getting low, so she bundled up and went out to the wagon for the firewood she'd brought. The snow fell harder. Flakes stuck to her eyelashes. She'd have to start for home as soon as she finished tending to the poor, sick widow.

After carrying in the supply of wood, she dipped out some bean soup she'd set warming in the fireplace. Then she sliced off a thick slice of bread from the loaf she'd baked that morning and poured some milk.

Miss Mamie sat up on the bed's thin mattress. "Bless you, my child. When I was a little girl, my mother used to cook bean soup, and the smell filled the whole house with goodness and love." A wistful look filled her eyes. "Now everyone is all gone, even my Albert." She glanced up. "Don't ever outlive all your people, Sidalee. The loneliness gnaws at you every minute."

What about her son, George? Had Miss Mamie forgotten about him? But then, she got confused at times.

"I'm sure it does." Sidalee fought back tears and held

Mamie's hand; it was lined with wrinkles and blue veins. "But you have me. And George, don't forget."

Miss Mamie's face lit up. "Oh, yes. I do have my George."

Her heart ached for this woman who'd borne a son and toiled beside her husband, trying to scratch out a living in the red Texas dirt. Even though she hadn't known Miss Mamie long, the woman had become like family.

Truth was, Sidalee didn't have anyone either. She'd buried them all during a cholera epidemic. She remembered the huge bonfire when she had to burn everything they'd touched to prevent the spread. It had about killed her to part with treasured keepsakes, the house she'd grown up in, and everything she owned. Stoker had found her wandering the streets of Fort Worth and brought her here to the Lone Star Ranch to give her a new start. He'd built a small town here on the ranch— complete with a doctor, a schoolhouse, and a telegraph. Since he'd built the businesses, she had been the third person to operate the mercantile and split both profits and expense with Stoker. Despite the loneliness, it was a good life and she was young and strong.

While the old woman finished her soup, Sidalee tidied up the room and stuffed rags into the cracks in the walls. Maybe that would help keep in some of the warmth.

Finally, she gave the room one last glance. She'd done all she could. "I have to go now, Miss Mamie," she said, washing up the soup bowl and putting it away. "Do you need anything else?"

"Nary a thing." Mamie fumbled for a little bag she kept near, pulled out a stone, and handed it to Sidalee. "For your trouble. Wish I had more than a blasted rock to give you." She waved her arm toward the door. "Now git."

"I told you I don't want any payment," Sidalee scolded.

"Do an old lady a favor and take it." Miss Mamie stuck it into Sidalee's pocket. "Let me show my gratitude, little though it is."

"If it puts a smile on your face, I reckon I won't argue." With a glass of fresh water on a crate beside the bed and the blankets tucked snugly around her friend, Sidalee bundled up. "I'll see you tomorrow. Get some rest."

"Be careful, child. Storms bring troubles. Don't be forgettin' that."

Sidalee nodded and went out the door. Darn it, she hated to leave. George had better hurry and see about his mother. She forced herself to climb onto the seat of the buckboard and set it in motion before she could change her mind.

A mile from the line shack, the weather worsened until she could barely see. She heard the barking dog before she spotted it. She pulled back on the reins when she made out the black-and-white fur. Why was a border collie out here?

She looped the rigging around the brake and climbed down. The poor thing would freeze to death. Maybe she could take him home with her until she could find where the animal belonged.

"Hey, boy, where do you live? I'll bet you're freezing."

The dog came close enough to pet. But when she tried to pick him up, he skittered away, barking furiously.

"Come on, boy, it's too cold out here. Let's go home."

Barking, the collie ran off the trail a ways and stood there, waiting. When she didn't follow, he came back, barking insistently. He stood there a second, then ran back out where he had been, waiting for her.

"I don't know what you're trying to tell me, but I'll follow you." She climbed back into the buckboard and eased off the trail, across the snowy ground, trying to avoid the drifts. Sidalee prayed she didn't get stuck. If she did, she'd spend the night here, for there'd be no one to come along.

She squinted through the haze, not sure what she was seeing. It was easy in a blinding storm to imagine things that weren't there.

But maybe the dark clothing she glimpsed was real. She moved closer, calling for the dog.

A little farther, she spied the dog curled up next to a snow-covered man. A horse stood nearby. With her heart pounding, she gave a sharp cry and plowed through the knee-deep drifts as fast as she could, praying, hoping it wasn't too late.

She brushed snow from the stranger's high cheekbones and chiseled jaw. Was he dead?

The dog gave a pitiful whimper. Sidalee put her cheek next to the man's mouth and was rewarded by a faint whisper of air.

He was alive!

"Mister, can you hear me?" There was no response. "I'm going to try to get you into the back of my buckboard." Sidalee glanced at the length of him. He stood at least six feet, maybe more, and was muscular. Standing at five feet four inches in her wool stockings, accomplishing this would be difficult for her.

Her eyes swept to a gun belt and the deadly revolver in the holster. Maybe he was an outlaw on the run. For all she knew, he could be a killer.

Still, this man needed help, and she'd give him that, killer or no.

She pulled him to a sitting position, holding him to keep him from falling back. "Mister, I'd sure appreciate some help, if you're able."

Again no response.

Gently letting him back down, she scanned the landscape. Spying a wide ravine that would work, she drove the wagon into it and backed up where it was even with the ground where the stranger lay. Then she brought his horse around and let the animal do most of the work. Between the roan, her, and even the dog, that pulled with his teeth, they managed to get the half-frozen man into the wagon bed. She wished she hadn't left every blanket with Miss Mamie. She could sure use one now. His threadbare coat would do little to warm him. The cow dog jumped up next to him and lay with his muzzle resting on his master's chest. Tying the roan to the back, she drove toward home as fast as she dared.

"Don't you die on me, mister!" she hollered over her shoulder.

She was not going to bury another soul. Not Miss Mamie and not this stranger.

Two

BEFORE SHE PULLED AROUND THE MERCANTILE TO HER home, Sidalee glanced toward headquarters—the big stone house and ranch office that belonged to Stoker Legend. But she spied no one, not even one cowboy. The weather evidently had the rancher and all the hands indoors by the fire. She'd have to unload the stranger by herself.

She chewed her lip and maneuvered the buckboard as close as she could get to the door. After pulling, grunting, and dragging, she got the man into the modest dwelling but had no strength left to get him off the floor of the small parlor. He'd have to lie there for now.

The collie rushed in barking before she shut the door.

Sidalee ran into the bedroom and yanked her quilt off the bed, tucking it around the lanky stranger. All the exertion had worn her out, but she couldn't rest yet. She threw several logs into the low blaze in the fireplace, then stoked the cookstove to add additional heat.

A glance out the window showed darkness falling. Soon it would be blacker than pitch. The snow had started to lessen some, however, and that was good news.

Now that she'd done all she could for the stranger at the moment, she trudged through the snow to Doc Jenkins's house and rapped on the door. Surprise lit his face to find her in the circle of his lantern light.

"I'm sorry to bother you, Doc, but I need you bad." She explained about the stranger and added, "Come quick."

The doctor nodded and got his coat, bag, hat, and

cane. Jenkins was a dapper man who dressed in three-piece suits like the important people of Fort Worth. It seemed to make no nevermind to him that he lived on a huge ranch in the middle of nowhere. He closed his door and hung his cane on his arm. No one had ever seen him use the cane. Just liked carrying it, she guessed. He was a good man of medicine, though, and often sat all night with his patients, so she supposed his fine airs didn't do anyone harm.

"Where exactly did you find this stranger?" Doc helped her across a snowdrift.

"I had delivered some food to...uh, someone, and was coming back. It was about half a mile from here." She'd almost messed up and mentioned Miss Mamie. She had to be more careful. "I noticed the dog first. He led me to the man. I'm not sure exactly how long he'd lain there. A good bit of snow had covered him."

"It was quite fortunate for him that you were out, or he would've died." He scowled at Sidalee. "I don't hold with you traipsing out across the ranch in this weather, though. You should've gotten someone to go with you. Or sent a cowboy to deliver the food."

Sidalee was saved having to reply when they reached her door. The minute she turned the knob, the doctor rushed in and knelt beside the stranger. She watched him take his temperature and listen to his heart.

"I need to get him off this floor, Sidalee." He glanced up. "If you'll run and get Jonas Harper from the black-smith shop, he'll help me get this man onto a bed. I don't know how you got him this far, to tell the truth."

"I'm stronger than I look, Doc," she said softly. Sometimes a person had to find a way to achieve the impossible. She couldn't leave him out in the cold. One more second could've made the difference between living and dying.

She wound the wool scarf back around her neck

and pulled on her gloves. "I have more blankets in the bedroom. Want me to put the hot-water kettle on to heat?"

"I'll do that and put some bricks in the oven to heat. Just go after Jonas."

Sidalee's breath lodged in her chest as she ran down the road to the blacksmith shop. She caught Jonas as he was leaving and told him Doc needed him. The man probably weighed three hundred pounds and stood six-feet-six. Jonas's arms were almost bigger around than her waist.

Back at the house, Jonas lifted the stranger and carried him into the bedroom. Sidalee waited in the kitchen while they undressed their patient and got him under the covers.

Thoughts turned to the man she'd found. That thread-bare coat he wore probably told the story. Everything the stranger had on him and in his saddlebags could be all he owned. Where did he live? She wondered if someone was expecting him to come home. Or...maybe this could be Miss Mamie's son. How wonderful, if that were true. Christmas was sad when families couldn't be together. This holiday was special and meant sharing, giving, and not being so very alone.

A few minutes later, the blacksmith came out, inter-rupting her thoughts. "Doc's working on that fella. I have to get home to the missus." He paused. "If you need anything, let me know. And I'll take those horses out there to the barn. I'm sure they're freezing."

"Yes, the poor things have to be. Jonas, you're a good man for doing that. Thank you. I didn't want to leave until I was sure Doc wouldn't need me."

"Yes, ma'am. Happy to do it. I'll give them some oats and brush them down." Jonas opened the door and stepped out.

Frigid air swirled into the room. Sidalee clutched her wool shawl closer and fixed a cup of hot tea for herself while she waited for the doctor to finish his examination. Thinking of supper, she put on the bean soup to warm.

She wondered how soon the man would be able to swallow some. That would thaw him out. And if he hadn't roused, Doc could do with a bowlful himself. He had no wife at home.

The rock Miss Mamie had given her crossed her memory. She took it from her pocket. The grayish-black stone looked just like the others the old woman had given her—rough and ugly. It appeared the kind you could find scattered anywhere across the prairieland, but if Miss Mamie thought it was worth keeping, so would Sidalee. She got down the tin box that held all the others and added the new one to the stash. Lord, they were ugly.

Strange how the woman needed to give her something for her kindness.

Doc Jenkins called, asking for a hot-water bag. She filled one and took it into the bedroom along with the heated bricks. "How is he?"

Doc tucked the hot-water bag at the man's feet, then wrapped the bricks in a light blanket and placed them along each leg. "I don't think he lost any fingers or toes, but he was close. I'll know more once I get his temperature to come up. He must have a guardian angel that led you to find him."

"His guardian angel's his dog." She glanced at the pooch lying next to his master, his head on the man's chest. "That dog wasn't going to give up until I followed him."

Doc scratched the dog behind the ears and was rewarded with a lick. "I've heard of dogs doing this when they're devoted to their owners. He's a pretty thing, and you can see love amid the worry in his eyes when he looks at his master."

"I wonder who he is—the man, not the dog." Sidalee stepped closer to look at him.

His midnight hair wasn't overlong and spoke of taking pride in his appearance. The stubble that darkened his jawline said he'd shaved in the last two days. High cheekbones and the dark lashes laying against his ashen face made his features handsome. She couldn't help but wonder about the color of his eyes. Would they be green, brown, blue, gray, or black like his hair?

"I know this is an inconvenience, but I don't want to take him back into the cold." Doc laid a hand on her shoulder. "I will, though, if you say the word. We don't know who he is or where he's from. He could be dangerous."

Again the thought hit her that he could be an outlaw.

Sidalee dragged her gaze away from the stranger and gave Jenkins a smile. "No, please. He's fine where he is. I don't mind one bit. I'll watch over him and keep heating the bricks."

"When he wakes up, he may be confused. I don't want to put you at risk."

"You're not." She shifted her gaze back to the sleeping man. Something told her he wouldn't be angry or violent. She sensed a gentle spirit inside him. "I made a nice pot of bean soup. Either that or hot broth will be good for him when he wakes."

"I smelled that soup when I walked in." Doc's eyes twinkled. "It's my favorite, you know. Maybe it's his too."

"Then I'll dip you out some. It's nice and hot."

"Those, my dear, are words from heaven."

"I'll feed the dog too, if he'll come." She called to the faithful pooch, and it took a good bit of coaxing to get him to leave his master's side.

With the dog eating leftover boiled chicken from a bowl, they sat at the table in the warm kitchen. While they ate, she asked Doc where he was from.

"San Francisco. I lived there many years, but one day I woke up and couldn't take the ground shaking any longer and came to Texas." He reached for another slice of corn bread.

Sidalee laid down her spoon. "Do you mind if I ask a question?"

"Not at all."

"Why do you carry that cane around all the time and never use it?"

Doc laughed and winked. "It goes with my suit, of course. I rather think it makes me look smarter. And rich."

She suspected he was pulling her leg. Her reply was soft. "You don't need a prop, Doc. You're the real thing. Anyone can see that."

"Bless you, child." He wiped his mouth with a napkin. "This soup and corn bread hit the spot. I don't think I've eaten better."

The border collie licked the bowl clean and padded back to his spot on the bed. The dog had such sad brown eyes.

"It's nice to share a meal," Sidalee said. "Gets lonely sometimes." For herself. For Miss Mamie. Maybe for the stranger too.

Doc pushed back his chair and went to check on their patient, buried under a mountain of blankets and quilts. Sidalee stood next to Jenkins as he listened to the man's chest and checked his breathing.

Finally, he stood and put his instruments back into his black bag. "I think we'll see him come around by morning. His chest is clear and his heart is strong. Refill the hot-water bag at his feet in a bit and through the night, if you're awake."

"I won't sleep," she announced firmly. Sleep wasn't important when a life was at stake. This man would live, if she had anything to say about it. Christmas was coming and the stranger was going to see it.

The doctor bundled up and collected his bag. With his cane looped over his arm, he went out into the cold. She made quick work of cleaning up. She couldn't stand mess and clutter, something she got from her mama. Their house stood ready for unexpected company at any given time—from the stocked larder to the beds. No one left the Kings' house hungry or cold. Nothing replaced family.

Unshed tears filled her eyes. How she missed her sweet mama's hugs.

Blinking hard, she went to the bedroom for the hot water bottle and refilled it. She couldn't wait for him to wake up so she could find out if he was Miss Mamie's George. The woman would be so happy. After tucking the warmth again at his feet, Sidalee went to the man's clothes and hat lying on the floor, hoping to find something to indicate who he was. The pitiful coat lay on top. She lifted it up and her chest tightened at how thin the fabric was in places. Someone had patched it numerous times, but even those had frayed.

Surprisingly, his shirt and trousers were clean, although they too were well-worn. His gun belt rested nearby with the big revolver in the holster. Doc had wrapped the belt around the gun into one tight bundle. She picked it up and put it in a drawer. Guns scared the daylights out of her. With it hidden away, she felt safer.

Sidalee glanced at the drifter. What had he been through? The clothes told a story of hardship. What had happened to him?

Everything was sodden from the melting snow. She carried his clothes to the kitchen and spread them out to dry before drifting back. The dog raised his head at her return, looking at her with curious eyes as she sat next to the bed. He chuffed once, then stretched out beside the stranger.

The hours passed slowly. She worried about Miss Mamie, wondering if the woman was warm enough. She'd bake an apple cake in the morning to take when she went to check on her.

But of course, that would depend on the man in her bed.

She pulled her wool shawl around her shoulders and stood to feel his forehead and cheeks. He was warming up nicely and the pink color confirmed it. His legs moved as though he was coming around. His eyes fluttered a few times, but still he slept.

While she watched, he drew his hand from under the covers. His long, slender fingers rested on top, but they constantly moved as though tapping out something. Very odd.

Midnight neared when she leaned over him again to adjust the covers up around his neck. His eyes flew open and he stared at her with alarm. Sidalee jumped back, her heart almost leaping from her chest. But she quickly collected herself and gave him a cheerful smile. "I'm glad you woke up. I'm Sidalee King. I'm sure you're wondering where you are. I found you in the snow, loaded you in my wagon, and brought you to my home. You were in bad shape. Doc came and, once we knew you were going to make it, left you in my care."

"Thought I was dreaming," he rasped.

"Not this time. You're safe and warm now."

His brows pinched together. "What town?"

"Not exactly a town. You're on the Lone Star Ranch. Stoker Legend built a small town here for the ranch hands and their families, since it's too far to the nearest town of any size for them." Light from the oil lamp beside the bed shone on his face. Sidalee thought he had the most arresting eyes she'd ever seen—gray with a dark outer edge around the rim. They left her strangely flustered as they followed her.

"Where are you from?" She handed him a cup of water, ignoring the flutter in her stomach.

"Nowhere."

"Were you coming to the Lone Star, Mister…?"

"Destry. Hank Destry. And no. I'm headed no place."

Sharp disappointment ran through her. He wasn't Miss Mamie's son.

Then his eyes met hers and she saw the pain this thread-bare man tried to hide, heard the bleak tone of his voice, felt his despair seep into her. She understood the obvious.

Hank Destry had no hope.

No future.

No life.

Three

HANK DESTRY STARED AT THE WOMAN HE'D MISTAKEN for an angel. The way the light caught on her blond hair, drawing out the red running through it like thin strips of flame, made him think of a heavenly being. He was glad it hung free, not twisted up on the nape of her neck in a tight little knot like a lot of women's, marking her hair out of bounds to a man's touch.

Not that he'd be touching this woman's. She wasn't meant for someone like him.

This one was too sweet, too pure for a man like Hank. The only type that gave him a second glance was found in saloons and brothels. They didn't care where he'd spent the last eight years of his life. As long as he had money to pay, they welcomed him.

His destination, she'd asked?

Probably hellfire and brimstone, if you believed the preachers. At least that's what they always told him. Enough times that he figured it was true.

The dog whimpered and licked his hand. Hank petted his fur.

"Where's my gun belt?" His dry mouth made his voice scrape like sandpaper.

"I put it away for safekeeping. You won't need it here."

"I always need it. Can you get it?" He hated to be insistent, but he'd feel better once he had his Colt close. Beau gave a sharp bark, evidently sensing his panic.

Without a word, she pursed her lips, strode to a dresser, and opened a drawer.

What the hell was her name? It was something odd. Lee was the last part. Becky Lee? Sibie Lee? Sally Lee? Sid? Then he remembered. Sidalee. It was pretty, like her.

Thick disapproval sat on her face as she laid the gun belt on his chest. It was clear what she thought of him, and he winced. He'd give anything for this angel to look on him with favor—though even as he thought it, he knew he shouldn't.

But one thing he knew, he couldn't let his blackened life touch her. He'd seen things, heard things, even said things no decent woman should see or hear. Not a refined woman like Sidalee. He wondered how old she was. He guessed early twenties.

Hank's hand curled around the gun and he found peace in the cold, hard iron. "Thank you. Where's my horse?"

"Warm and dry in the barn. Probably full of oats by now."

That was welcome news. He couldn't bear for his animals to suffer. "If you'll bring my clothes, I'll get out of here."

She planted her hands on her hips. "No. If you think I'm going to let you waltz out of here in the middle of the night in this snow, you're crazy. Besides, they're wet and cold, and putting them on will for sure hasten your death."

Beau glanced from Sidalee to him and barked three times. Hank didn't think he'd bite, but he kept a grip on the collie's fur to be safe.

The mulish woman had gumption, he'd give her that. And the flash of fire shooting from her eyes told him the only way he was getting his trousers was over her dead body.

He decided to call her bluff. "Well, I'll just find them myself. Surely you wouldn't mind seeing a man in long johns. Of course, I'd hate like hell to have your tender eyes see me through a big hole that just happens to be where something really needs to be covered. How many men have you seen in their holey long johns, Sidalee?" he asked, quirking an eyebrow.

"You just try to get up, mister, and I'll…I'll…I'll sit on you."

The exasperation on her face only made him want to bedevil her more. He hadn't seen that expression on a woman in a long time. It might be kinda fun to have her sit on him, feel her saucy bottom next to him, but he wasn't about to point that out.

Or that he must outweigh her by more than a hundred pounds. He'd play along—just to see what this tantalizing woman would do next.

Hank laced his fingers together behind his head. "So I'm your prisoner?"

He hadn't known true freedom for such a long time. But he'd give up a little to spend a few hours with Sidalee.

"For now. At least till morning. You have your gun, so go back to sleep. You need your rest in order to keep bullying the kind woman who saved you."

Shock rippled through Hank. "You found me?"

"Yes, although in hindsight, if I'd known how much trouble you'd be, I might've let you lie there." Her hands moved from her hips as she crossed her arms. "It wasn't easy getting you into the back of my wagon and then into the house. You must weigh a ton. You're solid muscle."

"I got lots of exercise, where I was." The kind no man wanted every day, six days a week. On Sunday the warden made them attend services. That's where he got preached to about his rotten soul and how there was no hope for him—not now and not in eternity.

She thawed a few degrees. "Would you like me to heat the bean soup I made yesterday?"

"Sounds good. Throw in a cup of coffee and you got a deal."

"I'll be back in a minute." She stopped at the

doorway. "You get out of bed and I'll holler for Jonas. He'll keep you in line."

Hank frowned. "Is he your husband?" Somehow the thought of that pricked him.

"No. Jonas is the blacksmith, and you wouldn't want to mess with him."

Beau barked, staring after her with his tail wagging to beat all.

"Lay down, Beau. Don't get us thrown out," he said low. "This is a good place."

He glanced around the bedroom. A woman's touch was evident everywhere he looked—from the painting of multicolored flowers in a vase, to the quilt on the bed, to the soft shade of pink and green wallpaper that bore pretty flowers inside wide vertical stripes. He bet there were rugs on the floor. He raised his head and leaned over. Sure enough, a deep-rose rug lay beside the bed. Another lay at the doorway. He swiveled to look behind and found the brass bedstead had a heart fashioned of metal with angel babies in the center.

Yes, Sidalee was all woman.

And she isn't for the likes of you, he reminded himself firmly for the second time.

But he was half tempted to get out of bed just so she'd sit on him. A smile curved his mouth, the first in so long. He admitted he was more than a little rusty, but the impertinent woman made it hard to stay grim. In fact, she made it difficult to breathe when she came into the room.

Soft footsteps sounded a few minutes later and she entered with a tray. Heavenly smells drifted from the bowl. She couldn't know how long it'd been since he had a home-cooked meal. He could barely remember. He sat up against the metal headboard and she placed the tray in his lap. Hank sniffed the fragrant steam rising from the bowl and the piece of corn bread resting beside it. He lifted the spoon and found heaven in the taste filling his mouth.

With eyes closed, he savored the soup, letting memories drift through his head. His sweet mama calling him to supper. The touch of her hand, smoothing back his hair. Her smile that lit up his heart on days so dark, he didn't think he'd ever see the sun again. He fought tears that tried to spill and didn't open his eyes until he'd pushed them back.

"How is it?" Sidalee asked.

"This tastes"—he swallowed the thick longing—"of home. Better than anything I've had in a while."

"Good." She was silent a second before asking, "Where is home, if you don't mind me asking?"

"Gone." Everything was gone. Friends had buried his mother and father in the church cemetery while he was locked up. He winced. Their only child had brought them shame and broken their spirits. Guilt stabbed him. His hardworking parents stood by him through it all, never losing faith that one day the nightmare would end. The house where he'd grown up was gone too—turned to ash after squatters set it on fire. At least that's what the neighbor told him when he gave Hank his father's horse and gun. He'd lost everything he had.

Hank lifted the coffee cup. "I'd rather not talk about it."

"I'm a good listener, if you ever change your mind."

The dim light bathed her in shadows, but he could see caring in her eyes. How fast would she run if she found out prison had been his home until a month ago? Then her kindness would come to an abrupt halt.

Pain rushed through him and it wasn't from the pinpricks in his thawing fingers and toes. This pain was the sort that lasted—the kind that rose from disappointing friends. He'd leave come morning, before Sidalee learned the truth. She would never have to know anything about the drifter she'd saved.

He finished the last swallow of coffee and set down the cup. "I refuse to take your bed. Give me a blanket and I'll sleep on the floor."

"Absolutely not, and I'll hear no argument." She leaned to take the tray.

Her fragrance circled around him. He'd never smelled anything so fresh, and the scent gave life to the part of him that had died waiting for justice. The brush of her hand against his made him long for the life he'd been denied. A home—a wife—a fresh start.

But it was too late for that now. Far too late.

"I insist." He threw back the covers, shivering when cool air touched his skin. But he couldn't let her spend a sleepless night because of him.

Sidalee plunked down the tray with a resounding noise and yanked the covers back over him before he could say a word. Beau jumped and growled low. "Am I going to have to make good on my promise, Mr. Destry? You're the stubbornest cuss I've ever seen."

"I could return the compliment."

"You're sick," she huffed. "Just you wait until Doc hears about this."

"You're a pain in my backside," he answered with a scowl, wishing she weren't so pretty and god-awful determined to butt heads with him. He'd never had a woman affect him like this in his life. "Here's a compromise. If you'll lie down beside me on top of the covers, I'll stay where I am."

"And if not?"

"Then I'm walking out that door, and there's nothing you can do to stop me. I'd rather sleep in a snowbank than turn you out of your bed." He watched her hesitate as she weighed her safety against the need to get her patient well. "I won't touch you, and that's a promise."

"And that's the only deal you're willing to make?"

"Take it or leave it. Your choice." Hank patted the

collie to keep himself from reaching for the red-haired angel with curves that could make a man forget his honor.

"You drive a hard bargain, Mr. Destry."

"Hank."

A smile flirted with her lips. "Hank."

After taking the tray to the kitchen, she wrapped a quilt around herself and lay down on the bed. The low light of the lamp bathed her delicate cheekbones and that stubborn chin. He was glad she left it on. He'd been in too much darkness.

He closed his eyes to soak up the softness lying next to him. It was all he could do not to put his arms around her and draw her close. Her scent taunted him, swirling about his head. He'd missed the scent of a real woman, one that wasn't soaked in heavy perfume.

Beau snored from the blanket on the rug next to the bed, probably dreaming of some lady dog that had caught his eye.

"Do you have enough room, Sidalee?" Hank turned on his side to face her.

She squirmed like a squirrel digging for a pecan. "Yes." She lay there a minute before she spoke softly. "Did you know I ordered this bed from the Montgomery Ward catalog?"

He wanted to ask what that was but he didn't. "You don't say."

"This is the deluxe Queen Anne, model number 24, complete with a thick feather mattress. It cost a pretty penny but was money well spent. I think a good night's rest is worth any price, don't you?"

Memories of his hard bunk, which had consisted of a thin mattress on a cement slab, ran through his head. Rest on any given night was out of the question. If he hadn't been keeping one eye open for trouble, it was his aching bones that kept him awake.

"Yes, ma'am."

"I apologize for rattling. I do that when I'm nervous."

"Are you afraid of me?" he asked.

"Not exactly. It's just that I've never slept with a man before and I find it strange."

Hank scowled up at the ceiling. He had to keep her from giving up the bed somehow, but a fine woman like Sidalee didn't go around sleeping with men—not even half-frozen ones like him. "Just think of me as a big dog, and that should fix it."

"Somehow, you don't feel much like a dog."

That was good news. One thing was sure: she definitely felt all woman—one he had no business lying next to.

Even if it *was* on a deluxe Queen Anne bed, model number 24.

Four

THE SMELL OF BACON FRYING TICKLED HANK'S NOSE. He opened his eyes and found no sign of his sleeping partner with those tempting curves. The bed felt empty without her slight weight beside him and the accidental bumps in the night. Once when she turned over, she'd laid a hand on his chest and kept it there as though it belonged.

The scent next to him overrode the bacon. Hank pressed his face into the pillow, inhaling Sidalee's fragrance.

He'd known such peace and comfort for just a little while. He saw no sin in that.

The few timid rays of dawn sneaking through the window were a welcome sight. The clouds had lifted. Beau whined and jumped up beside him.

"Hey, boy. You're looking chipper." His hands were stiff as he reached to scratch the dog's ears, but they didn't ache like the pins and needles that shot through him when thawing. He wondered if his clothes were still drying in the kitchen. He needed to find his horse and get out of here—before leaving became impossible.

A knock sounded and he heard Sidalee talking to a man. No, two men—Hank heard a second, deeper voice but couldn't make out the words.

A few seconds later, a dapper middle-aged man carrying a black bag strode into the room. "Good morning. Sidalee tells me you had a good night. I'm Doc Jenkins." He stuck out his hand.

Hank shook it and propped himself against the

headboard. "Folks call me Hank Destry. Miss Sidalee told me about you coming last night to tend to me. Sorry she dragged you out in that weather."

"It's what I'm here for. You're a very lucky man, Mr. Destry. You could still be lying in the snow, and would be, if not for your dog." Doc shook a thermometer and placed it under Hank's tongue, then listened to his chest and checked his feet and legs. After what seemed an eternity, the doctor removed the thermometer. "Almost normal. You'll have to bundle up when you go out for the next few days—and not in that coat you were wearing, either. Get one that will actually keep you warm."

"It's all I have."

"I know. That's why you're getting a new one." Doc put everything back into his bag.

"I don't take well to charity," Hank said tightly. The very thought made something shrivel up inside him. He was poor and destitute but he was no charity case.

A tall, lean cowboy spoke from the doorway. "Not going to be. Got a job for you, if you want it. You can work out the cost of a coat and warmer clothing."

When Hank opened his mouth to protest, the man held up a hand. "I can't have my employees freezing to death. My name's Houston Legend. My family owns the Lone Star. I'd be obliged if you'd help us out. I'm short some men to the grippe."

"What kind of work?" He might consider sticking around a few days until he figured out where to head next.

"Take your pick. I need more hands to go out and feed and water the cattle." Houston raked his fingers through his brown hair. "This is a 480,000-acre spread. There are always jobs to go around. Say, is there any chance you know how to operate a telegraph? Our operator had to go back East until spring, and my father has some urgent matters to take care of."

Odd that they would have a telegraph on a ranch. But

then Sidalee had mentioned that the owners had formed a small town out here.

"Strange you should ask. I used to help my father run the telegraph where we lived. I'm going to be rusty though." Hank never would've guessed he'd have need of that skill one day.

Houston grinned. "We don't mind one bit. Pa needs to get some telegrams sent as soon as you're able. We have some pressing business matters as well as personal things to attend to." He narrowed his gaze. "I'm serious about getting new clothes and a coat. You refuse, we have no work for you. We take care of our people."

"Understood." Hank had never met anyone like Houston Legend and he liked his honesty. "Don't you want to know anything about me? Where I come from?"

"Figure that's your business. Everyone is running from something. This is a good place to get your feet under you. You can stay in Wheeler's house for a while. I'll take you there after you get through at the mercantile." Houston moved aside to let Sidalee through.

She carried a stack of clothes that Hank recognized. "Out, both of you. Hank needs to get dressed and eat, if he's to fill in for Jim Wheeler," she said. Her tone was a tad bossy, but not in an unpleasant way. She wrapped the words in pure silk.

The grin was back on Houston's face as he met Doc's glance. "I guess we've been told, and in no uncertain terms."

"That's right," Sidalee said with a pretty smile, her blue eyes twinkling. "My house, my rules. I have to get the mercantile opened so Hank can go shopping. And Houston?"

"Yep," the man answered.

"I think Jonas has Hank's saddlebags. Can you find them?"

"Sure," Houston replied.

Hank watched the exchange and noticed how the

men treated Sidalee with respect. She did have that effect on people. She was sassy and bold…and soft. She was the kind of woman who would make a man proud to have next to him. Sidalee would probably be there not only in the rosy times, but the dark ones as well, with her backbone stiff and that stubborn chin daring trouble to knock her down.

As the two men filed out, she turned to Hank. "By the time you've dressed, breakfast will be on the table. Do you like your eggs over easy?"

"I do." He'd take them any way she fixed them. He wouldn't put her out any more than he already had. "Sidalee, I owe you my life. Thanks."

She put down the stack of clothes and laid a hand on the quilt covering him. "Just a friend helping a friend," she said softly. "That's what we do here. Everyone cares about each other, and I'm just glad I found you when I did. This Christmas is going to be extra special."

Yes, it would be. He hadn't celebrated Christmas in a long time, but this year he had a reason. He'd stay to run the telegraph through the holidays, then he'd move on.

He gave Sidalee a nod and hoped he could manage the emptiness that would again settle inside when he left. "I'm glad you found me too. The smells coming from the kitchen are making my stomach rumble. Be there in a minute."

"Take your time. You're likely to be a bit wobbly after your ordeal." With a swish of her skirts, she disappeared through the door, closing it behind her.

Beau whined and glanced up at him.

"Yeah, I know. She has that effect on me, too, boy." He reached for his pants. "We have a home for a little while. Don't get too comfortable though. This is only temporary."

The dog gave a pitiful huff and placed a paw over his eyes.

Hank buttoned his pants and reached for his shirt. "I mean it. We can't stay."

But his heart was saying something totally different. Hope had a way of sneaking past all of a man's defenses.

✎

Sitting across from the drifter, Sidalee reached for the plate of eggs. "You might as well finish these off, and the bacon too."

She'd enjoyed watching him eat. No telling how long he'd gone without before she found him in that snowdrift. The early morning light streaming in the window curled around the edges of his dark hair and nuzzled his chiseled jaw. From the best she could tell, Hank had been through some pretty trying times that could've hardened a man and turned him into a piece of granite. Yet somehow it hadn't appeared to. Last night he'd smiled and even joked a little.

After she'd given him his gun. She remembered the panic in his eyes until she laid the weapon in his hand, remembered him saying tightly that he always needed it.

Sidalee didn't think he'd felt safe in a long time.

A fresh start was exactly what he needed. The Lone Star Ranch could give him that.

When his hands were idle, his fingers constantly moved as though they had a will of their own. Even now, the fingers on his left hand tapped on the table. It was a curious habit.

"Can I ask you a question?"

Hank glanced up and she fell into his gray eyes. "I reckon."

"Why are your fingers always tapping? I doubt you're even aware of it."

"Sorry. An unconscious reflex." A strange sadness crossed his face. "Must be from my days working the telegraph."

"Maybe so. Habits are hard to break." But he'd said he hadn't manned a telegraph in a long while.

"I don't think I've ever eaten better food." He put

the other two eggs on his plate and reached for a biscuit. "These biscuits are so light, it's a wonder they don't float right off the plate."

A smile curved her mouth. "My mother taught me how to make them. In fact, she showed me the way around a kitchen." Her voice broke.

"Can I ask how long since you lost her?"

"Six years. Cholera took both my parents and three brothers." Sidalee glanced at Beau. The dog finished eating from his bowl and lay down by the warm oven. "Fire is the only way to stop the spread of the disease, so I had to burn everything. Stoker Legend found me and brought me here. The big rancher gave me a chance just as his son Houston is doing for you."

Hank studied her. "You must've been pretty young, I'm guessing."

"Eighteen. I knew nothing about running a mercantile, but I learned under the previous owner. When he had to return back East, I took over the business." She met his arresting eyes. "From what you said last night, I take it you don't have anyone either."

"Nope." He turned back to his food.

Sidalee watched him struggle with emotion and wanted to ask more, but he'd made it clear he wasn't talking about that subject. She poured him another cup of coffee instead. "Life is just hard. After you get finished, I'll take you to the mercantile and you can pick out those clothes and a new coat. I'm sure Houston would like you to get started right away, but you might find his father, Stoker, instructing you on what he wants sent."

"Like I said, I'm a little out of practice." He laid down his fork and pushed back his plate.

"I'm sure you'll pick it up again in no time and run the telegraph like an expert." She collected the dishes and took them to the dishpan.

Hank lifted his cup to his lips. "We'll see about that.

Thank you for finding my saddlebags. I wondered where they got off to and prayed I hadn't lost them."

The saddlebags would probably have everything that remained of Hank Destry's life. To lose them would leave him with nothing.

"I know how important a man's belongings are." Especially when they were so meager. She met his gray gaze and the gratitude she saw made the backs of her eyes sting.

"I'll pay you back—for everything."

"For goodness sake, Hank, I need nothing in return. It's been pounded into our brains since birth the importance of giving, but we also need to know how to receive." She pushed back her hair. "We shouldn't feel beholden for everything people do for us."

"Yeah, well, I do." Hank stood and instantly the dog was at his side with his tail wagging nearly off. "Point me to the barn. I'll go see about my horse. Boots and Beau are all I've got."

"You don't have a proper coat yet." She yanked her hands from the soapy water and dried them on her apron, then reached behind to untie it. "These dishes can wait. Let's go to the mercantile so you can get started."

He could get on that horse and ride out. If he did, she'd feel a great loss for some odd reason. What if she never saw him again? What if that one night was all she'd ever know about the sound of a man's soft snores and the hard feel of his body? What if she lost the man who'd come into her life and brought her hope?

For a second his gaze tangled with hers. He finally threw up his hands. "Whatever makes you happy, Sidalee."

He helped her into her coat, and the brush of his hands against hers brought a yearning she'd never felt.

Though the snow had stopped and the sun shone bright, the blustery wind bore a hint of ice in it. Beau ran across the white ground, jumping into a mound, then emerging with a snow-covered nose. Shivering, Sidalee pulled her coat tight around her and glanced at her tall escort. Hank had to be freezing in that threadbare coat. Except for his breath fogging, he gave no indication of being cold as he helped her across a snowdrift. She had a feeling he'd long grown accustomed to meager comforts.

That feeling persisted a few minutes later as he helped her light the big potbellied stove, then browsed the clothing in the store. The dog lay next to the fire's warmth, his dark eyes never leaving his master. Hank compared the prices of everything and appeared to weigh the cost over quality.

Sidalee put her hands on her hips. "Hank Destry, don't you dare pick out that thin shirt and thin jacket that couldn't keep a flea warm. I have to warn you—Houston Legend will march you right back over here, so you better do it right the first time."

Hank turned, and his voice had a slight edge. "I buy what I can afford."

It seemed prudent to get off her bossy high horse and button her lip. In the end, though, he focused on inexpensive but sensible clothes, and she approved of everything he selected. The clothes were well-needed, and she was glad to help him out. Her thoughts went to Miss Mamie, which led Sidalee to grab a soft wool scarf to take to the woman that afternoon.

She watched a smile steal across Hank's face as he slipped on the new coat and ran his hands across the thick wool. He glanced up and caught her staring, immediately dropping his hands to his sides, his features settling again into grim lines. Her heart broke for him and all that those small things revealed. He'd suffered something horrible. Something that stole his laughter and sealed his heart shut.

"I think I'm set. Can I chop some firewood to repay you?" He slowly moved toward her, his large presence filling the store.

"Find joy in *getting* for a change. There's nothing

wrong with accepting help." She laid a hand on his arm. She didn't need anything—except, some small part of her whispered, to be held and cherished.

Before she withered and died on the vine, a lonely spinster whose life had passed her by.

Hank came still closer until only a foot separated them. Her heart fluttered as she stared up into his eyes. The gray had darkened to blue. "I confess, I find happiness in being with you." He inched closer until his scent wound around her like a piece of leather. "Would you mind if I kiss you?" he suddenly asked. "Just once. It's been a long time since I held any softness."

"I'd like that." Sidalee's voice came out breathless and odd, almost in a whisper.

He placed a large hand on her back. Sidalee lowered her eyes as his lips gently settled on hers. A longing swept through her that she'd never felt before, followed by a hunger that consumed her every thought.

The room seemed too hot, her coat too stifling, her knees too weak.

She leaned into him, clutching him to keep from falling.

Just as her breath ran out, he broke the kiss and stepped back. Before Sidalee could utter a word, Hank turned and went out the door with his packages under an arm.

Her heart pounding, she ran to the window and quickly wiped off the fog with an elbow.

The man who'd slept beside her through the night strode toward the huge barn with his dog scampering around his feet. With the collar of the wool coat pulled around his neck, Hank moved as effortlessly as water, his stride fluid and easy, the gun hanging from the holster.

He stopped to pick up a handful of snow, packed it together, then threw it as though a ball for Beau to fetch. Sidalee laughed. She touched her lips that still tingled.

It looked like Hank Destry had some hope in his heart after all.

Five

HOUSTON LEGEND CAUGHT UP WITH HANK AS HE CAME from the barn after seeing to his horse. Thankfully, Boots appeared none the worse for the blizzard.

"Destry." Houston's boots crunched in the snow. A grin brought a twinkle to his brown eyes. "I see you have proper clothing. If you're ready, I can show you the house where you'll stay. Thanks for helping us out. Pa is fit to be tied. He wants Christmas perfect, and nothing less will do."

"I'm ready." Hank blew out a worried sigh. He couldn't let himself think of what would happen if he messed up, whatever Houston's father wanted.

"After I show you where you'll bed down, I'll take you to meet my father. Don't let his gruff ways scare you. You'll find most of it is bluster."

"Yes, sir." His breath fogged as he strode beside Houston. They were evenly matched in height, but Houston had him beat on weight.

The small one-room house fit Hank's needs perfectly. A bed, a flat oak chest at the foot on which his saddlebags lay, and two straight-back chairs completed the furnishings. Someone appeared to have put Jim Wheeler's personal effects away. Probably in the chest.

Houston pushed back his Stetson. "It's not much."

"It'll do. I'll move on after Christmas." Before Hank's past caught up with him.

"Maybe we can change your mind. Let's go meet my father."

A few minutes later, Hank entered the office of

headquarters. A silver-haired man rose from behind the desk and came around. His voice boomed. "You must be Hank Destry. I'm Stoker Legend."

"Glad to meet you, sir." Hank shook his hand and liked the firm grip.

Stoker waved Hank to a chair and propped himself on the edge of the desk. "It was pure luck that you rode along. Houston tells me you can work the telegraph."

Hank gave him a wry smile. "I won't lie. It's been quite a while since I've done it with my father. I've probably forgotten most of it."

"You'll do fine." Stoker's piercing stare seemed to see down inside where Hank couldn't bear scrutiny. "Where were you going when you ended up here, son?"

"No place in particular. Just drifting." Trying to find a place that would welcome him. Hank steadied his breathing and set his jaw. "I have to be honest with you, sir. I got out of prison a few months ago."

The barrel-chested man opened a cigar box and offered one to Hank and Houston before taking one himself. They cut the ends off and lit them. Smoke filled the room. Hank hadn't had a cigar in so long, he couldn't recall, and the taste satisfied a craving he'd had for years.

"What were you in for?" Stoker puffed on his fat cigar, his eyes never leaving Hank.

"Murder." Hank waited for the reaction, daring to wager how this would go.

The big rancher never batted an eye. He put his cigar in an ashtray. "You do it?"

"Nope. I learned money can buy a man's freedom, even if he didn't have it coming."

"Not here," Stoker snapped.

Hank glanced at Houston. The man's face hardened. "We know those kind," Houston said.

Stoker's eyes drifted to Hank's gun belt and Colt. "You looking to get even?"

"Nope. Just want to be left alone. Had enough trouble for a lifetime." The false charge cost him eight years of his life that he'd never get back. Hank got to his feet. "Look, I'm not the man you need. I'll get my horse and ride out."

"Hold on, son." Stoker rose. "Texas is full of good men who got caught up in messes." He laid a hand on Hank's back. "One thing you'll find with me and my sons is, we don't judge and we don't have any time for anyone who does. Sit back down and I'll tell you what I want you to send over the wire."

Hank dropped back into the chair.

"Now, I've got to find my son, Luke. I want you to pepper Texas with wires until you locate him. He goes by Luke Weston, though why the hell he does escapes me. I have a list of contacts. I want him here for Christmas. Maybe for once, our family will all be together. Send one also to my other son, Sam, in Lost Point."

"Yes, sir."

"Nope, don't call me sir. I'm Stoker."

Houston grinned at Hank. "We're a bit loose on formality. Guess we'd best get started."

Hank thanked the big rancher and left with Houston. On the walk over to the telegraph office, Houston told him a little about his brothers. Sam was the sheriff where he lived, but Luke seemed to be a man without a home, and Hank didn't really know why. There was something Houston wasn't telling him.

They arrived at the small office and Hank glanced around. It was as if he'd stepped back in time and half expected his father to walk through the door. He shook himself, made a fire in the potbelly stove, and located everything he'd need. Houston wished him luck and left. Soon his finger was tapping out messages as he got started on the list Houston had given him.

Beau gave a sharp bark and glanced up, covering his eyes with a paw.

"Stop that, for God's sake. You're not a person, no matter how hard you try to be. You're a dog. Accept it." Hank snorted. "Have some pride in yourself. You're not a bit cute, either."

As though to prove it, Beau whirled in a circle then stood on his back legs, his tongue lolling out the side of his mouth.

"Stop that grinning too, while you're at it. I ought to sell you to a circus. I can't play right now." Hank turned back to his work.

Noon came and Sidalee walked through the door. "I brought some lunch."

Hank glanced up and was struck by her brilliant smile and the sun caressing her blond hair. The rays fired the golden strands with red glints. He didn't think he'd ever seen a woman so breathtaking. All he could think about was their kiss.

When he could unglue his tongue, he managed to speak. "I don't have time for lunch. I have to find Stoker's son Luke, or he won't have time to make it here before Christmas."

"It won't take long to eat," she answered firmly. "Hot soup, and ham between two slices of my homemade bread. Plus slices of my famous apple cake. We have two weeks. Besides, I have a favor to ask."

"Whatever you need, just say the word." He'd do anything for the woman who'd saved his life—in more ways than one.

Sidalee wagged her finger at him. "Nope. Eat first."

There was no arguing with a lady. He poured two cups of coffee and sat down with her. Between mouthfuls, they talked.

"What do you know about Stoker's son Luke?" Hank asked.

"Not a lot. He stops by every once in a while, but never stays long. I always wondered why he uses the last name Weston. I get the feeling he has to keep moving. No one talks much about him around any of us." Sidalee's forehead wrinkled in thought. "Luke wears deep sadness inside, but he's always polite and kind when he comes into the mercantile. Once he removed his coat and worked one entire afternoon lifting heavy boxes for me. I'm not sure what secret he and his family keep, but I figure it's their business."

"You're wise not to pry." Hank reached for one of the ham sandwiches and his hand brushed Sidalee's. He could've sworn sparks bounced off their fingers—some kind of strange electricity that built up inside until it either had to escape or burn them up.

Sidalee's eyes met his. "I liked this morning. It was nice being with you, Hank."

"Same with you." What a stupid thing to say. He didn't know what happened to his brain when she was next to him. "What was the favor you mentioned?"

"Do you think you can ride with me out to an abandoned line shack? There's an old woman living out there and she's sick. I'm going to go get her and bring her in." She flashed a smile. "It wouldn't hurt to have reinforcement, in case she refuses again."

"I'll be glad to." Riding next to Sidalee anywhere would make his day perfect. "You don't need to go out there by yourself anyway. The snow is too deep and you could get stranded." Or hurt. He knew way too much about enduring the cold.

"Thank you." She covered his hand with hers.

"People helping people, isn't that what you said? Holler when you're ready." Hank helped her pack up the remnants of lunch, making sure to get his hands in the way of hers. He was starting to like these not-so-accidental touches too much.

When she left, he stood in the doorway, watching her maneuver the narrow path through the snowdrifts. He wished he could answer all the questions she had. Maybe someday, with luck, he could share everything. But he'd have to stick around first.

Thoughts filled his head.

What if he had her to go home to at the close of the day? What would it be like to sleep next to her for real in the deluxe Queen Anne bed, model number 24?

A smile spread at such crazy daydreams.

⌒∞⌒

Sidalee's heart raced like a herd of wild horses when Hank climbed into the wagon box and took the reins in his gloved hands. Beau leaped into the back. The snow glittered like diamonds under the weak sun and the horses' hooves crunched on the frozen ground. Sidalee didn't think she'd ever known more happiness.

When she glanced down, her breath caught to see her skirt resting against his leg. Warmth flooded her. Hank must think her forward, but she didn't move it or herself away. Memories of his gentle kiss washed through her mind like a treasured secret.

Even if she never got another, Sidalee would always remember how Hank took her in his arms and placed his lips on hers.

They talked about life with her family, and Hank's at his father's side, running the telegraph office in Still Valley, Texas. As he spoke, she pictured life there.

A few minutes later, his face hardened. "I've said enough."

"No, please. I want to hear more. What happened to make you leave there?"

"Sidalee, some things are better left alone." Then Hank turned to watch a rabbit scamper across the white landscape.

Sidalee loved how the snow wrapped them in a white cocoon and made it seem they were the only two people in the world. It was their own private sanctuary. Beau sat between them and laid his head in her lap, begging to be petted.

Suddenly she gave a cry. Only a thin, barely discernible column of smoke rose from the chimney of the line shack. Something wasn't right. She willed the horses to go faster and jumped down as soon as Hank stopped.

"Miss Mamie, are you all right?" Sidalee burst through the door with Beau.

The old woman sat in front of the fire with a blanket wrapped around her. She wiped her eyes and turned. "Girl, of course I'm all right. Why wouldn't I be?"

"The fire is far too low. It's freezing in here and you're sick." She hurried to the wood supply and threw on two logs. "There, that should have us warm in a minute."

"I was just trying to save wood in case you didn't come back today, dear. I—" Miss Mamie froze when Hank ducked his head and stepped inside. "George! You came!"

Sidalee whirled. Her son? No, it wasn't possible. Hank grew up in Still Valley. Her heart broke for the poor dear. She swung from Miss Mamie to Hank to see his reaction, praying that he let the old woman down gently.

Hank stared in confusion. "Ma'am, I think you have me mixed up with someone else."

"Miss Mamie, this is Hank Destry," Sidalee explained.

The sweet lady drew herself up. "I should know my own son." Her attention shifted back to Hank and she shrugged. "I don't know why you changed your name, but you must have your reasons. To me you'll always be George Tabor."

"Can I speak to you a minute, Sidalee?" Hank ushered her back out. "What's going on here?"

"I honestly don't know anything, except that she's been waiting for her son George." Sidalee chewed her lip. "Are you sure you don't know her?"

"Never saw her before in my life. There's no way I can be her son. Just age alone will tell you that much."

"She's been terribly confused. Some days she talks about things that couldn't possibly have happened. Maybe her son George died and she can't accept it."

"I've heard of things like this happening. A woman I once knew lost her mind when her baby died, and she started carrying a doll around, thinking it was real."

"Is there any way you can go along with this?" She rested her hand on his arm. "Let her have some happiness at Christmas."

"I wouldn't dream of doing anything different. Clearly, she needs to believe in something. I'll be whoever she needs me to be for however long. I'm glad we're taking her out of here. This is no place for a frail old woman." Hank strode to the wagon with Beau running circles around him. He lifted a heavy blanket and Sidalee followed him inside.

Her chest tightened. Hank Destry was a man with a big heart, and what he was giving Miss Mamie couldn't be measured in money.

She just prayed he could accept what the poor widow could give him in return.

Six

"MOTHER, I DIDN'T EXPECT TO TAKE SO LONG IN COMING for you. Now that I'm here, I'll take you somewhere warm. Put your arm around my neck." Hank lifted her into his arms, concerned that the skin barely stretched across her bones. The old woman probably didn't weigh ninety pounds.

Sidalee finished gathering up the last of Miss Mamie's things and stuffed them into a bag.

"Don't forget my bag of rocks, dear," the old woman said.

"I got them," Sidalee assured her and followed Hank out to the wagon, where he gently lowered his pretend mother onto the warm bed Sidalee had made. Then Hank helped her up beside Miss Mamie and watched her tuck blankets around the woman who needed a son so badly, she had to invent him.

At least that was Hank's theory. He'd send some telegrams out as soon as he learned the town she came from.

He climbed up into the wagon box, and with Beau perched beside him, he set off for the ranch town. The sun had faded behind heavy clouds, and the icy wind had picked up. He prayed they wouldn't have any trouble. This wasn't a night to be out in the elements. Every so often, he glanced back and always found Sidalee leaning close, talking to Miss Mamie and patting a thin, blue-veined hand.

Sidalee had no one either. She'd spoken of deep loneliness that cut through her at times. The gnawing was bad for a man, but for a sensitive, refined woman? It could destroy her and make her shrink into herself.

There were worse things than taking refuge at the Lone Star Ranch. Lots of worse things.

For no reason at all, Hank smiled.

The return trip didn't take long. Before he knew it, he was pulling up to Sidalee's door. He carried Miss Mamie inside and lowered her into a rocking chair in front of the fireplace.

"Thank you, son." She glanced up at him. "I can't seem to remember you getting so tall. You're a handsome boy. You take after your father."

"How long has it been since you've seen me, Mother?"

"What kind of fool question is that? You know it was only a few months ago."

"Of course. How were things in town when you left there?" Hank met Sidalee's questioning glance with a quick shake of his head. He'd explain later.

"Well, you know Benton Falls never changes. Except our place. It burned, you know. Your bedroom went up in flames. Nothing survived."

Hank gently wiped away Miss Mamie's tears. Here was someone who desperately needed something to believe in. He could be that for her. "That's all right, Mother. I can replace them. You rest and get your strength back." He took Sidalee into the kitchen and told her why he needed the name of the town.

"That's a great idea, Hank. Maybe you can figure out what's going on. My heart breaks for her. It did when I first saw her freezing to death in that line shack, and it's only gotten worse."

"I'll not turn my back on her, and that I can promise you." Hank met her blue gaze, sudden longing rising inside so fierce he could barely breathe. He lifted a tendril of her hair, wishing he could kiss her again, but he'd only asked for one, and any more would only make the leaving unbearable.

"Will you stay for supper, Hank?"

He didn't have the power to refuse. "I'll be back after I take the horses to the barn."

A rosy blush colored her cheeks. Hank didn't think he'd ever seen a more beautiful woman. To share supper with her—and Miss Mamie too, of course—would feed his soul, which had been hungry for so long.

But he wouldn't make a habit out of it. He just needed a little more of her company to store up for the lonely days after he left the ranch.

∞

The following morning, Hank set to work trying to uncover information that would shed light on Miss Mamie's insistence that he was her George. It didn't take long to get an answer from the sheriff in Benton Falls.

Albert and Mamie Tabor buried their baby boy, George, back around 1823 or so. The sheriff didn't know the specific year. The child had been about a year old.

Also, their house and all their belongings did not burn as Miss Mamie claimed. She and Albert had gotten evicted from their land by a bunch of land-grabbers. The sheriff hoped they found a better climate at the Lone Star.

Hank sat staring at the telegram for a long time, his heart aching for the old woman. Anger rose. The loss of their land must've been too much, and something in Miss Mamie's head broke. He'd be her son as long as she wanted.

Sometimes people just needed a little something to cling to, something to get them through the long days. To have hope. Lord knew he had—and still did. The thing that gave him strength in prison was the daily tapping on the wall, the conversation with his friend, Robert Gage.

For Miss Mamie, it was pretending her son was alive and well.

The door opened and Stoker Legend strode in. "How's it going, Destry? Have everything you need?"

Hank stood. "It's going fine, boss. I picked up the code just like I never stopped. I suppose you came for a report."

"No. It's early yet, and if you had anything, you'd have brought it." Stoker removed his gloves. "I need you to send a telegram to Joe Jameson right away. I have business to conclude with him before Christmas."

Ice froze the blood in Hank's veins. Dark foreboding rippled through him, and there was a foul taste in his mouth. He should have known this was all too good to be true.

After what felt like an eternity, he forced himself to focus and handed Stoker a tablet and pencil. "Write out what you want me to send, and I'll get to it."

Then he'd have to decide if it was time to saddle up and ride out.

Stoker scribbled out the message and drew on his gloves. "I'm real glad we found you. You're sure a godsend, no doubt about it." The big rancher's gaze swept over Hank. "Christmas should be spent with family though. I'll understand if you need to leave."

"I have no family."

"Then I'm glad you can join ours. The Legend and Lone Star families are one and the same. I throw a dance on Christmas Eve and you'll be welcome."

"Thank you, but I don't much like crowds."

"I know a few pretty ladies who'll be very disappointed." Stoker strode to the door and turned. "Maybe you'll change your mind. My day will be made if all my sons get to be here. A man can't ask for more than that."

"I reckon not. I'll keep burning up these wires until I find Luke."

With a nod, Stoker stepped out into the snow. The

fire crackled and popped as Hank focused on the message to Joe Jameson. The boss was telling Jameson to be there in four days or the deal was off. From the strong language used, it appeared Stoker didn't think any more of the man he was doing business with than Hank did.

The owner of the Lone Star rose even higher in his estimation, but either way, Jameson was coming to the Lone Star. Hank had four days. Did he stay or run?

If he stayed, Jameson would only make trouble for him. The man had more money than God and more lies than the Devil, with a lack of a conscience to match. Jameson had destroyed Hank once.

A muscle worked in Hank's jaw. This time the man would find out just how much Hank had learned about surviving. He'd aged far beyond his twenty-eight years.

He wondered if Jameson's boy would come. If he was going to show, Hank might be tempted to stay. He'd like to see if Seth was still a spoiled braggart. But likely someone had silenced him by now.

A troubled breath left him as he sat down to send the telegram. Soon he immersed himself in work, and the bitter taste in his mouth left. He was on the hunt for Stoker's son, Luke Weston. Hank still thought it odd that Luke didn't go by Legend. Maybe he'd ask Houston—if he got to know him well enough.

That wouldn't happen if he decided to leave before Jameson arrived.

Still undecided, Hank refocused and found comfort in the tapping sound. He was narrowing down Luke's location. He only had a few more days, or it would be too late for Stoker's son to arrive in time. It was important to give the man who'd offered him a second chance the Christmas he wanted.

When Hank was growing up and before he learned what a dark place the world could be, Christmas had been exciting. Hank could barely wait to see what he'd get—not that he couldn't guess. His mother always knitted a scarf, gloves, or a warm cap. His father would make some toy by the light of the lantern after Hank went to sleep. He missed those times where the love of family wrapped around him like soft wool. But Christmas had ceased to exist for him.

There wasn't any use in pretending it did.

A handful of ranch hands wandered in to send telegrams to family, making plans to spend the holidays together. Those left and more came. One tall cowboy sent a note to his sweetheart, saying he loved her. An older one, his face weathered by the sun and wind, told a woman named Alice that he couldn't make it this year. A young homesick cowboy asked Hank to write out his message for him on account of never learning to read and write. It was to his mother, apologizing for not making it.

Hank watched them, wondering about their lives and what they dreamed about at night when they stumbled to their beds, dead tired after a long day. They weren't much different from him—except they seemed content. Hank was still searching for a home and a place to belong.

Sidalee had said this was a good place to start over. He'd like to think she was right…but he had a feeling it wouldn't be long before he'd have to say goodbye.

Seven

SIDALEE GOT MISS MAMIE ALL SETTLED AND LEFT HER dozing by the fire, then rushed around to fix a nice, warm supper. Excitement hummed below her skin just thinking about Hank Destry sitting across the table from her. She wanted this to be perfect.

Tears stung her eyes as she remembered how tender he was with Miss Mamie. Not too many men would pretend to be the lonely old widow's son. Yet he hadn't batted an eyelash. Hank was cut from the same fine cloth as the Legend family. He wore honor and compassion like a second skin.

During the woman's morning nap, she'd fetched Doc Jenkins. He'd frowned when he listened to Miss Mamie's chest and told Sidalee to keep her warm and give her plenty of fluids. "She has pneumonia and is very weak. I'm glad you brought her from that line shack."

"Me too, Doc." She'd thanked him for coming.

Now with the shadows gathering, she made them a cup of tea and sat down with the homeless widow. "How are you feeling? Your cough doesn't seem quite so frightening."

"I owe everything to you, dear. Do you know where my sack of rocks went?"

Sidalee scowled. "Now, Miss Mamie, I hope we don't have words, with Christmas upon us, but if you keep trying to pay me for following my heart, we will."

Miss Mamie harrumphed. "Well, if this doesn't beat all. I'll bet my son wouldn't talk to me like this."

Sidalee rose and wrapped her arms around the woman. "I love you, don't you know that?"

"I reckon I do." She patted Sidalee's hand.

They sat there sipping their tea and finding comfort in each other's company. Not long after, a knock sounded at the door. She rushed to let Hank in. He stood there tall and broad-shouldered, with the low hat brim shading his unreadable eyes. Beau was at his side. The dog glanced up at her with a whine, and she smoothed his fur and crooned.

"I'm glad you came," she said, smiling. "I wasn't sure you would."

He stepped inside, taking off his hat. "One thing you should know about me—I keep my word." He sniffed and grinned. "What is that?"

"Fried rabbit. Jonas, the—"

"Blacksmith," he finished.

"Very good. You remembered. Jonas went out hunting and brought a couple of rabbits by. I'd been wanting fried chicken but didn't want to traipse out in this weather. Not with Miss Mamie here."

He glanced around and lowered his voice. "I got a telegram from the sheriff in Benton Falls." He quickly told her about the death of Miss Mamie's son and the reason they left.

"Oh dear." A stabbing ache filled Sidalee. "No wonder she'd rather live in a pretend world. Her husband's death must've pushed her over the edge."

"Is that you I hear in there, George?" Miss Mamie called in a frail voice.

Sidalee watched Hank still. It was apparent he was still getting used to his new role.

"Yes, Mother." He moved on into the parlor. "It sure is."

Sidalee swallowed the thickness in her throat and listened to Hank tell the woman about his day. She was sure he made up a good portion of it, but the fact he did spoke well for him. She dished up the fried rabbit and set the platter on the table along with the cream gravy and hot biscuits.

"It's ready," she called. Hank came through the door with his arm bracing Miss Mamie. The way the old woman glanced up at him with such adoration in her eyes touched Sidalee. It didn't matter that they bore no blood relation to each other. Their hearts had formed the only ties that mattered.

Beau padded to his dish filled with meat and wasted no time gobbling it up.

Sitting with Hank and Miss Mamie at the table, Sidalee didn't think she'd ever been happier or felt more cared for. They talked about everything and nothing. She caught him looking at her strangely all during supper and wondered why.

"This is the best meal I've ever had," Hank declared. "How about you, Mother?"

Miss Mamie wiped her fingers on her napkin. She seemed lost in a memory. "Often when I was a girl, at the first snow, we'd go rabbit hunting with my father. Then mother would cook them and we all ate until we popped." Her hand trembled as she wiped her eyes. "This makes me feel like I'm young again. What I wouldn't give…"

"You two are spoiling me." Sidalee patted Miss Mamie's arm. "We can always go home to visit in our minds, and that's a very good thing. Anyone want dessert? I made a pie out of canned peaches from the store."

"Yes, ma'am." Hank was quick to hold out his plate.

After they finished, he helped her clean up. Then she helped Miss Mamie to bed and sat with Hank on the settee in the parlor in front of a cozy fire.

"Hank, you just added another star to your crown," she declared.

His lopsided smile made her heart lurch. "I don't know what you're talking about."

"You could've easily straightened Miss Mamie out and hurt her very badly. It's the mark of a real man to put someone's need over his own," she said softly.

He took her hand in both of his. "Don't make me into something I'm not. I'm no different than you. I couldn't stop staring at you over supper. I've never met anyone with such depth of compassion. I kept thinking about you lying next to me in that bed last night, keeping me warm, making sure I didn't want for anything."

Sidalee's heart fluttered. He sat so close, the pleasing scent of him swirled around her as though it were a rope, binding them together. "I would've done the same for anyone else."

"Maybe, but I doubt it." He turned her hand over, studying it.

"Do you mind if I ask something?"

"Not at all."

"Why do you have this habit of tapping on things?"

The crackling fire filled the silence. Finally, Hank said, "In prison I had this friend, Robert Gage, in the next cell with a thick wall separating us. We talked to each other by tapping out a code. One of my biggest regrets is that I never got a chance to meet him. Our talks helped both of us get through the hard times. That way of communicating was a huge part of my life for so long."

"What happened to Robert? Is he still there?"

"He died." Hank rose to tend the fire.

"I'm so sorry." Now it made sense, but she wished she hadn't asked.

Hank returned to the sofa. "I had a decision facing me, but an answer came just now. I know exactly what I'm going to do."

"Anything you care to talk about?"

Sadness in his gaze spoke of torment and despair. "I've

kept things to myself all my life, thinking it was the only way left for a man. Sometimes I don't think I can bear the burden a second longer. You deserve honesty above all else, and if I make it to Christmas, that will be my gift to you. You'll have a full accounting."

What did he mean, if he made it to Christmas? He was so serious, and she knew he didn't say it lightly.

"I'll just ask one thing—is your life in danger?" She searched his face.

"I won't lie. It could well be. But I won't drag you into my mess."

"I never worried for one second you would." Hank was the kind of man who'd take a bullet so it wouldn't strike anyone else. He drew circles on her palm and the sensitive skin of her wrist. She'd never felt a gentler touch and yearned to lay her hand on the side of his face and tell him she'd stand with him. She longed to trace the curve of his lips and brush a kiss onto them.

This man who had trouble opening up communicated best by touch. She took his hand and tapped on his palm. "This can be our secret language too, and maybe you won't feel so lost. This way, you can honor Robert and never forget him in this new life as well as the old."

Hank allowed a smile as he tapped a message on her hand. "That says I've never met anyone like you, Sidalee. Your compassion astounds me. Thank you for caring."

"I see how much you grieve for the loss of your friend, and this will help ease that loss." Tapping on a hand was little enough. She'd do anything to give Hank hope again.

"That brings me to a question," he said. "Boss told me about a dance on Christmas Eve. Will you do me the honor of going with me?"

Thoughts of dancing with Hank filled her. "I can't think of anyone I'd rather go with."

Worry deepened the lines of his face. "Just one thing—I don't know how to dance."

"We're in the same boat. I never learned. My brothers used to tell me I had the grace of a donkey." She chuckled softly at the memory. "How about if we just stand there and sway? We can do that."

She could do anything if it meant being next to him—even fake dancing.

Hank brushed her cheek with his fingers. "I like the sound of your laughter. You're easy to be with."

"So are you." She paused, then added, "I know you consider being here only temporary, but I hope you'll stay."

"We'll see how the cards play out. It wouldn't set well to disappoint a pretty lady." His half smile made her heart do funny things. My, he was a handsome man.

He leaned toward her and she held her breath, hoping he was going to kiss her. Instead he bypassed her lips and pressed a light kiss on her cheek. Disappointment swept over her. It was nice though, real nice, and she'd take it.

This drifter she found in the snow had made her dream again. Maybe, just maybe, it wasn't too late for her.

⌘

Hank spent the next three days scouring Texas for Stoker's son. Finally, a telegram arrived from Luke. He was coming but might not arrive in time for Christmas, saying he'd do his best.

Stoker's face lit up when Hank handed him the message. "He'll be here if it's humanly possible. Good work, Destry." He opened his cigar box and offered one.

"Glad I could help." Hank cut off the end of his cigar and lit it.

He turned to leave when Stoker stopped him. "Doc told me about an old woman that Sidalee had found staying out in an abandoned line shack. What do you know about her?"

Hank filled him in on the old woman's plight, adding, "Miss Mamie has nowhere to go."

"Doc said she has a bad heart and may not have long. I want to make her last days comfortable."

"That's one prideful woman, boss. And stubborn. But she thinks I'm her son, George—the baby she lost before his second year."

"Perfect. You can persuade her to do most anything, if it comes to that." The rancher looked deep in thought. "I'll let you know after I think about this."

With a nod, Hank returned to the office. He gathered up a handful of telegrams in preparation for delivering them to the ranch hands, but Joe Jameson was heavy on his mind. He still had a window of opportunity to ride out. But he liked it here, and for the first time in a very long while, he felt he belonged. To the ranch, to Miss Mamie…and maybe to Sidalee.

And he had the Christmas dance to look forward to. If he left, he'd really miss that, miss a chance to hold Sidalee close and sway to the music, miss the laughter that set her blue eyes twinkling like stars. And he'd miss stealing another kiss.

Hank hesitated, then firmed his jaw. He wasn't leaving. He'd draw a line in this north Texas sand and make a stand.

Joe Jameson had better get ready. Hank Destry wasn't running. He'd face the man who'd framed him and risk everything. He had no money or power, but he would look Jameson in the eye one last time and tell him that he refused to be destroyed by him.

Some things freed a man's soul, and his already felt lighter.

Low, heavy clouds made for frigid wind as he made his way outside. He pulled his collar up around his neck and saddled his blue roan. He'd named the horse Boots because of the black stockings on his legs. The animal needed the exercise and Hank could take care of two things at once. Light snow was falling by the time he delivered all the telegrams and turned for home.

A smile formed. Yes, he was home—for however long they let him stay.

Eight

JOE JAMESON ARRIVED ABOUT NOON THE NEXT DAY. HANK spotted him from the office window and struggled to swallow the bitter memories that rose so thick and deep. His hand automatically caressed the Colt at his side.

Jameson walked with the same swagger, the same aloof bearing that demanded everyone's attention. He'd bet everything he owned that Jameson wore the same smug expression.

With luck, Hank would find an excuse to run into the man. He would have his say before the day was out, one way or another. He turned from the window and went to the potbellied stove for coffee. The telegraph machine began to clatter.

It was a message for Stoker from his son Sam. His boss would want this right away.

This was the chance he'd waited for. Hank stilled his breath and pulled on his coat and gloves. Facing down Jameson wouldn't accomplish anything except give Hank satisfaction. After all, the sorry piece of humanity had ties and money. But Hank would have peace in his soul. The dog padded to the door, and the minute Hank opened it, the collie dashed out. He made a beeline for one of the ranch dogs and promptly sniffed his hind end. Hank set his sights on Jameson and strolled toward his fate. A few minutes later, he entered headquarters and knocked on Stoker's closed office door.

Voices from the other side silenced, and Stoker barked, "Come in."

"A telegram from Sam, boss. It seems urgent." Aware of Jameson's angry glare, Hank handed the message to Stoker. The big rancher read it, wrote a reply, and instructed Hank to send it.

"Yes, sir." He turned and locked eyes with Jameson, glaring into the face of evil. He dared the man to utter one word. Jameson's face flushed and he appeared about to explode, but he couldn't in front of Stoker.

That gave Hank power, and he did the unthinkable—he smiled.

As he left, Hank heard Jameson ask to be excused for a moment. This was the moment Hank had prayed for. He stepped around a corner and waited.

Heavy footsteps neared and Hank stepped into Jameson's path. "Looking for me?"

The surprised man's eyes widened and he took half a step backward. "What are you doing here?"

"Working. I have that right," Hank answered smoothly, his eyes narrowing.

"One word from me and the judge will throw you back in prison to rot."

"I'm not afraid of your threats. You haven't destroyed me. I've only grown stronger. Now I have work to do." Hank turned. Jameson grabbed his arm but released it when Hank pointedly glanced at the man's hand and growled, "Never touch me again."

"I'll do as I damn well please," snarled the man. "A word of warning—keep your mouth shut. I can destroy you and will, if you mess with me." The man's heavy jowls hung down on each side like a big bulldog's, and the large paunch around his belly strained his waistband. "But who's anyone going to believe? A man of wealth or a penniless ex-con and drifter?"

"You seem to think that I'm afraid of you. You're sorely mistaken. By the way, how's Seth doing?" Hank's voice was silky and quiet.

"My boy is doing what he was destined to do," Jameson spat. "He's an important man in Still Valley. Seth is the mayor and is a pillar of the community with his lovely wife. They have three children."

"A pity that a murderer could rise to such heights. But then, he learned how to fool people from you." Hank stared into the face he'd hated for eight years but suddenly found he only pitied the man.

Jameson's voice grew loud and more bullish. "I warn you. Say one word and I'll put you in the ground this time."

Fury rose. Hank pinned him against a wall, a hand around Jameson's throat. "Come after me and you'll find yourself outmatched. I'm not a young kid anymore. You might think about that. And remember the witness to the crime that day. He might just spill his guts now."

"You wouldn't dare!"

Movement behind alerted Hank. He turned to see his boss in the office doorway.

"Both of you step inside." The anger in Stoker's voice was clear.

Hank's stomach knotted as he followed Jameson. They took a seat in front of the huge desk. This was it for him. Just as he'd started to think of the Lone Star as home, he'd have to leave. But he wouldn't take back his words or apologize for standing up to the liar.

Joe Jameson got the first word. "Did you know you have a murderer working for you?"

"I know Hank was jailed for killing a man." Stoker leveled a steely glare on the wealthy landowner. "I also know he didn't do it."

The man snorted. "Just because he denied it doesn't make it so. Whose word carries more weight—someone you've known for years or a drifter?"

"I have no patience with lowlife, cheating scum like you, Jameson," Stoker thundered. "You should know

I overheard everything. Hank, tell me what happened back then."

"I'd be happy to." Hank shot Jameson a glare. "His son, Seth, and I were the same age, but not exactly friends. I was in the bank with my father when Seth walked in with Jameson. Seth argued with the teller, then took out his gun and shot the man between the eyes. The sheriff ran in and Jameson told him that *I* shot the teller. My father's word meant nothing, because Jameson quickly lined the sheriff's pockets. I got sent to prison and Seth got off scot-free."

"Now, look here, Legend. You're not going to buy that preposterous load of manure. We've had plenty of business dealings, but if you're going to believe him over me, I'll never buy another bull from you. Men like Destry prey on the wealthy. He came from a poor family and he'll always be poor. He has dollars in his eyes."

"Strange that he hasn't asked for one cent," Stoker said calmly.

"Just give him time." Joe Jameson glared at Hank, his jowls quivering. Sweat beaded his brow. "He was trying to rob the bank when Seth walked in and stopped him."

Hank watched the exchange silently and waited. He'd said his piece. Now all he could do was wait to see if justice would abandon him again, or if Stoker Legend was made of sterner stuff.

"The problem is that I do know you," Stoker said. "Only too well." He turned to Hank. "Who is this witness you were talking about?"

"Back then, the kid was a ten-year-old and the judge wouldn't let him testify." Hank glared at Jameson. "He saw everything and he's grown up now. I spoke to him a month ago, and he's ready to say Seth Jameson killed the teller."

Jameson's face turned ashen and he steadied himself against the wall.

"There you go. Hank couldn't fight back before, but now he has me. I'm putting my considerable money and influence toward seeing justice done." Stoker pinned Joe Jameson with a seething stare. "I have a telegraph here on the ranch now, and I'm instructing Hank to wire the U.S. Marshal and have him place this witness in protective custody. You're about to have more trouble than you can wiggle out of, Jameson."

"You haven't heard the last of me," Jameson blustered. "If you want a fight, I'll damn sure give you one."

"You've always gotten under my skin with your shady dealings. I want you out of my house." Stoker's yell was so loud it rattled the windowpanes. "If you don't go to jail over this, I'll miss my guess. Come back on my land again and I'll have my men throw you off."

"You don't have to worry on that count." The rich bag of wind stalked to the door. "Seth is my boy, Stoker. We have to protect our own."

Stoker's face darkened. "I'm also going to instruct Hank to have the U.S. Marshal arrest Seth for the crime he committed."

Jameson struck the doorframe with a fist. "I was only doing what any good father does. I didn't want one mistake to ruin Seth's life." The slamming door rattled the hinges.

"Thank you, boss." Hank stood. "I've never had anyone stand up for me before."

"How does it feel, son?"

"Pretty good. In fact, it feels great." Hank shook his hand. "I don't know how I happened to find my way here, but I'm glad I did."

"It was meant to be. I've stopped trying to figure these things out." Stoker laid a hand on Hank's shoulder. "I started with nothing, so I know how you feel. I meant it when I asked you to wire the U.S. Marshal. I want the witness protected and Seth Jameson arrested."

"I'll be happy to." Justice had been a long time coming. Hank wiped his eyes, thinking of all he'd endured. His name was finally going to be cleared.

∽∾

Sidalee sensed a change in Hank as soon as he and Beau entered the empty mercantile she was decorating in green and red. He wore a real, honest-to-goodness smile for the first time—one that revealed a row of white teeth. He strode toward her with his hat in his hands.

With shaky fingers, she secured the last bit of Christmas holly and festive ribbon to the counter and stepped back. A length of red ribbon that she hadn't used draped around her neck. Beau nuzzled her hand, begging for attention. She knelt to hug the collie and let him lick her cheek before he padded off.

Sidalee stood and studied Hank's face. "You look happy. Really happy."

"That's because I am." He glanced around the store, evidently making sure he wouldn't be overheard, before going on. "Do you remember me saying that if I made it to Christmas, I'd answer all your questions?"

"I recall that. You also spoke of danger. Is that over now?"

"Yep." He took her arm and led her to some chairs at the back close to the stove, where Beau had found a warm spot. "I want to tell you everything. Then you can decide if you still want to be friends."

"I assure you nothing will change my mind about you."

"Even learning that I'm an ex-convict?"

Shock ran through her. He'd been in prison? She would never have guessed that. Sidalee touched his arm. "Not even that, Hank. I can see the man you are, and I like him very much."

"You're a special kind of woman, Sidalee." And he knew he'd never find another like her in all the world.

Over the next hour, they talked and she learned about the cruelty of Joe Jameson. Anger washed over her. Hank had paid for Seth Jameson's crime. But worse than that, his parents had died of broken hearts, buried by people who hated their son.

"I can't imagine the horrors you faced. You're a strong man, Hank."

"To be clear—I'm no saint. I just did what I had to. I sent the telegram to the marshal like the boss told me. Now Seth will finally have to face justice." Hank shoved his fingers through his hair. "I don't think he'll fare well in prison. A part of me feels sorry for him."

"They never gave a care about you. I'm sure his father's money will buy him plenty of friends," Sidalee said dryly.

"Joe Jameson may face charges of his own, as well as the sheriff," Hank pointed out.

"The town can stand a good cleaning. But what about you? What are you going to do now?" He still might decide to leave, and that worried Sidalee.

Indecision reflected in his face. "I'm not sure yet. It's a wonderful feeling to have choices and the freedom to make them." His eyes met hers as he toyed with the festive ribbon around her neck. "I do know I'm taking you to the Christmas dance. I won't miss that for anything. No doubt I'll have to beat off the single men with a club, though."

She grinned. "You'd fight for me?"

"Quicker than you can whistle 'Dixie.'" He took a tendril of hair between his fingers. "I'll fight, scratch, or shoot any man who tries to cut in."

"I've never had a man fight for me before." She captured her bottom lip between her teeth to stop the goofy smile.

"Then they must all be as blind as suck-egg mules." Hank slowly pulled the long silk ribbon from her neck, trailing it down one arm as he leaned closer. "There's some mistletoe right over your head. I hope I'm not pressing my luck, but do you mind if I kiss you again?"

A happy, warm glow swept over her. "I don't see anyone trying to fight you," she whispered.

He pulled her up into his arms and drew the ribbon around her, tethering her to him. Sidalee had never felt more alive, more breathless, more...hot.

She tilted her face to him, feeling the wild beat of his heart that matched hers. He gently anchored her against the hard wall of his chest. The moment his lips touched hers, an aching hunger swept through her, turning her knees to pudding.

The yearning for him was so strong, she clutched him to keep from falling in a puddle at his feet. One arm curled around his neck just under his hair. The strands brushed her skin like tiny feathers.

That's when she knew she was falling in love with Hank Destry.

His hand slid down her back, leaving a heated path. He broke the kiss but kept his lips on hers. "I don't know what it is about you, but when I'm near you, all I can think about is doing this. Reckon why that is?"

"Mistletoe?" She leaned back to meet his smoldering gaze. "I once heard that mistletoe can cast a spell on you."

"Is that right?"

Sidalee nodded. "It works the same as moonlight."

Beau scolded with a sharp bark, lay down, and covered both eyes with his paws as though to say he didn't go for this mushy stuff. Sidalee laughed.

"Kiss a lot of men to test your theory?" His voice was soft, teasing, but it hit too close to home.

"No." An ache filled her as she pushed away from him. She'd fallen in love with a drifter. Any moment he'd ride off and leave her alone again with only her work and the constant wind to keep her company. How could she go back to that after losing her heart to him?

"What's wrong?"

"This is a silly game, and I'm much too busy to indulge you." She whirled and fled to the front to her Christmas decorations.

"What did I do?" Hank followed her. "Tell me what I did. It's not a game to me."

"Isn't it?"

He took her arm and gently turned her. "What I feel is real, and for the first time in my life, I think about more than just this moment." He pushed back her hair and kissed her forehead. "You make me think that maybe I do have a future beyond tomorrow. For so long, all I've prayed for was to see the next sunrise. You have me dreaming and have given me hope."

She melted into his embrace. "You've done the same for me, and I think that's what scares me most. What if it all ends and you ride out? I don't think I could face that." Her voice shook, but she had to put her greatest fear into words. "You have the power to destroy me," she whispered.

"I'll never do that. Not intentionally."

His gentle touch was like the whisper of a breeze where the earth meets the sky. She had to trust that this could last. If not, what did she have left but loneliness and sorrow? She had to believe he spoke from his heart.

"You drifted in. Will you also drift out, or do you intend to stick around?"

Silence spun between them, broken only by her loud heartbeat in her ears.

"Yes," he answered. "Yes, for you I'll stick around."

With a soft cry, she buried her face against the corded muscles in his throat and held on to this stranger who'd come to mean so much. Hank Destry was everything she'd wanted.

"I want you, Sidalee," he murmured against her hair.

"I have this hunger inside to touch you—all of you. I know we haven't known each other very long and I shouldn't even ask, but—" He raised her face and stared into her eyes. "Would you be willing?"

Her pulse raced. She'd wanted him ever since he woke up in her bed and challenged her threat to sit on him if he didn't stay put.

"Yes. But Miss Mamie is at my house."

"If you're willing, we'll go to Wheeler's place."

Her hands trembled as she lifted the Closed sign and hung it on the door. She had no doubts as she strode beside Hank and a minute later waited while he put another log on the fire in the one-room house. Her eyes flew to the bed. Nervous anticipation filled her, but she knew this was the right decision.

Hank lifted her into his strong arms, his gaze locked with hers. "Are you sure?"

"Never more so." Sidalee ran her hand across his strong jaw and watched passion darken his eyes. "I want to feel you next to me, your skin on mine, our hearts beating as one. I love you, Hank Destry. Some would say it's impossible in this short time, but I know this is real."

Silently, he carried her and sat her on the soft quilt that covered the bed, then slowly removed the pins from her hair. "Your hair is beautiful." He ran his fingers through the strands. "The color reminds me of a wheat field under the morning sun, and it's softer than corn silk. It's a shame to keep it bound up."

"It's easier that way when I'm working. And I've never had anyone want to see it like this."

"More's the pity." He worked at the buttons of her dress. Slowly, piece by piece, he undressed her and then himself.

The light revealed scars, mostly from prison, she guessed, and tears bubbled in her eyes. This innocent, proud man who had more strength than twenty men had suffered greatly. But they hadn't broken him, and that was more important than the scars. She took his hand and brought him down beside her.

Hank lay facing her and kissed her eyes and cheek before covering her mouth with his lips. Sidalee closed her eyes and let the warmth flood over her. She didn't know how he felt about her, but she loved him, and that was enough.

With a feather-light touch, he slid his hands down to the swell of her breasts, then the curve of her hip. She'd never known such soft caresses. Hank made her feel as though she were a queen.

She laid a palm on the hard planes of his chest as he deepened the kiss and knew she never wanted to be separated from this man. She'd show him how to open his heart and let love in.

He finally let her up for air. Staring into his eyes, she ran her fingers down his body, leaving a trail of kisses in their wake. "Hank, I want you—all of you. And don't ask me if I'm sure, because I am."

"I have this hunger for you that's unlike anything I've known, Sidalee. You don't know how often I dreamed of this moment."

Hank rolled atop her and, kissing her long and deep, filled her with all the feelings he couldn't express, making her a woman in every sense of the word.

Sidalee knew the memory of this day would remain forever. Hank Destry was hers.

Nine

IN HER HOME BEHIND THE MERCANTILE THE NEXT MORNING, Sidalee's sweeping was interrupted by a knock. She set the broom aside and opened the door, surprised to find Stoker Legend on her stoop.

"Good morning. Won't you come in?"

Stoker removed his hat. "I'd like to see the old woman you found, but if this isn't a good time, I'll come back."

Sidalee smiled. "I think a visitor would do Miss Mamie good." She led him into the small parlor, which shrank considerably with his large form, and introduced the two.

Taking a chair, Stoker leaned forward. "You remind me so much of an aunt I used to have. She died many years ago, but I really miss her."

Miss Mamie smiled. "They say we all have twins running around."

"You know, I think that's true." Stoker laughed, then grew serious. "All of my kin have passed on. It's just me and my boys now, and they've all flown the coop. I get so lonely sometimes in my big old house that I think I'm going to go stark raving mad. Do you ever get lonely, Miss Mamie?"

"Oh land sakes, yes. But I have my George now."

"Would you take pity on me and come stay in the headquarters? At least until you get well? It would feel like having my aunt back, and you can give me pointers on running the ranch. I have a feeling you might know something about that."

"I reckon, if it would ease your loneliness." She gave Sidalee a sad glance. "I hate to leave here."

"I'll come to visit often." Sidalee gave her a reassuring hug. "It's not like you're moving to Montana."

"And George?"

"Han—George will always be welcome." Stoker rose. "I'll get a room ready and be back to get you this afternoon."

Sidalee leaned against the door after letting Stoker out. Happy tears trickled down her face. This was going to be a Christmas she'd remember for the rest of her days.

∞

Fat snowflakes floated around Hank as he carried Miss Mamie to the huge barn for the Christmas Eve party. Sidalee strode at his side, making sure to keep the cold from seeping under the warm blanket he'd wrapped around his pretend mother.

"Am I too heavy, George? I can walk, you know," Miss Mamie said.

"You're as light as a feather, Mother." He tightened his arms, wondering how a woman he'd never met had come to mean so much. His glance slid to Sidalee. *Two women*, he amended. Both had changed his life in ways he'd never dreamed back in the darkness of his cell.

Life had a funny way of turning on a man. Just when he was at his very lowest and didn't care if he lived, Sidalee found him and gave him hope and a dream.

Music already filled the night air and anticipation hummed under his skin. Tonight he'd hold Sidalee in his arms and try his best to dance. At any rate, he'd be happy with however this turned out. Three steps from the barn door, a man galloped up on a solid black horse. He was covered in snow, and he had a piece of fur wrapped around his mouth and nose.

Stoker, Houston, and his youngest son, Sam, strode

to meet the horseman. Hank smiled. This must be Luke, home at last.

Sidalee held the door and Hank stepped inside the warm barn with Miss Mamie. He sat his new mother on a chair closest to one of the fires that burned in large clay contraptions spaced along the walls. He'd seen them in Spanish yards, and they worked like an outdoor chimney that kept the fire contained, which was good with children around.

With the exception of Miss Mamie's chair, scattered hay bales provided seating.

At the front, where the ranch hands–turned–musicians played, stood the tallest Christmas tree Hank had ever seen. It had to be at least twenty feet tall. Bare of candles or decorations, the fragrant pine appeared to hold its breath in anticipation of something grand.

He glanced around at all the people, a good portion of whom were already dancing, and part of him wanted to run. He wasn't sure about this. Him and crowds didn't go together.

"You look like a scared jackrabbit. Relax. Try to smile." Sidalee took his arm. "Let's sit down for a bit beside Miss Mamie and let you get comfortable. These people are your friends." She let him remove her coat and he took advantage, letting his hands brush her shoulders taking it off.

The first glimpse of her dress dried the spit in his mouth. The gown fell slightly off her shoulders, made of red and green fabric with gold splashes woven throughout. "You're breathtaking."

Her wide smile put a twinkle in her eyes. "Thank you, Hank."

"Now, you two don't have to keep me company," Miss Mamie scolded, waving her arm. "Get on out there and dance."

"We will a little later, Mother." Hank didn't sit until Sidalee did.

They no more than got seated on a hay bale before a lot of the ranch hands wandered up to speak and to thank Hank for his help in making Christmas special for them. In some instances, they introduced him to their wives or girlfriends.

"See?" Sidalee said. "Their friendship is real."

"I was simply doing my job. Didn't think it was anything special."

"It meant the world to them, Hank. A cowboy's life is very lonely, with family often living a long way off. Sometimes they don't get together but once every couple of years." She leaned close. "See the woman in the pretty pink dress dancing with that cowboy?"

He followed her eyes. "They look really young."

"She gave birth a month ago and their baby almost didn't make it. But here they are, ready to celebrate."

Stoker and his sons entered with Houston's and Sam's pretty wives. Hank had met the women the previous day and liked them both. If that man who rode in was the third son, he hung back behind his father, removing his black leather gloves. Maybe he didn't like crowds any better than Hank.

Hank stood as Stoker aimed the group toward him.

"Thought you should meet the man you worked so hard to find. Hank, meet Luke—my boy," Stoker boomed in his commanding voice.

"Hank, thanks for tracking me down." Luke shook his hand. "It was probably just a job, but it meant everything to me. I don't get to come very often."

"Glad to help." Hank met the dark eyes of the mysterious man and saw the deep sadness and pain that Sidalee had mentioned. The low-slung gun around his hips wasn't there for appearance. Luke was a gunslinger and had more in common with Hank than he'd ever imagined. "I hope you plan on a long visit. Your father misses you."

A tiny grin flickered then faded as Luke's gaze lit on Stoker, who'd moved to chat with Miss Mamie. "Maybe one day I can come and stay. For now, it's not healthy for him or my brothers."

"You remember Sidalee?" Hank asked, drawing her into the conversation.

"Of course." Luke lifted her hand to his lips. "Always a pleasure, Miss Sidalee. I think you've gotten even prettier than the last time I saw you."

A pretty blush stained Sidalee's cheeks. "Luke, you're a silver-tongued devil. It's good to have you home. Will you stay awhile?"

"Can't. Too much—" Luke turned when Stoker called. "Looks like I need to go." He thanked Hank again and moved to join his father.

"I see what you mean, Sidalee," Hank said. "Luke is lost. I hope he finds what he's looking for."

He'd wanted to tell Luke he'd fight beside him if he ever needed him to. They'd obviously both ridden fifty miles of hard road. But he'd saved his words for another time.

The band struck up a waltz. Hank turned to her. "Care to try to dance?"

With the light casting red and golden glints in her hair, Sidalee floated into his arms. That same soft light brought out the blue of her eyes as she tilted her face to meet his gaze. The lady—his lady—had put a spell on him.

Hank had trouble swallowing. She was all he'd ever dreamed of finding. He tightened his arm around her and murmured against her hair, "Who knew when I landed in your bed that it would lead to this? I've waited a long time for this moment, and I pity anyone who tries to dance with you."

A smile teased her lips. "Will you fight them for me?"

Hank tucked her hand against his heart. "I'll beat them to a bloody pulp."

"Oh my!"

"You light a fire inside me. I can't sleep, eat, or work for thinking about you. You've ruined me, lady."

"If that's a complaint—"

"I can assure you, it's not that." He pressed his lips to her forehead and held her as he would a priceless treasure, which she was to him.

They swayed from side to side, lost in each other, and had no idea the music had stopped until Stoker's booming voice penetrated Hank's daze.

"I'm sorry to interrupt, but it's only for a bit. We'll have lots more dancing after we trim the tree."

Hank broke his hold and turned, feeling heat flood his face. "Sorry, boss."

Stoker chuckled. "I was young once too. But now that I have everyone's attention, I have a few words. This Christmas is very special to me because I have all my sons here for the first time. That wouldn't have been possible without Hank Destry's perseverance. I know he helped a good many of you too. Let's give him a round of applause."

Hating the attention, Hank wanted to duck his head. But instead, he raised an arm and thanked them.

"This Christmas is extra special for another reason. I want you all to meet a woman who reminds me of a favorite aunt I used to have. She's staying with me for a bit." He helped Miss Mamie from the chair next to him. "This is Miss Mamie Tabor. That big old house is less lonesome now."

People whooped and hollered. The old woman smiled happily, but her panic-stricken eyes searched for Hank. When she located him, she was all right. Hank waved and blew her a kiss.

After the noise settled down, Stoker went on, "Now, let's get back to business. It's been a long-held tradition here on the Lone Star to trim the Christmas tree together. As a family. Because that's what we are. This ranch wouldn't prosper without every single one of you, and thank God I'm smart enough to know it. The decorations are all here." He pointed where Sam, Houston, and Luke were opening boxes. "Let's make this tree the biggest and best we've ever had."

"Does he do this every Christmas?" Hank asked.

Sidalee grinned. "Yep. Do you see what you've become a part of? This tradition makes us all stronger. A lot of the men here are far from family. Some, like us, have no family. Celebrating together helps fill those voids." She tugged on his hand. "Come on."

Overcome with emotion, Hank stared as everyone rushed forward like excited children. He'd never seen anything like this or known a place like the Lone Star even existed.

He followed Sidalee but stopped to speak to Miss Mamie first. "Are you getting tired? Too cold?"

"I'm perfect, son." She took his hand and laid it on her cheek. "Everything is wonderful because you're here. Please don't ever go away and leave me again, George."

"I won't, Mother. Are you comfortable at headquarters with Stoker?"

She pulled him down. "It's real nice and all, but I miss Sidalee's cozy house. That bed is like sleeping on a cloud."

"I agree…uh, not that I know. I'll have to take your word for it." He lovingly brushed back some wispy silver strands that reminded him of his grandmother's hair. "Tell me when you get tired, and I'll take you back to your room."

"I ain't going to miss the tree lighting. Will you sit beside me, son?"

"I wouldn't dream of sitting anywhere else." He searched for Sidalee and contentment washed over him when he spotted her. "I'm going to help decorate so we can finish faster. Send someone for me if you need anything."

The old widow cackled and pointed. "Look at those fool dogs. They're trying to dance."

Following her gaze, Hank groaned. Beau and a cute little dog Houston had called Sissie turned around and around on their hind legs.

Hank rolled his eyes. He was going to have to have a talk with that Lothario.

Giving Miss Mamie a nod, Hank grabbed as many candle holders and as much tinsel as he could carry. With probably fifty or sixty people lending a hand, it didn't take long to finish.

Hank had no trouble locating Sidalee, because his gaze never left her, and asked, "What happens next?"

"We form two circles, an outer and inner, so all the people can fit. Then we sing while Stoker and his sons light the candles on the tree. I noticed you talking to Miss Mamie. Is she all right?"

"She seems to feel good. I promised we'd sit with her. I hope you didn't have any plans." He should've asked her first and would've, if she'd been there. He wasn't going to make a habit of speaking for her. For years, he'd watched other men do that and it belittled their wives. *Wives.* The thought of Sidalee maybe someday agreeing to be his *wife* sent a rush of warmth through him.

"There's no place I'd rather be. You should know that by now." Sidalee ran her fingers across his jaw.

"When this is over, I want to go someplace to talk." He had lots on his mind, and this was the night for it.

While the people were still forming a large circle and holding hands, Hank lifted Miss Mamie's chair and sat her in the line with the rest. No one should be left out at Christmas. After the opening chords of "Silent Night," everyone began to sing—one voice, one grateful heart, one spirit of friendship.

One candle at a time, the Christmas tree came to life. The tinsel glittered like stars under the glow. Hank didn't think he'd ever forget this moment. He'd yearned for a place to belong with every fiber of his being—one place where he'd be welcome—and he'd finally found it one snowy night.

They continued the song until Stoker and his sons finished and joined them in the outer circle for several more verses. Hank's gaze went to Luke. It could've been the light that made Hank think tears filled the gunslinger's eyes, but he didn't think so. Tears also filled Stoker's as he looked at his boys.

Damn, Hank missed his father. If he could just have one more day with him, and his mother too.

All too soon the celebration ended. Hank asked Sidalee to wait until he carried Miss Mamie home.

She grinned. "You must be crazy to think I'd let you go without me."

He helped her into her coat, and after bundling Miss Mamie up good and proper, they carried her to her bed. Sidalee got her into a nightgown and tucked her in. Then Hank went in to give her a good-night kiss. He stared down at the frail woman who needed a reason for living, and warmth flowed through him, thinking that *he'd* given her that. It didn't matter that he wasn't her son by blood. He was, where it counted most. He kissed her cheek and promised to see her in the morning for breakfast.

"Wait just a minute." Miss Mamie pointed to a drawer. "George, open that and get out a leather pouch."

Hank glanced at Sidalee and complied.

Miss Mamie took out two rocks and handed them to him. "For your trouble. They aren't much, but I want you to have them. Your father and I used to pretend they were gold."

Taking them, Hank held the rocks to the light, turning them this way and that. "They're not gold, Mother—they're raw silver. Where did you get these?"

"In New Mexico territory, where we lived for a time. Albert said they weren't worth anything. Why?"

"Mother, you're sitting on a fortune, if you have more."

"Are you sure, Hank?" Sidalee asked.

"I'm positive. The warden put me to work digging silver out of a hillside. I know what it looks like."

Miss Mamie leaned on an elbow. "I have two large sacks of these in my old wagon where it broke down. I'm sure they're still there."

"When this weather clears up, I'll ride out and get them." Hank put the silver back in the leather pouch. "Hang on to this. You're rich, Mother."

Sidalee patted Miss Mamie's leg. "What do you think about that?"

"Take the rocks and make a wedding ring, George. I have a suspicion you might need one." Miss Mamie rested her head on the pillow. "I found my son. I'm already the richest woman on earth."

cᐁ⌒ᐁ⌒

Outside the house, with snow gently falling around them, Hank took Sidalee in his arms. The embers he'd banked earlier flared, sending hunger like he'd never known through him.

Sidalee tilted her head back to meet his lips and leaned into him, her mouth slightly parted.

Hank let his fingers trail down the column of her slender throat. The kiss shattered everything inside him. For a moment the world silenced and stopped turning. They were safe in a cocoon where nothing else existed— not time or space or other people. Just the two of them and this impossible love they'd found.

He broke the kiss with a murmured, "Lady, I love you. I can finally say the words."

A grin curved her lips. "I was in no hurry. You

showed me how you felt, and actions are far more lasting than words."

"There'll be no need to sit on me to keep me in your bed, or mine. I'm saying that I want you there beside me—under the covers this time. For real. No pretending. And this will be for all of time until it runs out." He took her hand and tapped a message on her palm. "Do you know what I just asked?"

She tilted her head to one side. "Are you proposing?"

"I'm not doing a very good job of it if you have to ask," he growled teasingly. "If you want me to do it proper on one knee and all, we'll have to get where it's warmer."

"Oh, Hank." She took his hand and tapped out a reply. "Do you get my answer?"

"To be clear—you are saying yes?"

"Yes." She laughed. "Yes, I'll marry you. I'll sleep beside you for the rest of my life. Just one request."

"Anything."

"I have to keep my deluxe Queen Anne bed, model number 24."

He lifted her high and swung her around, whooping with happy laughter. Lowering her, he found her lips for a searing kiss that left no doubt about the depth of his love.

Everything he'd lost in the dark gloom of a prison cell, he found here on the Lone Star Ranch one snowy Christmas Eve where family, tradition, and love abounded.

He was finally home.

About the Author

Linda Broday resides in the panhandle of Texas on the Llano Estacado. At a young age, she discovered a love for storytelling, history, and anything pertaining to the Old West. There's something about Stetsons, boots, and tall rugged cowboys that get her fired up! A *New York Times* and *USA Today* bestselling author, Linda has won many awards, including the prestigious National Readers' Choice Award and the Texas Gold Award. Visit her at lindabroday.com.

A TEXAS
RANGER FOR
CHRISTMAS

A MATCH MADE IN TEXAS NOVELLA

—◆—

Margaret Brownley

One

Two-Time, Texas
November, 1879

SADIE CARNES SENSED TROUBLE THE MOMENT SHE STEPPED foot outside her farmhouse. Holding her six-month-old son in her arms, she anxiously surveyed her property. She had good reason to worry. A pack of wolves had been spotted the day before, and only last week a black bear was seen lurking by the woodshed. For now, at least, all looked calm—except for the dark clouds gathered on the distant horizon.

Convinced it was just the threat of an early winter storm making her uneasy, she sat her son in his wicker carriage next to the clothesline, where she could keep a close eye on him. After tucking a warm blanket around him, she handed him a piece of hardtack to chew.

"There you go," she said, ruffling his wispy blond hair. His toothless smile made her sigh with motherly pride. Adam was the best thing that had ever happened to her. She couldn't believe that something so precious could come out of what had been the worst mistake of her life.

Gripped with a fierce need to protect him, she scanned the yard again. Only after every shadow had passed inspection did she fetch the basket of wet wash off the porch.

Just as she pegged a towel on the clothesline, she noticed a cloud of dust on the road running parallel to her property. Watching with narrowed eyes, she hoped the single horseman would pass her by. No such luck. Instead he rode his horse beneath the rusty iron archway leading up to her farm.

Swiping a strand of blond hair away from her face, she chewed on her bottom lip.

"That better not be another bill collector," she muttered. The fool tax man had taken the last of her egg money. Before him, the general store owner had insisted she pay in full before making any more purchases. Even the druggist had demanded she make good on what she owed before he would sell her tooth balm for her teething son. Well, a pox on all of them!

The horseman kept coming. Astride his brown gelding, he looked larger than life. Though he appeared to be in no hurry, Sadie sensed an urgency in him that put her nerves on edge. Face half-hidden beneath a wide-brimmed hat, he looked sober as an old bone. The Colts holstered at his hips looked like they meant business too, as did the shiny cartridges circling his waist in a looped leather belt.

"That sure ain't no creditor," she said beneath her breath. "And he sure don't look like no peddler either." As encouraging as that was, her relief lasted for only as long as it took for the man's true identity to dawn on her. As much as she hated to think it, his erect carriage marked him as a Texas Ranger. The carbine slung on the side of his saddle seemed to confirm it.

A shiver rushed through her that had nothing to do with the cool breeze. Only one reason a ranger would be heading her way, and it sure in blazes wasn't to bring good news.

Willing her knees not to buckle, she balled her hands by her side. Her heart was beating so fast she could hardly breathe; her mouth felt like it was stuffed with cotton.

Greeting her with a finger to the brim of his hat, the stranger dismounted. Dressed in dark trousers, flannel shirt, and knee-high boots, he looked just as tall and commanding on the ground as he did in the saddle.

He wrapped the reins around the clothesline post and stepped in front of her, spurs jingling. He glanced at her son before turning back to her. "I'm looking for Mrs. Carnes," he said, his blue-eyed gaze sharp as an arrow.

She braced herself with a ragged breath. "You found her."

A muscle tightened at his jaw. "I'm Captain Cole Bradshaw, Texas Ranger." He studied her for a moment, and she had the uneasy feeling that he didn't miss a thing. Not the patches on her calico dress, or the stained apron, or even the messy strands of hair that had strayed from her bun. Feeling self-conscious, she hid her callused hands in the folds of her skirt.

"Well, get on with it," she snapped. Bad news was best delivered quickly.

His eyes widened briefly before he spoke. "I'm sorry to inform you that your husband, Richard Carnes, was killed in the line of duty."

She gulped back the bile in her throat. It wasn't the first time she'd heard those words. At the age of ten, she'd been told the same thing about her Texas Ranger pa. Still, familiarity didn't soften the impact. Swaying slightly, she clasped her hands to her chest.

He caught her by the elbow. "You all right, ma'am?"

Nodding mutely, she forced a breath and forbade herself to faint. Though his touch was strangely comforting, she nonetheless pulled away.

For a long moment, neither of them said a word. His eyes, however, spoke volumes as he gazed past her to the farmhouse, with its peeling paint and sagging porch. The last norther had done a number on the roof. What few shingles remained curled up as if waiting to hitch a ride on the next strong wind. The barn was in no better shape.

He turned his gaze back to her. "Just so you know, ma'am, we gave your husband a proper burial."

She stared at him and said nothing.

His forehead creased. "That yours?" he asked with a nod at her son.

It seemed like a strange question. Who else would he belong to? The nearest neighbor was more than a mile away. "He's mine," she said.

Something that looked like sympathy flickered in the depth of the captain's eyes, and she grimaced. The last thing she wanted from him—from anyone—was pity.

Pivoting toward his horse, he reached into his saddlebags. After a moment he turned and handed her a brown-wrapped package. "Your husband's belongings, ma'am." She heard him inhale. "I'm afraid his horse didn't survive the gun battle that killed him." After a beat, he added, "I'll make arrangements to ship his saddle to you."

She clenched her jaw. A million questions flitted through her head. "Was it...Indians?" The Texas-Indian wars had ended, but last month Comanche renegades had raided a ranch up north in the Panhandle.

He shook his head. "No, ma'am."

As if to discourage further questioning, he placed a small leather pouch in her hand. "My men took up a collection for you and"—he slanted his head toward the carriage—"your son."

Her back stiffened. The business about her son was a bald-faced lie, but curiosity kept her from calling him on it. She set the package next to her wash basket and fingered the bulging pouch he'd handed her. It felt heavy with coins. Though it was an answer to a prayer, she didn't want his charity. The Texas Rangers had robbed her of her father and now her husband. No amount of money could make up for such losses. Just as she was about to hand the pouch back, her son cooed, reminding her that necessity came before pride or even animosity.

Reluctantly, she tucked the pouch into the pocket of her apron. Since the ranger was watching her, she directed his attention back to her son. "His name is Adam. He's six months old."

"Nice-looking boy." He hesitated as if sensing her disapproval. "I'm sorry for your loss, Mrs. Carnes," he said at last. "Please, if there's anything I can do…"

She refused to give in to the tears burning her eyes. "Can you bring my husband back?"

"Would if I could, ma'am." His gaze traveled from the barn to the house and back to her. "If there's nothing else…"

She shook her head.

"Well, then…" He gave her an apologetic look. "I've got a long journey ahead. Better get a move on." With a tip of his hat he untied his horse, jabbed a foot into a stirrup, and mounted in one easy move. Astride his saddle, he gazed down on her. "Sorry I had to bring you such bad tidings."

She drew in her breath. "Me too."

With one more glance at the house and barn, he tugged on his reins and rode away. She watched him until she could no longer hold back the tears. The wash forgotten, she reached for her son and made a quick dash across the yard and into the house.

Two

The sign on the door of the Silver Spur saloon forbade floozies, suffragists, Methodists, and other troublemakers from entering the establishment.

Since it said nothing about Texas Rangers, Cole strode inside and bellied up to the polished oak bar. Still early in the day, the saloon was empty except for two other patrons—one a drunk slumped over a table, the other a bearded man the size of a bear.

The sound of distant gunfire failed to merit so much as a flicker of curiosity by the saloon keeper. Hammered and Bear didn't react either; the one kept snoring and the other kept working on the bottle of whisky in front of him.

For such a small town, Two-Time sure did have attitude. Already, Cole had witnessed more brawls on Main Street than could be found in the Huntsville penitentiary. Even the dogs roaming the streets seemed more ornery than most.

He rested a dusty boot on the gold railing.

The proprietor swiped a cloth across the bar. Bear had called him Stretch, and it was easy to see why. He towered over Cole's six-foot height by a good four inches. Now he looked Cole up and down.

"Haven't seen you in these parts."

"Just passing through," Cole said. Actually, he'd expected to be on the way to headquarters in Austin by now, but at the last minute had decided to spend the night in town and get an early start in the morning. He wasn't feeling all that well. Maybe he was coming down with something. Or maybe he was just tired. It had been a hard day. He couldn't stop thinking of Mrs. Carnes and her little boy. He felt sorry for the woman, and not just because she was a widow.

She'd looked exhausted, her hands callused. Keeping up a farm that size was no easy task, especially with a young child. Most women in her shoes would have collapsed upon hearing of a husband's death, but not her. She bore the news with the same sort of grit Cole expected from his men.

"What can I do for you?" Stretch asked.

"Just water," Cole said. He was hot and his mouth dry.

Stretch placed a glass of water in front of him. "Much obliged," Cole said, and took a long sip. The cool liquid quenched his thirst but did nothing to alleviate his dark thoughts.

It was his job to keep his men safe. Not to have seen the ambush coming was pure carelessness. He'd been warned that the Carpenter brothers were tricky and would do anything to keep from getting caught. He should have known they'd pull a trick like that. Now a child was without his father and a woman without her man.

Cole reached into his pocket for his watch and grimaced. It hurt to move his arm. Hurt like the dickens. The doctor had warned him not to exert himself, but he'd wanted to deliver the news to Carnes's widow in person. It was the least he could do.

He waited for the pain in his shoulder to subside before asking, "What time you got?"

"That depends."

Cole clamped down on his jaw. He was in no mood for games. "I just want to know the time so I can set my watch."

Stretch shrugged. "Like I said, that depends."

Cole gave the man a fish-eyed stare. "On what?"

"On whether you go by Lockwood time or Farrell time."

Bear set his empty glass on the bar and reached for the half-filled bottle. "That's how the town got its name, Two-Time."

Stretch tossed his rag aside. "If you know what's good for you, you'll go by Lockwood time, but stay clear of his three daughters. When it comes to them, the old man's a tiger."

"I'll keep that in mind. So I ask again, what time is it?"

Stretch pulled out his watch and flipped the lid open with his thumb. "Three thirty-five."

Cole set his watch and hoped that his next question would have a less complicated answer. "Do you happen to know Mrs. Carnes?"

"Yeah, I know her from church. Haven't seen her around much, since her baby was born."

No one in town knew of Carnes's death, and it wasn't Cole's place to break the news. That was up to the widow to do whenever she was good and ready. "Does she have family around?"

"You mean other than her no-good husband? Not that I know of."

Cole rubbed the back of his neck. No-good husband? Carnes hadn't been his best ranger, but neither had he been the worst.

"I take it there's no love lost between you and Carnes," Cole said.

"The man owes me money. So whadaya think?" Stretch narrowed his eyes. "Who are you, anyway? Why you askin' all these questions?"

"Just curious, is all."

"Yeah, well, here in Two-Time, curiosity can git you in a whole peck of trouble."

Cole flipped a coin onto the bar. "I'll keep that in mind."

Loud voices greeted Cole as he stepped outside, along with another round of gunfire.

Hand on a holstered pistol, Cole stood on the board-walk and stared at the mayhem in front of him.

A group of women marched down the street, carrying signs demanding the right to vote. Since they held up traffic, the suffragists were partly to blame for the curses that rent the air.

Two men shot out of the saloon across the way. Rolling off the boardwalk and onto the packed dirt road, they battered each other like angry rams. From farther down the street came the sound of gunfire, setting off a chorus of barking dogs.

Cole shook his head. He'd traveled through some pretty wild towns, but this one took the cake. Where was the sheriff? Did they even have one?

Since the road was blocked, Cole left his tethered horse and started on foot toward the hotel. After securing a room, he'd stable his horse. It was still afternoon, but he was dog-tired and his shoulder throbbed to high heaven. A good meal and some shut-eye should put him in good stead for tomorrow's journey.

As he passed the general store, something caught his eye. Though Christmas was still a few weeks away, the window was decorated with a tree surrounded by gaily wrapped packages. But it was the little wooden horse that caught his fancy. Carved out of pine, the horse sat on a wagon that had four wheels and a string for pulling.

The toy reminded him of something.

He slapped his forehead and groaned. He'd forgotten about the little wooden soldier Carnes had whittled. He walked back to his horse and checked his saddlebags, finding the carving at the bottom of one.

Holding it in the palm of his hand, he tried to decide what to do. The widow Carnes was still very much on his mind. She and her little boy. Her husband had carved the figurine, and no doubt she would want it. He could mail it, of course, along with the saddle, but somehow that seemed cold and impersonal.

With a shake of his head he stuffed the wooden soldier into his saddlebag. Shut-eye was what he needed right now. The rest he would figure out in the morning.

⚬∞⚬

Sadie had just finished giving Adam his morning bath when the chickens started making a god-awful racket.

"Oh, no! Not again." She placed Adam in his carriage where he would be safe, grabbed her broom from the kitchen, and dashed outside.

Panic reigned in the hen yard. Chickens squawked and ran in frantic circles, flapping wings and tossing feathers. At first Sadie couldn't see what had them all up in arms. Then a strong musky smell drifted through the air, telling her that the old fox was back even before she spotted a flash of reddish-brown fur behind a bale of hay. Fortunately, he hadn't yet made it into the chicken yard.

Wielding her broom—and wishing she'd grabbed her shotgun instead—she started after him. She wasn't about to lose more precious egg-layers to that furry thief. "Scat! You yella-bellied scoundrel!"

The fox dodged under a bush. Crouching low, Sadie peered beneath the leafy shrub. Yellow eyes stared back, followed by a low growl and bared teeth.

She brought her broom down hard and the fox raced away. But once started, she couldn't seem to stop, and a knot of emotions broke loose. She raised the broom over her head and slammed it down again and again. The animal forgotten, she continued beating the bush.

"Dang you, Richard Carnes!" Feelings she had held back for more than a year spewed out of her like wildfire. "I begged you not to go. You shoulda listened to me!"

Long after the fox had wiggled under a hole in the fence and vanished in the chaparral, she vented her anger and frustrations on that hapless bush. Richard had promised to quit the rangers if she married him. Always wanted to have a family, he'd said. Always wanted to own a farm. The man had a way with fancy talk. He knew what to say and how to say it and, fool that she was, she had taken him at his word.

If he'd kept his promise, he would still be alive. Adam would have a father, and she wouldn't be standing in her backyard, acting like a madwoman.

She beat that bush until it was ground to a pulp. She was breathing hard and still she kept wielding that broom. All the frustration and anger bottled inside gushed out of her like hot lava.

"I think you can stop now, ma'am."

The male voice startled her and she whirled about. The ranger stood a short distance away, holding Adam in his arms. His gaze dropped to the broom she held like a weapon. "I don't think that bush will give you any more trouble."

Embarrassed to be caught in a fit of temper, she lowered the broom, but nothing could be done about her flaring red face. What a frightful sight she must look, her hair falling down her back in tangled waves and her hands and face covered in dust.

"W-what are you doing here?" she asked.

"I forgot to give you something." He slanted his head toward the house. "The front door was open, and this little fella was airing his lungs."

She moistened her lips beneath the ranger's steady gaze. "A fox was after my chickens," she said.

His gaze traveled to the pile of crumbled leaves. "I guess you showed it," he said. Adam began to fuss, and the captain jiggled him up and down.

"He's ready for his morning nap," she said. "Would you mind waiting for me inside? I'll just be a minute."

"Take your time." Holding Adam in one arm, he walked back to the house with long, easy strides.

In an effort to calm both the chickens and herself, Sadie tossed a handful of corn on the ground. She grabbed a shovel from the barn and filled in the hole under the fence, for all the good it would do. The fox dug more holes than a gravedigger. Picking up her broom, she leaned it against the barn. Then she straightened her shoulders with a sigh and marched to the house.

After wiping her feet on the rug, she stomped through the back door to the kitchen. Adam's laughter drifted from the parlor and, despite her harried condition, she couldn't help but smile.

She splashed cold water on her face at the kitchen sink. After drying herself off, she gathered up her hair and twisted it into a bun, pinning it to the back of her head.

Her apron was soiled, but it hid the patches on her dress. For that reason, it stayed.

She found Captain Bradshaw on the parlor sofa, her son on his lap. Even seated, the ranger's presence seemed to crowd the room.

"Everything okay?" he asked.

"For now," she said, lifting Adam off the ranger's lap. "You certainly have a way with children. He doesn't usually go to strangers."

"Maybe he's just a good judge of character."

She met the ranger's gaze. "Maybe." Straddling her son on her hip, she studied the man's rugged features. Now that she thought about it, he had a nice face. Some might even say a kind face. His sun-bronzed skin was the color of tanned leather, and his eyes were as blue as the bluebonnets that popped up in the spring. She liked that he was clean-shaven and his brown hair neatly trimmed. Liked even more the way he smiled, though his smiles were for Adam, not her.

Embarrassed to be caught staring, she jerked her gaze

away. The man stood for everything she hated, and she'd best not forget it.

"If you don't mind waiting, I'll just put him down for his nap. I won't be long."

He said something, but she'd already left the room. Fled the room, more like it. She was still embarrassed—horrified—at having been caught in a fit of rage. What must the ranger think of her?

Reaching the safety of her bedroom, she laid Adam in his bassinet. The boy had almost outgrown his temporary bed and would soon have to sleep in the iron cot in the other room.

She covered him with a blanket and rubbed his forehead until his eyes drifted shut. Smiling, she tiptoed away. With a quick glance in the mirror, she braced herself with a sigh before rejoining her guest.

"Can I get you something, Mr.…Captain?"

"No, thank you. I can't stay long. I'm leaving on the afternoon train."

"You said you forgot to give me something."

He stood and reached for the little wooden soldier on the end table. "Your husband wanted his son to have this."

She stared at the carving in his hand and something snapped inside her. There was nothing she hated worse than lies, and this was a bald-faced lie if she'd ever heard one. "You have some nerve coming here, pretendin' to know what my husband wanted."

He reared back, brow furrowed. "Whew, now. I apologize if I offended you in some way, ma'am. Carnes…your husband…was always whittling." He glanced at the two wooden dogs on the windowsill. "But I guess I don't have to tell you that." When she made no effort to take the wooden soldier from him, he stood it on the end table next to the oil lamp.

She regretted her hastily spoken words. Under normal circumstances she might have felt sorry for the man.

Telling a woman her husband was dead couldn't have been easy, but she was having a hard time conjuring up sympathy for anyone associated with the Texas Rangers.

Forcing herself to breathe, she smoothed her apron and tried to calm her tense nerves. His presence only reminded her of Richard in the worst possible way.

He glanced at the door as if measuring the distance before he could make his escape. "I best get a move on." Grimacing, he mopped his forehead with a handkerchief. Though the fire had died down, the ranger looked flushed and beads of sweat dotted his forehead. "First, could I trouble you for a glass of water?" No sooner were the words out of his mouth than he swayed.

Hand extended, she started toward him. "Are you all right?" she asked in alarm.

He nodded and tugged on the collar of his shirt. "Just a little—" He seemed to be having trouble breathing and the color drained from his face.

"Maybe you better sit for a spell," she said.

He opened his mouth to say something. Instead, he swayed like a windblown tree and, before her startled eyes, toppled to the floor at her feet.

Three

THE SOUND OF GUNFIRE STIRRED COLE INTO ACTION. HE reached for his gun, but came up empty. His Colt was missing. So for that matter was his holster. He opened his mouth to warn his men, but nothing came out.

More gunfire. This time his body jerked and his eyes flew open. Battling his way through the fog, he struggled to make sense of his surroundings.

He blinked. Was that an infant's bed on the far wall? What the…?

He closed his eyes and tried to think. A vision of a pretty round face with big blue eyes and a pretty pink mouth came to mind. Shaking his head, he waited for the fog to clear before battling off the confining bedcovers. By George, it *was* an infant's bed!

Grimacing, he sat up slowly and swung his legs over the edge of the mattress. Another shot rent the air. This time his instincts kicked in and he rose unsteadily to his feet.

He staggered around on rubbery legs, looking for his guns. Unable to find them, he made his way from the room and through the parlor to the kitchen. Hands on the counter, the walls, the cookstove to keep from falling, he followed the sound of gunfire to the mudroom and cracked the back door open.

Blinded by the bright sunshine, he peered through the crack with one eye before swinging the door open. A blast of cold air struck his bare chest, and the last of the fog cleared from his head. That was when it hit him. Not only were his guns missing, but so were his trousers. He was wearing his long johns, but nothing else.

He spotted the widow, her honey-blond hair ablaze in the bright golden sun as she fired her shotgun.

Stepping outside, he lumbered to the edge of the porch. "I think you can stop shooting, ma'am."

At the sound of his voice, she lowered her gun and spun around.

"I reckon whatever you were shooting at is in the next county by now."

She looked like she meant business, even with her lowered shotgun. Her gaze lit upon him with a frown. "That old fox was back. Won't leave my chickens alone." She started toward him. "You should be in bed."

He squinted against the yellow glare to get a better look at her. "I was just telling myself the same thing," he said.

He swayed and he heard her gasp. "You better go back inside. If you pass out again, you'll be stuck here on the porch till tomorrow. I sure in blazes can't pick you up by myself."

He frowned. "What happens tomorrow?"

"That's when my friend Scooter comes to help out. His father owns the bakery. He's the only one strong enough to carry you. Mr. Watkins tried, but he has a bad back. Mrs. Compton wanted to help, but she's expectin' her tenth child, and I wasn't gonna take the chance on her havin' the baby here." After a beat, she added, "Mr. Peterson couldn't lift you either, on account of his wooden leg."

Cole stared at her. "How long was I out?"

"Three days."

"Three—!" He rubbed his forehead. It didn't seem possible.

"Yeah, but don't go worryin' none. Scooter saw to it that your modesty stayed intact."

He studied her. "I wasn't worried."

She eyed him with a thoughtful frown. "Got yourself a bad infection. I'm no expert, but I'd say you owe the hole in your shoulder to a bullet. Probably from the same gun that shot my husband." After a beat she added, "Sure hope you returned the favor."

"I tried, ma'am. I'm sorry to say...the killers got away. But don't you worry none. The Texas Rangers always get their man." He fingered the bandage at his shoulder. Something felt sticky. Thinking it was blood, he drew his hand away and stared at it.

"Sugar," she said, as if to guess his thoughts. "Can't beat sugar for drawing out the poisons."

"You did that?" he asked. "You doctored me up?"

She shrugged. "No one else 'round to do it."

"I'm...mighty obliged to you. Didn't mean to add to your troubles." He still couldn't believe it: three days. "My horse?"

She pointed her thumb over her shoulder. "In the barn." Stomping the mud off her boots, she started up the porch steps toward him. "Like I said, we better get you inside before you go passing out again."

He grimaced and willed his rubbery knees not to buckle. "I've got to get to Austin," he said, surprised to find that even talking was an effort. "That's where my company is camped. They're waiting for me."

She stood her shotgun in the corner of the porch. "Right now, you don't look so good, mister. You might not even make it as far as the bedroom."

Feeling light-headed, he thought better than to waste his energy arguing with her. She grabbed him by the arm, her grip surprisingly strong. Ever so slowly she walked him into the house. He wasn't used to having to depend on someone. The fact that she was such a small package—barely reaching his shoulders—made him feel all the more helpless.

Slipping an arm around his waist, she steered him through the kitchen and down the hall to the bedroom. He fell groaning onto the straw mattress, breathing hard.

She pulled the quilt over him. "I'll get you some coffee."

Coffee sounded good. Still, business had to come first. He rubbed his forehead in an effort to clear his thoughts. "I need you to do somethin' for me." His voice was low, so low that she had to bend over to hear him. She smelled of soap and something else that reminded him of a spring meadow. Distracted by the pleasing fragrance, he forced himself to concentrate.

"I need you to send a telegram to my men."

Drawing back, her eyes flashed with blue fire and her hands balled at her waist. "Well, mister, here's the thing. I've got a child to take care of, a cow to milk, butter to churn, laundry to wash, and a sick man to feed. Frankly, I don't have time to drive into town."

"Take my horse." The swaybacked mare he'd spotted in the corral could barely stand on all fours. "My horse's name is Hercules, and he'll get you there and back in no time."

"Your horse? You're joking, right? What am I supposed to do with Adam? Tie him to your horse's tail?"

"Leave him here with me."

Her eyes widened. "*You?* Look at you. You can barely stand. And what if he needs changing?"

"I've changed the ways of some of the most ornery and cantankerous outlaws this side of the Big Muddy." The fact that he did it with the help of a well-aimed gun was beside the point. "I reckon I can change a child's britches."

Doubt clouded her face. "What if you pass out again?"

"I won't."

"You might."

"I said I won't."

She drew in her breath and stared down at him. "Why

should I believe anything a Texas Ranger says? You've already lied to me twice."

Scratching his temple, he frowned. He wasn't used to people questioning his honesty. "If that's true, ma'am, then it must have happened when I was out of my head. I assure you, I'm normally a man of my word. When I say I'm gonna do something, I do it, and that includes takin' care of your son. All I'm asking is that you ride into town, send a telegram, and ride back." When she said nothing, he added, "I'll pay you for your time." That got her attention, or at least made her look less opposed to the idea. "So what do you say?"

"I'll think about it."

"Fair enough. While you're thinking, I'd appreciate that coffee you mentioned and maybe some grub. That is, if it's not too much bother. The sooner I get my strength back, the sooner I can get outta your hair."

Turning to leave, she stopped at the doorway and glanced over her shoulder. "Anyone else I should notify? A wife?"

He shook his head. "Not married."

She studied him for a long moment. "If you're smart, mister, you'll keep it that way."

∞

Sadie felt guilty for leaving her son with a man who was little more than a stranger.

It was the first time she'd been away from Adam since the day he was born. It wasn't that she didn't trust the ranger to take care of him. But now that Adam was beginning to crawl, he could wear out a string of mules. He certainly wore her out. Who knew what effect he'd have on the wobbly-kneed captain? The thought made her urge Hercules to go faster. The sooner she conducted her business, the sooner she could return home.

Still, it felt good riding into town on the ranger's fine

horse, the sun at her back and the wind in her hair. As she continued down Main Street to the telegraph office, she imagined everyone looking at her. She could almost guess what they were thinking. *What is Sadie Carnes doing on such a fine horse?*

The thought brought a smile to her face, and she threw her shoulders back another notch. She might look like a pauper, but by George, she didn't feel like one, and the shiny gold eagle the ranger had paid her was partly responsible. She hadn't wanted to take his money but he insisted. Told her to consider it payment for room and board.

"Buy something for Adam," he'd said. "Or something pretty for yourself."

Pretty. She tried recalling if she'd ever bought anything pretty and couldn't. Any store-bought purchases were out of necessity practical and cheap. Fabric to make clothes for herself and Adam. Cheap cuts of meat for stew. Sacks of flour. Bags of rice.

At the telegraph office, the youthful dispatcher greeted her with a nod. Nervously, she sidled up to the counter. She'd never sent a telegram. Had no reason to. Couldn't have afforded to even if she did.

The dispatcher must have sensed her hesitation, because he set pen and paper in front of her. "Just write your message down, and I'll take care of the rest."

She pulled off her threadbare cotton gloves and drew a piece of paper out of her drawstring purse. The ranger had written down what he wanted the telegram to say, and she copied it word for word. The whole thing took less than a minute or two. If the dispatcher thought it odd that she'd addressed her message to the Texas Rangers, Austin, Company B, he kept it to himself.

She paid with two coins and left. Not wanting to leave Adam any longer than necessary, she intended to ride straight home, but Main Street was blocked. Amanda Lockwood was at it again. The girl never gave up. Hardly a week went by when she wasn't marching down the street for one of her many causes. Today, she was leading some sort of protest outside the mayor's office.

While Sadie waited for the road to clear, she gazed at the window of the general store.

Buy something for Adam. Or something pretty for yourself. She reached into her purse and fingered the heavy coin.

Dismounting, she tethered the horse and, shoulders back and head held high, marched into the general store. The proprietor, Mr. Cranston, didn't look particularly happy to see her. An older man with white hair, his missing teeth caused him to lisp.

"I told you. No more credit."

"I know what you told me," she said, letting the shop door slam shut behind her.

Mr. Cranston went back to arranging the stock, leaving her to browse in peace.

What should she buy? A pair of kid gloves caught her eye. Picking them up, she rubbed the soft leather against her cheek and imagined sinking her hands into their silky depths.

The gloves were both pretty and practical, but she kept looking. Adam was growing like a weed and would soon outgrow the flannel gowns she had made for him. She considered buying more fabric when a ready-made dress caught her eye.

It was a simple blue calico dress and she could make something similar a whole lot cheaper, but she had always dreamed of buying something off the peg. She fingered the soft fabric and tried to imagine what the captain would think if he saw her in it. Would he smile at her as he smiled at Adam? Would he think her pretty?

Startled by the thought, she pulled her hand away. She had no business thinking such thoughts. Even if she weren't a recent widow, the captain was totally off-limits.

She'd already lost two men to the rangers. She sure in blazes didn't plan on going down that same path again!

As for Adam's father, he deserved her respect, if nothing else. That meant mourning him like a proper wife would do. If she purchased anything, it should be black crepe to make widow's weeds. Spirits dropping, she pulled her gaze away from the blue dress.

Aware, suddenly, that Mr. Cranston was watching her, she made a hasty retreat, the gold eagle still tucked in her purse.

Four

COLE COULDN'T REMEMBER THE LAST TIME HE'D HAD A home-cooked meal. The widow Carnes sure did know her way around the kitchen. Tonight's fare was chicken and dumplings, and the savory dish was every bit as good as it smelled. It was a vast improvement over the rations that made up the Texas Ranger diet, that's for certain.

Though it had been five days since he'd collapsed on the parlor floor, he still didn't have his full strength back and tired easily. Nevertheless, he'd insisted upon getting out of bed for his meals. If he had any hope of gaining back his stamina, he needed to get moving.

The three of them sat at the table in the small but tidy kitchen. Mrs. Carnes had strapped Adam to a chair so he wouldn't fall.

The lady was full of surprises—contradictions, more like it. She was plainspoken and ran the farm in a direct, no-nonsense way, yet her windows were dressed in ruffled curtains. Vases of late-blooming sunflowers graced her tables and counters. She was brusque at times with him, but always gentle with her son. She used words like *ain't* and *druthers*, yet set the table with a linen tablecloth and an assortment of fine-looking china. Odder still, she spent her evenings poring over a book of grammar as if it were some sort of treasure map. When questioned about it, she'd said she wanted to learn to speak good and proper-like for her son.

Drawing his napkin to his mouth, Cole sighed with contentment. He'd almost forgotten what a real home was like.

It was only three weeks till Christmas. That meant his company would remain camped in Austin till the first of the year. The thought of spending another holiday in cramped winter quarters with a bunch of rowdy men hadn't bothered him before. Shouldn't bother him now, but it did.

The realization made him grimace. A week away from his line of duty, and already he'd grown used to the comforts of home. Another week of Mrs. Carnes's hospitality and he'd be a goner for sure.

He'd fully expected the Carpenter brothers to have been captured by now. Blast his bullet wound! Lying around was not in his nature. Come January, he expected to be fully operational and would make up for lost time. Meanwhile, he may as well enjoy the widow's hospitality. Starting tomorrow, he intended to show his gratitude by doing a little work around the farm, strength permitting.

He reached for another biscuit. "I have to say, ma'am, this meal is fit for a king."

Mrs. Carnes smiled and color rushed to her cheeks. It wasn't often that she smiled, but when she did, it lit up the whole room, and tonight was no different. Aware suddenly that he was staring, he set to work mopping up the last bit of gravy on his plate.

"Hope you saved room for apple pie," she said, clearing the table.

He met her gaze. "You bet."

There it was again, that smile. Suddenly he was having trouble breathing. Adam babbled something that sounded like "oh, ah, ah," and Cole gratefully used it to break whatever hold she had on him.

"I think he wants pie too," Cole said.

She carried the dirty dishes to the sink, laughing, a sweet musical sound that reminded him of a songbird. "That boy sure does have an appetite."

Sucking in his breath, Cole reminded himself that she

was a recent widow. "How did you and Richard meet?" Hearing her talk about her late husband was bound to take his mind off the intriguing way her eyes softened when she looked at her son. Or how she puckered her pretty pink lips to drop a kiss on the child's blond head.

Now he could almost see the wheels turning as she considered how to answer his question. "Richard and I pretty much grew up together," she said at last. "Old man Carnes was a preacher and started the church here in town." She returned to the table carrying a pie and knife. "He wanted his son to follow in his footsteps, but Richard had other ideas. Soon as he turned eighteen, he left to join the Rangers."

She stopped to dab the drool off her son's chin before continuing. "He returned to town for his father's funeral. When he found out my grandfather had died and I was struggling to save the farm, he asked me to marry him. Said he had enough of the Rangers and wanted to settle down." She scoffed. "Turned out to be a lie."

Cole tried to picture Richard as a farmer and couldn't. Richard had avoided doing anything that required physical labor. "How long were you two married?"

She sliced a piece of pie before answering, her face tight as it always was whenever she spoke of her husband. "We were married for a year and a half, but he took off after only three months."

Cole's eyebrows shot up. "What happened?"

"He said farming wasn't for him. It was too much work, and he missed the excitement of the Rangers. We argued and that was the last I saw of him."

It wasn't the first time Cole had heard such a story. Hard as it was to be a ranger, it somehow got into a man's blood, and woe to the woman who loved him.

"Surely he sent you money. Something for the boy."

Her eyes blazed with accusatory lights. "He didn't know about Adam."

Cole sat back in his chair. "Didn't know?"

"He never told me how to reach him." She shrugged. "Figured he didn't want me to know."

Cole shook his head. Great Scott! No wonder Carnes had never mentioned a child. Come to think about it, he'd hardly mentioned having a wife. "So that's why you accused me of lying to you."

She shrugged. "Hard to believe Richard would whittle something for a son he didn't know he had."

Cole felt bad—real bad. He hated knowing that one of his men had made such a mess of his personal life. He prided himself on picking the best men, men who were of good moral character. Men who didn't get drunk or cause a ruckus. Men who didn't shirk responsibility.

"I just wanted the boy to have something to remember his father by. I'm sure that's what Richard would have wanted."

She cut a second slice of pie and scooped it onto a plate. Before handing the pie over to him, she sought his eyes. "Was…Richard a good ranger?" When Cole hesitated, she slammed the plate on the table in front of him. "And I want the truth. So don't go saying he was, if he wasn't."

The truth? If only it was that simple. Carnes had deserted his responsibilities here at home. That made him less than a man in Cole's eyes, but he couldn't say that, however much he was tempted.

"You can tell Adam that his father was a fine ranger and died a noble death," he said.

A look of gratitude and maybe even relief crossed her face. "I'll tell Adam that," she said. "Soon as he's old enough to understand."

∽∾∽

Sadie had just put Adam down for his afternoon nap that second week in December when a hammering sound drew her to the kitchen window.

"Dang that man!" Now the ranger was on the barn roof, hammering down shingles. Last week, after he spent the day repairing the fence, he'd run a fever and had to spend two days in bed.

Now here he was at it again, overdoing it.

She pulled a woolen shawl from a peg by the back door and stepped outside. The wind was cold, and angry clouds crowded in from the north like a bunch of wooly sheep.

Upon reaching the barn, she yelled up to him, "If you fall and break your neck, don't come runnin' to me!"

He peered over the edge of the roof. His nose was red from the cold and his hair tossed about like sails in the wind, but he sure was a sight for sore eyes. "I guess I'd just have to wait till your friend Scooter came."

She balled her hands at her side. "I'd think you'd have a little consideration for my reputation."

His eyebrows quirked upward. "I'm not sure I understand what you mean."

"How do you think it looks for a woman to entertain a man that's not her husband?"

She'd not yet told anyone of Richard's death. She didn't want friends and neighbors coming to her door to express condolences until after the ranger was long gone.

He shrugged. "Isn't it a little late to worry about that? Some of your neighbors already know I'm here."

"I told them my husband sent you here to recover from your bullet wound."

"Your *husband* sent me. That might be hard to explain when the truth comes out."

"That's my problem." She tossed her head. "I mean it, Captain." She grabbed hold of the ladder and gave it a good shaking. "If you don't come down, I'll see that you're stuck up there for good!"

"Why, Mrs. Carnes, is that a threat?"

She glared up at him. "You've already had one relapse, and I'm not about to take care of you for another."

"Okay, okay, I'll come down, but only on one condition."

She straightened, hands at her waist. "What?"

"You stop calling me Captain. My name is Cole."

"Not gonna happen," she said. Calling him by his given name would only strengthen the bond between them, and she couldn't allow that. It was hard enough trying not to like the man more than was absolutely necessary.

"Why not?" he asked.

"I never name an animal I plan on eating, and I sure don't aim on naming a man who'll soon be gone."

"All right, Mrs. Carnes. Have it your way. But could you at least tell me what your Christian name is? I promise not to use it unless you say it's okay."

She chewed on a bottom lip. "Sadie," she said. "And I don't want you calling me that, you hear?"

"Nice name," he said. "It suits you."

She didn't know what he meant by that and she wasn't about to ask. "So what's it gonna be, Captain?" She grabbed hold of the ladder and rattled it. "You coming down or ain't you?"

"Oh, I'll come down, Mrs. Carnes. But only because I don't want you complaining about me to your *husband*."

Five

A WEEK LATER, SADIE PEERED OUT OF HER KITCHEN window and shook her head. Cole was at it again. If he wasn't on the roof or mucking the barn, he was oiling the windmill and repairing the farm equipment.

Under Cole's watch, the battle with the fox had turned into an all-out war. Traps now dotted the yard, and fences were reinforced with wire. So far, nothing had worked, but today he had a new plan and that was to drench the yard with ammonia. She only hoped it was as offensive to the fox as it was to her.

She dropped the curtain in place and finished washing the breakfast dishes. Just as she placed the last bowl in the cabinet, Cole stomped into the house, hauling a tree.

She blinked. "What in the world?"

"It'll soon be Christmas," he said. "Thought the little fella needed a Christmas tree."

She followed him into the parlor. "Is that what you call it?" The drought had taken its toll on trees and shrubbery. By the time Cole stood the pine in a bucket of coal, the branches had parted company with half the needles.

"Sorry." A sheepish grin spread across his face. "It's the best I could find. Have any ornaments?"

"In the attic," she said. "I'll get them." It didn't take long to locate the box of Christmas ornaments stored there.

Moments later, she set the box on the floor in front of the fireplace. "It's been a while since I've seen these," she said as together they pawed through the wrappings.

She hadn't bothered decorating the year before, the worst Christmas of her life. Her friend Meg Lockwood had invited Sadie to dinner, but morning sickness had kept her trotting back and forth to the outhouse for most of the day. Never had she felt so scared or lonely in her life.

This year she was actually looking forward to the holiday, and that surprised her. It was because of Adam, and no other reason. Certainly, it had nothing to do with the captain.

Chewing on her bottom lip, she tried to decide where to hang the shiny ornament she'd pulled from its wrappings. Her gaze soon found its way to the captain's back as he hung a wooden angel on the tree, muscles rippling beneath his shirt. Clamping her mouth shut, she took a deep breath and hung the ornament on a lower branch.

They reached into the box at the same time. The touch of his fingers sent warm tingles up her arm and she quickly pulled back. "Sorry," she murmured, refusing to meet his gaze.

She blew out her breath and waited until he'd turned his back before reaching into the box for the tiny pair of mittens.

"I remember the Christmas my grandmother made these," she said softly. "She tried to teach me how to knit, but I was all thumbs."

Cole turned and regarded her with a thoughtful look. "Sounds like you miss her."

"I do. After my parents died, my grandparents raised me. After Grammy died, Grandpappy drank himself to death." She sighed. "Why do people do that? Drink themselves silly?"

Cole reached into the box for a toy soldier attached to a string. "I guess some people don't know any other way to ease their pain."

Her gaze met his. "Richard sure did like his firewater.

More than once I had to drive into town and drag him out of some saloon." She knew how much he hated the farm, especially at the end. Was that why he'd started drinking so much? "That's not why he got shot, is it? Because he was drunk?"

"Your husband never drank on the job. It's against company policy. Drunkenness, along with any rowdy behavior, is cause for immediate discharge."

She drew in her breath. Knowing that Richard had died stone-cold sober didn't make her feel any better. Dead was dead, no matter how it happened. Feeling suddenly self-conscious beneath Cole's steady gaze, she turned to hide her reddening face.

"Sounds like you had a tough childhood," he said.

She hung the mittens before answering. "Didn't know there was any other kind." She chanced a look in him. "What about you?"

He pulled a glass ball from the box and lifted it to hang. "My mother died in childbirth, so I never knew her. Pa remarried a couple of years later. He owned a general store." His face darkened. "One night as he was closing up shop, he was held up and shot to death."

"How awful for you," she said quietly. "How old were you?"

"Twelve." He rubbed his forehead and added, "The killer got away. But the Texas Rangers tracked him all the way to Indian Territory. That really impressed me, and I was sold on the idea of becoming a ranger myself."

She moistened her lips. "Any regrets?"

He arched an eyebrow. "About being a ranger? None." He named some of the outlaws he'd helped capture. It was an impressive list, and the pride in his voice reminded her of her father. Papa had helped catch a number of outlaws too. Whenever he spoke of his work, his eyes had shone much like the captain's eyes shone now.

Her gaze dropped to her empty hands. "What about the man who killed my husband. Will you get him, too?"

"You can count on it," he said, without a hint of doubt. "Sometimes it takes a while, but like I said, eventually we rangers always get our man. Or in this case, our men."

She reached into the box and pulled out a tiny wooden sleigh. "Men?" she asked.

"The Carpenter brothers. They're responsible for your husband's death."

Her mouth ran dry. "Did the Carpenters put that hole in you too?"

A muscle quivered at his jaw. "'Fraid so."

She drew in her breath. "Did he...did he suffer?"

He shook his head. "Didn't know what hit him." After a moment, he added, "I'm sorry. Like I said, we'll catch the men responsible."

Fingering the sleigh, Sadie tried to take comfort in his promise, but it was no use. Her father and husband had made promises too, none of which were kept.

Not wanting to spoil the fun of decorating the tree, she pushed her dark thoughts aside and concentrated on the present. These past couple of weeks had been a dream come true. Cole had been a tremendous help around the farm.

Each night they'd sat in front of the fire with Adam between them. Sometimes Cole played her grandfather's fiddle while she made up ridiculous lyrics. Their songfests always ended in laughter. At other times, she'd read aloud from her grammar book, and she and Cole would try to make sense of the complicated rules. But whether working, playing, or just relaxing, the three of them had seemed like a family. A real honest-to-goodness family that she'd always wanted.

Now she was reminded of something she didn't want to think about—Cole was a Texas Ranger, a temporary guest. A man on the move. She had no right thinking of him as family, or anything else for that matter.

"My father was a ranger," she said as a way to remind herself what was at stake. "His name was Jack Carter, and he was killed in the line of duty. I was only ten at the time."

His eyes filled with sympathy. "Sorry to hear that. It's gotta be tough losing both a father and husband like that."

"Tough don't—doesn't—begin to describe it."

"We rangers don't always make the best family men, but we do a lot of good. I hope knowing the good that your father and husband did brings you some peace."

She hung the sleigh and busied herself untangling a string of beads. "I'll be sure to tell that to Adam when he asks why the other children have fathers and he doesn't."

Cole lifted a tin star out of the box and attached it to the very top of the tree. While he tackled the high branches, Sadie concentrated on the lower ones. Sometimes his arm brushed against hers or they'd reach for an ornament at the same moment. Such occasions were met with quick glances and murmured apologies.

By the time all the ornaments had been hung, hardly a needle remained intact. That was the least of it; the tree tipped to the side as if looking for a place to land.

Cole stood next to her as they admired their work, and she basked in the warmth of the shared moment. It was the saddest, most wonderful tree Sadie had ever seen.

"I love it!" she said and giggled.

Cole laughed too. "I can hardly wait until Adam wakes up from his nap and sees it."

The softness with which he spoke Adam's name touched her deeply. Gazing up at him, she knew she was in trouble. Every accidental touch had triggered a jolt of awareness. Every unguarded look had tugged at her heart. A single whiff of his masculine scent was enough to quicken her pulse and steal away her breath.

As if he shared similar thoughts, his gaze met hers briefly before they quickly moved away. While he swept up the pine needles as if his life depended on it, she carried the empty box back to the attic, her senses still spinning.

Oh, yes, she was in trouble. Big trouble. And she didn't have the slightest idea what to do about it.

Six

THE WIND BLEW SOMETHING FIERCE THAT NIGHT. THE storm shutters outside Sadie's bedroom window had broken loose, and the banging woke Adam on three separate occasions.

At times, the wind sounded like a herd of mavericks running across the roof, and that worried her. The ranger had chinked the walls of the barn, but both roofs were beyond repair.

She lay in bed listening to the roar of the wind, and a distant noise made her sit up. Something…

Planting her feet on the bare wooden floor, she reached for the dressing gown at the foot of her bed. She shoved her arms into the sleeves and tiptoed from the room so as not to awaken Adam.

Reaching the kitchen, she lit a lamp and peered out the window. The rain beat against the glass pane, but it was too dark to see the source of the banging. Still, she had a pretty good idea where it was coming from.

Plucking Richard's mackintosh off a wooden peg, she worked her arms into the overly long sleeves and donned her grandfather's old Wellington boots. They were too big for her but offered some protection. Reaching for a box of safety matches, she lit a hurricane lantern.

Holding the lantern in one hand, she opened the door with the other. The wind blew the door clear out of her hand, and it banged against the outside wall. Rain pelted her like icy needles, and the wind threatened to knock her over. Head low, she stepped outside and battled the door shut.

Slipping and sliding in the rivers of mud, she made her way through the yard. It was just as she'd thought. The barn door had come unlatched. The wind simultaneously hurled it open and banged it shut. The sound of wood against wood had panicked the horses. She could hear them thrashing around in their stalls, their high-pitched whinnies bouncing off the barn's beamed ceiling.

She would have to calm the horses before they harmed themselves. Setting the lantern inside the barn, she grabbed hold of the door with both hands. It was a heavy door, and the slick wet wood made the tug-of-war with the wind a losing battle.

A shadow loomed toward her and she jumped.

"It's just me," Cole shouted over the rain and frantic neighs. His shoulder pressed against hers as together they pulled the large, heavy door shut, closing themselves inside.

The barn was cold, but at least it was dry. So far the roof had held. "You okay?" he asked.

"Yes," she said. Even though she was cold and wet, his presence helped. She tried not to stare at him, tried not to follow the rivulets of water running off his shoulders and down his bare chest to his trouser waist.

She shivered and his gaze sharpened. "You're cold." The concern in his voice matched the look on his face. "Go back to the house. I'll calm the horses."

"I should stay…" She pointed to her horse. "Daisy don't…doesn't…take kindly to strangers."

"Okay, then," Cole said, walking toward his horse's stall. "Let's make this quick."

Seeing his owner, Hercules rose on his hind legs and pawed the air.

Letting herself into her horse's stall, Sadie ran her hands along Daisy's slick neck and back. The old mare trembled slightly beneath her touch and pressed her soft nose into Sadie's hand.

"Good girl," Sadie murmured softly, her attention directed at the stall next door and Cole's soothing baritone voice.

After making sure Daisy had water and oats, Sadie checked Izzie, the cow, who appeared unfazed by the storm still raging outside.

After the animals were settled, Sadie followed Cole into the still-pounding rain. Her back toward the wind, she held the hurricane lantern while Cole battled the door shut and secured the latch.

Heads down, they started toward the house. A tree branch suddenly plunged to the ground, missing Sadie by mere inches.

Startled, she cried out and almost dropped the lantern.

Cole pulled her away from the fallen branch. "I've got you," he yelled over the roar of the storm. "Come on."

She buried her face against his wet shoulder, and his sturdy arm around her made her feel safe. It had been a long time since she'd felt so protected and secure.

Once inside the house, he helped her out of the dripping raincoat. She sat on the bench to pull off her boots, and he dropped on a knee to help her.

"You're frozen," he said, his eyes, his voice, filled with concern. After pulling off his own muddied boots, he said, "Wait here." He left the room and returned a moment later with a fluffy white towel. He dried her face, his touch as gentle as a warm summer breeze. Tossing the damp towel aside, he reached for her hand and pulled her from the bench.

"The hem of your robe is wet. You better put on something dry." His heated gaze lingered on her lips before lifting to her eyes. Something intense flared between them, something she dared not name.

"You too," she whispered, trying not to think about his nearness.

He stepped closer and put his hands at her waist.

"Sadie…" He looked like he wanted to say more, but instead slid his hands up her arms, drawing her so close she could feel his warm breath. Sense the pounding of his heart.

A moment of alarm flashed through her, but the tenderness of his touch was too tempting to pass up. Melting against him, she curled her hands upon his still-damp chest. He tightened his hold and her pulse quickened.

His lips on her forehead, followed by a series of warm shivery kisses down her face to her neck, made her forget her reservations. In that moment, nothing existed but the two of them. With a deep-rooted groan, he covered her mouth with his own, sending shockwaves of desire racing through her. His firm, moist lips demanded her full attention. No room existed for anything else.

They were both out of breath by the time their lips parted, but even then she didn't want to let him go. She wanted their kiss to last forever.

He laughed softly. "As much as I hate to put an end to this, I believe Adam needs you."

She drew in her breath, and that's when she heard the faint cry in the distance. Normally, she heard Adam's every sigh, but not this time.

He pressed his palm against her heated cheek. "I'll go to him, if you want," he murmured.

She shook her head and backed away, surprised at how hard it was to leave the comfort of his arms. "I'll go."

Dazed by what had just transpired between them, she left him standing in the mudroom.

It was only later, as she gazed out of her bedroom window at the black stormy night, that the full implication of what had happened hit her. She had kissed a man not her husband and had liked it. Liked it more than she'd ever thought possible. He made her feel pretty and desirable, and no one had ever made her feel that way before. Certainly not Richard.

"Oh, God!" She pounded a fist into the palm of her hand. It wouldn't take that much to fall in love with Cole Bradshaw, but that she could never do. She had already loved and lost two men to the Texas Rangers. Never would she allow herself to love—and lose—another.

Seven

THE NEXT MORNING, SADIE WALKED INTO THE KITCHEN with Adam in her arms. Cole stood at the cookstove, whistling.

Forcing herself to breathe, she strapped Adam into his chair. How could Cole sound so cheery when she was in a state of utter confusion? She'd not slept a wink. Whenever she'd closed her eyes, she'd imagined herself back in his arms. Imagined his lips upon hers.

He turned to greet her, coffeepot in hand. "Morning," he said with a smile.

She sat at the table without returning his greeting. If only she could forget the feel of his mouth. The touch of his hand. The sound of his heartbeats next to hers.

He filled a cup with coffee and placed it on the table in front of her. "Trees down. Lost more shingles on the roof, but nothing that can't be fixed."

"That's good," she murmured, handing Adam a spoon. If only matters of the heart could be so easily repaired.

"One thing can be said in the storm's favor—it kept the fox away."

She sighed. "He'll be back." Nothing could keep that creature away. The fox's return was the only thing she could count on for sure.

"Maybe you should think about raising cattle instead of chickens."

Her eyes widened. "You're kidding, right?"

"I'm serious. You have a large enough spread. Cattle

would solve the fox problem and make you a lot of money to boot."

She glanced at him sideways. "I know nothing about cattle."

"If you can figure out those crazy verbs in that book of yours, I reckon you can learn to raise cattle."

When she said nothing, he poured himself a cup of coffee. He regarded her with questioning eyes before sitting opposite her and changing the subject. "I think we ought to talk about last night."

She cradled the cup in her hands. "Nothin' to talk about. We took care of the barn door and the animals. No damage was done."

"I meant what happened when we came back to the house."

She lowered her cup. "Nothin' to talk about," she repeated. "What happened was a mistake."

Adam dropped his spoon and Cole bent to pick it up. He studied her for a moment before placing the spoon in Adam's grasping hand. "I didn't mean for that to happen. You only recently found out about your husband's death. I have no excuse for my poor behavior. Except to say that these last couple of weeks have meant the world to me. It's been a long time since I've known a real home. A real family."

She stiffened. Oh, God. There they were again, all the right words. Richard had said he wanted a home and family and she had believed him. That was one mistake she never intended to repeat.

"These last couple of weeks have meant a lot to me, too," she said, her voice choked. No sense denying it. She'd almost forgotten what it was like not to feel alone or afraid. He'd made her feel safe again. Made her feel special. Made her feel cherished.

She drew in her breath and let out a long sigh. If only…

"But…it's too soon," he said. "That's what you're thinking, right?" He reached for her hand. "Trust me, Sadie, I'm not trying to move in and take Richard's place. I'm willing to wait till the time is right."

She pulled her hand away. His presence was torment-ing enough without having to feel his touch. "The time will never be right," she said, each word tasting like gall. "You're a Texas Ranger."

His eyebrows knitted. "That's what I want to talk to you about. I've been a ranger for going on eleven years now. Ever since I was seventeen years old. Been thinking that maybe it's time I settled down. Being here has made me realize there's life outside the Rangers. A good life. Crazy as it sounds, I like working on the farm. And I meant it when I said I would love to run cattle here and—"

She shook her head. "Cole…"

"Please, Sadie, hear me out." An eager light flashed in his eyes. "I'm thinking of retiring from the Rangers. That is, if there's a chance that you and I could…you know…be together."

She sat back in her chair with a feeling of despair. This couldn't be happening. Not again. Oh, God, not again! "What about the Carpenter brothers?"

"They'll get what's coming to them, with or without me." His eyes held a hopeful glint. "Sadie, I care for you. I really do. I care for Adam too. Is there a chance you and I can—?"

The question hung between them, the air taut with tension. At least he didn't say love. Had he said he loved her, she would have been a goner for sure.

"No. No chance," she said. Bad news was best deliv-ered quickly and with as few words as possible.

He looked like she had hit him. "After last night I thought…"

"You thought wrong," she snapped. Afraid of losing

control, she curled her hands tight by her side. "All that fancy talk about retirin' is just that—talk. You'll always be a Texas Ranger. You won't be able to help yourself. Rangers don't make very good husbands. Don't make good fathers either."

"I told you I planned on quitting and I meant it."

She heaved a sigh. "Richard told me the same thing, and he lasted here at the farm three months. Three lousy months!"

"I'm not Richard."

"No, but you're one of them. Just like Richard and my pa. Pa promised to quit too. But there was always another outlaw to chase. Another call to adventure." As a child she couldn't compete with the lure of the Rangers. But neither had she been able to compete as a grown woman.

Cole's burning eyes held hers. "I'll always be there for you," he said, "and that's a promise."

She scoffed. "Those are mighty pretty words. They were pretty when Papa said them. They were pretty when Richard said them too. But you know what? They don't mean beans."

For several moments the only sound was Adam banging on the table with his spoon.

"Sadie," he said at last, his voice thick with emotion. "How can I prove that I mean what I say? What will it take?" His tender gaze met hers. "How can I make you believe that I will never leave you?"

"You can't," she whispered. It nearly broke her heart to say it, but it was better to lose him before the first stirrings of love turned into something deeper. As hard as it was now, it would be so much harder later. "You can't."

⟨∾⟩

After two days, the rain had stopped and Sadie threw open her bedroom window sash to let in some fresh air just as Adam woke from his nap. Hearing voices, she peered outside to the yard below. Cole was deep in conversation with a stranger, and her stomach knotted.

Things between them had been strained since the night they'd kissed. Every word, every look, every move had to be carefully planned in advance so as not to open up the floodgates of emotion that now simmered between them.

He'd told her he no longer planned on staying till Christmas. She didn't want to see him go. Not yet. But if she was right about the stranger's identity, things were now out of both their hands.

After changing Adam, she lifted him in her arms and joined the two men outside. Cole turned as she approached. "Sadie, I'd like you to meet Major Comstock. Major, this is Mrs. Carnes and her son, Adam."

The major pulled off his hat and tucked it beneath his arm. "Pleased to meet you, ma'am. Sorry about your husband. He was a fine ranger."

"Thank you," she said.

"The captain here was telling me that you took good care of him while he was laid up. We're mighty grateful to you."

"He was a good patient," she said.

The corners of Cole's mouth quirked upward before he turned dead serious. "The major was just telling me that they have a good idea where the men responsible for your husband's death are holed up."

"That's right," the major concurred. "That's why I'm here. I wanted to make sure the captain was fully recovered before he joined us. We'll spend the night at the hotel and take the train back to Austin first thing in the morning."

The news hit her like a rock. She met Cole's gaze, but the eyes looking back were dark and unfathomable.

"S-so soon?" she stammered. She'd hoped Cole would change his mind and at least stay until after Christmas.

"If we wait, we might lose 'em," the major said, "and I don't aim on takin' the chance." He pulled his watch out of his vest pocket and flipped it open with his thumb. "We better get a move on."

Cole nodded. "I'll saddle up."

Major Comstock glanced around. "Where can I find water for my horse?" Cole pointed to the horse trough next to the windmill. "Much obliged," the major said and led his gelding away.

Cole waited until he was out of earshot. "I'll stay, Sadie. That is…if you want me to. You only have to say the word. I give you my solemn promise I won't leave. I'll always be here for you and Adam."

Sadie tried to breathe but it felt as if someone had squeezed her lungs in a vise. She wanted him to stay more than anything in the world, but life on a farm paled in comparison to what the Rangers could offer him.

"You'll leave," she whispered, her voice hoarse. "You won't be able to help yourself." She turned and walked away. Letting him go was the hardest thing she'd ever done. It was also the most necessary—for both their sakes.

◦⟋⟍⟍◦

The hours following Cole's departure crept by so slowly, Sadie kept thinking her clock had stopped. She wandered aimlessly from room to room, pausing only to run her hand over his chair, his bed—anywhere he might have touched. The house felt empty, lifeless, like a tomb. Neither the Christmas tree nor the blazing fire could chase away the gloom.

Adam seemed to sense her dark mood. He had been fussy and clingy since that afternoon. He wasn't interested in his toys or even his favorite game of peekaboo. He even refused to nurse, but the heaviness in her breasts hardly compared to the heaviness in her heart.

"What's the matter, little fella?" she asked, rocking him in her arms. "You miss him too, eh?"

Never had she felt so lonely. Not even after Richard had left. She'd only known Cole a short while, but somehow a bond had been forged between them unlike any she'd ever known. At times it seemed as if he knew what she was thinking even before she knew herself.

Aware, suddenly, that Adam had fallen asleep, she carried him to the bedroom. After placing him in his cradle, she fell facedown on her bed, sobbing.

Eight

COLE TOYED WITH HIS GLASS. HE WASN'T MUCH OF A drinker. Never had been. Never believed in drowning one's sorrows in a bottle. Tonight he was tempted to try.

The major sat across from him, rolling a cigarette with the precise movements of a safecracker. With his stern face and military stance, he hardly looked like he belonged in the rowdy saloon, let alone the feisty town. Even the good-time gals avoided their corner table.

A group of men clapped to the tune of the foot-stomping fiddle music. In one corner, a noisy faro game was in progress. But the loudest sounds of all were the voices in Cole's head.

How can I make her believe that I meant what I said about never leaving?

No matter how many times he'd rephrased the question, the answer echoing back was always the same. *You can't.*

Major Comstock said something, yanking Cole away from his thoughts. "I'm sorry."

"I said, you've hardly spoken a word since we left the farm." The major slid the pouch of tobacco into his coat pocket and licked the edge of the rolling paper. "You haven't even asked about the plan for capturing the Carpenters."

"Figured you'd tell me when the time was right."

The major finished rolling his cigarette. "I've known you a long time. Ever since you were wet behind the ears and showed up at headquarters, demanding to join the Rangers."

Cole studied his commanding officer. "Why do I get the feeling this is leading to something?"

The major shrugged and continued, "You were a bright kid. Passionate. After talking to you I was convinced you would give heart and soul to the Rangers. To fighting crime. Turns out I was right." Comstock stuck the cigarette in his mouth and reached in his pocket for a box of safety matches. After lighting his cigarette, he took a long drag and blew out a stream of smoke. "The question is, will you still give me all you've got?"

Cole stared at him. "Why are you asking this of me?"

"I'm no fool. I saw how you looked at her. How she looked at you." The major leaned forward. "When you stayed away for weeks, I worried that you were more injured than you'd let on. That's why I came here. I wanted to see for myself that you were well enough to work again. Now I know that it was no bullet wound keeping you away. It was Cupid's arrow."

"That obvious, eh?"

Comstock shrugged. "I may be an old bird, but I remember how it felt to be in love. Believe it or not, I was once in your shoes." After a long pause, he added, "I chose the Rangers."

"Any regrets?"

"There're always regrets. You just have to choose the ones you can live with." Sitting back in his chair, the major took another puff and blew a smoke ring.

"She won't even let me make the choice." Cole stared into his drink. "She lost a father and husband in the line of duty. She refuses to get involved with another ranger."

The major flicked ash on the sawdust floor. "Can't blame her for that."

"I offered to hang up my spurs, but it did no good.

She believes that once a man's a ranger, he's always a ranger and can't stay put. At least not for long."

Cole took a quick swallow of his drink. The whisky burned his throat, reminding him why he normally avoided the stuff. Why he should have avoided the thing called love.

Elbows on the table, he held his head in his hands. No matter how many times he'd sworn not to leave, he still couldn't make her believe him. Oh, God, there must be a way, but how?

He scrubbed his hands over his face and stared at the wall. A sign read Troublemakers Will Be Asked to Leave.

Just as he drew his gaze away from the sign, an idea popped into his head. A surge of excitement rushed through him. Would it work? Would she believe him then? Maybe, maybe not. All he knew was that he had to try.

∽∾

It was dark when Sadie woke to Adam's frantic cries. She rolled off the bed and lit the lamp before rushing to her son's side. He was burning up with fever.

Taking a deep breath, she willed herself not to panic. She raced to the dry sink and poured water from the pitcher onto a washrag. She sponged off his face and legs and arms, but the fever persisted, as did his croaky cough. Even more worrisome, his lips were tinged blue and he had trouble breathing.

Oh, God, Cole. Tears sprang to her eyes. Never had she needed anyone as much as she needed Cole at that moment. *If only you were here. You would know what to do.*

She glanced at the clock. It was after 9:00 p.m. but she didn't dare wait till morning before taking Adam to the doctor.

Leaving Adam in his cradle, she grabbed an armload of blankets and pillows and dashed outside to the barn.

After making Adam a soft bed in the back of the wagon, she quickly hitched the wagon to her horse.

Less than twenty minutes later, she was on the road leading to town. Fortunately, there was a full moon to light the way. Though it was cool, the night air was still—eerily so. Even the wolves were silent.

The movement of the wagon seemed to have a calming effect on Adam, as he'd grown quiet. Her relief was short-lived, however, as a terrifying thought crossed her mind. What if he had stopped breathing?

With a frantic tug on the reins, she set the brake. Jumping to the ground, she froze. The memory of finding her grandfather dead in his bed flashed though her head. He had been so still, so cold. Now, as she froze, petrified, on the side of that lonely road, it was as if the very earth had stopped turning.

Shaking away her inertia, she crept to the back of the wagon. The sound of Adam's breathing made her cling to the side of the wagon in relief. The rattling in Adam's chest worried her, but nonetheless offered a measure of comfort.

The drive to town took the best part of an hour, mainly because she kept stopping to check on him. Banjo music, laughter, and occasional gunfire greeted her as she turned down Main. It was Saturday night and the saloons were packed.

Dr. Stybeck's office was on the corner of Eighth and Main across from a noisy saloon. He lived on the second floor of his office with his wife.

Sadie pulled her horse and wagon to the side of the road. Setting her brake, she jumped to the ground. Three horsemen galloped by. Dogs barked, a horse neighed. Two men exited the saloon across the street. One of the men was so drunk, he couldn't walk without help.

Wrinkling her nose in disgust, she reached into the back of the wagon and lifted Adam into her arms. He was still burning with fever and hardly stirred. *Oh, God. Please don't let him die.* She was so focused on Adam, she almost missed the familiar voice wafting from across the street. Her heart jolted. Was that…?

She turned to give the two men a second look in the yellow glow of the streetlight.

It was Cole, all right, singing at the top of his lungs. He was drunker than a sow in a peach orchard, and if it weren't for the major, he'd have been flat on his face.

Eyes burning, Sadie watched the major struggle to keep Cole upright. Tonight when she most needed him, Cole was in no condition to help even himself.

Turning away in dismay, she carried her son up the steps to the boardwalk and jabbed the doctor's night bell.

⟡

"Is it pneumonia?" Sadie whispered, the mere thought striking terror in her heart.

Dr. Stybeck pulled his monaural stethoscope away from her son's chest. "Croup," he said.

She frowned. "Is it serious?"

"Can be." He applied a poultice to Adam's chest and covered it with a cloth. "I think we caught it in time." He called to his wife. "We need steam."

Moments later, Mrs. Stybeck entered the room carrying a hot teakettle. Wearing a gingham apron and a knitted yarn snood over her gray hair, she moved with a quiet efficiency that could only have come from years of practice.

"Here we go," she said, arranging the kettle in such a way that the steam flowed directly on Adam.

The doctor nodded with approval. "That'll help him breathe."

Both he and his wife insisted Sadie stay the night. "We'll see how Adam is in the morning," the doctor said.

With Adam in her arms, she followed the doctor's

wife to the living quarters upstairs. "Your little fellow is breathing better already," Mrs. Stybeck said. "If you need the doctor in the night, just ring the bell by the side of the bed."

Sadie smiled in gratitude. "Thank you."

The guest room was small but comfortable and Sadie fell onto the bed, exhausted, Adam by her side. Sleep, however, escaped her.

Between Adam's raspy breaths and the noise outside her window, she was too tense to sleep. Fiddle music wafted from the saloon across the street till the wee hours of the morning. It was well after two when a group of raucous cowboys barreled down Main on horseback, whooping and hollering and firing pistols in the air.

But worse than the mayhem outside was the memory of Cole falling down drunk.

I'll always be there for you.

Thumping her pillow with her fist, she shuddered to think how close she'd been to asking him to stay.

I'll always be there for you.

"Oh, Cole," she sobbed. The tears spilling onto the pillow carried pieces of her broken heart. *I needed you tonight and you weren't there. How can I trust that you'd be there in the future?*

Nine

THREE DAYS LATER, SADIE HAD JUST FINISHED COLLECTING eggs when she spotted a lone horseman riding up to her farm. Recognizing Cole, she almost dropped the basket. They had nothing to say to each other, so what was he doing here? Why wasn't he out chasing bad guys?

Reaching the porch, she set the basket down and battled back the tears burning her eyes. She had less success willing her heart to keep from hurting any more than it already did.

Cole rode up to the porch and greeted her with a nod before dismounting his horse. "Sadie."

She curled her hands by her side. "I thought you would be gone by now."

"That was the plan, but..." He gave her a sheepish smile. "I came to tell you that I'm here to stay."

She shook her head and turned. "We've been through this. I can't..."

He placed his foot on the lower step. "Wait! Hear me out."

Her back to him, she reached for the doorknob.

"Please."

Something in his voice made her stop. Turning, she was surprised to see him smiling. Her temper snapped. His mere presence tormented her, and here he acted as if it was some sort of joke. "Say what you have to say and leave."

He took another step up the porch. "I can't return to the Rangers even if I wanted to."

She narrowed her eyes. "What's that supposed to mean?"

"This will explain." He reached into his coat pocket. Pulling out a letter, he handed it to her.

The parchment suggested it was an official document; the letterhead confirmed it. She quickly scanned it before looking up, puzzled. "It says you were dishonorably discharged from the Texas Rangers." She frowned. "I don't understand."

"That letter is proof I'm here to stay."

She stared at him, incredulous. "Dishonorably discharged?"

He rubbed his neck. "'Fraid I got me a full-grown case of booze blind. I'm not usually that friendly with a bottle, but"—his eyes pleaded for her to understand—"I missed you something terrible and…" He grimaced as if his drunken behavior had been as distasteful to him as it was to her. "Disorderly conduct is grounds for dismissal."

"Oh, Cole. I'm so sorry. I never meant… I know how proud you are of your service. To have it end like this…"

Something flickered in the depths of his eyes—a look of sadness, maybe even regret, but he quickly hid both behind a feigned smile. But the smile came a tad too late. She had seen the unguarded look and she knew. Leaving the Rangers under such a dark cloud had cost him dearly.

"I can live with it if you can," he said, his voice thick with emotion.

She doubted that. Doubted that he could so easily discount years of honorable service. Oh, God. How she hated knowing that she was partly responsible for his career ending in disgrace. Still, she couldn't help feeling a sense of relief and joy. She no longer had to worry about losing Cole to the Texas Rangers. He couldn't go back even if he wanted to.

"I'm not the one who has to live with it," she said.

"Now, that's still open for discussion," he said, and the tenderness in his eyes took her breath away. "Sadie, when I said I would stay, I meant it. I didn't need that letter. I love you."

The word *love* wrapped around her heart like a warm blanket. It was the one word she'd hoped not to hear him say, and for good reason. For now that he'd said it, there was no holding back.

"Oh, Cole. I love you too."

His face brightened. "Does that mean—"

For answer she flew into his arms and hugged him tight.

But even as he held her and kissed her and whispered sweet nothings in her ear, worrisome thoughts nibbled at her happiness. What if their love wasn't enough to overcome the shame of a dishonorable discharge? What if he came to resent her for the way an otherwise stellar career had ended? What if the discharge that had brought them together was the very thing that would eventually tear them apart?

∼∞∼

Two days before Christmas, Sadie drove her horse and wagon into town and went straight to the general store. Cole was staying at the hotel, but he spent his days at the farm. Today, he insisted upon watching Adam while she shopped for Christmas.

Mr. Cranston greeted her with a rare smile and for once didn't remind her that she was on a cash-only basis.

She wandered up and down the aisles, fingering the golden eagle in her purse. The blue dress was no longer on display. Not that she would have purchased it. She had more important things to do with her money.

She picked out a leather ball for Adam, but finding the perfect gift for Cole was more difficult. She finally settled on a silver money clip. It was far from the perfect gift she'd hoped to give him, but it would have to do.

She paid for her purchases and left the store. On the way to T-Bone's meat store to pick up a roast for Christmas dinner, she ran into Major Comstock.

He greeted her with a tip of the hat. "Mrs. Carnes. Perhaps you can help me. I'm looking for the captain. He's not at the hotel. Would you happen to know where he is?"

"He's at the farm. What…what is this about?"

"I wanted to inform him that the Carpenter brothers have been caught. The man who killed your husband has been charged with murder. He also has to stand trial for shooting a ranger. I was just passing through and thought I'd stop and give the captain the news in person."

"He'll be so happy to hear it," she said. It seemed like the perfect Christmas gift. "Do you want to come to the farm and tell him yourself?"

The major pulled out his watch. "Thank you, but I can't. The train will leave in less than an hour, and I need to get back to headquarters." He tucked his watch back into his vest pocket. "Would you be kind enough to convey my message?"

"Yes, of course. Thank you."

"No need to thank me."

"Oh, but there is. Knowing that my husband's killer has been caught means a lot to me."

"Yes, well, we Texas Rangers always get our man—and in this case, our men."

"I know," she said. How well she knew.

His frown told her he'd heard the sudden edge to her voice. "Mrs. Carnes, may I be forthcoming with you?"

She narrowed her eyes. "Yes, please do."

"I happened to see you last week in town."

She drew in her breath. "Yes, my son was ill and I was there to see the doctor."

"I trust that your son has recovered?"

"He has, thank you."

The major hesitated. "I'm in a dilemma, and I'm not sure how best to handle it. Perhaps you'd be kind enough to help."

Sadie frowned in puzzlement. It was hard to believe that anyone as important as the major would ask for her help. "It sounds serious."

"I'm afraid it is. At the captain's request, I gave him a letter relieving him of duty. He insisted upon it. Said he didn't expect to be treated any differently than he would treat his own men who might act rowdy."

"He…he showed me the letter."

"I thought he might have. Then you know the letter stated he was dishonorably discharged. What you don't know is that I can't in good conscience allow that to stand."

"I don't understand, Major."

Reaching inside his vest pocket, he pulled out a folded document and handed it to her. "That replaces the one in his possession."

She quickly read what it said, her gaze freezing on the words *honorably discharged*. "But the letter he showed me…"

"Completely false. I have to admit, he had me fooled at first. I left him for maybe twenty, thirty minutes to play a round of faro. The next thing I know, he had started a fight and had to be dragged outside. I suppose it's possible to get drunk in the amount of time he was alone, but given the circumstances, unlikely."

"I don't understand. What circumstances?"

"The bottle of whisky was still three-fourths full. I thought it strange at the time. But the next day when I returned to pay our tab, the bartender assured me that only the one bottle had been delivered to our table."

Again, she lowered her gaze to the document in her hand. "Then how… Why?"

"I think you know the answer to that," he said.

Her gaze flew up. "Are you saying—?"

He nodded. "It was all an act." He allowed those words to sink in before adding, "And I believe we both know why a proud and honorable captain would throw away his career and ruin his reputation like that."

She stared at him, speechless, her mind in a whirl.

The major continued, "I couldn't in good conscience leave things as they stood. And if you're half the woman he says you are, I don't think you can either." He tipped his hat and walked away.

The certificate in her hand suddenly felt like a steel weight. What had looked like a bright future was now clouded with uncertainty. Nothing, absolutely nothing, was keeping Cole from rejoining the Rangers. And as he always said, sooner or later, the Rangers always got their man.

Ten

THAT NIGHT SHE BROKE THE NEWS OF THE CARPENTER brothers' capture to Cole over dinner. She'd fixed his favorites: beef stew and apple pie.

He sat back in his chair, dabbing his mouth with a napkin. "And you're only just now telling me?"

"I wanted to tell you over dinner," she said and then explained how she'd bumped into the major in town. "He looked for you at the hotel."

"That's good news," he said. "Your husband's killers will get what's coming to them." He studied her with a frown. "I thought you'd be happy about that."

"I am happy," she said, sounding unconvincing even to her own ears. "Are…are you disappointed that you weren't there to capture them?"

"Disappointed? No." He laid his fork down and covered her hand with his own. "I'm just glad things worked out the way they did. For your sake." He tossed a nod at Adam. "For his sake too."

He pulled his hand away and reached for a biscuit. "What else did Major Comstock say?" he asked, as he mopped up the gravy on his plate.

"Nothing much." The lie felt like acid in her mouth. "Only that he was taking the train back to Austin."

She lowered her gaze. Keeping the honorary discharge from Cole was the right thing to do. It was the only way to protect her future. Protect Adam's future. She only wished their happiness and security didn't depend on deceit.

∽∽∾

A dispatch announcing the capture of the Carpenter brothers had been sent to the sheriff's office, and soon news of Richard's death traveled through town like wildfire. On the day before Christmas, Meg Lockwood was the first to lead the parade to the farm.

"Oh, you poor dear," Meg said, her turquoise eyes wide with concern. "What are you going to do?"

"What I normally do," Sadie said. "Take care of Adam and the farm." It was too soon to tell even her friend that she had fallen in love with another man.

The bank president's wife, Mrs. Mooney, was the next to land on Sadie's doorstep, followed by the pastor's wife.

Sadie felt guilty for accepting their condolences. Richard's death had hit her hard, but she was still angry at him for deserting her. Eventually, she would forgive him for leaving her, just as she'd forgiven her father; she had to for Adam's sake. But it would be a long and painful ordeal, and one she wasn't yet ready to undertake.

For now, something else was on her mind: the certificate of honorable discharge hidden in a bureau drawer. The document that could rob her of a happy future with the man she loved.

She'd hardly slept a wink since her conversation with the major. Even if she didn't feel like a grieving widow, the bags under her eyes made her look like one.

For the rest of the day she went through the motions. She attended Christmas Eve church service and later stood outside with Adam in her arms, singing Christmas carols around the tall decorated tree on the church lawn. Some of the other women took turns holding Adam, and he looked like he was enjoying all the attention.

Cole was there, too, but such was her guilt for not telling him about the document hidden in her drawer, she could hardly look at him. Apparently, he'd sensed something was wrong, because he appeared at her side and whispered, "Are you okay?"

"Yes, I'm just anxious to take Adam home. I don't want to risk him getting sick again."

He chucked Adam under the chin. "I understand." He locked her gaze in his. "See you tomorrow."

Nodding, she quickly moved away. It wouldn't look right for a new widow to be seen with another man. For that reason, they had agreed to keep their distance in public. As far as anyone knew, Cole was a farmhand she'd hired.

As she reached her wagon, she heard the carolers singing "Silent Night" and swiped away the tears that had suddenly sprung to her eyes. Moments later she drove away, holding Adam on her lap. She had everything she'd ever wanted. She had a darling little boy. Her husband's killer would soon stand trial and be brought to justice. And then there was Cole—a man she loved more than life itself. So why, oh why did she feel so utterly miserable?

∽∞∾

Cole appeared on her doorstep early that Christmas morning. Sadie had prepared them both a special breakfast, complete with flapjacks and bacon.

"The fox was back this morning," she said.

Cole quirked a smile. "Sounds like it's time to bring out the big guns."

"What does that mean?"

"You'll see," he said mysteriously.

After they'd finished eating, Cole carried Adam into the parlor and sat him on the floor in front of the Christmas tree.

"There you go," he said, helping Adam open his gift. Cole pulled a little wooden pull toy out of the box, and Sadie clasped her hands to her chest.

"What a lovely gift," she exclaimed.

"Glad *you* like it," Cole said. "Looks like Adam's more interested in the box it came in."

Sadie laughed.

Cole laughed too as he pulled two packages from beneath the tree, one small and one large, and placed them on her lap. "Now it's time to open your presents."

Never had Sadie received such prettily wrapped gifts, and she fingered the big red bows.

"Well? What are you waiting for?" he asked.

Laughing at his impatience, she worked off the ribbon on the smaller box. Inside was a book titled *How to Raise Cattle*. Thumbing through the pages, she tried to imagine herself a cattle baroness.

He grinned. "I told you it was time to bring out the big guns. I just hope that's more interesting to read than that grammar book of yours." He took the book from her and placed it beneath the tree while she opened the larger box.

Upon seeing the blue dress from the general store, she gasped. "Oh, Cole!" She lifted the dress out of the box and held it close. "How did you know?"

"A little birdie told me you were seen admiring it," he said.

Tears filled her eyes. "This is the nicest gift anyone has ever given me."

He grinned. "Try it on. I'll watch Adam."

"I will, but first...you have to open your gift." She set her dress aside and reached beneath the tree for his present.

He tore off the wrapping and drew the money clip out of the box. "It's perfect," he said, holding it up to the light from the window. He looked at her with such tenderness, it took her breath away. "You're perfect."

His eyes were so full of love and admiration and trust, it nearly broke her heart.

Trust. Such a beautiful word and so full of promise.

He trusted her with his whole heart and soul. In

return, she couldn't even allow herself to trust him at his word, and this pained her more than words could say. She didn't deserve him. At that moment she didn't even feel like she deserved Adam.

A silent sob welled up inside. When did this happen? When had the fear of losing him turned her into someone she didn't recognize? Didn't know. Didn't want to know.

She'd searched for the perfect gift for him, but that gift had been in her possession all along. She just hadn't been brave enough to give it to him.

All at once she knew what she must do, and a terrible weight lifted from her shoulders. "There's…more," she said.

He raised his eyebrows. "More?"

"Wait here." Leaving the room, she returned moments later with the discharge document in her hand.

He held her gaze. "What is this?" he asked.

"My trust," she said. "My trust in you. My trust in us. My trust in a long and happy future together."

Eyebrows raised, he unfolded the parchment. Frowning, he shook his head. "This is—"

"An honorable discharge," she said.

He was momentarily speechless. "I don't understand," he said after reading the document again. "How did you get this?"

"The major gave it to me when he told me about the Carpenter brothers."

"But this makes no sense. Why would he give me an honorable discharge after the way I acted?"

She moistened her lips. "I guess you didn't make a very convincing drunk."

He rubbed his forehead. "I don't know what to say. Getting myself dishonorably discharged was the only way I could think to convince you I was here to stay."

"I know," she whispered, touching a finger to his lips. "I…wasn't going to give it to you." Beseeching him to understand, she held her breath, searching for the least bit of censure in his eyes, the least bit of scorn on his face. But his tender gaze held none of the things she feared, and the love and acceptance in his eyes erased the last of her lingering doubts.

"I finally realized that if you stay here with me and Adam, it has to be because you want to. Not because you have to."

"Oh, Sadie, if you don't know by now…" Setting the document aside, he pulled her to her feet and crushed her in his arms. "I'm crazy as a fox in love with you. And just like that ole pest, nothing's gonna keep me away." He kissed her forehead, her nose, her mouth before adding, "I feel the same about Adam."

The tenderness in his eyes took her breath away. But no more so than the happy future she envisioned ahead. She would trust him because she loved him; it was as simple as that. She wrapped her arms around his neck and ran her fingers through his hair. "A cattle ranch, eh?"

"The biggest and best in the county," he said, grinning. "What do you think about calling it the Fox Haven Cattle Ranch?"

She laughed and rose to her tiptoes to kiss him.

"The Fox *Hollow* Cattle Ranch?" he asked.

Shaking her head, she kissed him again and this time targeted the intriguing indentation on his chin.

"The Running Fox Cattle Ranch?"

She laid her head on his chest with a contented sigh. "I think we should call it the Happy Hearts Cattle Ranch."

"Hmm," he murmured, his breath in her hair. "I like that. I like it a lot." He ran his fingers down her cheek and tilted her chin upward.

"Oh, Cole," she said, her heart nearly bursting with joy, "this is the best Christmas ever!"

He smiled. "I can think of only one thing that will make me happier," he said between kisses. "And that's the day you become my wife."

About the Author

Bestselling author Margaret Brownley has penned more than forty novels and novellas. Her books have won numerous awards, including the National Readers' Choice and Romantic Times Pioneer awards. She's a two-time Romance Writers of America RITA finalist and has written for a TV soap. She is currently working on her next series. Not bad for someone who flunked eighth-grade English. Just don't ask her to diagram a sentence. You can find Margaret at margaret-brownley.com.

A Christmas
Baby

A Last Chance

Cowboys Novella

— • ◆ • —

Anna Schmidt

One

Arizona Territory, 1891

LOUISA JOHNSON WAS LATE SLIPPING OUT OF THE HOUSE, but she knew Rico would be there waiting. She had come to a decision and she would not be denied, not even by her father—a man she had adored her entire life, but one who now stood in the way of her being with Rico. She had no idea how to make things right with her father. What she knew with more certainty than she had ever known anything in her nineteen years was that she loved Rico Mendez and he was devoted to her. If her father couldn't accept that—couldn't look past their differences and see Rico for the kind, hard-working man he was—then she would have to force his hand.

Dressed only in a nightgown that covered her from chin to ankle, she ran barefoot down to the creek. Clutched in her hand was the rosary she'd been given at her First Communion—long before she'd become a grown woman capable of making her own choices.

When she reached the creek, her breath came in gasps—a combination of the exertion of running, the chill of a spring night, and the excitement she felt for what she was about to do. Rico stepped out of the shadows. The moon lit the water behind her. She stood very still, knowing the blend of the thin fabric of her gown and the moonlight hid nothing from him.

"Louisa, no," he whispered, but he did not look away. And he could not stop himself from walking toward her.

"Yes," she replied. "It is time."

Rico had always counseled waiting, giving her father the time he needed to adjust to the idea that they loved each other despite the differences in their backgrounds. But she knew her father was unlikely to change. He was waiting for *them* to change. "You say you love me, but—" she said.

"It is because I love you that I cannot disrespect you or your family," he replied, interrupting her.

The two of them had spent long hours on this creek bank, lying on the soft grass, touching and kissing, but while they had found ways to pleasure each other, they had always stopped short of the final union. "Then make me your wife," she said.

He smiled and touched her cheek. "I thought that a proposal was my job," he teased.

She did not return his smile but stared up at him. "Then do your job." She was trembling now with the dew wetting her bare feet and the realization that she might have gone too far and he might refuse. She thought she understood his hesitation—the differences in their stations in life, in their heritage. "I love you so, Rico," she managed to say before she began to cry.

He pulled her fully into his embrace then. She felt the soft cotton of his shirt soak up her tears. "Oh, Louisa, do you know what you are asking?"

"Yes. I also know what it might cost me, but surely once we are legally wed…"

Rico rested his chin on top of her head, and she knew that he was considering her plea. "I don't know, Louisa. Maybe you're right," he said. "But have you thought this through? Our life will not be easy. You must be very sure that this is what you want."

"What I want is to be happy, and the only path I see to that is for us to be together openly—and legally. Papa will have to make his choice then, and at least we will know."

"And if he chooses to fully disown you? To keep you from your sister and mother, and them from you—what then? How can you find happiness then?"

"We will find it together." She stood on tiptoe to kiss him.

He tightened his hold on her, kissing her with all the pent-up passion each of them lived with day in and night out. He stepped away, took in a deep breath, and slowly released it as he stared up at the dark sky. For a moment she thought he would refuse her. But then she saw his fingers working free the buttons of his shirt. He spread it on the ground. She knelt and waited for him to join her. Kneeling, he faced her and gently took the rosary from her. He twined it around her wrist and then around his own, joining them in simulation of the *el lazo* tradition that was a part of the wedding ceremony for people of his culture.

"Louisa Johnson, I will be your husband, caring for you, protecting you, loving you from this day forward."

"And Rico Mendez, I will be your wife, caring for you, following you wherever you may go, and—forsaking all others—loving you with all my heart from this day forward."

They kissed and he stretched out beside her, their wrists still joined.

"Can you get away tomorrow?" he asked.

"Yes."

"Meet me here after dark. We will go to Tucson, to the justice of the peace, and make this official," he continued.

"But let this be the wedding of our hearts," she whispered as she raised herself onto one elbow and bent to kiss his bare chest. "Let this be our wedding night, Rico, in celebration of the vows we have just shared."

He said no words, but answered her by opening the row of tiny pearl buttons that closed the front of her nightgown and branding her as his with a row of kisses that moved from her throat to her breasts. She arched, offering herself to him. He sat back on his heels and ran his fingers over the fabric of her gown, easing the hem higher and then finding the core of her—a place he had taught her to expect a pleasure so irresistible that she would cry out with sheer ecstasy.

She pushed his hand away. "We are one," she said huskily, for in her mind no official service could replace the vows they had just given and received. In her mind they were man and wife. "Show me that way, my husband."

Rico removed the rest of his clothes and then pushed her nightgown over her shoulders and down her bare legs. Once they were both naked, he stood, held out his hand to her, and led her to the creek. The water ran fast, still engorged with the runoff from the winter snows of the high country. It was cold but thrilling. Rico led the way to a place they both knew well—a place they had discovered as children was deep enough to swim in. A place where as adults they had stood in water up to her shoulders. He bathed her now, scooping water and caressing her shoulders, breasts, hips. She followed his lead, reveling in the sight of his naked body, which was so strong and so beautifully fitted with hers.

He lifted her and she felt his erection coaxing her to open to him. She braced her hands on his shoulders and he filled her. In that moment she accepted that nothing would ever be the same for them again. She was joined to this man forever now, and together they would face whatever challenges life might bring.

∽∞∾

Two days later, on a beautiful April afternoon, Louisa and Rico arrived at the ranch after a courthouse wedding in Tucson and their first night as husband and wife, spent in a hotel. Louisa held Rico's hand as they climbed the steps to the porch where her parents sat. Her father stood and stared at them for a long moment as they delivered their news. When Rico stepped forward and extended his hand, George Johnson ignored the gesture and without a word went inside and firmly closed the front door of the house. In the weeks that followed, he refused to see or in any way have contact with them.

Her mother counseled the need to give him time and suggested it might be best if they stayed with Rico's family on the Porterfield ranch. But the days and weeks passed with no change. If her father saw her or Rico in town, he crossed the street or turned away. In the Catholic church both families attended, Louisa and Rico sat with his family. Louisa's mother would glance over at her but made no move to speak with her in the churchyard following services. Her younger sister, Helen, sometimes slipped away for visits at the Porterfield ranch, but when their father discovered these meetings, he forbade Helen from going anywhere without being accompanied by her mother or him.

"I'm a prisoner," Helen moaned one afternoon in June as she and Louisa walked along the banks of the creek that ran through both properties.

"Give him time," Louisa advised. "Surely once he realizes he's to be a grandfather, things will change."

Helen squealed with delight. "When?"

Louisa smiled and laid her hand on her still-flat stomach. "Rico's mother thinks sometime in January, and Doc Wilcox agrees."

"Wait till I tell Mama!"

But to Louisa's surprise, the news of her pregnancy only deepened her father's resolve. She had been so sure once she and Rico started a family, all would be forgiven and the necessary steps for reconciliation would be taken. For the first time, Louisa doubted she would ever be reunited with her family.

"I don't know what to do, Rico," she admitted

one afternoon as they worked together, whitewashing the walls of the anteroom that had been added to the Porterfield house. Mrs. Porterfield had offered them the space rent-free as her wedding gift. "Since they refuse to see me, I sent them each a note. I told them how happy we are and assured them I am in good health and we are so very blessed. The notes were returned—unopened."

Her husband was a quiet man—tall, slender, with dark eyes that always seemed to hold answers somewhere in their inky depths. He continued to spread paint on the rough walls, but she couldn't help but notice how his hold on the brush tightened.

"Tell me what to do," she pleaded.

But this time Rico had no answers, and Louisa began to fear this might be because there simply was no solution. Like Louisa and her mother—and his mother—Rico had assured her that with time George Johnson would accept their union. She knew Rico had always looked up to the man who had urged him to learn more of the business, had bragged to his friends and fellow ranchers about Rico's talent with a lasso and branding iron, had even joked with the Porterfields that one day they just might find Rico leaving them to work his place full-time.

Of course there had been other signs, signs Rico always excused as the pressure of the times or perhaps embarrassment caused by some comment made about how close Rico was to the family. Louisa had not always heard of those incidents from her husband. Her mother-in-law, Juanita, had revealed the most telling episode one day as the two of them sat in the Porterfield's court-yard waiting for their husbands to return from a day on the range. Louisa was mending one of Rico's shirts while she spoke openly of her frustration that not even the idea of a first grandchild seemed to have penetrated her father's resolve.

"I know he feels the pressure of others who

believe—wrongly—that we should not be together, but honestly, Mama Mendez, this is his grandchild I'm carrying."

The older woman was unusually quiet as her wooden knitting needles clicked off each stitch.

"Tell me I'm wrong," Louisa challenged.

Rico's mother reached over and took hold of Louisa's hand. "*Mi'ja*, I think perhaps you have underestimated the depth of your father's feelings," she said.

"But he always cared for Rico," Louisa protested.

"*Sí.* What he did not care for was Rico with you. He thought he had solved that problem, and then the two of you defied him by running away."

"Solved it how? I never once…"

Juanita hesitated for several seconds, her lips twitching as if she wanted to say something but was afraid. Finally she let out a long breath and began. "Do you recall a time, a week or so before you went away to Tucson, when Rico was injured? When you came here to see about him because he had not come to see you?"

"The time his horse threw him," Louisa replied, nodding with certainty.

"*Sí.*" Juanita Mendez lifted one eyebrow and then returned to her knitting. "No horse threw him," she said softly.

"What do you mean?"

Juanita glanced up at her and pursed her lips. "Your *papá* sent for him that morning, and when he arrived at your ranch, Rico went into the barn. Your father was waiting. He had a shovel and he struck him hard across his shoulders. It was a warning—one George Johnson had every reason to believe would be heeded."

"I don't believe you. It must have been an accident. Papa was surprised and thought Rico was an intruder or…"

"The other caballeros were right outside. There was no intruder—and no intrusion into what your *papá* was doing."

"You're accusing my father of trying to kill Rico?"

Louisa fought to control the instinct to shout at her mother-in-law.

Juanita smothered a hoot of derisive laughter. "Make no mistake, *mi hija*, if your father had intended to kill Rico, my son would be dead." She rested her knitting on her lap and continued her tale. "And then a week after that, the two of you…"

"It was me," Louisa said softly. "I was the one who said we should run away. Rico was always the one trying to talk me out of it, reminding me of all the comments and insults I had had to endure already for just being seen with him or daring to dance a reel with him. He tried to convince me that it would only get worse if we married."

"And that was exactly what your father feared—what he fears to this day, Louisa. You ask why the baby has not turned his mind around? It has doubled his fears. Your child will be branded as a mestizo, a half-breed, and for all that you and Rico must face, that baby will be caught in the middle as well."

Louisa bit her lower lip. "So you agree with him that we have made a mistake, Mama Mendez?"

"Love is never a mistake," she replied. "But it can be a challenge. You cannot go back and undo what has been done, Louisa—nor would I wish for you to do that. But you must face reality, and the reality is that for some people, perhaps for your *papá*, fear of the unknown makes them dig in their heels."

"But you and Papa Mendez…"

Juanita smiled. "Our people are used to finding a way to come to terms with things we cannot change. I can see how much you love my son and how he loves you. Your journey will not be easy, but then few are, and you and Rico have the added blessing of the Porterfields standing with you. Just do not base your happiness on changing others." She stood. "Time for me to start supper. Do not sit in the sun too long."

Louisa set her sewing aside and hugged her mother-in-law. "Thank you for telling me this, but Rico and I will find a way," she assured her. "Someday my family will just have to accept that I was the one who pushed Rico—not the other way around."

Juanita cupped her cheek, her gaze filled with sadness. But she said no more, just gathered her knitting and slowly walked to the house.

Louisa found a place in the shade, folded the mended shirt, and rested her hands on the slight swell of her stomach. She and Rico had known each other since childhood, and her parents had welcomed Rico into their home on multiple occasions. George Johnson had relied on the cowboy to help out on the spread when he was shorthanded. And in spite of his work at the neighboring Porterfield ranch, Rico had never failed to do what he could. In fact, Louisa's father had on more than one occasion referred to the young man as the son he'd never had. Given that history and her parents' love for her, Louisa had to believe eventually her father would do what he had always done in the face of circumstances he could no longer control—he would find his way to acceptance.

But as sure of the future as she felt whenever she and Rico were together, he was often gone for days at a time working the herd, branding new stock, and driving the cattle to market. It was on those lonely nights that the full force of her decision hit her, and as summer turned to autumn, she could not help but question if her parents would ever forgive her.

◆◆◆

Every November the Porterfields gave a party to celebrate the successful delivery of stock to market and the end of another season. Everyone from the area attended, and this year was to be no exception. Louisa had been pressed

into service by her friend Amanda Porterfield to help
with the plans—always elaborate whenever Amanda
took charge. She was grateful for the opportunity to
concentrate on something other than her estrangement
from her family, now going into its seventh month and
worse than ever. What had begun as her father's refusal
to accept Rico or their decision to marry had escalated
over the summer and fall to include her mother and
Helen and a good many of their friends and neighbors.

For months she had clung to the idea that in time her
mother would persuade her father to see reason—Louisa
and Rico were married and expecting a child. Right up
to the moment when she crossed paths with her mother
and Helen at Eliza McNew's dry-goods store, she had
believed her mother would finally stand her ground and
take her side in the matter. Early one morning, she went
to town with Amanda to shop for fabric for dresses for
the party. Although Louisa's pregnancy was advanced,
Amanda had assured her Eliza would not open the shop
to others while they were there. So when the bell over
the shop door jangled and Louisa saw her mother and
sister enter, she was sure Amanda had arranged this
meeting, and squeezed her friend's hand in gratitude.

"Mama," she cried as she hurried forward, but she
stopped when she realized the toll their estrangement had
taken. Dorothy Johnson had aged, her usually dark hair
now streaked with gray and her normally luminous skin
sallow and lined. But the biggest surprise was she did not
return Louisa's joyous greeting. Instead she locked eyes
on Eliza McNew, who appeared to receive the message
as she steered Amanda to the far side of the store.

"Hello, Louisa," her mother said finally. Helen said
nothing, fiddling nervously with the strings of her purse
as she pretended an interest in a display case near the
front door. "You're looking well," her mother said, but
this comment was delivered with a frown as she focused

on Louisa's obvious pregnancy. As was the custom, once Louisa began to show, she did not attend church or other gatherings. This was the first time she had left the Porterfield ranch in weeks.

"Amanda insisted we come today," Louisa began, thinking her mother disapproved of a pregnant woman in public—especially when that woman was her daughter. "We came straight here and will go straight back," she promised.

Her mother waved off any explanation. "Something must be done, Louisa. I agreed for us to meet here, because your father is distraught and unwell. Once I had thought to ask you to come to your senses and accept an annulment, but of course now it is far too late for that. We would be the talk of the territory. And so it occurred to me that perhaps once the child is born…"

"Rico isn't going anywhere. He is my husband, Mama, and the father of our child."

"And George Johnson is my husband and your father and deserves respect. Your actions have broken his heart, Louisa. Have you no pity for the man?"

"What would you have me do?"

"I would have had you wait and discuss this matter with your father and me instead of allowing that boy to persuade you to slip away in the dead of night. Honestly, child, those people…"

And that was the moment that Louisa understood Juanita Mendez had been right. She might never make this right with her parents. "And what would you have me do with this baby?" she asked quietly as she smoothed the fabric of her dress over her rounded stomach, deliberately emphasizing the evidence of her pregnancy.

"I am quite sure that Juanita would raise the child as her own. After all, this baby is her grandchild."

"And yours," Louisa reminded her, wanting to scream the words at her. She noticed Helen had joined Amanda and Eliza, and although all three were pretending to examine a bolt of fabric, there was little doubt they were hearing every word. "Mama, please. If you and Papa would only allow Rico and me to call on you, to sit down and talk calmly, surely…"

"If you refuse to follow the commandment that instructs you to honor your father, Louisa, then I give up. Helen, we should go."

Louisa watched as her mother walked to the door without a backward look or word of farewell. Helen glanced her way, giving her an expression of helpless sympathy, and hurried to catch up to their mother, who was already outside, walking stiffly down the street.

The jingle of the bell over the closing door was the only sound inside the store. Neither Eliza nor Amanda said a word. Instead they waited to see what Louisa would do. Stunned by the encounter, she stared out the window until she saw her mother and sister climb aboard their buggy and pass by the store on their way out of town. Neither of them looked her way.

Then she felt her child move inside her, and as was always the case when she felt that life, she smiled. The meeting with her mother and sister was not the end of things, she decided. Once her parents met their grandchild—held their grandchild—everything would be all right. Another two months of this, coupled with the coming of Christmas, and everything would work out. She was certain of it. She turned to face her friends, then crossed the store to finger the bolt of fabric they still held.

"This is lovely. Amanda, it is the perfect color for you. You must buy it and perhaps a few yards of that wonderful lace as trim. You'll be the belle of the ball."

As usual Amanda was distracted by the turn of their attention to her, and Louisa could see that Eliza understood exactly what she was doing, so she went along with her. "And now to find the perfect fabric for your gown,

Louisa," she said, turning to scan the bolts stacked on the shelves behind her. "Something in a rose, I should think. Or perhaps that lavender there."

Louisa was sure her parents would be at the party, and she would not further embarrass them by making such a public display of her pregnancy. "I won't need a dress for the party," she said quietly. "I'll enjoy it from the kitchen—helping Rico's mother."

Amanda's eyes went wide with surprise. "But…"

"Please don't fight me on this," Louisa pleaded. Her lower lip trembled and she bit it to keep the tears at bay. But when Eliza and Amanda wrapped their arms around her, she lost the battle and let the tears come.

Two

THE PARTY WAS LIVELY AND NOISY. THERE WERE SO MANY guests that Louisa and Juanita were constantly refilling platters and sending them out with Amanda and her brother, Trey, to set on the long table positioned under the tiled roof of the portal. From time to time Louisa would glance out the open door, hoping to catch a glimpse of Rico. He was playing guitar with a band put together by the Porterfields' top ranch hand, Bunker. When Rico played, he bent his head to the instrument, his straight black hair falling over his cheek. She knew he was humming softly along with the music.

"You should sit," Juanita said, nodding toward a chair near the door. "You're very flushed. Take some air."

Juanita was an imposing woman who spoke in tones meant to be obeyed without question, but Louisa had always liked Rico's mother—his entire family. On the ride home after they had eloped, Rico admitted that he had told his parents and the Porterfields of their plan.

"I couldn't just not show up for work," he'd explained.

And to Louisa's surprise, after she and Rico had gone to her family's ranch as a newly married couple and had been turned away, Juanita and Mrs. Porterfield had seen them coming and called others to gather in the courtyard. As they approached the rambling adobe house, they had been surprised to see Rico's family, all the Porterfields, and even the ranch hands cheering their arrival. Whistles and shouts and smiles greeted them as Rico lifted Louisa from the buggy he'd rented in town and led her into their midst. The men shook hands with Rico, congratulating him, and then shyly planted a kiss on Louisa's proffered cheek. The women were far less restrained, hugging them in turn and peppering them with questions about the ceremony.

And that was the homecoming Louisa chose to remember as she watched the guests enjoying the dancing and the food.

Once the waltz ended, Bunker announced that the musicians were taking a little break. Rico put down his guitar and hopped down off the platform that served as a stage. Louisa pulled at her dress, stretched to its limit by her expanding girth, and waited for him to come to her. He was so very handsome, but she knew it was not his good looks that had drawn her to him. Rico was kind and caring—to people and animals alike. His love of all things in nature gave him an aura of being at peace with the world, and that calmness brought him the respect of others.

"*Está bien?*" he asked when he reached her, after she had returned his embrace and kissed his jaw.

"You really have to stop asking me that every five minutes," she teased. "It's a baby, not some dire disease."

He smiled and pressed his palm to her stomach. "It's our baby," he reminded her, "and I worry about both of you. And you can do nothing about that." He turned to his mother. "I'm taking Louisa for a walk, Mama. I'll send somebody in to help you."

"No, *gracias*. Go, the two of you." Juanita shooed them away and then stood at the open door fanning herself with her apron, watching them go.

"Mama is so excited about this baby," Rico said as hand in hand they made their way down the path leading to the creek that connected the Porterfield ranch to that of Louisa's parents. "She brags about her first grandchild to anyone who will listen," he continued and chuckled as he added, "The other day I heard Papa tell her she needed to stop."

Louisa giggled, imagining her shy, quiet father-in-law, Eduardo, standing up to his wife for once. "I would like to have witnessed that," she said.

The walk to the creek took them past the barn, where the conveyances the guests had driven to the party were lined up. People were still arriving, so Rico took hold of her elbow to steer her clear of the moving horses and wagons, lifting his hand in greeting to those he knew— those who still spoke to them, Louisa realized, as a couple from church pointedly looked the other way in passing.

"Don't let them see you upset," Rico counseled when Louisa stopped and turned back, prepared to call out to the offending couple. "That just shows them they can get to you. It makes them feel like they're within their rights to disrespect you."

"Well, they do get to me, and they are definitely not within their rights—and besides, it is both of us they disrespect, not just me," she fumed, although she knew he spoke from experience she needed to learn to heed, experience they would have to teach their child to follow.

"Dance with me," Rico said.

She knew exactly what he was doing, and she loved him for it. Over the months of their marriage, there had been many times when someone in town or visiting the ranch had either pointedly ignored Louisa or covered some insult with a smile. And then there had been those occasions when Mrs. Porterfield insisted she join her and her guests for a glass of lemonade. Not infrequently there would be some comment made about the value of Mexican servants, followed by a sly glance at Louisa and an assurance that, of course, they didn't mean to imply Rico or his family were simply hired help.

"Come on, Louisa, let it go." Rico held out his arms to her.

"There's no music," she grumbled.

He hummed and swayed in time to the tune. He grinned at her and swept his hat off as he gave her a deep bow. He was, as always, irresistible.

Louisa managed an awkward curtsy. "I'd be delighted to dance with you, kind sir."

Laughter and conversation drifted their way from the party. The fragrance of Juanita's cooking mingled with the scent of juniper and sage used to stoke the fires that burned in the yard for guests to warm themselves. They moved slowly to the music he hummed.

"After the ball is over, after the break of morn," he sang, his lips close to her ear.

It was a popular song of the time, but so very sad in its story of love lost. She knew Rico wasn't thinking of that, but she pulled back anyway. "Bunker is headed back to the stage," she said. "Break's over."

She kissed his cheek and together they walked to the house, passing small gatherings of guests as they went. It took her a moment to realize one of those groups included her parents. She heard her father's voice, heard him break off in midsentence as she and Rico walked by, heard the silence that seemed to drown out everything else. She let go of Rico's hand and quickened her pace until she reached the sanctuary of the kitchen.

❧

Louisa's hand slipped from his as she gathered her skirt and hurried past her family and into the kitchen. Rico paused, taking in the uneasy silence that had enveloped those gathered around the small bonfire. He removed his hat, looked directly at Louisa's mother and father for a long moment as they avoided his stare and gazed into the fire. "*Buenos noches*, señor, señora," he said as he replaced his hat and kept on walking. But afterward, as he followed Bunker's lead and played reels and waltzes, he wasn't hearing the music. He was thinking about Louisa and how, through the months of their marriage and her pregnancy, she had put such a brave face on things when it came to her family. Surely, as her husband, it was his job to mend that fence once and for all.

The following morning he asked for time off. "Got something I need to do," he said.

Chet Hunter, the ranch foreman and the husband of the eldest Porterfield daughter, raised his eyebrows but did not pry. "You'll be back by noon?"

"Maybe sooner," Rico agreed. He liked Chet—liked working for him.

"You don't think you ought to give this a bit more thought?" Chet asked, and Rico understood he had guessed the reason for his request.

"It's been long enough."

Chet nodded and then clapped him on the shoulder as he walked with him to the corral. "Hold your temper," he advised. "George Johnson is a good man, but he will try to prove that what he thinks of you is right."

"Funny how his opinion of me changed when he realized I was in love with his daughter."

Chet held the reins as Rico mounted one of the ranch horses. "His opinion changed when he realized that Louisa was in love with you," he said. "He can't understand that."

"Past time he found a way," Rico replied as he turned the horse toward the open trail and rode off.

Even though the Johnson ranch bordered that of the Porterfields, it still took over an hour of steady riding to cover the distance between the two properties. That gave Rico plenty of time to consider how best to approach his father-in-law. It also gave him time to have second thoughts. Maybe he should have made an appointment. Just showing up might not be his best choice. Of course, for much of his life he hadn't thought twice about riding over to the Johnson place unannounced. In those days, George Johnson had always welcomed him with a handshake and a smile. As a rancher with no sons, he seemed to look forward to seeing Rico join him for chores and to sit with him while they discussed the changing role of ranching.

That had been before he realized that Rico's visits were not always about helping out.

"I'll remind him that in those days, before Louisa and me…"

He shook off the idea as he rode past the open land where the cowboys from the Johnson place were working their herd. A couple of the hands sitting near the chuck wagon called out to him and he raised his hand in return, but did not stop. Seeing those men, it occurred to him Mr. Johnson might not be at home—he might have gone into town on business or for a meeting of the cooperative several of the smaller ranches had formed. And that's when he decided perhaps a conversation with his mother-in-law might be the wisest first step toward healing the breach between his wife's family and him. And the more he thought about it, the more certain he was Mrs. Johnson was the key to the matter. Even though Louisa had told him of the ill-fated meeting at Eliza McNew's store, Mrs. Johnson had always had a soft spot for Rico.

He switched his thinking to how he might make his case to her, and lost in those thoughts, he failed to notice the rider coming toward him at full gallop.

"You lost, boy, or just trespassing?"

George Johnson was a heavy man, and that plus the exertion of the ride had left his face flushed to a mottled red and his barrel chest heaving to catch his next breath.

Rico reined in his horse. "I was coming to see you, sir," he replied, shaking off the insult. He tipped his hat back so Johnson could see his face—his eyes. "Louisa misses her family, and in her condition…"

"You defile my daughter and have the nerve to speak of her 'condition'? Get off my land. Tell Louisa she is welcome any time, once she has come to her senses and understands her mistake, but you are not welcome under any circumstances."

"Louisa is my wife."

"So you say, but until she takes her wedding vows in a proper church service delivered by a priest, she is no man's wife."

"And that will end this? If we stand before Father Sanford and…"

"Not with you—never with you or any of your kind. You tricked my daughter into sneaking around behind our backs, and then when she ended up in a family way, she thought she had no choice. And that's when you got her to agree to slip away with you and go down to Tucson and…"

Rico tightened his grip on his saddle horn. How much was he supposed to take before he stood his ground? Spoke for himself—and his people?

"Louisa was not defiled by me or anyone else." He forced himself to speak calmly. "We were legally married, and now we are to have a child together—a child conceived weeks after our marriage. I will provide for my family following the fine example set for me by you and Mrs. Johnson and by my *familia*, and I will love your daughter until the day I die. My heritage plays no part in any of that. I am as much a man of honor as you, and there was a time when I believed you knew that."

George Johnson pulled a rifle from its sheath at the back of his saddle, cocked it, and aimed directly at Rico's heart. "For the last time, get off my land and never let me catch you anywhere near here again." His voice shook with emotion and his hand on the gun was unsteady.

Rico tugged his hat low on his forehead and gathered the reins. "Please let Mrs. Johnson and Helen know they

are welcome to visit Louisa any time at the Porterfields—
and that goes for you as well, sir. I can accept that you do
not wish to see me, but please do not punish my wife in
the bargain. Good day."

As he rode away, he kept his horse at a slower pace,
half expecting the sound of the rifle firing and the
blaze of a bullet striking him in the back. And he knew
shooting him would carry no penalty. Shooting him
would achieve what Johnson wanted most—the return
of his daughter to the fold. It surprised him to realize
how much he understood what it must take for George
Johnson to not pull that trigger.

That night, as he and Louisa prepared for bed, he
studied his beautiful wife for a long moment as she sat
on the side of their bed, brushing her hair. "I went to see
your father today," he told her.

She paused in midstroke. "Oh, Rico, why? There is
nothing to be gained and…"

"I want you to go visit your family after they get
home from church on Sunday afternoon. I've asked Mrs.
Porterfield to go with you—at least the first time. They
won't turn her away."

She resumed brushing her hair, and the fierceness of
the strokes told him he had upset her. "You spoke of this
to Mrs. Porterfield, but not me?"

"Your father…"

"And you went to see my father without telling me?"

"He is hurting, Louisa, and…"

"And we are not?" She stood and paced the confines
of the anteroom. "I cannot believe you did this. My
family has made their choice. It is not for you or anyone
else to try and dissuade them, and it is certainly not for
you to go groveling to my father…"

"I did not grovel." He and Louisa had argued before,
and he had learned the only answer to her fiery temper
was to remain calm and silent, allowing her to get out

all of her fury before he attempted to reason with her. The minute he spoke, he knew he should have remained silent a little longer.

Louisa stared at him, her hands instinctively cradling their unborn child. "You went to him, when you have done nothing but love me. It is my father who is in the wrong here. It is his stupid prejudice that has made a mess of everything. It is his refusal to remember what you have meant to our family even before we…"

She burst into tears and threw up her hands as she turned away from him.

He wrapped his arms around her, turning her so that her head rested on his shoulder, her sobs sending shudders through her entire body. "Shhh," he whispered. "You'll wake the baby." It was a private joke they had used in the early months of her pregnancy, when in the throes of lovemaking, one or the other of them would cry out. As he stroked her hair and felt her relax against him, he led her to their bed. Once she was settled against the pillows, he stretched out beside her, fingering a curl as her crying subsided into hiccups.

"Louisa, we have to keep trying, and I see these Sunday visits as one way to do that. It will be difficult in the beginning, but that's why if Mrs. Porterfield goes with you, they might listen to reason, and in time…"

She stroked his face. "Rico, I don't want to have to choose you or my family—I want both."

"You can have both, *querida*. Just not at the same time—at least for now." She started to protest but he laid his finger against her lips. "You are unhappy, Louisa, and that can't be good for our child. I'm just trying to be a good *papá* here, so how about it? Will you give this a try?"

She frowned, then smiled. "I love you so, Rico."

"But?"

"No buts. You are going to be the best *papá*." She

placed his hand on her swollen belly and he felt his child moving. Louisa ran her finger down the center of his chest.

"Louisa," he said, his voice breaking with wanting her.

"I mean, as long as the little darling is already awake…"

"But Doc Wilcox said at this later stage…"

"Seems to me before we were married you had all sorts of ways to love me—and taught me what pleasured you in return." She pressed her hand lower and grinned when he groaned in reaction to her touch.

"You'll go see your family on Sunday?" he managed.

"That depends," she whispered as she pulled him close and stroked his ear with her tongue.

"On?"

She didn't say a word but moved his hand so that it rested on the apex of her thighs. He chuckled and pushed aside the fabric of her gown.

∝∾

The visit was a disaster. Not even the presence and charm of Constance Porterfield could soften Louisa's father. While his wife served tea and cake, he sat stone-faced, his arms folded across his chest, refusing to look at Louisa. Mrs. Porterfield kept up a lively conversation filled with tidbits of news she had gathered in town. Louisa's mother smiled and nodded as she sipped her tea and glanced nervously at her husband. Perhaps if Helen had been there, things might have gone better, but Helen had spent the night in town with her friend and had not yet returned.

"George," Mrs. Porterfield said, addressing him directly for the first time, "do you recall the time you and my Isaac decided to go camping over the New Year and got so terribly lost in the snow?"

Louisa's father turned his attention to Constance Porterfield, which meant he was also looking directly at Louisa for the first time since she had arrived. She smiled at him, for everyone in both families remembered that misadventure. For years it had been a source of good memories and laughter.

"What of it?" her father grumbled.

Mrs. Porterfield did not miss a beat. "I was just recalling how young Rico finally tracked the two of you down. Even as a child, that young man could find the proverbial needle in a haystack." She laughed and took a sip of her tea.

Louisa's father stood and addressed his daughter. "If it is your thought that bringing Mrs. Porterfield here to remind me of that boy's positive qualities in order to have me come round to what he has done to you and this family, you have seriously misjudged the severity of the situation, Louisa." He nodded to Mrs. Porterfield and left the room, crossing the center hall to his study and firmly closing the door. Louisa could not help but think that it seemed as if lately every occasion with her father ended in a closed door. The symbolism of that was not lost on her, and she set her teacup back on the tray.

"Perhaps it would be best if we left, Mrs. Porterfield," she said softly. "The days are so short now and we want to be home before dark."

Mrs. Porterfield stood, but she faced Louisa's mother, who remained seated on the settee. "Really, Dorothy, this is your daughter," she entreated.

Louisa's mother twisted her napkin and nervously glanced at the closed door across the hall. "Just go, please, before you make matters worse—as if things could get any worse."

"Dorothy," Mrs. Porterfield continued gently as she reached over to cover her friend's hand with hers. "You are to be a grandmother. This rift between you needs to be repaired if for no other reason than for the good of the child. Louisa…"

Now Louisa's mother stood and led the way to the front door. "My daughter has made her choice and now I must make mine. It seems we have each decided to choose our husbands. Goodbye, Louisa, Constance. Please do not attempt to visit again."

Once they were in the buggy and Constance Porterfield had taken up the reins, Louisa stared out at the horizon. Had her mother just disowned her? Surely not. And yet…

"Thank you, Mrs. Porterfield. I am sorry Rico has involved you in what should be a private family matter."

"You and Rico are part of *my* family, Louisa. Be very clear about that. His parents are among my dearest friends, and I have known Rico since before he was born." She gave a nod toward the swell of Louisa's stomach. "As I now am getting to know you and that baby there."

"Still…"

"Your father is a good man, but even good men can be wrong, and George Johnson is wrong in this."

They rode in silence for a while.

"Did you know he threatened to shoot Rico?" Louisa watched Mrs. Porterfield's face, carefully gauging her reaction to this news.

Constance dismissed this tidbit with a wave of her hand. "Men are always trying to prove their virility, and thankfully, in most cases the threat is an idle one. Once that baby comes into this world, I am sure your parents will come around. You must not give up—or give in, Louisa. If you love Rico…"

"There is no *if*—I love him, have always loved him, and will always love him," Louisa snapped irritably.

Constance Porterfield smiled. "Attagirl," she murmured, and for the rest of the ride back to the ranch they did not speak further of the estrangement between Louisa and her family.

Three

DECEMBER ROARED IN WITH A WINTER STORM, THE LIKES of which had not been seen in a decade. Cattle strayed from the herd and had to be hunted down and rescued. The work meant long, cold hours on the range, but the worst of it was that Rico was away from Louisa for days on end. When Louisa worried they had misjudged the timing of the baby's arrival, Doc Wilcox had told them the baby would come when it was good and ready and not a minute before. He also continued to assure them Louisa was weeks away from delivery. "In my years of experience, a first baby tends to be late, not early, Louisa. Come January, you'll see I'm right. Never met a first-time mother yet who didn't think I had miscalculated."

After the fiasco of the meeting with Louisa's parents a few weeks earlier, Mrs. Porterfield had taken Rico aside and quietly advised him to leave things alone. "The best thing you can do for your wife and child now, Rico, is to love and protect them. They are your priority now."

"But Louisa misses her family, and with me away so much, her mother should be with her at the birth and…"

"Sadly, that is unlikely. However, she will have Juanita and me with her—and Maria and Amanda. My goodness, Rico, this child is going to be so welcomed into this world."

He had to smile. Mrs. Porterfield had always been one to see the more positive side of things. Even after her husband died and she was in mourning, she had traveled that difficult road at first by simply refusing to believe he was gone, speaking aloud to him and mistaking Maria's husband, Chet, for the man on at least two occasions. But when she was ready, she had come out of her delusions and accepted that life must move forward. He understood that this was what she was telling him to do—move on.

"We cannot know the future, Rico," she had advised, "but shame on us if we waste the present."

And so the days had passed. Louisa did not speak of her family but talked instead about the baby and all the hopes she had for their child. "If it is a boy, you must teach him to ride and rope and all the skills he will need for making his way," she had announced one morning as she served Rico his breakfast before he left for the range.

"And what will you teach him?"

"Manners—and to read and write. The world is changing so very fast, and he will need every skill we can give him."

"And if our child is a girl?" Rico's grin faltered. "Not sure what I have to teach a girl."

"Nonsense. You will show her how to ride and how to form good judgments when it comes to others. You will make sure she knows how to stand up for herself."

"And you will teach her to charm a line of unsuspecting young caballeros that I will have to run off because she is far too young and far too—"

"But once she finds true love," Louisa interrupted, her lightheartedness gone, "then you will see that no matter who he is, if she truly loves him, then you must accept him as a son."

"I promise," he whispered and kissed her forehead before gathering his hat and yellow slicker and heading out to the corral. But as he rode with the others through the blowing snow that made it hard to keep count on the herd, he understood that in reality—boy or girl—this child would be considered a half-breed by many, and the struggles to be faced would be monumental.

"Rico, over here!" Chet Hunter's shout carried on the wind, and Rico kneed his horse to follow the sound.

Chet was standing near a barbed-wire fence, where a cow had gotten trapped. "It's one of Johnson's," Chet said, pointing to the brand.

Without hesitation Rico slid from his saddle and knelt in the snow. Gently he freed the animal of the sharp wire prongs. "She'll be all right," he reported as he held back the wiring and the cow struggled to find her footing. "I saw some of the Johnson hands just over that rise. I'll make sure she gets back to them."

Chet nodded and studied the sky. "Looks like the worst is over. Once you've returned that cow, head on back to the ranch. Me and the others can handle things from here."

Rico grinned. "You're spoiling me."

"Don't get used to it."

Rico herded the stray along a trail covered with snow, but one he knew well. Chet was right. The snow had stopped falling and there was a break in the cloud cover that had kept the skies gray for days now. He felt his spirits lift with the change in conditions. Christmas was coming—their first Christmas as man and wife. And with the New Year would come the responsibilities of fatherhood. He let out a whoop of pure joy and the cow paused.

"Git along now," Rico instructed, crowding the animal with his horse to prod it into action. "Time we both got home."

But when he reached the trio of Johnson hands, he realized his father-in-law was one of them. He tipped his hat as the cow loped away to join the rest of the herd. "She got tangled up in some fencing," he said. "A few scratches, but she'll be fine."

The two cowboys rode off to make sure the stray rejoined the herd. But George Johnson remained where he was, astride his horse, staring back at Rico.

Rico replaced the bandana to cover his mouth and nose—protection against the wind and icy snow. He nodded to his father-in-law and turned his horse to head home.

"Baby come yet?" Johnson shouted above the wind and noise of the cowboys whistling to the herd behind him.

Rico hesitated and looked back over his shoulder at the older man, trying to decide what this might be. Once again he lowered the bandana. "Not yet...Doc still says January," he replied and inched his horse in Johnson's direction.

"Storm's kept us from getting any news," Johnson called out. "My wife was worried."

"Louisa…"

But the word was lost on the wind as Johnson kicked his horse to a full gallop and rode away.

All the rest of the ride back to the ranch Rico thought about the encounter, studying each exchange. *My wife was worried.* Not *her mother* and definitely not *I was worried.* Still, it signaled something, surely.

But that night as he lay next to Louisa and told her about the encounter, he felt her go still. And then she turned to him. "Did he thank you for rescuing his stock?"

"Well, no, but…"

"If he cannot show you the most basic gratitude and respect, then nothing has changed, and I doubt it ever will."

"But he said your mother…"

"If my mother is so worried, where is she? No, she has not only chosen her husband—as she once told me—she has chosen to agree with his position, and that goes against everything she ever taught Helen and me about the importance of making up our own minds based on whatever the facts might be."

"Louisa, I know you are hurting and…"

"How can you defend them? They have disowned

their own daughter as well as this innocent child who is their own blood."

"A decision they will come to regret—one they may well already regret," he argued.

Louisa grimaced and he realized the pain in her expression was more physical than emotional.

"Louisa, what is it?" In spite of the doctor's assurance that the delivery was weeks away yet, Rico worried. Louisa was so big, bigger than his mother had been with any of his siblings. "A Christmas baby might be just what's needed," his mother had commented one morning—her way of saying she agreed that it would not be long.

But surely it was far too soon. "I'm going to get help," he announced as he reached for his hat.

"No! Wait!" Louisa reached out to him. "It's a twinge and will pass." She forced a smile as she tried to find some position that might offer more comfort. "Your mama warned me this might happen as my time came closer. You cannot worry about every little thing, Rico."

But when she rolled onto her side, Rico saw a pink stain on the bedding. "Humor me," he said, not wanting to alarm her. "My mother might have some advice or one of her special teas that could help."

Louisa wrinkled her nose at the mention of tea. Juanita was well known for her home remedies that she assured friends and family alike could cure everything from a simple head cold to pneumonia. More than once during Louisa's pregnancy, Rico's mother had arrived bearing a steaming pot of foul-smelling liquid intended to lessen morning sickness or leg cramps or some other malady. He was always surprised when his wife gamely drank down the potion and thanked Juanita profusely.

"Be right back," he promised and hurried away.

When he described what he had seen to his mother, half hoping she would laugh away his fears, she did not even smile. "Addie Wilcox is staying the night with Amanda," she said. "And that young woman knows almost as much as her father does, when it comes to doctoring. You get back to your wife and make sure she stays put. I'll wake Addie and we'll be right there."

By the time his mother and Addie arrived, Rico had endured Louisa's annoyance that he was making far too much of a little discomfort and managed to keep her lying still in the bargain. But when she saw Addie, she bit her lower lip. "I really don't think it was necessary to…"

"I was in the neighborhood," Addie said as she sat on the side of the bed to take Louisa's pulse. "Besides, my father has been very selfish about allowing me to be a part of this wonderful adventure that you and Rico are on."

But Rico saw Louisa was not fooled. "What's going on?" she demanded, looking first at her husband and then back at Addie.

"Rico noticed a little staining on the bedding here," Addie replied calmly as she walked to the other side of the bed to examine the evidence. "It could be nothing, but let's be sure, all right?"

"Blood?" Louisa's eyes went wide with distress.

Rico sat where Addie had sat and held Louisa's hand while they both watched Addie touch the stain and then bring her fingers to her nose. They did not have to ask what she'd found. Her expression told them that it was blood and it was fresh.

⤜∞⤛

Louisa tightened her grip on Rico's fingers. "Are we going to lose our baby?" It was a whisper.

"Nonsense," Addie said, her voice cracking a little as she attempted to reassure them. "It's not uncommon at this stage for there to be some fluid leakage. We're going to change these linens, and once dawn breaks, I'll take this sample to my father just to confirm, but I am fairly sure that it is nothing you need overly concern yourself with."

Juanita turned to the cupboard and pull out fresh bedding. "Saves us doing this in the morning, when we would have anyway," Juanita commented as she loosened the covers on the unoccupied side of the bed and wadded them in a line next to Louisa's body.

"Let me…" Louisa gripped Rico's shoulder as she attempted to sit up.

"You stay right there," Juanita ordered. "I've changed many a bed with the person lying in it and this is no different. Rico, make yourself useful and tuck in that corner there." She pointed to the bottom of the straw mattress. "You've overdone, Louisa," she continued as she smoothed half of the sheet into place. "For the duration, I will not allow you to…"

Louisa did not listen to the rest of her mother-in-law's monologue. She was well aware that when Juanita was upset, she tended to babble on about everything and nothing. So whatever was going on with her pregnancy, it was serious. And looking at Rico, she knew he had come to the same conclusion. As usual, his response was to try and find a solution.

"What can we do?" he asked.

Addie glanced at him and then back at Louisa. "Well, your wife here needs to stay put—bed rest for at least a week, unless my father overrules me. And you," she said, turning to Rico, "need to stay calm and make sure Louisa follows doctor's orders. Now, let's get her moved to the other side of the bed so we can finish changing it and all get some sleep."

Louisa did not tell Addie what was most worrisome about her situation—that she could not recall feeling the baby move since earlier that day. She would wait and pray and hope. She would not tell Rico.

Her mother-in-law fluffed the pillow and replaced

it in its freshly washed case under her head. "You rest now," she murmured. "Everything is going to be fine." But she could not hide the tremor in her voice nor the unshed tears that brightened her eyes in the lamplight.

"I'll stop by before I head back to town," Addie promised. "The real Doc Wilcox will come out to see you tomorrow as well, so no reason to worry." And as Rico walked his mother and Addie to the door, Addie told him to not hesitate to come get her should anything happen before morning broke.

So everyone was trying to put a brave face on the matter, when in fact they were all clearly every bit as worried as she was. Well, they did not know her when it came to facing adversity—and they did not know her child. Together they would do whatever it took to make it through the rest of this time.

After he shut the door, Rico remained standing there for a long moment, his back to her. His shoulders sagged and she knew he was crying.

"Come here, Rico," she said softly.

"I'll sleep in the chair," he managed, swiping at his eyes with the back of one hand before pulling his shirt free of his trousers.

"No. We want you here with us. We're *familia*, Rico." She laid one hand on her stomach and patted the bed beside her with the other.

"You're sure it's okay?"

Louisa felt a bubble of laughter well within her. "It had best be all right," she said, smiling. "After all, you lying next to me was how I got to this condition in the first place."

He sat on the bed and pulled off his boots, then tentatively lay next to her.

"Sing to us, Rico," she said as she rolled to her side and laid her head in the crook of his shoulder. He hummed a melody she had heard his mother sing softly as she kneaded bread or made tortillas.

"What are the words?"

"It's a lullaby," Rico replied. "I only know the Spanish."

"Our child will know both English and Spanish," she reminded him.

He smiled, leaned close to the mound of her pregnancy and sang.

"*Cierras ya tus ojitos. Duermete sin temor.* Close your eyes. Sleep without fear." He sang the Spanish, then spoke the translation. "*Duermete sin temor. Cuando tu despiertes, Yo estaré aquí.* Sleep without fear. When you wake up, I'll be here." He kissed her stomach and rested his head there.

She fingered his hair. For the first time in days she felt a sense of calm, a feeling everything would be all right. And just before she dozed off, she felt the baby shift and she smiled.

∞

A few days before Christmas, as Louisa sat by the window, bored by days and weeks of being cooped up in this small cottage, she saw Mrs. Porterfield leave the main house by the kitchen door. The older woman picked her way around puddles that had iced over during the night until she reached Louisa's door. She had a shawl wrapped around her head and shoulders, and she was carrying a wicker basket. She knocked twice and then opened the door.

"Louisa?"

The scare they had endured a few weeks earlier had passed and not been repeated, but everyone was determined to make sure that Louisa got her rest. Struggling to her feet, she shuffled toward the door. "Mrs. Porterfield, should you be out in this weather?"

She knew Constance Porterfield had been suffering from a bout of rheumatism for nearly a week now, but she also knew that once the woman made up her mind to do something, nothing would stop her. "Old age—nothing for it," she said dismissively. "The real question is, how are you doing? You know we all told Rico he could stay home this time? Plenty of hands to handle the herd."

Rico had left before dawn with the other men. They would be gone until Christmas Eve, but he had promised her nothing would keep him from being with her for their first Christmas as man and wife. He planned to have a very special surprise for her.

"My husband does not like the others to think he is being given special consideration, Mrs. Porterfield."

"Nothing we wouldn't do for any one of them, and they surely know that. Your husband is stubborn, Louisa." Her words were critical but delivered with a fondness Louisa knew spoke her true feelings. "I brought you a few things for the baby." She began laying out a variety of garments, including a christening gown. "Rico and his brother Javier were both christened in this gown, as were all my children. Juanita fussed and fumed, but I tend to get my way in the end."

Louisa fingered the fine muslin and lace of the garment. "It is so beautiful."

"It's seen its share of trauma. Amanda spit up all over it and the minister at her christening, and Trey…" She paused as she so often did when she spoke of her youngest. Trey Porterfield had been frail and sickly for much of his early life. Now he was a robust teenager who spent much of his time in the bunkhouse with the other hands. "Well, it swallowed Trey," she said with a smile. "Your mother-in-law had to sew a seam down the back to keep it from slipping off him."

Louisa looked down at her distended stomach. "I don't think that will be a problem for this baby," she said. "But are you sure? I was thinking perhaps I might write my mother and…"

Mrs. Porterfield continued to unpack items from the

basket. Louisa did not miss the way her lips tightened and a frown creased her forehead. "Well, you see, I saw your mother and sister in town a few days ago. They were shopping for last-minute gifts, and I thought it might be an opportunity to play upon their Christmas spirit of charity and mention…"

"You asked my mother to send our family's christening gown?" Louisa did not know whether to be touched or annoyed. Both emotions raced through her and must have shown in the tone she took, for immediately Mrs. Porterfield looked up, her face twisted into an expression of contrition.

"I know I overstepped, Louisa. It was not my place. My late husband used to say that if there was a time for not speaking, I had never observed it."

"Please do not concern yourself, Mrs. Porterfield. Rico will be very touched by your offer of this beautiful garment for our baby—as am I. Thank you." She forced herself to smile as she began going through the rest of the bounty laid out before her on the scarred but spotless wooden table. "You are making me realize that in a few weeks I will have need of all this—and more," she said, fingering a tiny pair of knitted booties. "Do you think these will fit? Rico has very large feet."

Mrs. Porterfield laughed. "How about I make us a cup of tea so we can have a nice long talk about the joys—and challenges—of being a mother?"

"I would like that."

"Let's get Juanita in here to be part of this. Better advice from two experienced mothers than just one, wouldn't you say?" She went to the door, opened it, and shouted Juanita's name.

"Is it time?" Juanita pushed her way through the door seconds later, her cheeks rosy with exertion and the effects of the cold. "What is it?" she demanded.

"A tea party," Mrs. Porterfield said cheerfully; then

she frowned. "I should have brought some of that wonderful cake you made us for supper last night, Nita."

"The last thing I need is cake," Louisa said with another nod toward her girth, and she realized that a day that had begun with the loneliness of long hours before Rico would return had turned into a celebration of sorts—a family gathering of women with one thing in common. She only wished her mother could join them.

◦◊◦

"Go home, Rico," Chet Hunter ordered as the men sat around the chuck wagon, finishing their breakfast. "And take Eduardo with you. Bunker can handle the wagon. You've got a day's ride and a night on the trail ahead of you, so go, the both of you." He jerked his thumb toward Rico's father, who was putting out the campfire. "We'll be starting back ourselves early tomorrow, and the two of you worrying about that baby are about as useful as a couple of adobe fence posts."

"At least fence posts serve a purpose," Bunker muttered as he started packing up the chuck wagon. When the others glanced his way, he grinned and added, "They hold up the fence."

The men all laughed.

Rico's father was watching him. Their eyes met, and as had happened throughout Rico's youth, he received the silent order his father gave him. "All right, boss," he agreed. "If you're sure."

"I'm relieved, is what I am," Chet replied with a snort. "Got enough to do keeping up with the herd, without worrying about you. Now git along…"

"Little dogie," the men chorused, and Rico grinned.

His father mounted one of the remuda—extra horses the cowboys traveled with whenever they were working the herd—and the two of them rode away. Wanting to get back as soon as possible, Rico led the way cross-country toward the higher cliffs that would cut the time it took to make the journey in half. Normally, with the chuck wagon and herd, they would take a longer route along the frozen creek.

But once they reached the base of the cliffs, it was slow going. The snow had drifted and made picking their way single file along narrow animal trails that offered a wall of rock on one side and sheer drop on the other more difficult. Twice Eduardo's horse slipped and they had to stop, dismount, and make sure the animal was not injured. In good weather they were only a couple of hours' ride from the ranch, but at this pace, Rico feared it might well be dark before they reached home.

"We should have gone the regular way," Rico said.

"We'll get there," his father replied as they pressed on.

What worried Rico as much as the treacherous terrain was the way the sky had started to darken with a thick layer of clouds that promised more snow. After another hour, they decided to camp near a cave opening that would protect them from the elements. Rico built a fire and began roasting two potatoes.

"Rico?"

"You all right, Papá?" Rico turned so he could see his father.

"Just thinking about you and Louisa. She's a fine woman and will make a good *mamá*. This business with her family, in time…"

"This business with her family is unfair, Papá. They have broken her heart."

"They would say she broke theirs first."

Rico realized that over the months since he'd married Louisa and her family had abandoned her, his father had said little about their situation. "How can you take their side in this? We're just two people who fell in love. What does our heritage have to do with any of that?"

Eduardo was silent for a long moment. "Times are

changing, son. You and your kind are seeing to that, but you have to be patient."

"Why? If something is wrong, then why wait? What are we waiting for?"

"You can't force something like the way folks think, Rico, and you need to consider what kind of world your baby is going to face because of what you and Louisa have started."

"You blame us too?" Rico was incredulous. He had thought his parents, of all people, not only understood but sanctioned what he and Louisa had done. "I did not defile Louisa as her father believes. I would never do that. I love her, but more than that, I respect her. What's so hard to understand about that?"

"Rico, you and Louisa need to accept that this is more than just the two of you."

"I know it's also the baby. Well, we'll protect our child and…"

"It is also more than your child. This is about history— decades of a divide you and Louisa have bridged. Can you not understand that as much as the Johnsons may have liked you, they are afraid?"

"Of what? Me?" He handed his father one of the roasted potatoes.

"Of the same things your mother and I fear—that you will be shunned, and worse. That our grandchild will be branded in a way that will color his or her entire life."

"But you and Mama have embraced Louisa."

"We have a longer history of accepting what we see cannot be changed and moving forward," his father replied. "For the Johnsons, that is not so. White people, especially those with power, do not like change foisted upon them by others. They don't understand it, and therefore it frightens them."

Rico pondered his father's words later as he lay awake, listening to Eduardo snoring next to him. He got up and walked out to the edge of the cliff. In the distance were outlines of the buildings that made up the Johnson property. He thought about the large house where Louisa had grown up, where she had had her own room and space to entertain friends in the impressive formal dining room and parlor. He thought about the cramped space where she had made a home for them now, and he wondered if his father was right. Was love enough, when the differences between them were so great?

"We're not trying to change the world," he whispered. "We just want to live our lives and raise our family." He hoped he spoke for Louisa, but he was no longer sure. For now she seemed content, but as the years passed, wouldn't she want more? Was love enough?

Four

It had been a long time since Louisa enjoyed a day like the one she had spent with her mother-in-law and Mrs. Porterfield. The tea party lasted long into the afternoon, making the hours fly by. Amanda had joined them, and her lively presence had only added to the laughter and joy of the occasion. Ever since Louisa was confined to her home, she had grown more restless with each passing day. She had spent long hours alone, and even when Rico returned, he was often exhausted and fell asleep soon after supper. She had tried to occupy herself with reading to pass the time but could not seem to concentrate. She was hopeless at knitting and had mended every single piece of worn clothing she could find. Housework was out of the question, and if she did give the cottage the good sweeping it needed, Rico or her mother-in-law were sure to notice and chastise her for not following doctor's orders.

Doc Wilcox and Addie took turns stopping by. Addie always pretended she had simply been in the area, and couldn't she take a minute to see a friend? But Louisa was not fooled. Addie was not as good as her father was at disguising her concern.

The morning after the tea party, Louisa was alone when she felt a pain in her lower back that stopped her cold in her tracks. It was so sharp, her yelp of protest went no farther than her open mouth and a gasp for breath as she bent over the table, gripping the edge for support. As she waited for the pain to pass, her mind raced with options for seeking help. Rico and the other men would not be back until the following day.

Before they left, Rico had assured her that he would never miss their first Christmas as man and wife. "Besides," he said as she lay in bed watching him tuck in his shirt and button the fly of his trousers, "I have a very special surprise for you and Little Bit there."

Since they had no idea whether their baby would be male or female, Rico had come up with the name Little Bit to distinguish their child from other unborn babies.

Little Bit had seemed interested in what Rico had to say, if the sharp jab from within was any indication. "Tell me the surprise now."

"Well, what if I told you I've gotten Doc's okay for us to go into town for midnight mass? And what if I told you that from then until Little Bit is born, you'll be staying with Doc and his family?"

"Truly?" It had been so long since Louisa had been allowed to leave the ranch for any reason, and the opportunity to partake in at least one of the Christmas traditions she and her family had always enjoyed was exciting. Her parents and sister would be at the service as well—not that it would be the same, but at least she would see them. She saw Rico's smile turn to an expression of doubt.

"But maybe…"

Because she knew he had worked miracles to have everyone agree to his plan, she stroked his cheek and smiled. "It's been months since I was in church. And Christmas Eve…how special that will be."

Rico had kissed her with a good deal of passion. "Gotta go, *querida*. You get plenty of rest and I'll be back as soon as the cows and the boss let me." He grinned as he laid his hand on the swell of her belly. "Be good, Little Bit."

Two days had come and gone since the men left.

Now, as the pain finally passed, Louisa drank down a glass of milk—cold from being set outside overnight—and nibbled on a crust of the bread Juanita had brought the day before. That's when the second pain struck. She closed her eyes and did a mental check of everyone's whereabouts. Juanita would be serving up breakfast for the Porterfield women in the large dining room of the sprawling adobe house. Amanda would be babbling on about plans for Christmas celebrations. And no one would hear if Louisa were even able to cry out for help.

She stood as still as possible, once again clutching the table for support. Gradually the pain eased. Instinctively she spat out puffs of breath, and that seemed to help some. After what seemed like forever, she realized she was able to loosen her grip on the table and stand up straight. She tentatively took a step with no return of the pain. She got a cloth and wiped up the droplets of milk that had spilled when she knocked over the empty glass—something she had no memory of happening.

"Are you planning on being a Christmas baby after all, Little Bit?" she murmured. A wave of happiness passed through her, a lightness she had not experienced in weeks, as she imagined everyone in church and then the labor starting, and surely in those circumstances her family would not turn away. No, a baby born on Christmas had to be seen as a gift straight from God. Once Little Bit was out in the world to be held and cuddled, her parents would realize details like heritage and the tone of a person's skin did not matter. What mattered was being a good person, kind and generous, and Rico was all of that and more.

Addie had explained that as her time neared, she was likely to have these pains. "False labor," Addie had assured her, "*unless* they keep on. One or two is nothing to worry about. Pain every few minutes means this child is coming."

Louisa started to hum the tune to "Silent Night." It sounded to her like a lullaby, and she hoped it would soothe the baby into holding on a little longer. It seemed to work. She washed the breakfast dishes without further incident. Drying her hands on a flour-sack towel, she looked around the small space. Not a single sign of Christmas. She saw Trey Porterfield outside the small kitchen window. He was calling to Chet's border collie. Louisa watched boy and dog frolic in the snow that had fallen overnight and then went to the door.

"Trey!"

He looked up and waved, then trotted over to the stoop. "You need me to go get Ma, Louisa?"

"What I need is a tree—a Christmas tree."

Trey frowned. "Well now, not sure I can help you there," he said slowly. Then he brightened. "I could make you some paper chains and we could string those around the door and windows…and maybe Juanita could pop up some corn for us to string with Juniper berries. I'll go get Amanda so we can get started." He dashed off, the dog at his heels.

The youngest of the Porterfields was a talented artist, constantly astounding his family and friends with his sketches and drawings of the landscape and even the people he saw every day. He was the perfect choice for someone to help her prepare the house for Christmas—a surprise for Rico.

Within the hour, the cottage buzzed with laughter and activity, and Louisa realized that between the tea party and now this, she had passed two whole days without the feelings of sadness and loss that had been her constant companions since her family disowned her and her child. What she felt as she watched Trey and Amanda loop strings of paper and popcorn around the window and doorway was joy—and hope.

◦◦◦

At dawn, Rico shook his father awake. "Will you be all right going the rest of the way on your own? I've got something I need to do in town."

Rico had not exactly told his father the truth. He was on his way into town all right, but not to run an errand or, as his father thought, to buy a present for Louisa. In the long sleepless hours, he had come to a decision. Things were changing all over the West. The coming of the railroad had made it far easier for ranchers to get their stock to market, and as a result, owners hired fewer hands. There had been a time when he thought he might have a chance to be foreman on the Porterfield place, but that wasn't going to happen—not with the arrival of Chet Hunter a year or so back. As for striking out on his own, the land had all been bought up by sheepherders as well as cattlemen, and even if there had been acreage available, Rico could never afford it. And most of all, if he could not find a way to properly support his wife and children, he would never earn the respect—and forgiveness—of Louisa's family.

He could promise her his undying love, but unless he could build a life for her that was at least close to the life she had grown up living, he would always be a failure in George Johnson's eyes. And then, just before dawn, he recalled that the last time he'd been in town, he'd seen a sign posted outside the livery: NEED HELP.

He hoped the sign was still there.

The blacksmith, Tolly Backus, had been shoeing horses and renting out wagons and buggies for as long as Rico could recall. The man had to be close to seventy and showed his age in the slowness of his movements and the grunts of pain he issued in time with the pounding of the hot iron of a horseshoe. Tolly was a man who didn't seem to care who you were, how much land you owned, or what the color of your skin might be. He treated everyone entering the hot confines of the stable the same—with a sneer of scorn and impatience.

"What do you want, Mendez?" The blacksmith didn't turn from his work when Rico walked to the door of the stable the day before Christmas Eve.

"Saw your sign," Rico said.

"Didn't hang it to just be seen."

"What's the job?"

Tolly turned and looked directly at Rico. "I need help running this place—fact is, I may need more than help." He squinted at Rico for a long moment. "Can you keep something under your hat, Mendez?"

"Yes, sir."

With a gasp and choking cough, Tolly fumbled for the three-legged stool he kept near the door of the stable and sat. "Doc says I got a bad heart and two choices. I can work myself into an early grave or I can start training somebody to take over this business and give me some time off. You interested?"

"Maybe." Rico's heart hammered with excitement.

"Pay ain't much, but it comes with living quarters, and in time you'd own the place. Not that I plan to kick off any time soon, but I seem to recall you have a reputation for knowing your way round a branding iron. That's good experience for this job…"

"Can I see the living quarters?"

"Not so fast, vaquero. First, let me see you handle that hot iron there." Tolly unhooked an extra leather apron from its place on the wall and tossed it to Rico.

An hour and two shoes later, Tolly clapped him on the shoulder. "You're a natural, kid. Cottage is out the back there. Door's not locked. Comes with whatever's still there. Nobody's lived there since my kids left and my Sarah passed on, so it might need a little dustin'."

A little dustin' was apparently Tolly's attempt at humor.

Cobwebs stretched across window frames and doorways. A couple of scorpions scurried across the floor as soon as Rico opened the door. The air inside reeked of trapped cooking odors and abandonment. But the place was filled with light from several windows, and a stairway leading up to a second floor promised more than twice the space they had at the ranch. What furniture there was would do them nicely for the time being, and he could just see Louisa standing at that kitchen window, humming to herself the way she did, while Little Bit played nearby.

He closed the door and returned to the stable. Tolly did not look up. "Well?"

"I got a kid coming any day," Rico began.

"Pay is fifty bucks a month plus the cottage. I hold back half the money toward payment on the business, should that day come. That's the deal—take it or leave it."

"You had any other interest?" Rico asked, knowing the sign had been there long enough for the ink to have run and the paper to turn yellow.

"That ain't none of your damn business, Mendez. If you want the deal, say yes and be back here the day after Christmas at sunup. You don't want it or you have to think it through, stop wasting my time."

"Fifty dollars, the cottage, and I keep working branding and calving seasons for the Porterfields. That, plus you hold back a *quarter* of the pay, not half. I expect you're stubborn enough to live for some years yet, and you wouldn't want me paying you off before you're ready."

Tolly actually chuckled. "You'll do," he said as he wiped his hand on the apron and stuck it out for Rico to shake.

"Merry Christmas," Rico said as he headed out the door.

Tolly grumbled a reply Rico didn't catch, because he was already mounted up and riding hard for the ranch to tell Chet Hunter his plans.

∞

Addie Wilcox arrived just after noon. As usual she stopped first to check on Louisa, and Louisa did not like the slight frown that marred her friend's otherwise placid face.

"I am going to that service tomorrow night, Addie."

"Never said you weren't," Addie replied as she put away her stethoscope and then wiped the lenses of her glasses on her skirt. "But I am going to be right there with you and we'd best sit toward the back, unless you've got an idea of performing some kind of live nativity pageant."

"You think the baby will come before the New Year?"

"I think that's within the realm of possibility. However—and this is a huge *however*—everything I know tells me you are not yet ready to deliver. My father agrees, which is why we're letting you go to town. But once there, you will stay there until this child arrives. My folks have set up a room for you at our house."

"I appreciate that," Louisa said quietly as she stood in the doorway, watching Addie go. What she didn't say was that no matter what anyone said, she was determined to attend Christmas Eve services. That might be her only chance to see her parents and sister during the holidays—or ever. She had not told Rico, but the truth was, with each passing day she lost a bit more hope she might ever reconcile with her family. On the other hand, surely once they saw Little Bit in the flesh…

From the yard she heard the muffled sound of a horse and ran to the door. "Rico!" she cried. She hadn't expected him before the morrow, and here he was.

"What's all this?" Rico stopped at the door as he entered the cottage and saw the decorations. "Lookin' like Christmas, if you ask me." He didn't even bother to remove his hat or slicker before taking her in his arms and kissing her. "And I have got the perfect present for my best girl and Little Bit," he said.

"Tell me you didn't spend too much." Louisa worried constantly about their finances. Rico didn't make a lot of money, and Louisa hadn't said anything yet, but one day she wanted a larger house. After all, there would be more children eventually and they would not all fit in the tight space they currently called home. She had been putting aside whatever she could of Rico's pay. She hoped that by spring they might have enough to at least start making plans.

"Not a dime," he said and kissed her forehead as he shrugged out of his coat and hung it on the hook near the door. "Looks nice," he added, fingering the paper chains and other decorations. "Our first Christmas, *muñeca*, and it's going to be one to remember."

"Oh, Rico, I'm so excited about going into town. I've been so cooped up here. It feels like I've forgotten what it's like to be out among people."

"We'll leave right after noon," he promised.

∽✑✍

On the morning of Christmas Eve, Louisa stood close to the small mirror as she fussed with her hair. "Do you think I look all right?"

"You are always beautiful, Louisa." The way his eyes burned, she had no choice but to believe him, and she felt her cheeks flush with pleasure.

"Well, you need to change your shirt." She held out the new one she had had Amanda help her buy for him. And because it was Amanda doing the choosing, it was unlike any shirt Rico had ever owned...a soft chambray cotton in a faded blue color with suede piping outlining the pockets and cuffs. "Merry Christmas, Rico," she said shyly.

He took the shirt from her and studied it.

"Do you like it?" She was nervous that perhaps he would think it too fancy.

"I've never had anything so fine," he said. "I mean, wait till Bunker and the others see me in this." He grinned as he removed the shirt he was wearing, slid his arms through the sleeves of the new one and began fastening the bone buttons. "Fits like it was made just for me."

"I thought it would be best if we exchanged presents before we leave for town," she said.

"Now that's not gonna work, when it comes to the present I have for you and Little Bit there. That present is in town, so I'm afraid the two of you will just have to wait, but I promise it will be worth every minute."

And it was. When they reached town just before twilight on Christmas Eve, instead of tying up the wagon by the church or the Wilcox house, Rico pulled around to the back of the livery and stopped in front of a small two-story house. "Come on," he said, his voice shaking with excitement.

"Who lives here?" Louisa was puzzled. They had reached the front door, and instead of knocking, Rico grasped the knob.

"We do—or we will." When the door refused to budge, he used his shoulder to push it fully open. "It's not much now, but a good cleaning and some paint and…" He lit a lantern, revealing a fully furnished parlor. He hesitated, seeing the place in all its tawdriness for the first time. *What had he been thinking?*

"Rico, we can't afford this—we can't live this far from the ranch and your work, even if we could."

He held her hands as he told her about the meeting he'd had with the blacksmith and livery owner. "Then I talked to Chet and to Mrs. Porterfield, and they thought it was a fine idea. We'll have a start on a solid future for us and our kids, Louisa."

She walked slowly through the small house—the parlor and dining room already furnished, a kitchen twice

the size of the one she had now, and on that first floor
a bedroom complete with a four-poster and a wardrobe
for their clothes.

"And two more bedrooms up here," Rico told her
as she slowly climbed the stairs, with him carrying the
lantern to guide the way. "And most days, instead of
being out on the range, I'll be right across the yard there,
within hollerin' distance, should you need me." He had
stepped past her to the window at the landing and was
pointing toward the livery.

"You did all of this for me—for us?"

"I love you, Louisa, and I needed to find a way I
could provide for my family. We can build something
together here—a better life for our children."

Tears welled, tears of surprise and joy and relief that
somehow this wonderful man she had married had found
a way to secure the future for them—one her parents
could not possibly condemn. "Oh, Rico, you have
given us the miracle I prayed for. How can my family
help but embrace you now?" She kissed him tenderly. "I
love you so much," she whispered. Then she grinned as
she cupped his face in her hands. "Now let's get to the
church and wait there so I can tell my father what you've
done for me—for us."

She turned to start back down the shadowy stairs. She
was looking back at Rico and laughing when she missed
the first step and tumbled forward. The last thing she
heard before passing out was Rico's cry of fear and his
boots heavy on the stairs as he rushed to her side. The
last thing she felt was a gush of liquid soaking her skirt
and legs.

Five

RICO'S HEART WAS IN HIS THROAT AS HE STUMBLED DOWN
the stairs and knelt beside Louisa. "*Querida*, speak to me,"
he whispered as he stroked her hair from her face. But
she looked as if she were sleeping, so peaceful that he
feared she was dead. "No!" he screamed as he gathered
her to his chest.

She moved then, nestling closer to him. Knowing he
had to get help, he laid her carefully back on the floor and
covered her with his coat on top of the cloak she wore.
That was when he noticed the water on the floor—a lot
of water mixed with something else. He leapt to his feet
and ran out the door, looking left and then right, trying
to decide where to go, who to call. Tolly had left for the
night to spend Christmas with his children and grandchildren. Addie Wilcox was driving back to town with the
Porterfields. They had arranged to all meet at the church,
but Doc Wilcox...surely he was at home. Desperate not
to leave his wife, but seeing no one he might send to fetch
the doctor, Rico started to run. He could see one wagon
arriving early at the church, and he ran toward it.

"Help!" he shouted and three people, two women
and a man, turned toward him. The women's faces were
covered by the hoods of their cloaks and the man was
turned away from him, tying up the wagon. But Rico
would know George Johnson anywhere.

"Mr. Johnson, it's Louisa," he called as he covered the
distance between them. "She's taken a fall and...we need
Doc Wilcox now."

"I'll go," he heard Louisa's sister say as she jumped down from the wagon and took off running toward the doctor's house at the far end of town.

Satisfied help would soon arrive and not really caring if his in-laws followed him, Rico ran back to the house. Louisa was lying where he'd left her, but now she was moaning and writhing with pain. As he entered the house he heard footsteps behind him, and looked around to see Louisa's mother pulling off her gloves and adding her cloak to the ones already covering her daughter.

"We need to get her off this cold floor, Rico. George, get in here!" Her voice was a command meant to be obeyed without question.

"There's a bedroom off the kitchen," Rico said, but as he prepared to lift Louisa, his father-in-law took charge.

"Don't you touch her. She could have broken her neck for all you know. We'll wait for Doc."

Rico knew his father-in-law had a point. He also knew the man already blamed him for Louisa's fall.

Mrs. Johnson surveyed her surroundings. "Which way is that bedroom?" she asked, and Rico pointed toward the back of the house. "It'll need some cleaning, I imagine," she huffed as she hurried off. Minutes later he heard the squeal of the pump, followed by water running into a metal pan and Louisa's mother muttering to herself. He realized she was praying.

Meanwhile Louisa seemed to drift in and out of consciousness. When Doc Wilcox arrived on the heels of Louisa's sister, Rico saw he had not even stopped to put on his coat. In his shirtsleeves, he paused at the door. "George, get a fire going. This place is freezing. Helen, see if you can find some more lanterns and bring them to the bedroom." Then he went to work, his calm voice doling out directions as he first examined Louisa and then instructed Rico and her father to help him carry her carefully to the bedroom. Louisa's mother had found a fairly clean dustcover to place over the bed. She had wiped off the top of a small dressing table and pulled it closer. Helen brought a second lantern as well as Doc's medical bag and set it there beside a pan of clean water. "We need rags," Mrs. Johnson said. "Helen, go find Eliza McNew. She'll have plenty of them in her store."

The girl left the room at a run.

Rico was aware of other voices, and soon Addie, Rico's parents, and the Porterfields all crowded around the doorway of the small bedroom. Rico stood on one side of the bed holding Louisa's hand, while her father stood on the other.

"You and you, out," Doc ordered, pointing to them in turn. "Addie, get over here. The rest of you go about your business."

"I'm not going anywhere," Rico heard his mother declare.

"Nor am I," Dorothy Johnson added. "This is my child and grandchild and I will not leave them."

"Dorothy," Mr. Johnson said softly as he tried to steer his wife to the door.

"No. This has gone on far too long, George." And with that she brushed off his hand and moved to one side of her daughter's bed.

As Mrs. Porterfield led Rico from the room, his father-in-law hesitated and then quietly followed. "I'll see if there's any tea in the kitchen," Mrs. Porterfield said after they had reached the parlor and she'd urged Rico to sit so he could warm himself by the fire his father-in-law had built.

"I'll help," Amanda murmured.

Rico's father stood uncertainly by the door and then stepped outside onto the porch. Through the window Rico saw him roll and light a cigarette. He stood on the edge of the porch fingering the turquoise cross he'd worn for as long as Rico could remember.

"What were you doing here?" George Johnson demanded after Helen had rushed past them bearing a stack of linens that she carried to the bedroom. He paced back and forth, his hands clasped behind his back.

The last thing Rico wanted right that minute was to hear a lecture from the rancher who had once respected him. "It's where we're gonna live from now on. I took Tolly Backus up on his offer to have me come in with him, and the house is part of the deal." He glanced around, recalling the way Louisa's eyes had sparkled as she took in the room and its furnishings. "It was—is— Louisa's Christmas present."

"So it was you insisting she get out of her sickbed to come out in this cold and take that rough ride into town." It was not a question.

Rico had had all he could take. He stood and stepped in front of George Johnson to stop his pacing. "First of all, sir, Louisa is pregnant, not sick. Second of all, she pleaded with everyone at the ranch as well as Doc Wilcox to be allowed to be here tonight, because she knew you would be here. She has not once given up hope that you will accept me and our child. Doc gave her his blessing and here we are. I think you know Louisa well enough to know she's that much like you—stubborn and determined to have her way."

The older man stared at Rico for a long moment as if trying to recall something, and then to Rico's surprise tears began to leak down the crevices of his father-in-law's weathered face. "I don't know what I'd do if we lost her," he blubbered. "I'd never forgive myself." He turned away, pulled a handkerchief from his back pocket, and blew his nose as he collapsed onto the settee, raising a puff of dust as he did.

Unsure of what to do as Louisa's father's tears turned to sobs, Rico sat next to him. "Louisa's not going to die," he said. "Doc won't let that happen."

"But if she loses this baby, it will kill her inside," Johnson replied. He looked at Rico, his eyes wild with grief. "If she loses this baby, we may never get her back."

Rico understood the man was not including him in that *we* but rather was admitting Louisa might never come home to him and his wife. "We're not going to lose this baby, sir," Rico said with a fierce certainty he did not really feel. His hand shook as he awkwardly patted George Johnson's shoulder. "Can't see God bringing anybody such heartache on Christmas Eve." He walked to the window and silently prayed he was right.

They remained that way for what seemed like hours— not speaking and really not moving until finally they heard someone leave the bedroom and close the door with a click. Rico held his breath.

"Rico?" Mrs. Porterfield stood at the door to the parlor. "You have a beautiful daughter."

And for the first time, Rico understood everything George Johnson had done or said in the past long months had been driven by one purpose—his love for his daughter and the belief he needed to protect her against the slings and arrows of this world. In that moment he understood the older man's fears, but he could not condone the man's animosity toward him when it had no basis in fact. He loved Louisa, had loved her for as long as he could remember. Surely that counted for more than a difference in the color of their skin. No doubt, they would face prejudice—they already had. But standing together, they would prevail, and perhaps by the time his children grew up, opinions would change. No, he understood the foundations of his father-in-law's feelings, but he also knew the older man was wrong.

"Rico? Did you hear me?" Mrs. Porterfield came into the room and touched his forearm.

"Louisa?" he asked.

"Has had a rough time of it, but she's resting now. Doc says she's going to be just fine."

"Can I see her…them?"

"Your mother and mother-in-law are making her more comfortable. Eliza sent over fresh linens for the bed and a nightgown. Give them a few minutes. Meanwhile Doc wants to talk to you." She turned to George and added, "And you. Wait here."

It was clear all the fire had gone out of Mr. Johnson. He remained seated, his hands dangling between his knees, his head bowed. "A girl," he murmured finally.

"Yeah." Rico headed for the door. "I'm going out to tell my father the news. Let me know when Doc is ready for us."

"Rico?" The call was so faint that he thought he might have imagined it.

"Yes sir?"

"Congratulations, son."

"Thank you, sir—and to you."

And just like that it was over. Louisa had been right in her belief that eventually her father would come around.

"He's afraid," she had said more than once by way of explanation.

"Of me?" Rico had been incredulous.

"No. Of us."

Doc's lecture was brief and to the point. "Your wife and both your daughters have been through a lot tonight, and I will not have either of you further upsetting them." He turned to George. "Either you get behind this thing and understand you can't change what is, or you stay away until Louisa has had the time she needs to regain her strength. She has her mother back—that much is clear."

"I hear you, Doc."

Doc grunted and turned his attention to Rico. "As for you, she's already babbling on with Addie and both mothers about fixing this place up. She's got no strength for more than caring for that baby in there, so do what you need to do to make sure she has what she wants without having to do the work herself."

"Yes sir, whatever she wants. Can I see her now?"

"Yes, but keep it short. She needs her rest."

Rico started down the hall, then turned to look at Louisa's father. He pointed over his shoulder toward the bedroom. "You coming?"

∽∾

Louisa couldn't seem to keep her eyes open, so when she saw Rico and her father standing side by side at the foot of the large bed, she thought she must be dreaming. Her mother and Rico's were in the corner with Addie, tending the baby.

"Rico," she said weakly, trying to bring him into focus. "We have a baby girl."

He sat on the side of the bed and took her hands between his. "I know. Are you all right?"

She laughed and then grimaced. "I'll be fine. Stupid of me to be so clumsy, but Doc Wilcox assures me I did no harm to our daughter."

"As if you could hurt anything," Rico murmured as he kissed her fingers. "Your father's here," he added, glancing back over his shoulder.

"Papa?"

"Right here, Louisa." Once again his voice shook with emotion and he swiped his eyes with the back of his hand. "I want you to know that me and Rico have…he's a fine man, Louisa. He'll make a good father."

"Oh, Papa, I've prayed for this day." She held out her hand to her father and he took it, standing on the opposite side of the bed. "Have you seen her?" she asked, looking from her father to her husband.

"Not yet," Rico said.

"Almost ready," Addie said as she wrapped the

newborn in cloth and then presented Rico with the bundle that to him didn't look much bigger than a small sack of corn meal.

"Hello, Little Bit," he whispered, then added in awe, "She's so tiny."

"She'll grow," George Johnson grumbled, "and cause you no end of worry, I promise you that."

Louisa's mother came to stand next to her husband, her head resting on his shoulder as Juanita and Eduardo held hands from their vantage point at the foot of the bed. Addie slipped quietly from the room.

"Listen," Louisa said. Everyone went still as they heard the bells from the church echoing on the cold night air. Louisa looked around at the two families. "It's Christmas Day," she said huskily.

Rico placed his little finger in the baby's hand. "You hear that, Little Bit?"

"That child needs a name," Rico's mother announced.

"We decided to call a daughter Mary," Louisa said. "Mary Isabel to honor my grandmother and Rico's." She looked directly at her father. "To honor them and her heritage."

Her father bent and kissed her forehead, then he straightened and cleared his throat. "Seems to me that everybody here has had a chance to meet this young lady except for me and Eduardo. How about giving her grandfathers their turn?"

Rico stood and passed his daughter to his father-in-law, who stared at her for a long moment before handing her to Eduardo.

Seeing both sets of grandparents huddled around the child, Louisa tugged on Rico's hand. "Merry Christmas," she whispered.

"Are you truly all right?" he asked.

She stroked his face. "I have never been more all right in my life, Rico. I have our perfect child and my family back in our lives…and you." She framed his face with her hands and pulled him to her, and the kiss they shared held the final release of all the anguish they had suffered over the last several months.

Her father cleared his throat and she and Rico broke apart, each grinning as they looked up at the others. "Doc said you need your rest, Louisa, so we'll be going."

"We most certainly will not," his wife announced. "You men go find a bedroll so Rico can get some sleep. We've set up a crib for little Mary here in this bureau drawer for tonight, but first thing tomorrow, I want you to go get that cradle from the attic and bring it here."

"And until then?" her husband demanded.

Addie stuck her head in the door. "We've got plenty of room at our house," she said. "Rico can stretch out in the parlor here, and Amanda and Helen and I can take shifts until morning. Now scoot."

Like her father, Addie was not someone to be argued with. Slowly the two families moved out into the hall after taking their turn to plant kisses on Louisa's cheek and take one more look at the sleeping baby that Rico held, looking as if he had held babies his entire life. Once the others were gone, Rico closed the bedroom door and laid the baby in Louisa's arms as he settled himself next to her, his arm around her shoulders. The two of them stared down at the infant.

"She's so beautiful," Louisa said.

"And why not?" Rico tenderly stroked her hair. "Just look at her mother. Now it's time you got some rest."

He reached for the baby.

"I wish she could be closer than that bureau drawer," Louisa said. "What if she needs me in the night?"

Rico glanced from the bureau back to the bed. "Here," he said, returning the baby to Louisa's arms. Then he pulled the dressing table next to the bed, pulled the drawer out of the bureau and set it on top of the table, then straightened the padding the grandmothers had put inside the drawer. He held out his arms for his daughter. With something that Louisa saw as akin to reverence, he laid Mary in the drawer.

"You can reach her from there," he said, "but promise me you'll call for Addie or your sister if she needs anything." He started toward the door. "I'll be right outside."

"Oh, no, sir," Louisa replied with a mischievous grin. She patted the space beside her on the large bed. "You are staying right here, and if our Mary needs something in the middle of the night, her Papa can see that she has it."

Rico laughed and pulled off his boots as he stretched out next to her so that her head rested in the crook of his shoulder.

From outside the window, Louisa could hear the muted voices of people leaving the church services, calling out holiday wishes as they headed home. From the makeshift crib, she could hear Mary making small sucking sounds as she slept. And from next to her, she heard the soft steady breathing of her husband, who had found so many ways to make all her Christmas wishes come true.

About the Author

Award-winning author Anna Schmidt resides in Wisconsin. She delights in creating stories where her characters must wrestle with the challenges of their times. Critics have consistently praised Schmidt for her ability to seamlessly integrate actual events with her fictional characters to produce strong tales of hope and love in the face of seemingly insurmountable obstacles. Visit her at annaschmidtauthor.com.

A CHRISTMAS REUNION

A RUNAWAY BRIDES NOVELLA

———•◆•———

Amy Sandas

One

Wyoming Territory
December, 1879

WARREN REED HAD LIVED IN THE NORTHEAST MOST OF his life and was no stranger to winter winds, snow, and ice. He had expected some degree of hardship when he decided to make the move from Philadelphia to the Wyoming Territory in the middle of December. But as he rode horseback with nothing to shield him from an increasingly biting wind except his brand new sheepskin coat, his new Western hat, and an old pair of leather gloves, he seriously doubted the sanity of such a decision.

It didn't help that he was blindfolded, with his wrists bound, and being escorted into the mountains at gunpoint.

⚬⚭⚬

Taking on an abandoned medical practice in the small town of Chester Springs at the base of the Shoshone Mountain Range was not the type of thing Warren had ever expected to do in his career. But when the opportunity arose, he had accepted it without much debate or introspection. It had been one of the rare moments in his life when he acted impulsively.

He'd been in the small Western town for only two days, not long enough to meet any townsfolk beyond the elderly lady who owned the boardinghouse where he'd gotten a room and the shopkeeper at the mercantile. With winter heavy on the ground, the citizens of

Chester Springs seemed inclined to stay indoors, leaving the narrow roads through town eerily quiet even in the middle of the day.

At least the mayor, with whom Warren had been corresponding, had left behind a key for the doctor's office before leaving town for a few weeks.

Determined to settle in, Warren had immediately begun the work of setting the abandoned office to rights and taking stock of supplies. Unfortunately, most of what he needed had to be ordered and could take weeks to arrive. It was with some disappointment and not a little frustration that he closed up his office just after sunset on his second night in town. He had hoped to be able to jump right into this new life he had chosen.

His feelings of dissatisfaction slid into a wary curiosity as he turned around on the boardwalk to find two men, who had obviously been waiting for him in the street, outside his office.

One of them was mounted and held the reins of two other horses while cradling a rifle in his arms. The other stood silently to Warren's left, just a few paces away. They looked much the same as all the other rough-and-ready men he'd seen out West. Both wore the clothes of cowboys, with wide-brimmed hats shadowing their faces. Their only distinguishing features, as far as Warren could tell in the gathering darkness, were that the one on horseback had a full beard, while the other had the black skin of African ancestors.

Something about them set him on edge.

"Can I help you, gentlemen?"

The man to his left stepped forward, lifting his hand to show a pistol pointed squarely at Warren's chest.

Warren stiffened, but knew better than to overreact. He'd been mugged his fair share in the big cities out East. But for some reason, this didn't feel like a robbery.

"No shouting or you get shot. No struggling or you

get shot," the bearded man on horseback said in an easy conversational tone. "Just come with us peaceful-like and you'll make it home again. Got it?"

"Where are we going?" Warren asked, keeping his eyes on the pistol.

"Can't say," the man replied.

The one pointing the gun at him gave a nod to the leather bag in his hand. "Does that hold your medical supplies?"

"It does."

The man gave another sharp jerk of his head, indicating he wanted Warren to mount one of the horses. Since there didn't seem much choice, he complied. Once he was in the saddle, they quickly tied his wrists and blindfolded him.

It would seem they wanted him for his doctoring skills, but why they felt they had to lead him away at gunpoint was beyond him.

Still, doctoring was what he had come here to do—to tend to the people of this wild territory. He'd fallen in love with this land seven years ago, when he'd spent a summer with his uncle up in Montana. So he wasn't going to resist or argue their methods—especially not with guns drawn and the promise that he'd be returned after his services were rendered.

They headed straight out of town at a swift, intentional pace. The longer they rode, the more Warren was able to gather about the situation he'd be facing once they reached their destination. It must be nestled someplace up in the mountains, judging by the incline they'd been traveling for the last couple of hours.

He was surprised his captors would talk so openly about their criminal behavior, but the bearded one seemed to have a penchant for idle chatter. Someone had been shot. And from the sound of it, the wound had been come by during unlawful activity. A stagecoach robbery was Warren's deduction.

Well, wonderful.

His first patient was going to be an outlaw.

Wherever they were going, Warren just hoped they made it there before he froze to death. His hands were already numb, as were his legs and face. He was not dressed for this kind of exposure.

"Damn storm comin'." This was offered by the bearded man, riding to Warren's right.

"Yep," replied his companion.

"We gotta push through the pass before snow starts fallin'."

"Yep."

That was the only warning Warren got before the three of them started loping at a pace that had him bending forward over the pommel of the saddle. They kept up that grueling speed at a steep climb for what felt like another hour, though it was probably less. Their horses couldn't possibly last much longer at such a pace.

And then they started a slow descent.

Not long after, Warren figured they had entered a valley, as there seemed to be some shelter from the wind that had been whipping at them for most of the journey. No more than ten minutes later, the horses came to a slow stop.

Warren was dragged from his horse. He couldn't do much to assist in dismounting with his hands tied, but he could at least have had some warning to get his feet ready to hit the ground. He heard a grunt of annoyance when he stumbled in the snow, followed by a derisive mumble about him being a city slicker.

"It would help if I could see where I was walking," Warren said. "Or do you expect me to tend to your friend blindfolded?"

There was a pause before the bandana was removed from his eyes.

They stood outside a long wooden building like the

sort of bunkhouse he'd seen on large cattle ranches in Montana. It was made of thick logs, and a long porch stretched across the front, with warm light spilling from the deep-set windows.

Warren turned to get a better look at his two captors. The one who'd remained mounted during his kidnapping was younger than he'd expected, maybe only in his early twenties. He had bright blue eyes, and the full beard covering his face did nothing to disguise his youth.

The other man stepped forward to take the horses' reins. He was clean-shaven, his black hair was shorn close to his skull, and his gaze was deep and intense, but he wasn't likely much older than his partner. He gave Warren a passing glance before saying to his companion, "I'll get the horses settled. You'd best get him inside."

"I'll need my bag," Warren reminded them.

The black-skinned man wordlessly released it from the saddle and handed it to Warren before turning to lead the horses away.

"Come on, Doc," the bearded one said. "Let's hope we ain't too late."

There was a note of strain in the outlaw's voice. The stakes must be high for these two to have traveled several hours to Chester Springs and back in order to fetch a doctor.

Warren followed him onto the porch and through the front door of the long building.

As he stepped inside, he was welcomed by a blast of heat from the big stone fireplace set into the far wall straight ahead. Unlike the bunkhouses he'd known in Montana, this place had an open living space spread out to his left, with a good-sized kitchen stretched along the wall to his right. A long wooden table with nearly a dozen chairs around it took up much of the space between the two areas. Two hallways extended from the front room, one to the left and one to the right, containing doors to what he assumed were individual bedrooms.

As they stomped the snow from their feet and Warren did his best to shake the numbness from his fingers, he heard someone coming toward them from one of the wings. Light stretched from a room at the far end of the hallway. At first all he could make out was that the silhouetted figure was a woman.

And she was in a hurry.

"It's about damn time you got back. Did you grab the doctor?"

Her voice hit him like a blow straight to his sternum. Warren took an instinctive step back. Old memories sliced through him like the sharp edge of a scalpel against raw flesh.

It *couldn't* be.

They were hundreds of miles from where he had last seen Honey Prentice in Montana. That distance was the only thing that had made it possible for him to come back out West. He had assured himself there was no chance he'd accidentally run into the woman who had torn his heart from his chest all those years ago.

But her gasp as she stepped out into the room told him he'd been wrong.

She was as beautiful as she had been as a girl of seventeen.

And she was not happy to see him.

She crossed the room with long, swift strides that had her cotton skirts whipping about her legs. In an easy movement, she pulled the bearded outlaw's gun from his belt before he knew what she was about and then turned the weapon on Warren.

Fire flashed in her brown eyes as she held the gun steady with two hands. "What the hell are you doing here, Warren Reed?"

Warren swallowed back the tight squeeze of his own fury as he stared coldly at the weapon and then at his former lover's face. "You should ask this gentleman that question, since he and his friend didn't give me any choice in the matter."

"Are you crazy?" asked the stunned man at her side. "This here is the new doctor from Chester Springs that Jackson told you about."

In the tense silence that followed, Warren noted a few telling details.

Honey's plain calico dress was streaked with dried blood and her hands were stained the same brownish red. She had grown slimmer since he last saw her. Her hair was drawn back in a loose bun at her nape with heavy strands falling about her face, but it was still the same rich golden hue. And her brown eyes, which had once looked at him with adoration and innocent passion, now glared hard and steady in his direction. More than anger flashed in their depths. Though still a stunning young woman at twenty-four years old, Honey had done some living in the last several years.

Well, at nearly thirty himself, so had he. And he was not going to be intimidated by her irrational fury or the gun she had aimed at his heart.

And what the hell did she have to be angry with *him* about? She had been the one to turn her back on what they could have had together.

"Get him out of here, Eli," she said finally in clipped and heavy tones. "Now."

At that moment, the other outlaw returned from seeing to the horses, entering from the back of the house. His black eyes took immediate stock of the situation. "I don't know what the problem is here," he said as he came slowly into the room, "but unless Luke made some miraculous recovery, he needs this doctor's services."

"It's Luke who's been shot?" Warren asked. "I suppose I shouldn't be surprised."

"You sonofa—" she muttered as she took a step forward, only to be stopped when the man she'd called Eli threw an arm out in front of her.

Luke was Honey's twin brother. When Warren knew him during that long-ago summer, he was always getting into trouble. That he had ended up part of an outlaw gang didn't really shock Warren. That he'd dragged his sister into the mess with him did. Luke had always been very protective of Honey.

"Come on, Jackson's right," Eli coaxed. "Let the doc at least take a look at him."

There was a flicker in her eyes, but she didn't budge.

Warren ground his back teeth. The history between himself and this woman did not change the oath he'd taken. He slid his gaze down to her dress. "From the look of things, Luke's lost a lot of blood already. Do you intend to let him bleed out while we rehash our past?"

With a fiercely narrowed gaze, Honey lowered the gun and turned away to head back down the hallway. "Dammit. Come on, then."

Another thing that had changed—Warren didn't remember Honey having such a harsh vocabulary.

Flicking a glance at the two men, who were obviously relieved by her decision, Warren asked, "Are you going to untie me so I can be of some use?"

Eli came forward, drawing a knife from a scabbard tied to his thigh, and sliced neatly through the ropes.

Before Warren could take a step to follow Honey, Jackson stepped in front of him with a scowl. "If I suspect that whatever just happened is having any effect on your performance in there, you'll feel my bullet before you have a chance to explain."

The truth of the threat was plain in the man's eyes. Though he was the less talkative of the two, he was proving to be the more articulate. Warren didn't feel it necessary to reply. He strode down the hall to the lit room at the end.

The patient lay sprawled on his stomach on a blood-soaked bed. Only taking a passing notice of the room,

Warren went straight to the side of the bed. A table had been pulled up close and held a pitcher, a large bowl filled with red-tinged water, and several soiled cloths.

Warren forced aside his personal turmoil over the unexpected reunion with Honey Prentice to focus on his patient.

Luke had changed far more than his sister had. He had been lanky and lean when Warren had last seen him. Though he was unconscious, it was clear that the years had toughened him up. Even sprawled out as he was on his stomach, the injured man's solid build was obvious.

Luke's physical strength should go a long way toward assisting in his recovery—as long as it was accompanied by a strong will.

"He passed out about three hours ago," Honey explained in tight, clipped words from where she had taken up a position on the other side of the bed. "I did what I could to keep it clean, but the bullet is still in there. I couldn't…"

She didn't finish.

Warren set his bag on the table, shrugged out of his heavy coat, and tossed it over a chair. His hat quickly followed, and then his tailored jacket.

"I need a bowl of fresh water, some clean cloths, and some whiskey," he stated.

He didn't bother to glance up to determine if his orders were being followed. He was already examining Luke's injury, taking in as many details of the situation as he could while he rolled up his sleeves.

The young man had been shot in the back of his upper thigh. A makeshift tourniquet was cinched high around his leg and had helped to stem the bleeding to a slow ooze. His breeches had been cut away from the wound site rather than being removed altogether.

Warren checked Luke's breath and pulse. Both were weak, but steady.

As soon as Honey returned with the items Warren had requested, he washed his hands and splashed them with antiseptic from his bag.

"Were those two men with him when he was shot?" he asked with a jerk of his head toward the front room.

"Yes."

"I will need to speak with them."

As she left to follow his instructions, Warren carefully probed at the wound. More blood seeped over his fingers.

A few minutes later, the two men entered the room. Warren tried not to put any significance on the fact that Honey did not return with them. She was not his concern right now.

"Eli, right?" Warren asked, looking at the bearded man.

He waited for the man's nod before he looked to the other outlaw. "And Jackson?"

Another nod.

"Who applied the tourniquet to his leg?"

"He did that himself," Eli replied.

"How soon after he was shot?"

"It couldn't have been long," answered Jackson. "We were riding fast and didn't notice at first that he wasn't right behind us. By the time he caught up, he already had the leg cinched tight."

Warren continued his clipped questions. "Did either of you see any spurting blood? Or did he mention anything of the sort?"

Jackson gave a negative shake of his head and Eli explained, "He didn't say much of anything, except to curse at the pain."

Warren nodded. "I want you both to stay close in case I need you to hold him down."

There was no way for Warren to know if an artery had been hit until he released the tourniquet. But first, he had to get that bullet out.

Two

HONEY TOOK BIG GULPING BREATHS. SHE STOOD IN stunned shock in the kitchen. She would go back to Luke's room soon enough to do what she could to help, but right now she needed to get herself under control or she would be of no use to anyone.

Having Luke come home with a gunshot wound had been a nightmare come to life. How many years had she been telling him his wild ways would get him killed? He'd already bled so much, and with the bullet still lodged in his flesh somewhere, he'd no doubt lose more blood before the ordeal was over. And then there was the risk of infection…

She pressed her hands flat to the scarred surface of the large dinner table and focused on the pattern in the wood grain as she counted each breath she took.

It had been terrifying to see Luke in such a state. The last thing she needed was the havoc inspired by seeing Warren Reed again.

Fury, physical pain, and the crushing, breath-stealing sense of emptiness.

She hadn't felt that emptiness in years, not since her heartache had turned to hatred. But all it took was one look into his silver-blue eyes to take her right back to the day she'd gotten his letter telling her he was marrying a girl out East and wasn't coming back for her as he'd promised.

She'd often imagined what she'd do or say if she ever saw Warren again. But she wasn't prepared for the overwhelming emotions that flew through her when she came into the front room and saw the man who'd broken her heart.

The fury had not been a surprise, not when she'd spent so many years hating the man. Even the raw, choking tightness in her chest was not completely unanticipated.

What she never would have expected, what warred with everything she held true about herself, was the wild unfathomable yearning that flooded her system the moment she'd looked into Warren's eyes after seven long years.

He was back.

What on earth had brought him out West again?

She didn't care. She *couldn't* care.

Obviously, he'd gotten that medical training he'd wanted so badly. Not that she'd ever doubted he would. Warren was destined to be a doctor; even though it was a profession considered beneath his family's social standing back East, he'd wanted to help people. Warren had been stubborn and determined. Not even his father's disapproval had managed to deter him from setting out after his dreams.

Had his father survived the illness that had called Warren home that summer?

Honey shook her head fiercely, straightening her spine. None of that mattered now.

She turned away from the table to start some coffee on the big wood-burning stove. The bitter brew might be needed before the night was through, and she'd learned long ago that keeping busy helped her to get through the darkest of days.

That's all she needed to do. Just get through this, the way she got through everything else.

As soon as Warren fixed Luke up, she would never see him again. Eli and Jackson knew enough to blindfold anyone being brought to their valley. Warren wouldn't be able to find his way back even if he wanted to.

And she would simply avoid Chester Springs like the plague. She'd send one of the boys in when she needed anything.

Right.

Dammit. Why was he here?

She lifted her hands to rub her face, but stopped when she noticed the dried blood caked under her fingernails.

Throwing on her coat, she grabbed a bucket and went outside to gather some fresh snow to boil over the fire. She'd run out of hot water and hadn't wanted to leave Luke unattended to get more. Now she had a chance to take stock of their supplies and maybe try to get some of the soiled cloths washed.

When she stepped outside, an icy gale hit her straight in the face, taking her breath away and making her eyes tear up. She lowered her chin to her chest and took short breaths as she stomped down the stairs to scoop a bucketful of snow. Wind whipped around her head and numbed her fingers.

She looked out over the moonlit valley that had been her home for more than six years. It had taken her and Luke months of travel to find this beautiful spot nestled in the mountains. Winter white covered everything around them, but she looked toward the copse of trees partway up the side of a steep incline. She couldn't see her own little cabin hidden in those trees, but she knew it was there. She knew it'd be warm and welcoming inside. Her refuge. Her sanctuary from the world.

She could not allow Warren to ruin it. He was from her past and he was going to stay there.

She tipped her face up despite the whipping wind as clouds skittered across the face of the moon. The storm that had been coming their way would hit in force tonight.

With a curse, she turned and headed back into the longhouse. There was much to do.

By the time the coffee was ready, the three buckets of

water she'd hauled in were boiling, and the clean sheets she'd torn into fresh bandages were folded and ready, she finally felt she could endure Warren's presence without disintegrating into that lovelorn young girl she had once been.

Entering Luke's bedroom, she saw Eli and Jackson bracketing her brother, holding him still as Warren bent over him to stitch up the wound. His hands were tinged with blood but steady and confident as he moved the needle in and out of the red, swollen flesh.

She glanced at the bedside table and saw a slug of metal in the bowl. He'd gotten the bullet out.

She hadn't doubted he would. From the moment he'd entered Luke's room, his focus had been apparent, his skill never in doubt.

Honey stood there in the doorway for a moment, willing her heart to stop racing.

Seven years ago, Warren Reed had been so handsome, with his dark hair and light twinkling eyes. He'd possessed an understated sort of confidence that had charmed her from the start, and the warmth and gentle strength of his nature had made her feel safer and happier than she'd ever been.

It had all been a lie.

But even knowing he wasn't worth the heartache she'd lived through, she was ashamed to feel that old spark lighting up inside her. The years had put a few hard lines and angles on his features, but it only made him more handsome.

Shoving aside the nostalgia, she strode forward and placed the stack of bandages on the table beside him, then gathered up the bloodied cloths and the bowl.

In silence, she moved back and forth between the bedroom and the front room, switching out the bloody water with clean, fetching whatever Warren requested in the clipped, precise tones he must have mastered while working in some prestigious hospital out East. After they got Luke's bedding changed and her brother was settled in for the long wait to see if any infection would set in, Jackson and Eli finally sought their beds, located down the opposite hallway. Their exhaustion led them to forgo the coffee she'd made.

Honey made a mental note to have a big, hot breakfast ready for them when they woke up. She might even fry up some of the precious ham she'd been saving for Christmas Eve dinner. They certainly deserved it, after riding half the night to fetch a doctor.

Honey put the soiled bedclothes to soak in a washing barrel in the kitchen end of the front room. She was too tired to do much more tonight, but hopefully that would keep the stains from setting so she could wash them in the morning.

Pressing her fists into the small of her back, she stretched.

She wanted nothing more than to go home, climb into her bed, and pull the covers up over her head. She doubted she'd sleep, but the solitude would be welcome.

But she didn't want to leave Luke yet.

"You should rest."

She spun in place at the sound of Warren's voice. His words were spoken softly, but something hard as iron was in his tone, suggesting he was as uncomfortable around her as she was with him.

She wished she hadn't reacted so violently to the first sight of him. It made it hard to pretend just then that his presence had no effect on her.

Lifting her chin, she ignored his comment and said, "You can take one of the unused bedrooms for the night. The boys'll take you back to town in the morning."

There was a pause before he replied, "Is that coffee I smell?"

Honey gestured toward the pot keeping warm on the stove. "Help yourself."

There had been a time she'd have given anything to care for him as a wife tended a husband. But that inclination had been crushed and ground into the dirt long ago.

She tried not to watch him as he came toward the kitchen to grab one of the tin cups she'd set out earlier. She didn't want to notice how tall and fit he was or how appealing he looked even though his fine white shirt was damp and streaked with her brother's blood. She hated that the way he moved, so confident and strong, brought back another rush of memories. Memories of running her hands over the muscles of his back, of feeling his legs slide along hers and his hips moving between her thighs.

She turned away and stalked to the far side of the big front room. There had to be something she could clean, some more tasks that needed doing. She had to find something to keep her hands and her mind busy.

Especially her mind. Her treacherous, lustful mind.

He was a selfish jackass and she hated him. She had to remember that.

Three

HE'D DONE EVERYTHING IN HIS POWER TO FORGET HER. It had never been enough.

Yet here he was.

Warren didn't dare to contemplate what workings of fate had brought him to this moment, standing with the heat of the fire at his back and tension in every cell of his body as he watched Honey bustling about with quick, efficient movements.

Anger still flashed in her eyes every time their gazes accidentally caught and held. But her anger couldn't hide her anxiety. She was nervous.

Dammit, so was he.

Nervous, confused, and fighting hard to control his arousal now that he was alone with her.

Passion had never been a problem between them seven years ago. Honey had been a sweet, vivacious young woman, just coming into herself after growing up a tomboy hellion with her twin brother. And Warren had been an optimistic young man just out of college with his sights set on the future.

No. Desire hadn't been a problem. It had hit them both like lightning from the start.

Perhaps Warren had been naive to think something deeper and more lasting came along with it.

When he got the urgent notice that his father was unwell, he'd packed up without a second thought. Frederick Reed's heart had never been very strong, and Warren had feared the worst. He hadn't been wrong, and he never regretted leaving Montana to be at his father's side when he died.

What he did regret, for a while at least, was leaving Honey behind with the vow to return for her as soon as he was able. He should have taken her with him to Boston right then.

Of course, then he never would have discovered the fickle nature of her heart or just how easy it would be for John Freeman to step in and claim her.

Freeman had been a local land baron in Montana, owning just about every parcel worth owning and still wanting more. He had been a frequent presence at Randolph Brighton's modest ranch, doing all he could to get Warren's uncle to sell his property.

The man was a bully.

After Warren left, he had also become Honey's husband.

That thought still managed to send an arc of raw pain through his insides. It was the kind of pain that had nearly suffocated him. He'd saved himself back then by throwing himself into his studies and then his work at the research hospital in Philadelphia.

It was only recently that he had begun to think of his time out West without the old heartache tearing through him. He remembered instead the way he'd been awed and inspired by the grandeur and power of the Rockies. The way the mountain air had stirred his soul and the great, expansive wilderness could spread around a person for miles. He'd begun to crave the wide-open spaces, the sunshine, and the meadows.

He'd come out West again, seeking that feeling of freedom. He had not expected to see Honey. He'd convinced himself he never wanted to.

It was the biggest lie he'd ever told himself.

With gritted teeth he turned away, then downed the last of the coffee, welcoming the bitter path it took down his throat.

Shoving thoughts of the past out of his mind, he strode down the hall to check on his patient. The bullet had not hit an artery, though it had torn an angry path into the biceps femoris muscle that ran down the back of Luke's thigh. Assuming he recovered from the blood loss and managed to avoid infection, there was still a possibility his muscle would not retain its full capability.

At present, Luke slept soundly. His breathing remained even and his body was not raging with fever. Yet.

Warren didn't care when they intended to bring him back to town; he wasn't leaving until he was certain the threat of infection had passed. After making sure there was no further bleeding from the wound site, he ventured back out toward the front room.

Honey was sitting at the end of the sofa by the fireplace with a cup of coffee wrapped in her hands, staring into the flames. She had added some wood to the fire and sat huddled, her legs tucked beneath her, her skirts drawn close over her feet, a woolen shawl wrapped around her shoulders.

Warren stopped in the doorway to watch her.

More than this, he soaked in the sight of her.

He wanted to hate her for marrying Freeman within only a few months of his leaving. But he could understand why she may have been seduced by the security and wealth Freeman offered.

Honey's father had been a miner until he died in a tunnel collapse when she was a young girl. Her mother was a frail woman, susceptible to lung ailments, and though Mrs. Prentice had done what she could to provide for her two children, the small bit of income she earned from sewing was not enough. Honey and Luke both had to help out from a young age. And with Luke rebelling every chance he got, Honey was often left to make up the difference.

The first time Warren saw her was out behind the

laundry where she worked most days. She had been hanging clothes on the lines to dry, and there was something so beautiful in the way the summer breeze lifted the gold-blond strands of her hair, falling free down her back. And the way she smiled as she hummed a tune he could barely hear. It was that smile that initially drew him nearer, but it was her warm brown eyes and the light constellation of freckles across her nose and cheeks that had him sticking around to strike up a flirtation.

She had been reserved and wary at first, but Warren had drawn her out, and soon she was teasing him for his city-slicker ways and what she called his "fancified" manners.

Their mutual attraction had been instantaneous and intense. Within a few weeks, he knew he wanted to marry her. A few weeks after that, she gifted him with her innocence on a night filled with romance and youthful passion.

Honey Prentice had completely stolen his heart that summer, and as he stared at her now, seven years later, he admitted to himself that despite her callous disregard, she held it still.

That realization was like a fist to the gut. But it was no less true. He felt it in every living cell of his body. Despite everything, he still loved her.

"Why are you here?"

Her softly muttered words jolted him out of his unexpected revelation. She didn't turn to look at him when she spoke, and he wondered how long she had been aware of his presence.

"Your brother's men—"

"No," she interrupted sharply. "I mean, why did you come back out West?"

How could he explain that the land had called to him? That the only reason he had stayed away as long as he had was to avoid her. Avoid the memories.

"I wouldn't have come, if I'd known you would be here."

She flinched at his reply. Her shoulders curved inward and her chin dropped a notch before she forced it back up.

Warren wondered at the reaction. He hadn't meant it the way it sounded. Then again, maybe he had. A part of him wanted to hurt her the way she had hurt him.

He came forward to retrieve his coffee cup and refilled it from the pot on the stove. Then he turned back to her, trying to remember his manners. "Would you like more coffee?"

She looked down at her cup before nodding silently and holding it out toward him.

"I will watch Luke through the night, if you want to get some rest," he said as he replaced the pot and took a seat in one of the side chairs. Sharing the sofa with her would be far too intimate.

"I won't be able to sleep anyway," she answered.

She kept her focus trained on the flames as she sipped her coffee. Then, still without glancing his way, she asked, "I am surprised your wife would so willingly move out to the wilderness."

"I have no wife."

His reply brought her gaze flying to meet his. The sudden connection sent arcs of electric awareness through his body. She was surprised by his answer.

"Did she die?" she asked, her voice tight.

Warren frowned. "I never married."

Her breath seemed to catch in her chest and distress spread across her features. Before he could question her reaction, she rose to her feet and walked to the corner of the kitchen, as far from Warren as she could get.

Confused, he did the only thing he could. He followed her.

Four

HE CAME UP BEHIND HER, AND EVERY NERVE IN HONEY'S body ignited with fire and life while her mind fought to find steady ground within the emotional storm his words had caused.

He never married.

It made no sense.

His letter had been clear and explicit. Enough to shatter her heart to pieces with only five lines. Five lines that she had read over and over for months on end to convince herself that the love she'd held so dear had to die.

The love had to die or she did, because she simply could not endure the pain of it, the soul-crushing sense of loss.

And now he said he'd never married.

Had it just been an excuse not to come back for her? A lie to cut the ties?

Fury raged like wildfire beneath her skin.

"Honey?"

She jolted at the sound of her name on his lips. His curiosity was clear despite his even tone. She had once found such comfort and peace in his voice, which like everything else about him had seemed created in perfect harmony with herself.

But now, hearing him say her name in that calm and questioning way was intolerable. She spun around to face him.

He stood barely a step away and she sucked in a tight breath at what his nearness did to her. Every scathing word she wanted to throw at him died in her throat. Her heart thudded so heavily and recklessly within her that it drowned out her thoughts.

His black brows tugged low over his eyes. He stepped closer, and though she tried to back away, to keep some distance between them, her back was already pressed against the counter behind her.

"Honey," he said again, this time in a barely audible murmur as he lifted his hand to brush his fingertips across her cheek in a quiet, tingling caress.

She held perfectly still, fighting against the treacherous will of her body, which wanted to lean into him, fall into his strength, and give herself to him as she had done so passionately before.

But she wasn't that girl anymore. Her innocence and trust had been obliterated by his abandonment and everything she'd faced since. So she held herself stiff and unmoving. Enduring his touch and refusing to give in to the urgings within her.

He swept his fingers down the side of her throat, stopping when his fingers pressed to the erratic flutter of her pulse, as though measuring her heartbeat.

"Where did your softness go?"

His whispered question brought her anger back in a rush. "You took it with you when you left."

Planting both hands against his chest, she gave him a shove and stepped to the side. But he hooked his arm around her waist and pulled her back until she was once again trapped between him and the counter. This time, he was not all gentle concern. Frustration had risen in his hard, beautiful features. His hands now pressed against the counter on either side of her, caging her in, keeping her in place to feel the heat of him. Everywhere.

When he spoke, it was through clenched teeth. "I told you I would return."

"Seven years later?"

His brows lowered in a dark scowl. "You know that's not what I meant."

"I know it's not what you made me believe," she corrected. "How you must have laughed at the stupid little country girl who thought a fine gentleman like yourself might want her."

His frown deepened. His jaw muscles clenched. "I did want you, Honey."

The words created a swirling mixture of pain, regret, and intimate yearning. She shoved down the yearning and focused on the rest. With a jut of her chin she replied, "Yes, I know. For a little fun before you went back to your studies."

"What on earth are you talking about?" he growled, his anger escalating along with hers.

"The truth, Warren. Something you apparently refuse to acknowledge even now."

"Oh, I know the truth." He made a show of glancing around them. "Where is your husband, Honey?"

She'd heard the question so many times, and always spoken with the same scathing judgment as Warren had just used. She answered automatically, in the way she'd always done. "He's dead."

As soon as the flat, emotionless words left her lips, something flashed bright and deep in his eyes.

His desire for her had always been tender, almost reverent. But despite her innocence and youth, she had sensed the deeper passions beneath his gentlemanly behavior, and she had practically begged him to make love to her that night under the stars.

What she saw now in the silver-blue windows to his soul held little resemblance to that gentle, loving passion. It was the unabashed hunger of a man holding nothing back.

And everything she'd ever felt about him came rushing back in one overwhelming wave—all the pain, heartbreak, anger, confusion. All the dreams, the passion, and the longing burst free.

Dammit, how she wanted him.

The press of his large male body. The warmth of his breath against her face just before his mouth crushed over hers. She even wanted the anger that transferred from his kiss.

It fueled her.

So that was how she kissed him back. With seven years of pent-up hostility over the lies he'd told her and the shattered dreams he'd left for her to sweep up into some sort of life worth living. She brought her hands to his head, her fingers curling into his thick black hair as she held him there to take every bit of aggression she could put into that kiss.

She had not expected how easily anger could dissolve into pure passion.

After the first taste of his lips, the first glide of his tongue as he accepted what she gave and returned it in equal measure, the heart-aching familiarity of his kiss transformed her fury into a desperate craving.

And when he shifted his hands from the counter to wrap his arms tight around her waist, locking her against him in a hold she had no wish to break free from, she knew where this was heading. And the acknowledgment only heightened her desire.

She broke from the kiss to gasp for breath, and though she tried to avoid his gaze, it caught her anyway for a brief flashing moment. What she saw there nearly changed her mind.

She didn't like the intensity in his expression. It made her feel the distrust and betrayal between them more acutely. She didn't want to think of that.

She wanted him as much as he wanted her. But this time, she did not have stars in her eyes. She was well aware of the realities of life. If she took him to her bed, it would have no promises for the future attached. She would never make that mistake again. But she could claim tonight and indulge in the fierce, overwhelming desire only he had ever inspired.

As her body hummed with sexual anticipation, Honey pressed her hands against Warren's chest, feeling the rapid beat of his heart beneath her palms. This time, he stepped back, and she turned and started toward the hall where there was an empty bedroom. Before rounding the corner, she looked back at him.

He remained where she'd left him, standing in the kitchen, looking after her. His body was rigid and his expression was strained, but his eyes...

His eyes sparked bright with hunger.

Honey met his gaze for just a second before continuing down the hall to the bedroom.

She didn't have to say it. He had always known when she wanted him.

She lit a small lamp on the bureau, creating a quiet contrast of golden light and subtle shadow. A ripple of intense awareness ran through her at the sound of Warren entering the room. She turned to see him standing with his back to the closed door, staring across the room at her.

No, she didn't want to think. And then, thank God, she didn't have to.

He closed the distance between them in two long strides and caught her face in his hands. Pressing his mouth to hers, he scooped one arm around her waist and started walking her back toward the bed.

Yes.

Just this. The passion and the fire. It's all she wanted. Nothing more. Nothing less.

She dove into the heat that swirled around them. Tangling her tongue with his, tugging at his clothing. Low sounds of need issued from her throat.

But no words. Words would only interfere. This was a time for feeling only. And she felt so much.

The rough and hurried way he released the buttons of her dress. The slide of his hand down her naked back when he finally got her clothing pushed down to her hips. The smooth feel of his bared chest pressing against her breasts after she pulled his shirt up over his head.

And his mouth as he kissed a hot and searing path down the side of her neck, across her bare shoulder, and then lower, when he wrapped his arms around her hips to lift her up so he could take one full breast in his mouth.

Pleasure flooded her body, making every inch of her ache with need.

It was familiar.

And it was easy. So easy.

They fell together onto the bed and somehow managed to shrug out of the rest of their clothes until they lay naked together. Flesh to flesh, heart to heart.

She couldn't stop touching him. Her hands flying over his body, relearning the contours of muscle and bone, discovering how he'd changed and how he was exactly the same.

When he nudged his thigh between hers, she gasped at the rush of excitement it inspired. Her belly danced wildly, sending deep arcs of pleasure and longing down between her legs, where her body craved his presence. The flare of hunger in her blood was like nothing she'd felt before. Stronger than it had ever been in her youth. Desire pulsed through her, taking over everything, demanding more.

And he gave it. Without any whispered words of love she wouldn't have believed anyway. He settled his hips between her thighs and entered her with one rocking thrust that had them both arching back. His breath was harsh and shallow as he withdrew from her slowly then charged forward again.

Honey's entire being strained at the rush of sensations. She gave herself over to it. It had been so long since she knew such a loss of control. She welcomed it with an abandon she might regret later. But not right now.

Right now, she surrendered to the storm of passion consuming them both.

She drew her knees up, allowing his thrusts to go deeper. Her eyes were closed tight and her arms were wrapped around his back as his mouth sealed on hers. This kiss was deep and demanding. The movement of his body over her, inside her, drew upon her last reserve. In a bright, consuming flash of light, pleasure exploded from her center and flew to the farthest reaches of her awareness, and she flew with it.

As the pulsing pleasure receded, Warren continued to glide in and out of her body in slow, beautiful strokes that sent little tingling sparks along her nerves. Her eyes fluttered open to see that he had propped himself up on his elbows and was looking intently at her face.

Something in the shining depths of his silver-blue eyes ensnared her and she could not look away. An invisible tether stretched between them, originating from a spot frighteningly close to her heart. The connection was as undeniable as it was unwanted.

Weakened and vulnerable after her release, Honey fought against the threat of tears clogging her throat. She was helpless to resist the draw of his gaze, but she didn't want him to know how deeply he touched her.

His brows lowered, briefly shadowing the light in his eyes as his jaw clenched tight. He gave one last possessive thrust that reached clear to her soul before his entire body went rigid. He pulsed deep and strong within her, but never took his gaze from hers as his pleasure finally claimed them both.

Five

WARREN SHIFTED, CAREFULLY DRAWING HIS LIMBS AWAY from Honey's warmth. He risked a glance to confirm what he'd suspected—that she'd fallen asleep almost as soon as he had withdrawn from her. Her skin was a soft gold in the low light, her features were relaxed and gentled by sleep, and her long blond hair was a tousled mess across the pillows.

A fist squeezed tight in his chest.

At seventeen, Honey Prentice had been open and joyous. Her easy love of life and quick smile had been an inexorable lure. Her unbridled heart and generous passion had bewitched him.

Though the last hour proved that her passions were fiercer than they had ever been, he'd sensed the wall between them. She didn't trust him.

Wariness flowed from her dark gaze. She claimed it was because of him, but it had been her choice to marry Freeman while he'd been attending his father's deathbed.

It made no sense.

And there was something else troubling him as he dressed quietly. The memories of that summer had not been exaggerated in his imagination. Whatever power had drawn them to each other then was still present, as strong and consuming as ever.

How was that possible after all this time and everything that had happened? He wanted to lay their past out on an exam table and dissect every little piece of it to find out what had gone wrong, why she hadn't waited for his return.

But he feared it would do no good. The past was done. This was now.

And right now, he needed to check on his patient.

It was hard to turn his back on Honey lying in that bed, but he did. He entered Luke's room two doors down to find the injured man awake and struggling to rise. Honey's brother looked up at Warren's entrance and his expression turned hostile.

"What in goddamned hell are *you* doing here?" he muttered with a menacing snarl.

Warren crossed his arms over his chest and returned the younger man's glower with a calm stare. "I am your doctor. I am here to see that you don't die from that gunshot wound in your leg. Toward that purpose, I suggest you lie back down so I can be sure you didn't tear open the stitches."

Luke grimaced in pain as he propped himself on one elbow.

"I don't want anything to do with your doctoring, Reed. Get yourself out of here before Honey sees you."

"She already has."

Luke lifted a brow at that. "And you're still alive."

"For the time being," Warren replied as he stepped forward. "She, at least, understands that my services are needed to keep your reckless hide alive."

"Well, shit," Luke muttered, "it's not like I planned to get shot. Damn cowards shot at me as I rode away."

Warren reached the bedside and gestured for Luke to roll to the side so he could loosen the bandage and get a look at the wound.

"I suppose you thought they'd be grateful to you for robbing them."

"Course not, but there's a code out here that says you don't shoot a man in the back."

"You were shot in the leg."

"From *behind*."

"As you made off with their valuables. I doubt the code of honor you describe applies to outlaws."

Luke snorted at that, then cringed as Warren probed around the stitches to find that they all held well and there had been no fresh bleeding. Fortunately, there were no warning signs of infection just yet.

Warren rewrapped the bandage and wordlessly helped Luke to a more comfortable position in the bed. He would have given the wounded man something to help him sleep, but Luke shook his head.

"I can't take any of that mind-dulling stuff," he said with a grimace toward the small green bottle of laudanum. "I gotta stay alert."

Warren debated arguing with him and decided to point out the obvious. "Even if you are alert, you won't be able to go anywhere."

"I've still got a working gun hand," Luke replied.

Warren replaced the laudanum in his bag. "Try to get some rest on your own then. If the pain gets to be too much, give a yell."

"Where is she?" Luke asked with tension bracketing his mouth.

Warren hesitated only a moment. "Sleeping."

"Here?"

"Yes," Warren answered, tipped his head in curiosity. "Does she usually sleep elsewhere?"

Luke shook his head. "I'm not telling you that if she didn't. But I'll tell you this." The outlaw's expression shifted, showing a hardness the young man had not possessed seven years ago. It made him look dangerous and unpredictable. "Before she wakes up, I want you gone from here. Head back to your Eastern city and never come back this way again. You're not gonna get another chance to break her heart, you understand me, Reed?"

Warren didn't understand. In fact, his confusion was only increasing. But Luke wasn't the one to ask for clarification. He turned and walked away, shutting the door behind him.

Honey was still asleep.

Warren stood at the side of the bed and tried to make sense of what Luke had just said and the way Honey had reacted to seeing him again.

Something was off.

"Honey, wake up."

He didn't expect her to stir so easily, but her eyes came open before he even finished speaking. She blinked a few times in rapid succession, then sat up with an incoherent mutter of annoyance as she grabbed at the bedsheets to cover herself. The grumpy little frown she turned on Warren might have made him smile if not for his determination to get to the bottom of what was bothering him.

His emotions coalesced into a rock, sitting heavy in his gut as he finally asked her the question that had been burning in his brain for years.

"Why did you marry John Freeman so soon after I left?"

"What?" The shock and incredulity in her face might have been residue from her sudden awakening.

Warren didn't think so.

"Why did you marry him, Honey? I thought you hated the man. Did he hold something over you? Did he threaten you?"

Warren had witnessed Freeman's bullying techniques when his uncle had refused to sell his small ranch to the man. The wealthy land baron had been willing to go to extremes to get what he wanted.

Honey angrily pushed her tangled hair back from her face as she turned to swing her feet down to the floor on the opposite side of the bed, giving him an excellent view of her slim, naked back.

"I don't know what you're talking about, Warren. Has your mind gone soft?" She stood, letting the sheet fall to the bed as she reached for her chemise and drew it over her head, then pulled her dress on over it. "I never married that pig. I never married anyone."

Warren's heart stopped. His brain lit up with a thousand questions.

"But you said your husband was dead," he said in a flat tone as a horrid suspicion began to form.

She made quick work of pulling her stockings and boots back on and was buttoning her dress as she replied. "I just got used to saying that whenever…" She stopped, then shook her head. "Never mind. It doesn't matter. But where did you ever get the idea I went and married Freeman?"

"From the letter I received from you the day of my father's funeral. It said you didn't want me to come back. That you had married Freeman and were starting a new life."

She spun around, breath held and eyes wide. "I never sent any letter, Warren. Not a one."

The mayhem erupting inside him at her words nearly felled him.

They had been manipulated.

"Oh my God," she whispered, shock set in her features. "Did you send me a letter saying you were marrying a girl out East? That I was nothing but a good time to fill your summer?"

Warren's hands curled into fists so tight, his knuckles ached. "No. I did not."

"Freeman! That good-for-nothing sonofabitch! I'm gonna kill him. I'm gonna ride up to Montana and put a bullet in that man's gut."

She turned and left the room in long furious strides.

Warren caught her by the arm just before she reached the front door, apparently intending to head out into the snowstorm as she was.

"Honey. Stop." He held tight. She still strained to get

away, but twisted her head to look at him with all her pain and fury showing plain in her face.

"Don't you see what he did?"

Warren nodded. A furious tornado of heartache and rage spun wildly inside him.

"He deserves to die," she growled.

"And he will someday, but not by your hand or mine."

She stared at him, disbelief written all across her face. "How can you be so calm about this? He tricked us to try to get what he wanted."

"I know." He forced the words through a tight throat. He knew the loss and anger she was feeling. He felt it too, down to his very bone marrow, but he knew something else as well. "But he didn't get what he wanted, did he? He's hundreds of miles away. We are here now."

His low murmured words seemed to have some effect on her as she stopped straining against his hold and turned toward him instead.

Was there hope in her eyes, mixed in with all that sadness?

"It's way too late," she whispered.

He frowned and lifted one hand to sweep some of her hair back from her face, letting his thumb brush gently over her cheekbone, where the golden freckles spread in a delightful pattern. "How do you know that?"

"Too much has happened, Warren."

He would have argued that it didn't matter, but something moving in the periphery of his vision caught his attention. A small girl-child shuffled in from the hallway. She was dressed in a long flannel nightgown, and the woolen socks on her feet slouched down around her ankles. She was rubbing the sleep from her eyes as she made her way into the kitchen.

Warren froze at the sight of her. An odd prickling sensation claimed every nerve.

His hand tightened involuntarily on Honey's arm,

alerting her to the newcomer. Noticing the girl, she stiffened like a board. The panic on her face told Warren nearly as much as the fact that the girl was right around six years old and had thick black hair tied into a messy braid that fell over her shoulder.

He got a feeling like his chest was caving in. He couldn't breathe.

Finally, the girl lowered her small fists from her eyes. Shock hit Warren like a train going full speed as he looked into the same silver-blue eyes he saw every morning when he shaved in front of his mirror.

A sleepy scowl hovered over the little girl's innocent eyes. "Why are you shouting, Mama? What's wrong?"

"Holy shit."

The curse was uttered by the outlaw named Jackson, who had just entered the front room.

"What?" Eli followed behind him, rubbing at his full beard. "What?" he asked again as he came to a stop and took in the scene.

"Isn't it obvious?" Jackson muttered beneath his breath.

Honey slipped from Warren's slack grasp and rushed toward the girl. "Nothing's wrong, baby. You should still be sleeping."

"But it's morning and I'm not tired anymore."

Warren glanced at the window over the kitchen counter. She was right. A muted white-gray light was expanding beyond the window. Snow covered everything.

"Let's get you dressed and we'll go home," Honey said as she began to shoo the girl back down the hall.

"Honey." Warren finally found his voice, but once again he was stopped short, this time by the appearance of Luke stepping from the hall between him and the two females. His shoulder was propped firmly against the wall to keep himself upright, and his expression was fierce with pain and determination. One hand grasped a handful of the blanket he'd wrapped around his hips for the sake of modesty, while his other hand held a gun pointed at Warren.

"You'll stay right there, Reed, if you know what's good for you."

Warren would have charged past that gun regardless of Luke's threat if two more weapons weren't instantly drawn on him by Jackson and Eli.

Apparently, they weren't going to give him a choice in the matter.

Six

HONEY RUSHED STELLA BACK TO THE LITTLE BEDROOM where she'd put her down to sleep when she realized she would be spending the night, tending to Luke.

Her brother's darkly muttered warning would keep Warren from following.

It was the only bit of security she had at that moment in a world that had flipped and spun out of control.

"Who was that man, Mama? Why were you yelling at him like that? Was he naughty?"

"I wasn't yelling *at* him exactly," she evaded, "and it's nothing you need to worry about anyway. It's time to head home."

"Is Uncle Luke gonna be okay?"

"I think so, baby. Your uncle is far too stubborn to let anything lay him low for too long."

Honey hustled her daughter through the motions of dressing her in her flannel underclothes, her dress, boots, and then her coat. A glance out the window suggested the snowfall had slowed to a few random flakes drifting here and there. She hoped they hadn't gotten so much through the night that they wouldn't be able to make the short trek home.

Once she had Stella bundled up, Honey grabbed the quilt from the bed to throw around her shoulders, not wanting to go back out to the front room to fetch her coat.

She needed time to think. Time would help her figure out this mess of thoughts and feelings flying through her. Time and distance from Warren's penetrating gaze, which looked straight into her heart without showing her a glimmer of his own. She needed to get home to her cozy little cabin. There she could be reminded of the safe and comfortable life she had created for herself and her daughter, with their handful of chickens and the garden they planted every spring.

She'd thought she hated John Freeman for how he had essentially run her out of the town she'd grown up in, but knowing the way he had tried to manipulate her into accepting his courtship made her angrier than she had ever been in her life.

"Why are you so mad, Mama? Did that man do something bad?"

Honey swallowed back the threat of tears at her daughter's innocent question.

"No, baby. He didn't."

Acknowledging that fact sent a crushing wave of regret through her.

Stepping through the back door at the end of the hall, just past Luke's room, she hustled them both through the freshly fallen snowdrifts, some of which reached nearly to Honey's thighs. A few times, she had to lift her daughter clear in order to get through.

Stella would have preferred to tromp through the snow on her own, pouncing and leaping over the drifts, her bright laughter echoing through their secret valley. But Honey rushed her along, glancing nervously over her shoulder every couple of minutes in fear that Warren would somehow get free of her brother to come after them.

Once they reached their cabin, Honey released a heavy sigh and set about starting a fire and settling in. She desperately needed a bath and a change of clothes. The dress she wore was probably ruined, but she had to at least try to wash the blood out. Ready-made dresses were nearly impossible to come by, and it took Honey an awful long time to sew her own, having never developed a talent for it like her mother's.

Staying busy was all she had to keep her sane, especially when Stella started in again with questions about Warren. Had the girl noticed the resemblance between them?

Honey couldn't think on that just yet.

She finally managed to get her daughter occupied with making some bread. Stella loved anything that could get her messy and provide a nice treat for later. Which left Honey to sift through the many and varied thoughts running through her head.

Her past was a lie. Warren's betrayal, completely false. Her hatred, unfounded.

And perhaps the worst thing—the whole time, he had felt betrayed by *her*.

Her chest tightened up so much, she had to stop in the middle of scrubbing her dress to force some deep breaths into her aching lungs.

She was not going to start crying now.

She had cried a lake full of tears seven years ago, so much that by the time her mother died, she'd only had a few tears left to give. After that, she'd sworn she was done with grief. That was the day she decided to leave Montana and raise her child away from the judging eyes of the town where she'd spent her life and the constant demanding presence of John Freeman.

She would always be grateful that Luke insisted on coming with her. She may have found a way to survive without her brother's support, but it would have been infinitely more difficult.

And she would find a way to survive this new twist on her past.

She had no idea what Warren might be thinking of all this. The temptation to hope was like a pounding drum in her chest. But the heartbreaking sadness had been

with her for so long and had cut so deep. A renewal of
their shared passion may have triggered that long-buried
yearning once again, but it held no promises.

She had to think of Stella.

She needed time to reconcile what she had believed
and what she now knew was the truth.

Luke would make sure Warren was taken back to
town. Christmas was not far off, and Honey still had a
lot to do in preparation. It was good to keep busy. It
was necessary.

∞

Warren was numb.

No, that wasn't quite right. This wasn't a total lack of
feeling. This was the exact opposite.

The discovery of his daughter had blasted through
him with such intensity that all he had left was scattered
debris. His thoughts were obliterated, his past inconse-
quential, his self now completely unfamiliar.

He had a daughter. He and Honey, together.

No. Not together.

Anger filtered through his shock, but he didn't want
to waste time on thoughts of a past that couldn't be
altered. It was the future that concerned him now. And
that thought was what finally motivated him to start
pulling his shattered awareness back together.

By the time Warren realized Honey wouldn't be
returning, he already had a plan forming in his mind.

When Eli left the longhouse to return a short time
later, declaring the pass clear enough to travel, Warren
didn't argue. He met Luke's hard gaze and didn't even
insist on checking the status of his wound. If Luke could
manage to be on his feet and hold a gun steady, he'd
likely be fine. If any infection set in, they knew where
to find him.

He did not resist when his two escorts tied the

blindfold back over his eyes and loaded him up onto horseback for the trip back to Chester Springs.

It was a silent ride this time, and no words were spoken until they stopped just outside of town to remove his blindfold.

"Leave the horse at the livery," Jackson instructed. "We'll come back for it."

Warren looked into the outlaw's dark eyes. "What is her name?"

Jackson gave a short shake of his head and said nothing. Eli wouldn't even meet his gaze. Their loyalty to Honey and her daughter was reassuring and irritating at the same time. *He* should be the one protecting them, not these outlaws.

Without another word, he nudged his horse into a lope.

He had a few things to work out in town before he could leave again. Chester Springs was likely going to need a new doctor, because Warren was not planning to stick around.

Seven

THERE HE WAS.

After nearly a week, Warren finally had the chance he'd been waiting for. Eli was back in town to fetch the horse.

Warren snatched up the bag he'd had prepared for days now, then grabbed his coat and a few other essentials. If all went well, he would come back for the rest of his belongings. And if he didn't make it back, well, so be it. Nothing he was leaving behind held any particular meaning for him.

He left the boarding house with determined strides, his feet crunching in the snow and gravel as he made his way down the road to the back of the livery. It was the day before Christmas and the town was mostly closed up. Only a few people could be seen rushing about on last-minute errands.

Eli must have left the outlaw's valley before dawn to get to town as early as it was. Which meant he most likely intended to head back today.

Warren quickened his steps until he reached the back entrance of the livery stables.

He could hear some shuffling about inside as horses scuffed their hooves in their stalls. There was no conversation, suggesting to Warren that if the livery owner had been there when Eli arrived, he wasn't anymore.

Warren spotted the outlaw in the last stall. The horse he'd ridden into town stood in the narrow alley between the rows of stalls as he readied the one he'd come to collect.

With a long, steadying breath much like the one he

employed before starting a particularly tricky surgery, Warren stepped into the stables and aimed the barrel of his recently purchased Colt revolver at the outlaw.

"Be sure to get that saddle nice and secure. I don't want any accidents on the ride into the mountains."

Eli didn't even flinch at Warren's interruption. He just tilted his head to get him in view, then went back to saddling the horse as he hissed a drawn out, "Sheee-it." After another minute, while Warren stood still and silent, Eli glanced back at him with a jeering grin. "You even know how to use that, Doc?"

Warren knew how to use a gun; his uncle had made sure of it that summer in Montana. He hadn't done any target practice in years, but then, he didn't actually intend to shoot anyone. He just needed to provide a bit of incentive to ensure his wishes were followed.

"What are the chances I would miss what I'm aiming for at this range?" he asked calmly in response.

Eli eyed the gun with a bit more wariness. "What do you want?"

"You are taking me back with you."

Eli tipped his hat back on his head, then scratched at his beard. "That's what I figured." He gave Warren a contemplative look. "You plan on hurting anyone?"

"Of course not," Warren answered automatically before he realized his admittance basically negated the threat of the weapon in his hand. Still, he didn't lower it. If Eli refused, he'd just have to find another way.

"Put your gun away, Doc," Eli said with a heavy sigh of reluctance. "I'll take you."

Elation rushed through Warren, but he eyed the outlaw with distrust. This had been easier than he'd expected. "Why?"

The other man led the gelding from his stall, then turned to mount his own pinto before he looked down at Warren. "Luke might put a bullet in me for it, but I'd be more afraid that Honey'd shoot to kill if she found out I refused you."

The muscles down Warren's spine tightened. "She has been upset?"

Eli laughed. "You might say that. The woman has been spinning around camp like a tornado. She seems to find work wherever she goes—and she's been giving plenty of it to us."

Warren frowned. "That doesn't exactly indicate she wants me to come back."

"Look, Doc, I grew up with eight females. That's six sisters, my ma, and an aunt. If there's one thing I learned, it's that they all got their own way of working through their emotions, and it ain't necessarily what you'd expect. I'd bet anything that the reason Honey's been going loco over these holiday preparations has more to do with your surprise appearance than anything else."

"Why would you agree to take me back if my appearance is what got her so upset?"

"The way I figure, if she didn't care about you, she'd've put you from her mind as soon as you left. The fact that she didn't tells me there's something unfinished between you two. I don't see getting any peace at camp until it's settled." Eli shrugged. "Besides, I didn't have no pa growing up. Seems to me that little girl deserves to have hers."

Warren stared hard at the man, wanting to trust him.

The outlaw stared back, unconcerned. "Are you getting on that horse, or what?"

Warren slid the Colt back into its holster on his hip. The weight of it felt strange, but he figured he'd have to get used to it, if he managed to convince Honey to give him a chance. After securing his bags to the saddle, he mounted the gelding and followed Eli from the stables.

"You are not going to blindfold me?"

Eli shrugged. "Nah."

Warren was really starting to like the man.

There had been two more snowfalls since the storm on the night he'd tended to Luke, and everything was covered in fluffy, pristine white. The late-morning sun shone brightly in a clear, pale sky. The air was still frigid and crisp, but there was no wind, and the snow sparkled in the sunlight.

Warren would have enjoyed the beauty of the landscape they crossed if he weren't so occupied by thoughts of what he would face when he saw Honey again. Everything—his future, his happiness, his heart—depended upon what happened when he reached his destination. Warren's mind ran obsessively through every possible variable and outcome. Though Eli attempted some casual chitchat, he was soon forced to accept Warren's nonreceptiveness and gave up.

A few hours later, they were making their way through a narrow pass between the mountains. The atmosphere grew shadowed and silent as they traversed this last stretch, and anticipation was like a flickering flame in Warren's blood. Finally the pass took a turn and opened up to the outlaws' valley.

Smoke drifted from the stone chimney of the longhouse, which was located near the center of the valley where it was widest. Fresh pine boughs had been hung along the porch railing, with a giant red bow tied festively at every post. Forest-covered mountains rose up on each side and formed a backdrop in the far distance behind. The scene was stark in its beauty yet welcoming.

A casual observer would never suspect the place housed a group of outlaws. Especially if they heard the burst of childish laughter and saw the small figure emerge from the tree line to the west to tumble head over heels down the snowy hill.

Warren's hands tightened on his reins, drawing his horse to a halt as he watched the scene with a sort of terrified awe spreading through his chest.

The girl came to rest at the base of the hill and immediately jumped to her feet to start the long trek back up. She wore several layered skirts and heavy boots. Her coat was thick sheepskin, buttoned up to the woolen shawl that covered her head and wrapped about her neck. Mittens protected her hands as she scooped handfuls of snow and threw them up into the air.

Warren tensed when the girl slipped back out of sight into the trees.

But a moment later, her laughter pealed again as she tumbled back down the hill. This time, she was followed by her mother, carrying a large basket in her arms as she rushed along with long strides and a soft laugh.

When Honey reached the girl, she said something Warren couldn't hear and the child took off for the longhouse.

That was when Honey looked up to see Warren and Eli atop their horses half the distance from the pass. Eli had stopped when Warren did and silently sat his horse a few steps behind him, as though waiting for Warren to make a move.

He couldn't.

If someone had asked, he would have readily admitted his trepidation as Honey stared at him across an expanse of sparkling white snow, their daughter's laughter still dancing in the crisp air. A daughter Warren hadn't known about until a week ago. A daughter Honey had given birth to and raised on her own.

That truth—the fact that he hadn't been there for either of them—filled Warren with a regret unlike anything he'd known. He could excuse his absence and say that he hadn't known about the baby. Hadn't known that the letter had been a lie. That he had spent the last years feeling as betrayed as she had.

But all he could feel was guilt and sadness.

He should have gone back anyway. He should have fought for her, done everything he could to win her back from Freeman. Then he would have seen the lie. And the last six years could have been so different for both of them.

He didn't regret his training as a doctor. His chosen path fulfilled him in ways that were personal and deep. But he could have done it with the woman he loved—and their daughter—at his side.

Honey stood staring at him for a long moment. She was too far away for him to read her expression, but he could see the tension in her body and he could imagine what she might be thinking and feeling. Then she hefted the basket she carried higher in her arms before she turned to continue on to the longhouse.

Only once she was in the building and out of sight did Warren release a full breath.

At least she hadn't drawn a gun on him this time.

"You're not gonna chicken out, are you?"

Warren frowned at Eli, who sat hunched forward in his saddle with his forearms resting on the saddle horn. The man wore an amused little grin that annoyed the hell out of Warren just then, but before he could reply, the outlaw laughed and nudged his horse forward.

"Come on, Doc. Let's stable these horses and get inside where it's warm."

They rode around behind the longhouse to where a nice-sized stable was tucked in along the tree line opposite from where Honey had emerged. Warren hadn't even noticed the building on his last visit and was surprised by its size and the number of horses already inside.

"Just how many men are housed here?" he asked as they brushed down their mounts after getting them fresh water and grain.

"At any given time, not too many."

Warren wasn't sure if the man's answer was intentionally evasive, or if that was just his manner. He was

getting the sense Eli was a bit more complex than he'd
first appeared.

"You'll see most of the gang today, though. Honey's
been prepping for this holiday feast for weeks."

His comments reminded Warren to take care with his
bags as he hefted them onto his shoulder and followed
Eli to the longhouse.

He had no idea what he'd face inside. If Honey had
told Luke he was here, it was possible he'd be walking
into a room full of guns pointed his way and an outlaw
army ready to escort him right back the way he'd come.

Eli muttered a quick "Good luck" beneath his breath.
Apparently, he wasn't too sure of Warren's welcome either.

❧

To Warren's relief, no one drew their gun when he
stepped into the front room.

About a dozen men were gathered. Most of them
hadn't noticed him yet, or if they had, they weren't
acknowledging his presence.

Jackson stood by the fireplace with two other men
and gave Warren a shallow nod as Eli led him in. In his
company was a short, wiry fellow with salt-and-pepper
hair, and a tall, lanky kid in possession of a baby face that
hadn't grown any whiskers yet. They both cast curious
glances toward Warren but seemed to take their cue from
Jackson and continued with their conversation.

Four men of various ages, one of them with a shock
of red hair and a deep rolling laugh, sat at a table playing
poker. Behind them, a large man of native blood stood
alone and silent, watching the game from his position
beside the front door, his thickly muscled arms crossed
over his chest. He made a striking image with his bronzed
skin, straight black hair plaited into two long braids, and
deep-set eyes. He cast a calm, assessing glance at Warren
before shifting his attention back to the poker game.

Luke, however, was a different story.

Honey's twin was seated in one of the armchairs placed near the fire. He shouldn't have been up and about yet, but he showed no signs that the wound had taken a turn. Warren was relieved until he saw the animosity in Luke's eyes. At least the outlaw's gun stayed in its holster and his hands stayed calmly on the armrests of the chair, one of them curled around a glass of spirits.

Warren wondered if Honey had told him what Freeman had done. If she had, apparently Luke had not made up his mind about Warren just yet.

Only then did Warren allow himself to look toward Honey, bustling about in the kitchen area. He'd been avoiding meeting her eyes, afraid of what he'd see there.

He needn't have worried.

Honey stood stirring a large cast-iron pot set on the wood-burning stove, turning every now and then to toss a bit of instruction to one of the two men who had apparently been assigned as her helpers. She wore an apron over a red dress trimmed in ivory lace, and her golden hair was twisted and pinned atop her head. After giving Warren a brief glance, she returned her attention to the pot she was stirring on the stove. Dinner preparations were going all out. One of the men, a stocky white-haired fellow with a deeply lined face, had an apron tied about his waist and a wide grin as he enthusiastically kneaded some dough on the kitchen counter. The other man sat in a chair, peeling potatoes and wearing an expression much like a schoolboy enduring punishment.

Now that he knew he wasn't immediately going to be run off, Warren figured he could allow her time to adjust to his presence. She wasn't the only person he was there to see, after all.

Honey's daughter—the only other female in sight—skipped out from one of the hallways and started weaving in and out of the men with a smile of delight and a twinkle in her eye.

She danced about in a pretty blue dress with white lace, her dark hair woven into a long braid with a bright blue bow tied at the end. He felt the tug of a smile on his lips when she made her way to the poker game and hovered behind one of the players for a couple of minutes before she pointed to his cards and whispered something in his ear.

Whatever she said made the man laugh out loud before she flitted off again.

The scene was joyous and festive. Delicious smells of savory cooking and mulled spices filled the air. An evergreen Christmas tree stood in a corner opposite the fireplace. It was dressed with dried cranberries and popcorn threaded on long strands, angels fashioned out of bits of cloth, paper snowflakes, and dozens of tiny, flickering candles. The long dinner table had been covered by a red plaid tablecloth, and fresh pine boughs interspersed with pine cones and red ribbon formed a fragrant centerpiece on the table.

In the kitchen, various pies were lined up on one end of the counter next to the basket Honey had been carrying across the valley when he'd arrived. He could see now that it held several loaves of bread and some jars of what looked to be homemade taffy.

A lot of effort had been put into making the holiday gathering festive and bright.

Warren glanced toward Honey again and caught her gaze quickly sliding away. She had been watching him. He wanted to talk to her, take her somewhere private and say all the things that had been circling in his brain for the last week.

But it wasn't time yet, and this wasn't the place.

He lowered his bags and set them against the wall. When he straightened, his heart jolted at the sight of his daughter standing in front of him with wide eyes that matched his and a curious tilt of her head.

"You were here before," she declared. "When Uncle Luke was hurt."

Warren crouched down, bringing his face more in line with hers. Such a beautiful face. A pert little chin and gentle brow, and a light dusting of freckles across her nose and cheekbones. Though she had his eyes and his dark hair, the rest of her features were her mother's—except for there, in the turn of her mouth. That curious little curve with the barely suppressed hint of mischief was entirely reminiscent of Warren's younger sister, Evie.

Seeing that made him smile as he replied, "Yes, I am the doctor who treated him."

"He is all better now," she said with a wave at the man in question.

Warren glanced up to see Luke was still watching. He nodded to him and brought his attention back to the girl in front of him.

"So why are you here now?" she asked. "Have you come to celebrate with us? Tomorrow is Christmas, you know."

"That is exactly why I am here." Warren took a chance in saying the rest, but he wanted to be sure he was honest in his intention from the start, especially with this child. "I was friends with your mother and your uncle many years ago. I would like to be friends with them again."

She considered that for a bit. Her eyes narrowed in thought. Then she glanced back at her mother, who was laughing with the white-haired man in the apron. Honey's quick glance in their direction proved she knew exactly whom her daughter was speaking to at that moment. That she didn't come over to draw the girl away gave Warren hope.

"It would be nice if you and I could be friends as well," he ventured.

The girl looked back to him with a smile brightening her face. "Mama always says that friends are the family you get to choose. We have a lot of friends," she said with an impulsive open-armed spin that made it look as though she were giving a swift hug to the entire room.

"I would love to have another," she said when she came to a stop again. Then she held out her hand. "It is a pleasure to meet you, sir. My name is Stella, what is yours?"

The name immediately brought to mind a memory from that summer long ago. He and Honey had slipped out of town in the middle of the night to find a quiet patch of earth beside a slow-moving stream. It had been a beautiful night, filled with love and hope. Forever had stretched out before them like the endless night sky. They'd lain side by side in the grass with her head on his shoulder and their fingers interlocked as they stared up at the blanket of summer stars overhead, and he'd told her the Latin word for each of the shining points of light. *Stella.*

"My name is Warren Reed," he said finally, his throat tight as he took his daughter's small fingers in his. "A pleasure to meet you, Miss Stella."

She smiled and gave his hand a vigorous, heartfelt shake. "There," she said, "now we're friends."

Eight

HOW WAS IT POSSIBLE FOR A HEART TO FEEL LIKE IT WAS filling up and breaking at the same time?

Seeing Warren with Stella was something Honey had never expected to experience. And now that she had, she feared what it could mean.

To Stella.

And to herself.

Her world had twisted itself inside out. She was desperate to do the right thing by her daughter, but she wasn't sure what that was. Not when her own heart's desires were too powerful and confusing to ignore.

With the truth about the past known and the anger that had sustained her obliterated—or at least shifted to the correct target—Honey was forced to acknowledge that she had never really stopped loving Warren. She had hated him, but only because of how badly she had been hurt by his abandonment.

Now all that was changed.

She did her best to stay occupied with preparations for the holiday dinner. But it was a challenge. Especially once Warren began to interact with the rest of the boys. It was unnerving to see him, so sophisticated and refined, in the midst of a gang of former cowboys, soldiers, and wanderers who had come together to form a sort of family. There was even a point when Warren approached Luke, and the two of them had what appeared to be a frank discussion that perhaps started out with an inquiry into her brother's condition and ended with a handshake.

It was all so strange.

Just before dinner was to be served, Honey claimed a moment to step outside and grab a few deep breaths of the crisp night air.

The sky was still clear and the moon was nearly full, casting a bright silver glow through the night as it reflected off the snow. Her breath puffed in the frigid atmosphere, but she welcomed the icy nip on her skin. Drawing her woolen shawl around her shoulders, she wandered down the length of the porch to the corner where she could peer up through the trees in the direction of her little cabin. Just knowing the home she'd created for Stella was there, comfy and secure, filled her with a sense of rightness.

Stella's happiness and safety were what mattered most. Honey's personal longing would never take precedence over her daughter's well-being.

Acknowledging that to herself cleared some of the anxiety she had been fighting since seeing Warren riding into the valley with Eli. She didn't know why he'd returned and she couldn't deny the combination of thrill and fear it ignited, but she wouldn't lose sight of what was most important.

Just as she turned to go back inside, the door opened and a large figure stepped out. The shadows of the covered porch concealed his face, but Honey knew it was Warren. She knew it by the fiery rush through her blood and the way her breath froze midexhale.

The door closed behind him, blocking out the light and noise from within as he approached her. Stopping only when they were nearly toe to toe, he looked at her with an expression she could not read.

And she looked back. Unable to turn away. Unwilling to break eye contact even though her heart pounded so hard, her ribs ached.

Then, still without a word, he lifted his hand to the

side of her face. The warmth of his bare palm contrasted against her cold skin. When his thumb brushed across the crest of her cheek, she knew he was going to kiss her.

Considering what they had done the last time he had been there, a kiss shouldn't have terrified her. But it did. This was different.

Because he had come back. Because they both knew the truth now. Because it felt the way it had that summer when she was seventeen.

Breathless, hopeful, new.

He leaned in slowly, his gaze holding hers. The touch of his mouth was warm and soft. Her eyes fell closed and her body swayed toward him. Though she still clutched her shawl with her arms folded tight across her chest, he wrapped his arms around her anyway, drawing her into the heat of his body.

He wore his heavy coat, but he hadn't buttoned the front. She pressed in against his chest and the edges of his coat came around her, enclosing them both. It felt safe and warm.

And then it felt hot as his kiss changed from soft to passionate with a tilt of his head and sweep of his tongue. She opened to him and returned the stroke of his tongue with more of her own. Relaxing her arms, she slid them around his waist and rose up on her toes, wanting nothing more than to get closer to him. To feel the way she remembered in her dreams.

He tightened his hold around her, and the hard evidence of his desire brought her back to reality. They couldn't exactly slip away to find a quiet corner somewhere, no matter how badly she wanted to.

She broke from the kiss, her breath puffing harshly as she dropped her forehead to his shoulder. He tightened his embrace even more.

"I have to go back in," she whispered.

"Not yet." His voice was raw and deep. The thick

emotion revealed in his words matched the weight of her own. "I'm not going to let you go this time."

A lump rose in her throat at his declaration. Heartache returned with the force of a winter storm.

"You have to."

"No."

"There is more than just my heart at stake."

"I would never hurt her."

Honey tipped back her head to see his determined expression. "Not intentionally, I know. But we have security here. A home and family—"

"With a bunch of renegades and outlaws," he interrupted, frustration coloring his tone.

Honey stiffened and drew back. He let her, his hands dropping to his sides as she grasped the edges of her shawl to fold it tight across her chest again. "Yes," she replied, pride in her tone. "I built a home here. It is a place where Stella and I are loved and happy. Why should I risk that?"

Warren frowned. "You don't trust me."

She didn't deny it. He may not have left her in the way she had believed, but he had left her. She had been on her own, forced to take responsibility for her life and her daughter's and make the most of what they had available.

Luke had done what he could to help, but his life was about taking risks. Honey's had been about the opposite.

And loving Warren again felt like the biggest risk she had ever faced.

"It's time for dinner," she said as she stepped around him and strode across the porch to reenter the house.

He did not immediately follow, only coming back in just as everyone was taking their seats around the long table for the Christmas Eve feast. The table was loaded with the results of her loving labor: a large ham glazed with a brown sugar syrup, a haunch of venison that had been basted with butter over several hours, thick gravy, mashed turnips, roasted sweet potatoes, cranberry sauce, mince pie, pickled beets, sugared nuts, and more.

Stella had helped in the preparations of nearly everything that was being served, and her little face glowed with pride as the men expressed their praise and gratitude for the delicious food.

It was hard to ignore Warren's presence throughout the meal, but Honey focused her attention on Stella and purposefully engaged in the raucous conversation flowing around the table.

Still, she felt his regard and knew their conversation was not finished.

Nine

AFTER DINNER, THE MEN WENT BACK TO THEIR TALK AND their cards as bottles of whiskey and brandy got passed around more freely. A new set of kitchen helpers cleaned up while Luke supervised the roasting of chestnuts over the fire, and the older man who had been talking with Jackson when Warren arrived pulled out a fiddle. He seemed to only know a couple of Christmas carols and the music soon shifted to more rollicking dance tunes. Warren assisted with the clean-up where he could, enjoying the sight of his daughter dancing through the room, delight evident on her face.

It wasn't long, however, before the girl's eyes began to droop and she curled up into a corner of the sofa. Honey noticed as well. She fetched the girl's boots and coat and started bundling her into her winter gear. The task was made difficult as Stella had decided she didn't want to leave just yet and resisted Honey's efforts even though her limbs were heavy with sleep.

"Let me help," Warren said.

Honey looked up at him, not saying anything. Her eyes were guarded, but after a moment she nodded.

He crouched beside the sofa and leaned toward Stella with a conspiratorial smile.

"You know, the sooner you get tucked into your bed, the sooner you'll wake up to Christmas morning, and I might just have a few packages in my bags with your name on them."

The girl gasped and her eyes grew wide. "Presents?"

Warren shrugged. "Maybe. You won't know for sure until Christmas Day."

The reminder of what the morning would bring gave her enough motivation to finish dressing.

Honey gave him a stern look as she secured a scarf over her daughter's head. "You didn't have to—"

"Yes, I did," he replied firmly.

While Warren fetched his bags and Honey said her goodbyes, Stella nodded off to sleep. Warren returned to her first and scooped her up into his arms to wait for Honey by the door.

The three of them left the longhouse in silence, stepping out into the crisp, white world. Warren followed Honey as she trekked along a well-trod path up into the woods. He breathed deep and reveled in the feel of his daughter's small body nestled against his chest and the sight of her mother leading them home.

He doubted he would ever forget the way he felt along that walk.

Not far into the forest, tucked in against the side of the hill, was a quaint little cabin with a small front porch decorated in pine boughs and red sashes, just like the longhouse. A couple of steps up, and Honey was opening the wreath-decorated door.

Warren took a deep breath and followed her across the threshold.

~∞~

The fire in the hearth was still lit but had dimmed to glowing coals. A little woolen stocking hung from the mantel, waiting to be filled with treats and surprises from Santa Claus. As Honey stoked the fire and added fresh wood, Warren set Stella on the sofa before the fire and started drawing off her winter gear. Soon the place was filled with warmth and flickering firelight.

"I'll put her to bed," Honey said quietly.

Warren was crouched in front of the sleeping child, pulling off her second boot. At Honey's words, he rose to his feet and backed away. She lifted the sleeping girl in her arms and carried her through a doorway into the bedroom beyond.

He turned in place, taking in the details of Honey's home.

It was a small cabin, tiny really by comparison to the longhouse down in the valley. The room was barely large enough for the sofa and one small end table, with a corner kitchen open to the living area. There was no stove, but a large black kettle rested on the woodpile beside the fireplace. It appeared she did the cooking here over the fire. Books were stacked in the corners and woolen blankets draped the back of the sofa, pillows were scattered on the floor in front of the sofa, and a braided rug covered the wood floor. A tattered and obviously beloved rag doll rested among the pillows.

Warren scooped it up before taking a seat on the sofa. He stared at the doll, noting the places where it was most threadbare, where its dress had been mended and lace had been resewn.

The doll had been made from the remnants of a dress he remembered Honey wearing a lot that summer. It was a beautiful pale green with a pattern of pink and yellow flowers. He had loved seeing her in that dress and had told her so, which in turn made her wear it more often.

And now the dress had been refashioned for Stella's doll. Something he had loved had become something she loved. It made him feel more connected to the daughter he had only barely met.

Honey reentered the room and he hastily swallowed the thickening lump in his throat.

"Would you like some coffee?" she asked from the kitchen. "Or tea? I think I have tea."

"Coffee would be wonderful. Thank you," he said without looking up.

As Honey bustled about, he set the doll aside and refocused his purpose. After a few minutes, she approached the fire and hung the coffeepot on a hook that moved on a swivel over the flames to heat up.

Then she turned to face him. Warren's heart nearly broke.

She looked so scared and strong at the same time. So proud and uncertain. Did she feel the fierce tug between their hearts like he did?

"Tell me what happened after I left," he said, doing his best to keep his tone neutral.

Honey took a deep breath and came forward to sit beside him on the sofa, far enough to keep their bodies from touching. Though she angled her shoulders toward him, she directed her gaze at the fire.

"Everything changed," she said simply.

"Tell me," Warren said again.

"Not long after you went back East, Freeman started making a nuisance of himself. He came around as often as he could, most times catching me when Mama or Luke were gone. He didn't force himself on me or anything," she said quickly when Warren stiffened beside her, "but he made sure his intentions were clear. He wanted to marry me. Said he'd been biding his time since I turned fifteen, thinking I needed to grow up a bit more." She grimaced and gave a little huff.

"I thought everyone in town knew how I felt about you, but when I said I wouldn't marry him, that I loved someone else, he got real angry."

Warren had never been a violent man, but his hands curled into fists at her words. "What did he do?"

Her brown eyes found his and held there. Sadness swirled in the dark depths.

"We know now that he sent us those letters. He also made things difficult for Mama. People stopped bringing her business. He put pressure on the sheriff to hassle

Luke for every little thing. It got so Luke couldn't walk down the street without breaking some obscure town ordinance and landing in the jail for the night.

"It was around the same time your uncle left the area." She tipped her chin to look at him questioningly. "I always worried that Freeman had done something to force them out."

Warren shook his head. "No. Uncle Randolph's a born wanderer. He never stays in one place for long. He and my cousin headed off on some whim or another."

"I always liked that girl of his," she replied with a wistful smile. "Such a bright little hellion."

"She was that," Warren smiled, thinking of his young cousin. "Alexandra has actually been in Boston with my mother for the last few years."

Her eyes widened. "In the big city? Now, that is hard to imagine. That girl was born to run in the wilderness."

"The last time I saw her, she had become quite a lady."

"Amazing."

"It is," Warren agreed with a nod, before he lowered his brows, "but I think this conversation has digressed quite enough."

She gave him a look that said she wasn't grateful for the reminder as she rose to her feet and crossed to check on the coffee.

"There's not much more to say. When I wouldn't be bullied by Freeman's tactics, he decided to make the whole damn town suffer. He made sure everyone knew that if I'd just agree to marry him, the troubles would all stop."

Warren wanted to punch something. Preferably, Freeman's fat nose.

Honey came to stand in front of him, holding out a steaming cup of coffee. He took it from her hand and then caught her fingers in his.

She tried to keep the emotions from showing in her

face, but the evidence of what that time had been like for her darkened her eyes.

"I should have been there," he said softly. "I wish I had known."

She lowered her lashes and pulled away.

He let her go.

"You had to leave and I don't begrudge you that, Warren. Truly. Maybe things would have been different if Freeman hadn't interfered as he did. But we can't change it now."

After pouring coffee for herself, she reclaimed her seat on the sofa, curling her legs beneath her.

"And when you learned of the baby?" he asked, his stomach tightening at the thought of her, so young at seventeen, discovering she was going to have a child. Alone.

"I tried to hide it as long as I could." Her voice lowered and her expression softened as she stared at the flames burning steady in her hearth. "But I was so happy. From the second I knew of Stella's existence, I cherished her." She paused to sip her coffee, both hands wrapped around the steaming mug. "Unfortunately, people in town did not have the same reaction, as you can imagine.

"Freemen used my disgrace as further ammunition against me and my family. Luke got in so many fights he was perpetually black and blue. And Mama…" She glanced down at her lap. "Mama couldn't take the strain of everything coming at her from Freeman, from the townsfolk, from my…situation. Her heart gave out one night while she slept."

Warren ached for her loss at a time when she had been so vulnerable. "God, Honey, I am so sorry."

She rushed on as though embarrassed by his sympathy. "Luke and I sold the house and left town as quick as we could, taking only what we needed. I owe so much to him for his support during those months. It was Luke who found this place and worked out a way to pay for it. There was just this cabin and the land then. But it was home, and just in time for Stella."

She smiled. "Even with his reckless ways, Luke has a way of earning people's loyalty." She turned to look at him. "They are not bad men, Warren. Each of them has his own reasons for going outside the law to survive. Just as Luke and I did."

As a doctor in one of the largest cities in the Eastern states, Warren was not as sheltered as his family had raised him to be. He had seen desperation and the human instinct for survival in some of the harshest of conditions.

He was grateful to Luke for doing what he had to provide for Honey and her baby. But it only added to the guilt and regret growing inside him as he listened to her story. He would give anything to have been able to prevent all that she had endured. She was right, he couldn't change the past, but he could have an effect on the future.

Setting his coffee aside, he shifted from his seat until he crouched down in front of her, bracing his hands on either side of her hips.

She said nothing. Just looked at him with sad eyes, her shoulders squared and strong.

"I never stopped loving you, Honey."

A sound caught in her throat and she shook her head wordlessly, making the rest of his words tumble out before she could try to refute him.

"I was hurt and angry and confused by the news that you married Freeman so soon after I'd left. But I never stopped loving you. I love you now, seeing what you've done for yourself and"—he swallowed hard around the thickness in his throat—"and for our daughter. I can't express how much I admire the wealth of strength and love you possess."

He lowered his head, then looked up again. The tears in her eyes nearly made it impossible for him to continue.

"I know you don't need me, Honey. And maybe you can't find your way to loving me again, but you should know how I feel."

The shaking of her head got more vigorous and she rose to her feet in a rush to shove past him.

He stood and followed her into the little kitchen area. He was not going to back down until he knew for a fact she didn't want him.

"No, Warren. You do not love me," she said sternly as she placed her mug on the little table and turned back to face him with her arms wrapped tight around her middle. "It is your guilt talking, nothing else," she said with a hard jut of her chin.

"That's not true," he argued. "Of course, I'm filled with remorse for what I couldn't do for you, but that does not mean I don't love you. Give me a chance to prove it."

"Warren, I…" She couldn't finish.

"What is it, Honey?"

She took a breath, but didn't answer.

He closed the distance between them and took her face in his hands, forcing her to meet his gaze.

"I know you feel something for me, Honey. I cannot believe that this longing in my heart does not fill yours, that this fire rolling through me does not burn through you as well."

He saw the flicker of response in her eyes, felt her body swaying forward. He ran his thumbs along the stubborn line of her jaw. His gaze dropped to her lips and he murmured, "Tell me you don't want me to kiss you right now."

Her lips parted and her breath came swift.

Warren eased closer until their bodies pressed full length to each other. He could feel her heartbeat and the unsteady rhythm of her breath.

"Tell me you feel nothing," he murmured, "and I will let it be."

Her eyelashes fluttered and the corner of her mouth curled unexpectedly. "Somehow I doubt that," she whispered. "But this—whatever this is still between us—is not enough. Too much time has passed. Too much has changed."

"I don't believe that," he said. The words were gruff with emotion. "Give us another chance."

She met his eyes steadily. "What happens when Stella comes to love you and you decide to go back East? I won't let her experience that heartbreak and I can't go through it again."

She was scared.

He was scared too, but he wasn't about to let it stop him.

"Nothing could take me from either of you," he vowed. "Not ever again."

He brushed his thumb once more over her cheek before he lowered his head. Warren put everything he had into that kiss, holding her face in his hands as he swept his tongue past her teeth to taste her deepest desires and claim her every wishful breath.

He wanted this. Her. Forever.

Only when the kiss had made them both breathless, and he felt her hands clutching at his shoulders as she moved intently against him, did he pause, easing the pressure of his mouth just enough to murmur against her lips, "Please say you'll marry me."

She pulled back with a gasp of surprise. Her eyes were wide and her lips parted in stunned silence. Warren took the opportunity to step back and fetch the small box he had tucked into the pocket of his coat.

"I bought this the first week I was back in Boston. I had expected to give it to you years ago, but perhaps you'll accept it now as my Christmas gift."

He opened the jeweler's box to show her a ring with five amethysts interspersed with tiny diamonds set along a gold band. The center stone was the largest, with those extending to each side gradually decreasing in size.

"Marry me, Honey."

She silently shook her head from side to side, but one of her hands lifted toward the ring.

Warren caught that wayward hand and took the ring from the box to slip it onto her finger. She didn't resist, and his heart began to sing.

Then she stuttered, "Marry you...I...but this is our home. I can't take Stella away from the only family she's ever known."

"Then I will come to live with you here."

She blinked at that. "In this little cabin?"

"Why not?" Warren glanced around. "We might want to add on another bedroom in the spring, but otherwise it's perfect."

"But your practice in Chester Springs..."

"I can make a trip to town a few times a month to see to people's needs. If that isn't enough, I will find a replacement."

"Being a doctor is all you ever wanted."

"Not all," he said with a smile, drawing her into his arms. "And right now, this is more important. I'll find a way to work out the doctoring bit."

"But Stella...she will have so many questions."

"We have all night to figure out how best to explain things to her."

"My brother—"

"Will have to accept it," he stated.

She fell silent.

"Any more concerns?" He kept his tone light though his insides were churning.

Her eyes glistened with emotion as she stared at him for a long moment. Then she released a slow breath.

"Just one," she admitted as she brought her arms up to encircle his neck. The smile curving her lips made his heart skip a beat and his blood run swift. "I do not have a gift for you."

"I cannot imagine a better Christmas gift than having you and Stella in my life." His arms tightened around her. "Forever."

"Then forever it is," she said before she rose up on her toes to seal her promise with a kiss.

About the Author

Amy Sandas's love of romance began one summer when she stumbled across one of her mother's Barbara Cartland books. Her affinity for writing began with sappy preteen poems and led to a bachelor's degree with an emphasis on creative writing from the University of Minnesota Twin Cities. She lives with her husband and children in northern Wisconsin. Visit her website at amysandas.com.

Howdy, Beautiful.

Looking for a cowboy of your very own?
Take this quiz to find your perfect match!

★ ★ ★

1. Where can you be found on a Friday night?

a. Spending quality time with the tight-knit family built with the man you love.
b. Riding the range alongside your hero to ensure the land is safe.
c. Working tirelessly with your man to impact the community.
d. Locked in the arms of your soul mate.

2. Your idea of a perfect date would be:

a. Walking by the river, hand-in-hand, as the sun sets.
b. Racing horses across fields of gold.
c. An impromptu picnic surrounded by wildflowers.
d. Locked in the arms of your soul mate.

3. Your perfect state is:

a. Texas
b. Montana
c. Arizona
d. Locked in the arms of your soul mate.

4. Your one goal in life is to be:

a. The beating heart of your fiercely loving family.
b. The protector of anyone who can't defend themselves.
c. An agent of positive change in the world.
d. Locked in the arms of your soul mate.

— RESULTS —

☞ If you answered **mostly A's**, your perfect match is the **True-Blue Hero**! Go to Men of Legend and Texas Rodeo for more information.

☞ If you answered **mostly B's**, your perfect match is the **Fearless Lawman**! Go to Night Riders and Navy SEAL Cowboys for more information.

☞ If you answered **mostly C's,** your perfect match is the **Last Good Man**! Go to Last Chance Cowboys and A Match Made in Texas for more information.

☞ If you answered **mostly D's**, your perfect match is the **Outlaw with a Heart of Gold**! Go to Outlaw Hearts and Runaway Brides for more information.

☞ If you answered a **mix of all four,** congratulations! You can't be tied down by convention—every hero is your perfect match. Go to Men of Legend, Texas Rodeo, Night Riders, Navy SEAL Cowboys, Last Chance Cowboys, A Match Made in Texas, Outlaw Hearts, and Runaway Brides for more information.

YOUR PERFECT COWBOY IS THE
True-Blue Hero!

You value deep family connections and a life built on mutual respect, love, and breathless admiration. Your hero is as true as the Texas skies and as devoted to you—and the children, animals, and other family you two found along the way—as you could ever dream.

Want to know more? Find your hero in:

— MEN OF LEGEND —

Three Brothers. One Oath. No Compromises. Meet the Men of Legend.

BY LINDA BRODAY, *NEW YORK TIMES* AND *USA TODAY* BESTSELLING AUTHOR

To Love a Texas Ranger
When Texas Ranger Sam Legend finds himself locked in battle to rescue a desperate woman on the run, he'll risk anything to save her—his badge, his heart, and his very life.

The Heart of a Texas Cowboy
Houston Legend swore he'd never love again, but with the future of his family's ranch on the line, he heads to the altar to marry a woman he's never met.

To Marry a Texas Outlaw
The last thing outlaw Luke Weston needs is more trouble. But when he stumbles upon a kidnapped young woman, he'll face any odds to keep the delicate beauty safe.

YOUR PERFECT COWBOY IS THE
True-Blue Hero!

You value deep family connections and a life built on mutual respect, love, and breathless admiration. Your hero is as true as the Texas skies and as devoted to you—and the children, animals, and other family you two found along the way—as you could ever dream.

Want to know more? Find your hero in:

— TEXAS RODEO —

A fun contemporary Western series featuring the
exciting and dangerous world of the Texas rodeo.
BY KARI LYNN DELL

Reckless in Texas
Rough and tumble, cocky and charming—Joe's everything a rodeo superstar should be… And he's way out of Violet's league.

Tangled in Texas
Thirty-two seconds. That's how long it took for Delon Sanchez's bronc riding career to end. Knee shattered, future in question, all he can do is pull together the pieces…and wonder what cruel trick of fate has thrown him into the path of his ex, the oh-so-perfect Tori Patterson.

Tougher in Texas
Rodeo producer Cole Jacobs has his hands full running Jacobs Livestock. So when he loses one of his cowboys and his cousin sends along a more-than-capable replacement, he expects a grizzled Texas good ol' boy. He gets Shawnee Pickett.

YOUR PERFECT COWBOY IS THE
Fearless Lawman!

You value hard word, grit, and an honor-bound drive to keep the people you love safe. Your hero is the kind of man people can't help but look up to—brave and true and always willing to go the extra mile to make things right.

Want to know more? Find your hero in:

— NAVY SEAL COWBOYS —

Three former Navy SEALs injured in the line of duty, desperate for a new beginning...searching for a place to call their own.
BY NICOLE HELM

Cowboy SEAL Homecoming
When a tragic accident sends Alex Maguire back home, he's not sure what to make of the confusing, innocently beguiling woman who now lives there. But something in Becca's big green eyes makes Alex want to set aside the mantle of the perfect soldier and discover the man he could have been...

Coming
Spring 2018

Cowboy SEAL Redemption
Jack Armstrong figured he'd never recover the pieces of his shattered life, but when he and local bad girl Rose Rogers pretend to be in love to throw his meddling family off his trail, he discovers hope in the most unlikely of places...

Coming
Spring 2018

Cowboy SEAL Christmas
When Monica Finley takes a job with Revival Ranch, she knows it won't be an easy transition for her or her son, but getting snowed in with charming, hates-all-therapists former SEAL Gabe Cortez turns this Christmas into one that'll change her life forever.

YOUR PERFECT COWBOY IS THE
Last Good Man!

You value a sense of community and coming together to build something bigger than yourself. Your hero is a natural leader—the kind of clever and honorable man who, with your help, can guide a whole town to do what's right.

Want to know more? Find your hero in:

— A MATCH MADE IN TEXAS —

Welcome to the quirky town of Two-Time, Texas, where finding love is nothing but sweet, clean, madcap fun.

BY MARGARET BROWNLEY, *NEW YORK TIMES* BESTSELLING AUTHOR

Left at the Altar
When jilted bride Meg Lockwood falls for the groom's lawyer, they'll do anything to stay together—even as the whole crazy town seems set on keeping them apart.

A Match Made in Texas
Amanda Lockwood has her hands full as Two-Time's first female sheriff...especially now that she's falling for an innocent man accused of murder.

"A great story by a wonderful author."
—Debbie Macomber, #1 *New York Times* bestselling author

YOUR PERFECT COWBOY IS THE
Outlaw with a Heart of Gold!

You value love and a passion that cannot be tamed. Your hero may be rough around the edges, but he looks at you as if you hung all the stars in the sky…and really, sometimes being a little bad can be so very, very good.

Want to know more? Find your hero in:

— OUTLAW HEARTS —

A decades-long love story of two people, united by chance, that proves love's lasting power and its ability to overcome all odds.

BY ROSANNE BITTNER, *USA TODAY* BESTSELLING AUTHOR

Outlaw Hearts
Miranda Hayes has lost everything. So she sets out to cross a savage land alone… until chance brings her face-to-face with notorious gunslinger Jake Harkner.

Do Not Forsake Me
Chance brought Miranda and Jake Harkner together. Now, the strength of true love is tested against a past that he can't leave behind.

Love's Sweet Revenge
Threatened by cruel men in search of revenge, the Harkner clan must be stronger than ever before. Yet nothing can stop the coming storm.

The Last Outlaw
Life has brought Jake Harkner back full circle as he rides into Mexico to save a young girl from a dreadful fate…leaving Miranda behind one final time.

YOUR PERFECT COWBOY IS THE
Outlaw with a Heart of Gold!

You value love and a passion that cannot be tamed. Your hero may be rough around the edges, but he looks at you as if you hung all the stars in the sky…and really, sometimes being a little bad can be so very, very good.

Want to know more? Find your hero in:

— RUNAWAY BRIDES —

A sensual historical Western series about runaway brides who find freedom in the untamed West.

BY AMY SANDAS, *USA TODAY* BESTSELLING AUTHOR

Coming **Spring 2018**	*The Gunslinger's Vow* Malcolm Kincaid has no desire to escort a pampered eastern lady to Montana, but the longer he and Alexandra Brighton travel together, the harder he's falling…
Coming **Fall 2018**	*The Cowboy's Honor* Courtney Adams is still in her wedding finery when she leaves her groom at the altar and finds herself mistaken as a mail-order bride for a cowboy who makes her blood burn.
Coming **Spring 2019**	*The Outlaw's Heart* Evelyn Perkins will never return to the husband who betrayed her—not even when a handsome outlaw threatens to hold her for ransom.